CORAM HOUSE

CORAM HOUSE

A Novel

BAILEY SEYBOLT

ATRIA BOOKS

NEW YORK   AMSTERDAM/ANTWERP   LONDON
TORONTO   SYDNEY/MELBOURNE   NEW DELHI

ATRIA
BOOKS

An Imprint of Simon & Schuster, LLC
1230 Avenue of the Americas
New York, NY 10020

This book is a work of fiction. Any references to historical events, real people,
or real places are used fictitiously. Other names, characters, places, and events
are products of the author's imagination, and any resemblance to actual
events or places or persons, living or dead, is entirely coincidental.

First Atria Books hardcover edition April 2025

ATRIA BOOKS and colophon are trademarks of Simon & Schuster, LLC

Simon & Schuster strongly believes in freedom of expression and stands against censorship
in all its forms. For more information, visit BooksBelong.com.

For information about special discounts for bulk purchases, please contact
Simon & Schuster Special Sales at 1-866-506-1949 or business@simonandschuster.com.

The Simon & Schuster Speakers Bureau can bring authors to your live event. For more
information or to book an event, contact the Simon & Schuster Speakers Bureau at
1-866-248-3049 or visit our website at www.simonspeakers.com.

Interior design by Kyoko Watanabe

Manufactured in the United States of America

1 3 5 7 9 10 8 6 4 2

Library of Congress Control Number: 2024015762

ISBN 978-1-6680-5700-1
ISBN 978-1-6680-5702-5 (ebook)

For Tim, of course

August 1, 1968—Coram House

Sarah Dale

There's a flock of shadows under the old oak. The one that grows at the edge of the graveyard. But no. My sun-dazzled eyes adjust. Not shadows. The sisters, their black habits hanging limp in the humid air. Sister Marguerite beckons me forward. Beads of sweat dot her hairline, soaking her wimple. It's like she's melting inside her robes.

"Cook is making lemonade," she says and points up toward the House, as if I didn't know where to go. "Bring it here, child."

The others are playing on the beach, shouting and splashing in the cool water while Sister Ann tries to hush them. But I'm not sorry to leave. A few minutes alone are more precious than even the most perfect summer day. I take the path up the hill through the sumac, which is just starting to put out flowers. They're still green cones—nothing like the fiery red clusters they'll be come autumn. The air is thick with growing things. The hum of insects drowns out the sounds from the beach. In here, I'm all alone.

I arrive at the old part of the graveyard. Some headstones go back to 1800, but most of the letters are faded or filled with green moss, so you can't tell who's who anymore. Overgrown grass tickles the soft skin behind my knees. The dead here have no one to visit, so Marcus only cuts the grass when Father Foster makes him. Even then, he grumbles about the extra work. But I think it looks nice all covered in feathery scarlet bee balm and purple spires of anise.

I take a roundabout path that leads through the fairy circle of white pines where someone named May Sullivan has a bench just for her. She must have been loved to have such a spot all to herself. On the other side, I follow a line of identical marble squares, each bearing the name of a lieutenant or corporal who died in 1918. The grass here is cut short and the graves usually have flowers or tiny flags on them. There are still living people who care about these poor boys, as the sisters always call them. The dead boys. Not the living ones. We're never poor boys or girls.

The path curves past a row of mausoleums that look like stone doll-houses, and there, at the top of the hill, is the iron gate leading to the House. A stone angel sits on each gatepost, her face buried in her hands. Why do they weep, I've always wondered, if everyone here is in a better place? Unless their tears are not for the dead at all.

Strings of spiderweb stick to my face as I step through the gate. Something crawls down my arm, but when I look there's nothing there. Today, the yard is quiet. Everyone is down at the lake or playing in the shady woods.

The kitchen door is propped open with a stone, but it's too dark to see inside. "Hello?" I call, but the word is all breath. The last part of the path was steep.

"Hang on," Cook's voice grumbles from the darkness. A dragon in her den. So I wait.

From up here, the whole of the lake shines, smooth as mirror. Way down at the other end of the beach, a rowboat bobs in the shallows. Sister Cecile stands beside it, waiting. Even from way up here I can tell it's her by the way she stands—straight and still as a statue. Someone must be getting a swim lesson. Worse for them.

"Well, what do you want, then?" says a voice. I jump and turn around.

Cook stands in the doorway, flour up to her elbows like gloves. Hot air billows from the kitchen behind her. "Sorry, ma'am," I say.

But she doesn't look angry. She's nicer than the last one.

"Sister Marguerite sent me up for lemonade?"

"Oh, she did, did she?" Cook's mouth presses into a thin line. "Wait here," she mutters and goes back inside.

I turn to watch Sister Cecile down on the beach. The boat bobs up and down, but she never moves.

Behind me, a crash from the kitchen. Before I can move out of the way, a boy bursts through the door, ramming his metal bucket straight into me. I go down in the dusty yard. The pain is sharp. Skin sliced from skin. My knee throbs, but once I look up into that red, freckled face, I scramble to my feet.

Fred holds his hand up to block the sun's glare. He leans forward, so I can smell his stale breath even over the bucket of garbage. "Watch where you're going," he hisses.

"You're the one who ran into me." I try to sound hard. He's worse if you seem afraid.

Fred picks up a stick, thick as my arm. It's smooth and bleached white as bone. He hefts it in one hand, testing the weight. My body hurts in anticipation of the blow.

But it doesn't come.

Fred's eyes catch on something behind me. Then he's pushing past, knocking me to one side like I no longer exist. I watch as he disappears down the path to the lake, his white shirt blinking in and out of view among the green branches. I count to one hundred to make sure he's gone. Blood runs from my knee and soaks my white sock.

"Should I just stand here all day, then?"

I turn back to see Cook framed in the doorway, holding a white ceramic pitcher. Beads of water cling to the outside.

"Sorry," I mutter and fumble to wipe the dust from my hands.

"Oh, drat. Hold on. They'll want glasses."

The dark kitchen swallows her again. This time, I stand at attention, waiting for her to reappear. It takes forever. The blood on my leg dries to a crust. She returns with four empty jars.

"Had to wash them up. Here, take them."

She thrusts the stack into my arms. But I don't understand.

"Where are the others?" I ask.

Cook's eyebrows knit together. "The others?"

"The glasses," I say. *Are we all supposed to share?*

But she misunderstands. "If Sister Marguerite expects me to send real glasses to the beach where they'll be smashed to bits, she can come get them herself."

3

Then she grumbles off into the kitchen.

Of course. Four glasses, four sisters. How stupid to think that the lemonade would be for us. I turn to go, already deciding to go back the long way. I'd rather walk an extra mile than run into Fred alone on the path.

The rowboat is out on the water now, floating right in the middle of the cove.

Sister Cecile sits in the stern and a boy sits in the bow, tall and lanky, his white shirt glowing in the sun. That's where Fred was going in such a hurry, then. The pitcher is slick in my hands. I try to get a better grip. Down on the water, the rowboat spins, blown by the breeze. Now I can see another boy, small and huddled, but I'm too far away to make out his face. Sister Cecile casts her arm toward the water, as if throwing a stone. In answer, Fred lunges forward. In a blur, the smaller boy goes over the side. His arms and legs thrash the water to foam. Time stretches forever.

A swim lesson. A swim lesson. The words repeat in my head like a prayer.

The frothing water stills to ripples, then goes smooth.

No small head breaks the surface.

I don't move. I can't move. The others in the boat are frozen too. Sister Cecile, a black triangle. Fred, a smudge of white shirt. Only two now. Time stretches forever. Then Fred lifts the oars and begins to row.

Cold needles sting my leg. I look down. They're wet. Shards litter the ground. I must have dropped the pitcher, but I never heard a smash.

When I look up again, Sister Cecile is watching me from the boat, which is almost back to shore. She can't possibly see my face from all the way down there, but I still want to hide. She'll send me back to the attic. I know she will.

A sound escapes my lips and I hold a hand to my mouth, stuffing it back in. The pieces of the pitcher lay in the dirt, jagged and white. I feel as if they might leap up and put themselves back together. As if I can turn back time and do things differently. As if I can know what's coming and hold on tighter.

Karen Lafayette

Alan Stedsan: Good morning, Ms. Lafayette. Thank you for coming.

Karen Lafayette: Happy to be here if it will help.

AS: All right, let's get started, then. You lived at the Coram House Orphanage from 1965 to 1970. Can you tell me a little bit about life there?

KL: [Laugh] Every single person who worked there should be in prison. Do you know they called themselves the Sisters of Mercy? Can you believe that? Forget prison, Sister Cecile—every last one of them—should be in hell.

AS: I understand your anger, Ms. Lafayette. But the more details we have—

KL: I know. All right.

AS: Could you tell me more about Sister Cecile? What were her responsibilities at Coram House?

KL: You mean besides torture?

AS: I—

KL: I know—details. She was in charge of the girls' dormitory. Making sure we said our prayers, made our beds. That kind of shit. Oh, and walks, swim lessons. She was a big believer in the power of the outdoors, Sister Cecile.

AS: How would you characterize her general treatment of the children?

KL: [Laugh] She's a monster. Unless you were her pet. She always had a pet.

AS: Maybe you could be a little more specific.

KL: Okay, you want details? How about the time Sister Cecile pushed a girl out the window.

AS: Out the window?

KL: She fell from the second story. I saw—she sort of bounced when she hit the ground.

AS: And this child—did she survive the fall?

KL: It was pavement. I'd think not.

AS: Do you know her name—the child?

KL: Amanda, maybe? Melissa? I think she was Seven.

AS: Seven years old?

KL: No. Seven. You know—her number. They called us by our numbers most of the time. So some girls, I never knew their real name.

AS: And why did—you said Sister Cecile—why did she push this girl out the window?

KL: I don't remember that either. We were cleaning them, I think. Me and Sarah and Seven.

AS: The windows?

KL: Yes, the windows. We were cleaning them and, I don't know, maybe she wasn't doing a good-enough job. Maybe that old bitch was just bored that day. Who knows. I heard there was a little girl who burned up. Sister Cecile told her to fetch a ball from the fire and her snowsuit went up in flames. And then there was the boy who drowned. Oh, and there's Father Foster, of course. But you know all about that. Let me tell you, Father Foster was the only good thing about being a girl in that place.

May 3, 1989—US District Courthouse

Sarah Dale

Alan Stedsan: Thank you for coming, Ms. Dale. I'd like to ask you some questions about life at Coram House. Is that all right?

Sarah Dale: Yes. All right.

AS: To your knowledge, were the children ever punished by the nuns or priests?

SD: Oh, yes. That happened quite often.

AS: What sorts of things would you be punished for?

SD: Speaking during meals. Talking back to the nuns. Not doing our chores well enough.

AS: And how would you be punished?

SD: Hit, you know, with a ruler. Or they'd make you stand in the corner with your arms out for hours, until you felt like they'd break. That sort of thing. If they were really angry, they'd send you to the attic.

AS: The attic?

SD: It was cold. And dark. There was no—what do you call it—insulation, I guess. Just wooden boards and then the roof above. In some places, you could see cracks where the light shone through. There were windows at either end. Huge round ones taller than me, even. But still it was dark all the time. I don't know why. Maybe because it was so big. And cold. Half the windows were broken so the wind just blew right in. And it was full of ghosts. [Laugh]

AS: You believed it was haunted?

SD: No, the ghosts were real. They were statues—big stone ones. Of the saints, I think. But they were all covered in white sheets. I can't

7

imagine how they got them up there. They must have weighed hundreds of pounds. When the wind blew in, the sheets would move around. They looked like ghosts. Dancing all together in the dark.

AS: That sounds frightening.

SD: They would take you upstairs. Usually Sister Cecile. And there was this old wardrobe. She made you get inside and then locked the door.

AS: She locked you inside the wardrobe?

SD: Yes.

AS: For how long?

SD: I don't know. Once they sent Mary up and she stayed the whole night. It was winter and her lips were blue when they brought her down. We thought she was dead.

AS: Ms. Dale, I'd like to ask you about something that Karen Lafayette mentioned.

SD: Fourteen.

AS: Excuse me?

SD: Karen was number Fourteen. I was Eleven and she was Fourteen.

AS: Do you remember an incident that happened when you were washing windows? This would have been sometime in the 1960s.

SD: Oh, you mean with Sister Cecile.

AS: Could you tell me what happened that day?

SD: Nothing much.

AS: Nothing much?

SD: Well, nothing out of the ordinary. I was washing windows up on the second floor, along the back of the building. It must have been one of the classrooms because they had these very tall windows made up of tiny panes of glass. They were a terrible pain to wash because you had to do each one individually with a cloth wrapped around your finger.

AS: It sounds tedious.

SD: It took ages. I was at the House for nearly twenty years, you know. That's thousands of windowpanes. Maybe tens of thousands. If you added it all up, I wonder how many months of my life I spent washing those windows.

AS: Ms. Dale, the day you were speaking about—

SD: Yes, of course. Anyhow, I was washing windows with Fourteen—Karen—and another girl. Missy, I think her name was. She hadn't been there long. Sister Cecile came in. She was furious about something. Nothing to do with us, but that's how it worked. She said something about the windows looking filthy and Missy pointed out that all the dirt was on the outside where we couldn't reach. She was right, you know, but it was a stupid thing to say. She was new.

AS: What happened next?

SD: Oh, Sister Cecile raged for a while and then told Missy that she better clean the outside then.

AS: The outside of the windows?

SD: The windowsills were very wide. So Sister Cecile told her to stand on the windowsill and we were supposed to hold her ankles from the inside.

AS: Jesus.

SD: Let me tell you, Jesus had nothing to do with it. We held on to that girl tight as anything. My hands ached after.

AS: And Missy—what happened to her?

SD: I'm not sure. Adopted, I think. She was a sweet little thing. Blonde curls like a doll. Those ones went pretty quickly.

AS: She didn't—I mean, that day—she didn't fall out the window?

SD: [Laugh] Of course not. I mean, she was frightened. We all were. But it wasn't—you have to understand—it wasn't even unusual, that type of thing.

AS: Ms. Dale, I have to tell you. Ms. Lafayette—Karen—she remembers the girl being pushed out the window.

SD: Fourteen always did love a story. But I don't know what to tell you, Mr. Stedsan. I can promise you no one went out that window who did not come back in. To be honest, I only remember that day because of how upset Karen was after.

AS: She also mentioned the incident of a boy who drowned. [Pause] Ms. Dale?

SD: Yes.

AS: Do you have any recollection of that?

SD: I meant, yes. That happened.

AS: What can you tell me about it?

SD: It was a few years later. Karen wasn't there that day, so I don't know why she's telling you about it.

AS: But you were there?

SD: Not *there* there. No one was there except Sister Cecile and the boys in the boat.

AS: Then how—

SD: I was up at the House. I'd come back to fetch lemonade for the sisters. It was strange, the timing of it. If I'd been just a few minutes earlier or later. God, that day was hot. I was sweating from the minute I got up. My dress stuck to me like I'd been painted with glue. There was a summersweet growing right outside the kitchen door. It had these big white blossoms hanging off that made the air smell spiced.

AS: [Pause] Ms. Dale?

SD: I was coming out of the kitchen. Down on the lake, there was a rowboat in this little cove. The water there was deeper so Sister Cecile would take us there for swim lessons. But you couldn't see it from the rest of the beach. That day, Sister Cecile was inside the boat with Tommy and Fred. Tommy was all hunched over like he was sick, maybe. Sister Cecile said something—I don't know what, she was too far away, but I could see her arms moving. Fred, he grabbed Tommy under his arms and he pushed, so Tommy went right into the water.

AS: And then what happened?

SD: I just stood there. But Tommy, he never came back up. He couldn't swim.

AS: And Sister Cecile—what did she do?

SD: Nothing. They rowed back to shore.

AS: How did they look?

SD: What do you mean?

AS: Did they seem upset?

SD: I couldn't see their faces. They were too far away.

AS: Then how did you recognize them?

SD: You'd know Sister Cecile from miles away just by how she stood. Like her spine was a broomstick. And I'd just seen Fred outside the kitchen, on the path down to the water. I'd been scared. He'd had this huge knobby stick through the handle of his bucket. A boy like that doesn't carry a stick unless he means to hit someone with it. But even without that, I'd have known it was him in the boat. Fred went wherever Sister Cecile did, you see. He was her favorite. And Tommy, well, I didn't know it was him until later, when he went missing.

AS: So the boat rowed back to shore. What did you do next?

SD: You mean, did I run screaming down the hill—jump in the water to save him?

AS: Ms. Dale, I wasn't suggesting—

SD: No, it's all right. That's what I should have done. What I would do now. You know, I'd dropped the pitcher of lemonade and it smashed on the ground. There was lemonade all over my legs. I was afraid of getting in trouble, for that, of all things. Back then, I was just so afraid. Of both of them. So I did nothing. Said nothing. At least not right away. A few days later I got up the courage, but no one believed me. And then Sister Cecile came to me after dinner. Told me how Tommy was missing. Had run away. And then— [Inaudible]

AS: Can I get you something—a glass of water?

SD: No. Thank you. She took me to the attic. There was a wardrobe there. She told me to climb inside and she latched the door from the outside. It was dark—so dark. And cold. Even though it was summer. I don't know how long she left me there for. At least through the night. Maybe longer? I don't know. At the time, I wondered if she'd leave me there forever. Call it an accident.

AS: Because of what you'd seen?

SD: She never said that was why. But I knew it was. I had nightmares about it for years.

AS: About the drowning?

SD: No. About the dark. Being locked in that wardrobe. Is that terrible of me?

AS: It wasn't your fault.

SD: I should have done something.

AS: You—

SD: No. I know that now. I carry that with me. There are times—well. There are times when it's hard to live with that. And that's the thing you have to understand. The years we spent there. You can leave Coram House but you can't leave it behind. Not all of it. The worst of it you carry with you. It becomes part of you. And sometimes I worry you pass it on.

PART 1

1

I leave Brooklyn before the rest of the city is awake. The day is bitter and damp. No snow. Just wet sidewalks and mounds of slush clogging the storm drains. Usually, I find the brick townhouses cheerful and bright, but today the gray sky drains the color from everything around me. I pull the building's door shut and hoist my suitcase down the stairs. Patches of confetti glitter on the sidewalk. Soon they'll be washed into the river along with the slush. It's unusually quiet this morning. As if, a day later, the city is still sleeping off its New Year's hangover.

New Year's Eve was particularly cold and clear, so the sounds of people celebrating carried all the way up to my empty third-floor apartment. A knot of girls passed beneath my window, laughing and drinking tiny bottles of champagne through straws. I'd shivered to see their bare legs glowing white. I've always hated New Year's.

A few days ago, Lola had come over with a bottle of wine to toast my new book. She knew the rough details: the old orphanage, the church, all the usual horror and abuse, the case that had finally broken everything open and then the settlement that had shut it back in the dark.

Sounds like bestseller material was all she said, even after I told her about the fine print: six months in Vermont and someone else's name on the cover.

Ghostwriter.

After everything that had gone wrong with my last book, the word appealed to me. Like I wasn't there. And besides, I had a pile of unpaid medical bills in a drawer. Three years since Adam died and they still keep coming. No one tells you about that part.

All right, Lola had said, *I'll help you pack.*

And she did try, pulling clothes out of my closet and holding them up. A chunky striped sweater. A long red dress with flowers. I hadn't worn any of it in years. She refilled my glass, tried to make it fun, but I'd begged off. After she left, I drifted around, finishing the bottle on my own. It seemed impossible to take things off the shelves. Like, over the years, they'd grown roots. Adam's closet was already empty, at least.

Alone, I'd made a pile of the things I cared about. Photos from our wedding. The cone of a giant sequoia tree, tiny as an acorn, from a trip to California. A perfectly round stone I'd found in a Peruvian temple and smuggled home. It's an ancient Ping-Pong ball, I'd told Adam. Each object came with a memory that I shoved into the locked cabinet in my mind to be dealt with later—on the advice of a therapist I'd seen a few times after Adam died. I'd never asked her what happened if you just leave the memories in there, the door firmly locked.

My pile had fit inside a single box. The box went into Lola's basement. Everything else went to the curb. The tiny bottles of vinegar. Brass candlesticks. A set of ugly brown sheets. Objects that had piled up over the years as if washed ashore.

Today, my car is parked right in front of the building—a small miracle I found the spot. I bought the car in some New Jersey suburb the day after I signed the book contract. A used Toyota with seventy thousand miles and two matching dents in the roof where the previous owner drove it into a garage with a bike on the roof. I like that the car comes with its own story. I load my suitcase into the trunk next to the boxes of work stuff. Laptop and reference books. Blank pads of paper, my favorite highlighters, index cards, empty binder. My stomach growls.

It's just past six in the morning, but the OPEN sign at the deli promises hot coffee. I order my usual bagel with cream cheese and tomato slices, even though I know they will be pale and mealy. While I'm waiting, I drink in the bare branches of the trees in the park across the street, the chipped green paint of the stairs leading down to the subway. Pantone 350. New York green. My stomach tightens.

I'm being maudlin. The book contract is six months for a first draft. Then I can come back. Even here, I hardly leave the apartment in the early stages of a project. Besides, this isn't even a real ending—that came three years ago. It's more like tearing off a hangnail. Painful, yes, to sever that thread of flesh. But also a relief.

I take my bagel, diapered in wax paper, back to the car. My phone pings as I slide into the driver's seat—a text from Lola wishing me luck and telling me it's supposed to snow and not to end up in a ditch. Also an email from Alan Stedsan, my new coauthor.

Dear Ms. Kelley, it begins, with the same formality as all his previous emails. Maybe lawyers can't help themselves. He wishes me a safe drive and asks if I'll come by his office tomorrow to get started. I type back a quick reply, agreeing.

We've only spoken once on the phone, but that was enough to paint a picture. Stedsan did most of the talking. He gave a brief overview of the case against the Catholic church and his vision for the book—history for true-crime fans. He needed someone good at both, he said. Like a young Erik Larson. His tone suggested this was the highest compliment.

That conversation was supposed to be an interview, but I got the sense he was searching for something inside my answers, some mysterious quality. Right before we hung up, he asked if I'd like any changes made to the draconian contract, though of course he didn't call it that. Full editorial control for him. A punishing nondisclosure agreement for me with a six-figure slap on the wrist should I violate it. Plus, a ruthless schedule and a move to Vermont so he could keep tabs on *our* progress.

I said no. It was fine, all of it.

My agent called an hour later with the offer. So I guess the quality he'd been searching for was compliance. Not so mysterious after all.

I pull up directions to the apartment I've rented sight unseen. Burlington, Vermont. Six hours north in an almost-straight line. The engine makes a metallic crunch as it turns over, but soon I'm merging onto Atlantic Avenue. Five blocks later, I realize I never took a last look at the apartment. A white van honks and cuts me off. Any regret is swallowed by the anxiety of trying to get on the highway without dying.

An hour north of the city, the traffic grows sparse. I reach for my bagel and coffee, both cold. Through the bare winter trees, I glimpse miniature towns down in the valley and snowy fields dotted with brown horses or cows. By the time I reach Albany, its office towers and smoke-stacks seem enormous.

After that, the towns get smaller and farther apart until I stop for gas in a town that consists of a post office and general store nestled in snow-frosted evergreens. I fill up at the gas pump out front, switching hands every ten seconds so I don't freeze.

Inside, I navigate racks of every imaginable type of potato chip—dill pickle, ketchup, shrimp—until I find the coffee nestled beside a case of sugared donuts. I once read about a man who slipped razor blades into gas station donuts. Someone had to get their tongue sewn back together. I fill up a cup and take a donut out of the case and pay. Outside, the cold winds around me like it missed me. The donut tastes of apples and cinnamon. It's delicious. No razor blades either.

Adam told me once that I see danger everywhere. He blamed it on my books. His theory was that if I wrote about kittens instead of people who were murdered, the world would feel less threatening.

No one wants to read books about kittens, I'd argued.

Everyone wants to read books about kittens, he'd said.

But I think I got the argument all wrong. Maybe I do see danger everywhere, but that's because the world is dangerous. Some donuts will slice your tongue off. My books aren't made up, is what I should have said to him. They're facts. He's the one who didn't see things as they are. He's the one who believed life would get better, right until the end.

I wonder what Adam would say about this new project. More darkness and death. Maybe he would have been excited at the prospect of leaving New York for a few months. Or maybe he would have hated it. For a while, I could summon his voice—imagine just what he'd say and how he'd say it. But it doesn't work anymore. In my head, his voice just sounds like my own. The pain of this is less sharp than it used to be. More like pressing on an old bruise.

I get back in the car and drive.

The next couple hours are uneventful. No traffic, no blizzard. Just a road unfurling across hills with the occasional small town or lonely barn rising up on the side of the road. I keep an eye out for Camel's Hump, a mountain whose distinct shape was all over my internet searches about Vermont, but I don't find it. I begin to understand how people enjoy driving.

As I top out on the next hill, I see the flash of the highway in the distance. Then a mint-green bridge carries me over a river and back into the present. A shopping plaza stuffed with giant budget stores—the siren song of stuff, cheap and plentiful. The pictures of Burlington looked charming enough. Lots of antique brick buildings with the wide expanses of Lake Champlain as a backdrop, but now I worry they were misleading. Maybe this is going to be six months of dumpy strip malls and Egg McMuffins. Even though I'd protested to Lola that Burlington was a city—the biggest city in Vermont!—I realize part of me has been expecting not the wilderness exactly, but at least something charming and Thoreau-adjacent.

I crest a hill crowned by a college campus. Historic buildings mix with a giant glass student center. In the rearview mirror, the distinct shape of Camel's Hump appears as if carved on the horizon. It feels like an omen that my first glimpse of it should be unexpected and through a mirror, but what kind of omen, I'm not sure.

I miss the next turn and get lost in a maze of one-way streets until I finally end up on Archibald Street. Most buildings look like they could use a fresh coat of paint, but the neighborhood is busy. There's a bakery with fogged-up windows, a corner store promising samosas, a mural of Muhammad Ali so big I could curl up inside his nostril. Then a tiny colonial graveyard tucked among a row of old Victorians, each house divided into many apartments, judging by the number of mailboxes.

My destination is the last house on the block, a rambling place painted acid-trip purple. I double-check the address, but my phone assures me I've arrived. I'm scrolling through my emails, trying to find the landlord's number, when someone raps on the hood.

Outside, a white-haired man motions for me to roll down the window. "You must be Alex," he says. "I'm Joe. I own the building. How was the drive?"

I scramble to get out while he launches into an explanation of snow-plowing and parking. The sidewalk is dotted in patches of ice, but he seems more confident on his feet than I am, despite his age and unlaced snow boots.

"Well," he says, holding out his arms to embrace that monstrous expanse of purple house, "this is it."

I wrap my arms around myself, regretting I didn't take the time to pull on my coat and hoping he'll take the hint, but he seems to be waiting for me to respond.

"It's very cheerful," I say finally.

"Well, it's gray around here six months of the year, so I thought, why not brighten up the neighborhood a bit."

He delivers the line like he's said it before.

"All right. Ready for the grand tour?"

He unlocks the front door and I follow him inside and up a steep set of stairs.

Joe's tour covers the hot water heater, the fire escape, how to flip the breaker if the stove overloads the system. *Old house* seems to be the explanation for everything. Finally, we stand in the kitchen, our boots melting onto the yellowed linoleum.

He nods at the doorway that leads into the living room. "I had an old table in the garage. Had my son clean it up and put it in there. Figured that would be better than a desk—more space and all—if you're going to be writing a book in here."

"Thanks," I say. "That's great."

He pauses, waiting for me to go on, but I just smile politely. People are always curious when you say you're a writer. Like it's not a real job and you owe them a better explanation, but I'd long ago gotten over the impulse to fill the silence. Any silence. Besides, Alan Stedsan had instructed me to be cagey about our project. *Don't tell people what you're working on*, he'd said. *Not until you have to.*

"Anyways."

Joe jangles a set of keys, then holds them out to me. The owl keychain looks at me with googly eyes.

"I usually swing by on Wednesdays," he says. "To check up on things. But you have my number. Let me know if you need anything. And good luck with the history project."

With that, he shuts the door behind him. Heavy footsteps thunk down the stairs and then the outside door slams shut.

I wander the rooms, taking inventory or maybe claiming them. The kitchen is clean and bare and smells of bleach and mildew. There's an electric stove, a small fridge, and a window looking onto the asphalt lot behind the house. The living room is covered in gray carpet. The couch, with its wooden arms, reminds me of dorm furniture. Beside it stands a laminate coffee table and a small television. The promised table, which takes up most of the living room, is like something straight out of a farmhouse with its scarred pine top and turned legs. In Brooklyn, you'd pay thousands of dollars for that kind of perfectly distressed paint job. I run my finger over a line of tiny dents on the surface. Fork tines.

In the bedroom, the mattress is still wrapped in plastic. It's the one thing I'd insisted on buying new after a decade terrified of bed bugs. The bedside lamp gives off a dim, yellow glow beneath a shade that's far too large for its squat body. The one window looks out onto the street at a corner store and the cemetery. The mattress crinkles beneath me as I sit and take stock of the situation, searching for any hint of panic at my new reality.

I go through it like a checklist. Walked away from the apartment I've lived in for seven years, check. Gotten rid of most of my belongings, check. Moved to a town where I know no one. Agreed to ghostwrite a book with a complete stranger. Check, check, check.

But the panic isn't there. I feel nothing but tired.

I'll get my boxes out of the car, I decide. Find a pizza place that delivers. Buy a bottle of wine. Outside the window, a few white flakes drift from the sky. Then a few more. The promised storm, finally here.

———

The sky is inky black when I wake, the silence so deep, I think it must be the middle of the night. But no. My phone says it's nearly six a.m. I untangle myself from the blankets and pad over icy floorboards to the window. The world is buried under a thick layer of snow. A plow scrapes somewhere in the distance, but the street below is untouched. The graveyard is painted in soft blue shadows.

My eyes feel like they're full of sand, but I don't go back to bed. Early morning has always been my favorite time. But I do need coffee.

In the kitchen it's disorienting to see the grocery bag from my apartment in Brooklyn on the counter—like it got lost and wandered into the wrong life. I put a piece of bread in the toaster. No butter, no milk. But good enough for now.

While the coffee is brewing, I turn on my laptop. Last night, I'd set it out on the table along with the slim folder that contained everything I had from Stedsan so far, which is not much. My contract. The book pitch. A proposed schedule—one month for an outline, which is punishing for a research book. Stedsan promised he had boxes of deposition transcripts, interview tapes, and historical photos, all waiting for me at his office. And also that there might be more documentation with the church or local historical societies.

I send my agent a quick email, letting her know that I've arrived. She's been quietly furious with me since I signed the contract. She'd assumed we'd negotiate—the money, the terms of authorship—but I said no. None of it. She sat me down in her office, actually crouched so we were eye-to-eye like a parent with a child. *I know this story is interesting*, she'd said, *and sure, it's been a dry spell, and yes, your last book didn't turn out so well, but you've been on the bestseller list twice, and now you're not even going to get a byline?*

But none of it changed my mind.

The story was interesting. A haunted orphanage for a setting. The terrible stories of nuns and priests. The settlement that buried the whole thing. But that wasn't the reason I took the contract. My agent thought I simply hadn't written anything for the last year and a half. That I was grieving. I never told her how I couldn't write. How I'd tried and failed. How I'd looked for that spark I felt with my first book, but couldn't find it. How I was starting to believe it was gone forever. But maybe if I was writing as someone else. If everyone in the story was already dead so I didn't have a chance to fuck up their lives. Maybe now, things would be different.

I unpack, which takes ten minutes. Then I drink my coffee. My appointment with Stedsan isn't until ten, but by eight it feels like the walls are closing in. At home, I'd go for a run—sweat out my impatience on the paths that crisscross Prospect Park or along the river. Before I came, I scoped out some likely routes, but none took a foot of fresh snow into account. I think of the sign I'd seen yesterday in the window of the minimart, promising samosas. Then I pull on my brand-new snow boots, grab my keys, and head across the street.

The floor of the minimart is already slick with brown slush. I fill a paper bag with samosas and pour a cup of hot chai so spiced the smell alone is warming. I eat while walking, past a Nepali restaurant and a school with an impressive treehouse, already busy with kids, their snowsuits blurs of color against the white snow.

The road ends at a park, though there's not much to it—an empty stone fountain and a stretch of piebald snow and brown grass all encircled by a retaining wall. If you rolled down the steep slope beyond, you'd land in the harbor. Granted, with a few broken bones.

I'd looked at Burlington on a map. Downtown is on a bay that looked like no more than a puddle-sized inlet off the rest of Lake Champlain. But now, seeing it in person, the bay is plenty big: a two-mile-wide expanse of solid ice dotted with fishing shacks. At the far end, forested peninsulas enclose it on both sides, like a forefinger and thumb nearly closed in a circle, cutting the bay off from the great expanse of open water beyond.

I bite into a samosa and grease dribbles down my chin. Sitting on the wall, feet dangling over the edge, is giving me vertigo, so I turn my back to the view to finish. On the far side of the park, three police officers cluster around a parked school bus. The nosy reporter in me wonders what's going on. Then a man in an apron passes a cup and foil-wrapped package out one of the windows.

The officer tucks a few dollars into a jar. Only then do I notice the smell of grease in the air. The side of the bus is painted with big blue letters: BEANSIE'S BUS. The officers cross the street into a squat brick building. BURLINGTON POLICE DEPARTMENT, announces the sign above the door.

My phone buzzes. A text from Stedsan. *Running late. 10:15 okay?*

It's almost nine thirty now. I write him back. *No problem! See you then!*

As soon as I hit send, I regret the exclamation marks. Then regret my regret. It feels pathetic that, at thirty-six, I can be sent into a spiral of self-doubt by punctuation. Five years ago, I don't think I would have had that same doubt, but I can't be sure. That's a land too foreign to remember clearly. The grease in my samosa has hardened in the cold. I crumple the rest in the bag and throw it away.

———

The dashboard clock says 10:05 when I park in front of a small brick building with the kind of antique white patina that home improvement shows covet. In front, a carved wooden sign hangs from a post. ALAN STEDSAN, ATTORNEY AT LAW—black with gold lettering. Stately homes with turrets and gingerbread trim keep watch over the rest of the street. The setting has the flavor of old money and deep connections.

I glance in the rearview mirror, but my reflection is not encouraging— dark circles under my eyes, thin pale lips blending into the rest of my skin. I riffle through the glove box, find a tube of half-frozen lipstick, and smear some on my lips and cheeks. Good enough.

There's no doorbell beside the red front door, just a brass knocker in the shape of a fist. I knock. After a few seconds, the door opens. Alan Stedsan is nearly seventy, but there's something ageless about him. Like he might actually be thirty and just wearing stage makeup to play someone much older. I'm five foot eight, but I have to look up into his bright blue eyes and cut-glass cheekbones. He looks descended from Viking kings. The expensive suit helps too.

"Alex," he says, holding out a hand for me to shake. "Alan Stedsan. Nice to finally meet you. Come in."

I step into the foyer, a dark cocoon of green, striped wallpaper and slate floors.

"May I take your coat? You can leave your boots just there."

He points to a copper tray beside the door. Below the hem of his suit he wears only socks, but makes it look elegant. I hand over my coat and pull off my boots, balancing on one leg and getting slush all over the cuffs of my jeans.

Stedsan guides me into the living room and then disappears to "get refreshments." The room is all blond wood and modern furniture. In the corner, an egg-shaped wood-burning stove descends from the ceiling on a long tube like a spaceship. The vibe is rich-person IKEA—not what I expected.

The entire back wall is glass and looks out onto a snowy garden, though the only sign of life now is a small, twisted tree with a stone bench beside it.

"In September, it puts out hundreds of apples."

I turn to see Stedsan holding a tray with a French press, silent as a cat in his socks. He offers a plate of delicate, flaky pastries but I decline, imagining crumbs all over myself and his expensive couch.

"Your office is lovely."

I gesture to take in the room.

"I'm mostly retired, so it's more home and less office these days. And how about you—how are you settling in?"

I think of the generic motel furniture and peeling linoleum in my apartment. It's funny how some things don't bother you until you see them in contrast to something else.

"Fine, thanks," I say.

We talk for a little while about the city, the restaurants I must try, whether I ski. *No*, I shake my head. I'd tried a few times with Adam when we first met, when I was still trying to impress him with my gameness. He'd looked so elegant, his poles lightly tapping the snow as he carved turns. While I'd felt like a newly hatched octopus, all these extra limbs I didn't know what to do with. It's not an experience I ever looked to repeat.

"So the case," I say, guiding us away from my personal life, back onto solid ground.

"Yes, the case."

I'd done a little digging. I knew it had been settled out of court for practically nothing in today's terms. In 1993, people had still been shocked by the idea of a priest doing *that* to a child. The unthinkable was still unbelievable. Then the *Boston Globe*'s Spotlight article in 2002 cracked the church open and let the light in. If the Coram House case had been ten years later, things might have gone very differently.

Stedsan leans back and folds his long legs in a way that makes me think of a praying mantis. "The case, frankly, was a mess," he says. "I inherited it from a senior partner who had taken it on pro bono from another lawyer. The plaintiffs couldn't agree on anything and kept dropping out and starting their own cases. When the publisher approached me about writing this book, I have to say, I was surprised. But the more I thought about my legacy—" He pauses, shrugs. "It's a story worth telling, and it appears I'm the one to tell it."

It's an interesting choice of words from someone who's hired a ghostwriter. A reminder, perhaps, to stay in my lane. Or maybe I'm reading too much into it.

"The timeline is aggressive for a book like this," I say.

He laughs, shrugs. "I'm not getting any younger."

I smile. It's probably true. Publishing is slow. But still, I sense something behind the words. A man who likes to control the room. He has a stare that traps you like the glare of two bright-blue headlights. It's probably very effective in the courtroom.

"You're not exactly what I expected," Stedsan says.

No one's exactly what anyone expects, I want to say.

"What were you expecting?" I ask instead, hoping he can't hear the quiver in my voice, the way my uncertainty has gone into overdrive.

"Perhaps we should address the elephant in the room?"

I've always hated that expression.

Stedsan puts down his coffee. I think he was going for a sense of finality, but the cup makes a tiny clink on the saucer.

"Your last book was problematic," he says, tone diplomatic. "Your agent mentioned that you had some personal circumstances. A breakdown, I suppose you'd call it, though she didn't use that word exactly."

The lump in my throat grows. But I keep my expression neutral. "A breakdown. That sounds very Victorian."

He studies me, waiting for what he's owed.

The anger leaks out like someone punched a hole in my gut. What does it matter, really. "My husband died," I say. "And, for a while, work didn't matter much. My last book suffered for it."

I hate myself for offering this up. It's true and not true. I had loved someone and he had died. After, all the things that used to matter—

work, food, friends—became cardboard props. But the book had still mattered. Maybe the only thing that did. But that didn't stop me from getting everything horribly wrong.

"To be honest, I wasn't sure I'd ever write another book."

It feels good to say this out loud.

"You know," Stedsan says, "my wife died a few years ago."

"I'm sorry to hear that."

He nods, but he's not really listening. It's just what you say.

"So why did you hire me?" I ask.

He drums his fingers on the table. "*The Isle* was a good book," he says. "And you were cheaper."

The laugh bursts out of me. I was waiting for a story about second chances. "Yeah," I say. "I probably was."

"Anyhow, you're here now," he says. "Shall we begin?"

Stedsan leads me down a hallway and into a large office. The room is dominated by a desk large enough to be a dining table. Behind it, a door leads out to the street. It would make me uneasy, having a door at my back while I worked. But I get the sense there's not much that ruffles Stedsan. He gestures to the corner where stacks of cardboard file boxes surround a brocade love seat.

"They're a mess," Stedsan says cheerfully. "Depositions, newspaper clippings, legal documents. Probably all missing pages. A box of unsorted photographs. The case dragged on for years and traded hands between God knows how many paralegals with their own filing systems."

Stedsan rests his hand on a box teetering precariously on top of the stack. I count at least ten more. CORAM HOUSE, someone's written on the side in all caps—like they're yelling it.

"I think you'll find my material is more organized," he continues. "Some of the videos were destroyed, mice probably, but the surviving tapes are here, along with transcripts of all the rest. You'll also want to request materials from the police."

"The police?" I turn to look at him.

He shrugs. "Not that it's likely to get you anywhere. And the church might have some documents too."

"That they're willing to share?"

The room smells faintly of old paper. The desire to cut through the tape and open the first box is an itch I'm trying to ignore.

Stedsan smiles, and there's something foxlike about it. "Oh, yes, they're very happy to be helpful. Speaking of . . ." He flips open a leather-bound calendar sitting on the desk. "What are you doing one week from Wednesday at nine a.m.?"

I want to laugh. I was contractually bound to move to a place where I don't know a living soul beyond Stedsan. "Nothing," I say. "What did you have in mind?"

"Father Aubry wants to have us over for tea."

"That's very . . . collegial."

"Isn't it? It's your call, but I'd play nice. Father Aubry isn't a bad sort."

For a priest, I think.

"This meeting—"

"Tea. I think Father Aubry sees this as a social visit."

I shrug, not caring what we call it. "Will it be at Coram House?"

Stedsan shakes his head. "No. The building has been turned over to the developer now. But the rectory is on the same property, just behind St. Joseph's—the church. You can't miss it from the road."

"Do you think the developer will let us go inside?"

Anticipation bangs in my chest. I need to see it.

Stedsan waves his hand, as if it's already done. "I'll call him. I've known Bill a long time and he loves being helpful, as long as there's an audience."

I file that one away for later. "Wednesday at nine," I say. "All right."

Stedsan goes off to see if he can find a VHS player for the deposition tapes. I run my fingers over the rough threads of the love seat. They glow gold in the lamplight. I wonder again why Stedsan is writing this book. I assumed it was for the money, but now that I've seen where he lives, that seems less likely. There are plenty of rich people foaming at the mouth to get richer, sure, but he wears his wealth casually, as if he barely notices it's there. His legacy, he says. And maybe that's true. I push aside the unease creeping up my spine. It's too late for second thoughts and I'm not going to let some fancy furniture send me into an anxiety spiral.

Stedsan reappears, empty-handed. "Sorry," he says. "I was sure I had an old VCR in the basement."

"No problem," I say. "I can find one."

I bring my car around the side. Stedsan looks doubtfully at the small trunk. "I could have the boxes delivered."

But I can already hear the rip of tape and feel the old, brittle pages under my fingers. "I think they'll fit," I say and start loading.

After twenty minutes of cardboard-box Tetris, they do fit. Barely. I refused to let Stedsan help, but now my back aches and I'm soaked with sweat under my jacket.

"Will you be all right on the other end?" Stedsan asks.

I picture the steep, narrow stairs up to my apartment. The icy front porch. "I'll be fine."

"I imagine it will take some time to go through all that. Call me if you have questions. Otherwise, I'll see you next week."

I nod, surprised. Considering the contract, I assumed he'd be hovering over my shoulder.

As I climb into the car, Stedsan calls my name. He's framed in the doorway, a hand gripping either side like some force is trying to suck him inside.

"There's one more thing you should know for our meeting," he says. "It's not called Coram House anymore. It's Sunrise House."

"Sunrise House," I repeat. The words taste bitter.

That foxlike smile reappears on his face. "Try not to mention it around Bill—at least not with that face. I believe he picked the name himself. Hold on."

Stedsan ducks back into the office and reappears a second later with a glossy brochure. *Sunrise House—on the Lake!*, it announces above a stock photo of attractive thirty-somethings drinking wine around a fire pit, the glimmer of water in the background. Why do developers always pick names that sound like a high-end prison?

"Right," I say, swallowing my grimace. "Noted."

"See you next Wednesday," he says and shuts the door.

2

The car starts with that same grating noise. The boxes are piled to the roof and every time I take a turn, cardboard rasps against cardboard. The farther I get away from Stedsan's, the more I feel my body relax—like I passed a test I didn't know I was taking until it was done. There's another sensation stirring, a hunger I haven't felt since my first book, and never with the second. I'm afraid to name it now in case it slips away.

The Isle was an accident. I never set out to write a book. Actually, I was working as an investigative journalist, though really in name only, producing three-minute pieces on what's really in your toothpaste for a morning news show. Adam and I had rented this tiny cottage on the coast of Maine for a week that summer. It was so damp the sheets and pillowcases were dotted with mildew and the walls were so leaky the sea breeze came right through, even with the windows closed. I loved it.

The story had been a local legend, dusty with age and telling. On the night of March 18, 1886, Inga Berg and her sister Mathilde were brutally murdered by axe on Channel Isle—a small rocky island six miles off the coast of Maine. A third sister, Agnes, survived. The next day, Elias Cobb, a drifter who had once boarded at the house, was discovered on the mainland with blood all over his clothes. A year later, he was sentenced to death by hanging. From the beginning, the pieces of the story didn't sit right with me. Nothing specific, just a feeling.

The weather on our trip had been terrible. Cold rain soaked through our jackets until they were permanently soggy. Adam was happy enough curled up with a book, but I'd gone down to the historical society to see what I could find about the case. It turned out there was a lot. Old newspapers, trial transcripts, even a self-published book by a local historian.

Newspapers had published Agnes's account of the night. Her words were vivid: the full moon over dark water, the rocky coastline of the mainland impossibly out of reach. The cold barren island, free of snow by March but the grass still matted and dead from the long winter. The house, small and gray-shingled, standing sentinel against the wind whipping off the Atlantic.

Agnes had been the last of the three sisters to emigrate from their native Norway, arriving just the year before. Immediately, she'd brightened up the small cottage, painting it white so it was visible from shore, rising from thickets of wild rose in the summer. The sisters had taken in boarders during the warmer months to supplement their meager income. More than one article had mentioned Agnes's industriousness as well as her proportions, the thick blonde hair, braided or left loose, that fell nearly to her knees. The world had fallen in love with the beautiful, tragic Agnes. *Eyes the color of the ocean*, they'd said. But how can that be, I'd wondered, when the ocean is always changing?

Not one report had questioned her account of that night. Her story was harrowing. Elias Cobb had broken through the door with an axe, killing her sister Mathilde, who had been sleeping by the fire. Agnes and Inga had barricaded themselves in the bedroom. Inga had fainted, overcome, and Agnes had escaped through the bedroom window just as the axe had splintered the door behind her. She'd crouched behind a rock, listening to the screams of her sister and the silence, which was worse. She'd been found eight hours later by fishermen, her nightgown covered in dried blood.

When I read the story, I had the feeling of looking at one of those optical illusions. At first, it looks like a rabbit and that's all you can see. But then your eyes shift and suddenly it's a duck. And it's always been a duck, you just couldn't see it before.

From there, it was easy. I made a list of questions and dug into each one methodically. Why was Agnes covered in blood if she'd escaped through the window before Inga was killed? How had she had time to put on shoes? How heavy was an axe? How long would it take a man in a rowboat to make a twelve-mile round trip to the island? What about rowing eight miles down the coast to Portland, where Cobb was eventually discovered? With each question answered, a piece of the story unraveled.

For one thing, the sisters' bodies had been covered in axe wounds. At least twenty each, mostly shallow cuts. But I'd seen a picture of Elias Cobb. He was tall and muscular from years of doing odd jobs, pulling in fishing nets, hauling boxes. He looked like a man who could kill with a single blow. Then I found a testimony the newspapers hadn't published. Another drifter had vouched for Elias, said they'd been fishing together the evening before. That the blood on his hands was fish blood.

Adam went home at the end of the week, amused by my obsession, but I stayed and read everything I could. Newspaper clippings, hundreds of pages of trial transcripts. I studied how newspapers printed *facts* in Victorian New England. Police department procedures in the 1880s. On my last day, I hired a boat to take me out to the island. I stood on the white stone ledges and saw the mainland six miles in the distance. I tried to imagine it was night and the air was heavy with snow. No light but the candles burning in the cabin. No sounds but the wind and the cry of gulls. The cabin had burned down decades ago, but the pieces were still there, a pile of charred rotting boards, a few shards of glass from a window.

The real breakthrough came a few months after I got home. It turned out Agnes had changed her name when she emigrated from Norway, so I hadn't known about her husband or his death. He'd been killed when someone broke into their home in Trøndelag. She'd inherited enough money to pay for passage to join her sisters in Maine. When her sisters died in turn, she inherited more. Then she'd gone to Boston, where she married a sailmaker—dead a year later of a stomach ailment—then her final husband, a merchant, died, leaving her a very wealthy widow at the age of forty.

Reframed, the story told of a relentless march upward. Of someone who flattened every obstacle in her path by any means necessary. Later, I had to keep a tone of admiration out of my voice. Agnes knew what she wanted and let nothing get in her way. If you take the facts away, there's something to admire there.

I'd written the book without telling anyone but Adam what I was doing, feeling both protective and ashamed of this strange project. I didn't think anyone would ever read it, even after I got an agent, a publishing deal. But I was wrong. It was an instant bestseller, a TV miniseries. And suddenly I had everything: Adam, the book I'd always wanted to write, the legitimacy I craved, the money. I'd thought that brief, shining moment was the beginning of everything, but now I see it for what it was: an ending in disguise.

———

When my building comes into view, bright purple against the white snow, I don't stop. Instead, I keep going, past a bakery that fills the car with the smell of dough like day-old beer. I turn right at the park where I ate my breakfast, drive past the police station and its greasy-spoon school bus. I keep driving north, past a gas station and a few houses. A corridor of trees appears on the left. From studying the map, I know most of this land—the peninsula that closes the bay—is still owned by the diocese but is used as a public park of sorts. A man emerges from the trees, tugging a dog's leash, just beside a sign that says ROCK POINT.

Then the trees are gone, replaced by a snowy field, dotted with headstones. I pass a brick church, dark and shuttered, too close to the road, which I assume is the church Stedsan mentioned. It feels out of proportion to the landscape around it with its huge neoclassical arches and high bell tower covered in flakes of white paint. More graveyard. Then, there it is.

Coram House.

Stedsan had included a grainy black-and-white photo in the materials he'd sent with my contract. But it's different in person. For one thing, it's much larger. Four stories of red brick topped with a slate roof, tiles smooth and shiny as the scales of a snake. The wooden front doors must be ten feet high. But even the building is dwarfed by the scale of the lake behind it.

I knew Lake Champlain was big—people call it the inland sea—but

I'm still not prepared for the way water stretches forever in either direction, dotted by an occasional island for scale. The mountains on the other side are faint charcoal shapes etched in a gray sky. Unlike the bay just to the south, the water here isn't frozen. White-capped waves churn the surface. A ferry plods into view, heading for the far shore.

Coram House looms. There's no other way to describe it. This desolate graveyard with the sweeping view of the lake beyond like a promised land just out of reach. An island in the middle of a graveyard. How strange it would have been to be a child here.

I park on the street and get out. The stretch of land between the church and Coram House is untouched. The north side of the building is a different story. An addition emerges from the original building like a growth—steel beams, rebar, corrugated metal paneling. The beginnings of Bill Campbell's Sunrise House condo development. Though, right now, the construction site is dormant. I want to go closer, to feel Coram House's door beneath my hands, to push until it cracks open and reveals its insides.

A flash of movement at an upper window makes me step back. I teeter on the curb as dark shadows swoop and dance. A throaty burble rings out, and I realize what I'm looking at. Ravens circle the parking lot, their dark shapes reflected in the windows. I take out my phone and snap a picture.

Then I get back in my car. The last thing I need is to be caught trespassing. Plus, my stomach is growling. I'll retrace my route back to that bakery, see what smelled so good. Then I'll unload these boxes. When I look in the rearview mirror, the ravens are gone.

———

It's afternoon by the time I stack the last box in the living room. Now the apartment smells of mildew and damp cardboard. I need to buy groceries, shampoo—all the settling-in errands that will be easier while the unfamiliar streets are still light. Instead, I sit cross-legged on the floor and cut the tape off the first box.

Stedsan was right. It's a mess. The contents look like someone's recycling bin. I pull out a sheaf of brittle receipts. They're faded, some so old they're handwritten. A hundred cans of beans delivered in 1964. Received by S. Marguerite. A receipt for the cleaning of fifteen marble statues from 1962. And on and on, back to the late 1950s.

Next comes a stack of VHS tapes, each in a cardboard sheath, bearing a handwritten name and date. Sarah Dale. Violet Harrison. Karen Lafayette. Sister Cecile. Eighteen tapes total. The dates are all from 1988 or 1989. A DVD player blinks at me from the shelf below the television. Do stores even sell VHS players anymore? I make a note to check and put the tapes aside.

The next box contains nothing but paperwork relating to the case. Motions filed back and forth. Requests for information. I label this box and set it aside, knowing that the contents won't mean anything until I have a better grasp of the case.

Suddenly, the room is bathed in an orange glow. The streetlights coming on. I should really get up and find something for dinner. It's going to take days to log everything and create some kind of order from this chaos. But I can't shake the feeling that I'm looking for something. *One more box.*

The next box is heavy. I'd had to wrestle it up to the apartment one step at a time. But now it slides easily across the carpet to my desk. I open the lid and the air fills with the scent of decay. Right on top is a mold-speckled shoebox. Beneath, thick reams of yellowed paper. I lift the shoebox into my lap and pry off the top.

Inside, the box is bursting with black-and-white photographs of various sizes. My heart accelerates like I've found a box of treasure. I hold the photos carefully, at the edges, and lift them out one by one. The first shows a group of unsmiling children in hats and snowsuits arranged in front of tall wooden doors that I recognize. I turn the photo over. It's labeled *Coram House, 1964* in neat cursive.

The next photo is larger with scalloped edges. Four nuns and a priest, all wearing long dark robes, arranged in front of a brick fireplace. The ink on the back is smudged but I can make out two names. *Father Foster. S. Marguerite.* No date.

Most of the photos are like this—portraits of various groups of children and their minders, arranged into stiff, formal poses. But halfway through the box, I come across a photo that feels different. Carefully, I flatten the curled edges.

First, there's the setting: a rocky beach, the bright summer sunlight. Four people stand around a rowboat that's been pulled up on shore, the oars resting haphazardly in the foreground. On one side of the boat, two small children—a boy and a girl—wear old-fashioned bathing suits that sag around their pale, skinny legs. They look wet and cold, hair slicked back, arms wrapped around themselves. Neither looks at the camera.

On the other side of the boat stands a nun wearing a long dark habit. It's so incongruous in the setting, it feels like she's been pasted from some other photo. Her face is a ghostly blur. She must have turned her head just as the photo was taken, which lends the scene an eerie feel. The nun is short, much smaller than the teenage boy standing beside her. He looks about fifteen or sixteen, tall and pale with gangly arms held stiff by his sides. Of the four, he's the only one looking at the camera. Not just looking, he's staring intently, a curl to his lip, as if there was something rancid in the air.

I stare at the photo for a long time, wondering if this is what I've been looking for—something with a sense of life. Not a tableau, but a moment captured. The back has only two names scrawled in faded ink. *Swim lessons. S. Cecile. Fred.* The second name is in a darker ink, as if it was labeled later.

As I finish going through the shoebox, I find a few other photos that contain the same sense of life. A young woman caught in the middle of a laugh, hand half covering her mouth. *Sarah D. 1970.* Children arranged in a neat row with a boy reaching up to pull a girl's braid, ruining the formal scene. The back is blank. Many photos are labeled, but so many names and dates are missing. The children unknown.

Once I'm done, I nestle each photo back in the shoebox. The main box is filled with stacks of paper held together by rusty binder clips except for a single loose sheet on top, ochre with age. A typewritten list of names, some of which I recognize from the labels on the tapes. Sarah Dale. Violet Harrison. Anthony Fiero. A list of the deposition transcripts, I realize.

My knees pop in protest when I stand and stretch. Tomorrow, I'll cross-check the list with the stack of tapes I found in the first box. Then I'll catalogue each of the photos, the receipts, everything I've found so far. But today, it's enough. I need hot food and a glass of wine. Even though it's barely seven, I'm exhausted. I put everything back in the box except for one transcript, chosen at random. *Sarah Dale—May 3, 1989.* I place it on top of my closed laptop. Tomorrow, I'll get started.

3

My arms and back ache from hauling boxes yesterday. I wash down a couple ibuprofen with coffee and then eat a bowl of cereal standing over the sink. I have one week before my meeting with Father Aubry. It's not enough time to familiarize myself with the case in the way I'd like. But a week's what Stedsan gave me.

Given that, I decide to start with the transcripts. I'm hoping they'll give me the best feel for daily life at Coram House—the mundane and the awful. Then I'll sift through the court documents about the negotiations around the settlement. I don't expect to be an expert in a week, but I need to know where to tread lightly and where to probe.

Pushing aside my laptop, I free the pages of Sarah Dale's deposition from the binder clip. My first thought is that whoever did the transcription did a good job. They capture every utterance and silence, so I can feel the rhythm of the conversation. For a while, Sarah talks about daily life—chores and meals. Routine cruelties like being slapped or locked in the attic as punishment. Her recall is impressive. The way she describes the frigid air of the attic, the heat of a summer day, her dress soaked with sweat—it makes me feel like I'm right there with her.

In my experience, it's rare to find someone who remembers things with all five senses. Sarah Dale either has a remarkable memory or a very active imagination. I don't think she's lying. But if you tell a story enough times, it can start to feel true. Then again, she did live at Coram House for twenty years. A lifetime.

Toward the end of one day's testimony, her tone changes. Even through a transcript, I can sense her distress. Her answers break like Stedsan is pulling the words from her. There are long silences, as if she's dredging up these memories from somewhere deeper than the others. She watched a boy drown while others stood by and did nothing. My throat clenches when I imagine her on the hill watching the events play out far below. I'd braced myself for horrors, for abuse, but this is cold-blooded enough to knock me breathless.

I think of that little boy in the water, gasping for air, reaching for a hand to pull him out and finding no help at all. I sift through the mildewed shoebox until I find the photo of the nun and children by the rowboat. *Swim lessons. S. Cecile.* I stare at the nun's ghostly blur of a face and the small pinched faces of the children. They look cold and scared. The nuns said he ran away. Cold seeps down the back of my neck. Wrongness has a temperature.

Once, while I was working on *The Isle*, I'd tried to describe the feeling to Adam—that moment when people who had only existed on paper suddenly become real. *It's a rush*, I'd said, *almost like they're sitting next to you, just out of sight, but you can hear them breathing. They're there.*

He'd asked me if I was high.

I'd laughed, but it was a little like that.

Tommy, what happened to you? I place the photo back in the box. Then I stack the pages of Sarah Dale's deposition and put them gently aside. My hand closes on the next stack—maybe there will be more answers here. Okay, Michael Leblanc. I read on.

The next few days are a blur. I barely leave my desk except to go across the street for coffee and cellophane-wrapped turkey sandwiches. The apartment is covered in stacks of papers—depositions, legal pads, photos. I spend hours drawing a map of Coram House and the surrounding area on a sheet of butcher's paper. I'd done the same when I was writing *The Isle*. It had helped me understand the space and see people moving through it. Now I label every place mentioned in a deposition. The dormitories. The kitchen door. The sections of Rock Point where the children went to play. The dump. The trails that crisscrossed

the graveyard and woods. The deepwater cove where Sarah Dale saw
Tommy drown.

Lola calls at one point and leaves a message asking what I'm up to
tonight. I'm not surprised. In college, she was always the one to pull me
out of the library—to a play, to a late dinner, to a movie. And in the last
couple years, she's started calling even when she's busy just to make sure
I'm not sitting home alone in my sweatpants, which is usually exactly
what I'm doing.

Lola and I met the first day of college. The first five minutes, really.
She rescued me then and, like we're in some fairy tale, I think a part of
her believes it's her responsibility to rescue me now. Our dorm was this
massive complex, an old hotel they'd turned into student housing. The
two wings—east and west—stretched around in a horseshoe. But the
rooms had been numbered by someone with a sick sense of humor. So
there I was at eighteen, my first foray into adulthood, and I was already
lost and foolish, dragging a massive suitcase and pushing along a cardboard box with my feet. When along came Lola.

She's not tall, but she's one of those people who feels tall. Something
about the bounce in her step, the wild curly hair bleached blonde just at
the tips, the massive gold hoop earrings, and overalls hand-printed with
woodblock stamps. She was so the opposite of me in my nondescript
jeans, my white tee that I owned seven of.

She'd stopped, smiled at me. "Lost?" she'd asked in a way that made
it seem like I was in on the joke.

"Maybe," I'd said. "The numbers don't make sense."

She laughed as she explained how they'd numbered the rooms so
odd numbers were in the east wing and evens in the west.

"Here, I'll show you."

She took my hand then, such an unusual gesture from someone who
was basically a stranger, and I'd felt—not a spark—more like a thunk.
The way a magnet feels when it meets its opposite—joined, inseparable.
A perfect fit. I've never felt love at first sight, not with Adam or anyone
else. Love was always something that grew quietly and slowly for me.
But those moments—the thunks, the sense that someone is going to be
important—that's the closest I've ever come.

Something inside Lola called out to something in me. Not just her intelligence, her wild clothes, the wilder theater crowd she hung out with. No, it was her sureness. About the things she loves, how sure they were worthy of her devotion. How unworried she was about what other people thought she was making with the clay of her life.

I, on the other hand, agonized over all of it. Where to intern. What to do with my love of words. Whether I'd end up as a penniless writer, whether I had anything original to say or was just regurgitating the ideas I found in other, better work. I took a fiction class, but whenever I tried to make something up, I'd just sit and stare at that blank page, paralyzed. I didn't know then that creating something from something else was an art form too. To take facts and assemble them into a story that made sense. It took me years to realize that too was a calling.

After college, Lola and I had moved to New York together, lived in a one-bedroom apartment the same size as the dorm room we'd shared our sophomore year. Except this had a kitchen and living room crammed in. We'd pursued our dreams in parallel.

When she'd met Kay, an actress in a play her theater company was producing, they'd moved in together, and I'd taken a year abroad. A supremely weird copyediting job at a newspaper in Bangkok. I'd spent the year sending emails back and forth with Lola, regaling her with stories about food—so spicy I'd eaten a napkin on my first day in a desperate attempt to get the chili oil off my tongue. The islands ringed in sand so white and fine it was like powdered sugar. But the truth was, I was lonely, had been relieved to go back to New York.

The plan was to couch surf with Kay and Lola. Their apartment always hosted at least one actor or musician between gigs. I'd wait for a sublet to come up. I already had an entry-level job at the news show lined up.

When I got on the plane and found my row, there was a guy sitting in the aisle seat. Dark wavy hair, glasses, and pale skin, sunburned pink. I paused, looked down at my ticket, and then up at him.

"Lost?" he said, and smiled at me.

The words tugged on me, and the gentleness of his tone too. I felt the strange echo across continents and years. The same words Lola had spoken to me in that hallway six years earlier. Years later, the four of us would laugh about this. How I'd fall in love with anyone who gave me directions. But even now it gives me a little chill, makes me wonder if I did look at him differently because of that moment. Because his words echoed Lola's.

"I think you're in my seat," I said.

We did the dance, rechecked our tickets, and settled into our seats for the sixteen-hour flight.

"I'm Adam," he said.

I wonder what would have happened if someone had sat in that middle seat between us. What path my life would have taken and with whom. But no one ever did.

By the end of the flight, I felt that same sense of two magnets clicking together. Thunk. *You will be important*, I thought. Then, with a thrill because I was twenty-four years old and the world was possibility: *What will happen next?* I shove the memory into the locked box inside my head and shut the lid. It's getting crowded in there.

It's only after listening to Lola's message that I realize it's Saturday. I've worked through half the weekend without knowing it.

My dreams are becoming eerie, full of empty halls and the feeling of being watched. I know I should take a break, so I drive out to a complex of big-box stores to buy a VCR, which turns out to be a challenge. I have no luck at the electronics store and the acne-faced teenager at Walmart acts like he's never heard of a VHS tape. I try calling thrift stores with no luck. Finally, I give up and order one online that promises it will be here in three to five days, all along cursing myself for waiting so long.

That night, I eat popcorn for dinner and read, turning pages with one hand so I don't smear cheesy residue on the brittle paper. By midnight, I'm turning the final page on the last deposition in the box. Then I wash my hands and pour a tall glass of wine. Back at my desk, I close my binder and push aside my notepad.

Most of the depositions had been what I'd expected. The former children of Coram House had been in their thirties and forties by the time they were interviewed, and their memories had dulled over time. Everyone remembers eating and sleeping. Attending classes in the schoolroom. The sting of being slapped. But most transcripts contain very few specific moments. They read more like a summary.

There were terrible stories, to be sure—and some of those were very sharp indeed. Stories of abuse at the hands of the priest and nuns who ran Coram House. But there was a depressing sameness to even the worst ones. I guess that's unsurprising. Predators tend to find something that works and stick with it.

But not all the testimony feels routine. Karen Lafayette describes a girl being pushed out the window by one of the nuns. Though her account is called into question by the testimony of Sarah Dale, among others. Anthony Fiero talks about a boy who was electrocuted trying to climb under a fence, how he was forced to look at the body, how for years after he had nightmares about his hands turning black. And then there's Tommy, who sticks in my head like a burr.

Based on what I'd read, many of the children hadn't remembered the abuse until they'd reconnected with other children from the orphanage in a support group, something I knew the church had made much of during the case. False memories, they'd claimed, painting a few as vengeful liars out to say anything to wring a settlement from the church. The attacks on Sarah Dale had been particularly vicious. But she'd been particularly insistent about Tommy's death and, after all, even child abusers balk at being accused of murder.

But that's just how memory works. Something horrible happens and you tell yourself it wasn't real; you lock it in a dark closet where the nightmares live. You make this true by the force of your will, at least until someone opens that door by mistake. We shape our reality as we live it. So, no, it didn't seem unbelievable to me at all.

I look down at my binder, now full of questions divided into research areas, starting with the deaths and injuries. The unnamed girl pushed out the window. The boy who crawled under the electric fence. Tommy, drowned in the lake. How many other unrecorded deaths and injuries existed in Coram House's past? And then, the other side of that question: How many of these could be creations by traumatized children, trained by terror to see monsters everywhere, even inside their own heads?

The wine is overly sweet, but I finish the bottle anyways. Soon the world is pleasantly blurred. In the bathroom mirror, I see my teeth are stained red. I don't bother changing out of my clothes. The bed is cold. I huddle under the comforter, shivering. Every time I close my eyes, the bed starts to rock gently, like I'm drifting on the water. I think of Tommy with his scraped knees and freckles and I want to shout at him to run, to lift him out of the boat and carry him away.

———

I wake as if no time has passed at all, except now sunlight stabs my eyelids. Paper crinkles when I roll over. My comforter is littered with folders and loose paper. I don't remember bringing them into bed with me. My head aches. Possibly something to do with the empty bottle of wine on the bedside table. I shuffle into the living room. A dusting of powdered cheese coats the table. Papers blanket the floor. It looks like a dorm room.

I gather the papers and wipe down the table. Then I splash water on my face and hunt through my suitcase for a pair of socks—the floor is like ice. All morning, I search for Tommy. Through the list of children, the intake forms, the sheaves of receipts. When that doesn't turn up so much as a mention, I search online—death records, police records, hospital records. But, without a last name, I don't get far.

Frustrated, I call Stedsan. He had years with the case; he spoke to Sarah Dale and the others. He must know more than what's inside these boxes. When he doesn't answer, I leave a message, asking him to meet. His reply comes when I'm halfway through a bowl of cereal, suggesting we meet tomorrow, Monday. Only two days until our meeting with Father Aubry, but it will have to do.

My body is twitchy from too many days at a desk. The need to move is constant and as annoying as an itch. So I pull on my sneakers and head outside with no plan except to run. The sky is pale blue and cloudless. The air crackles with cold. Within minutes, my thighs ache beneath the thin leggings, and every gulp of freezing air feels like a dagger inside my lungs. Still, I keep going. Past a brewery where people stand around fire pits drinking beer, past a playground with a slide built into the hillside so four children tumble down at once, and along a bike path full of other joggers, chatting in pairs or on the phone, running to nowhere.

By the time I get back to the apartment, my toes throb and the hair around my face is crusted with ice. My fingers fumble when I try to unlock the door and I feel a spike of real fear. Upstairs, I get straight into the shower, leaving my clothes in a puddle on the bathmat. The cold, which felt like a part of me just a minute ago, melts away, so easily forgotten.

———

The coffee shop where I'm supposed to meet Stedsan is tucked on a narrow street, barely wider than an alley. Deep snow covers the sidewalk, so I have to slog my way to the door. A bell rings as I step into air thick with coffee and cinnamon. Stedsan is folded into a green armchair, underneath a painting of a rooster. He sees me and lifts his cup in greeting.

I order a coffee and find the milk hidden among the antique glass bottles arranged on the counter. I take the chair next to his, this one red velvet draped in cowhide. Fur scratches my neck when I lean back. I suppress a shudder.

"Thanks for finding time to meet," I say. "I've read through the depositions and wanted to follow up on a few things before we see Father Aubry."

"You've read all of them?" Stedsan raises his eyebrows. "You do move quickly. All right, go ahead."

He leans back, getting comfortable. I open my notebook to a random page. People have an easier time talking if you're not looking at them.

"I want to talk about the children who died."

The words take flight, an insect crawling out of my mouth and fluttering across the room.

"There's a boy who was electrocuted on a fence—" I start, but Stedsan interrupts.

"That one was quite sad, but just bad luck. He'd found an army helmet, one of those old metal ones, and the fence was poorly marked.

These days you could probably make a case for neglect or sue someone, but back then . . ." He shrugs.

"Some of these incidents have conflicting accounts, though. There's a girl who went out a window—"

"Melissa Graves."

"What?"

"Her name was Melissa Graves, but the children called her Missy, I believe. She's buried in the graveyard behind Coram House. East section with some of the other children."

He ticks off the death matter-of-factly. I should find it encouraging that his memory of the case is so good. But instead I feel on the defensive—like he's preempting every question to show me how little I know.

"And Missy's cause of death?"

Stedsan shrugs again. "Complications due to flu. About six months after the incident you're referring to—with the window. Hard to believe children still died of the flu in the sixties but the medical care here wasn't exactly state of the art." He laughs.

I wait for him to go on, but he doesn't. *Case closed.*

"And how can you be sure that the records weren't falsified?"

He makes a visible effort at patience. "We can't be sure, not really. But to have the local doctor faking death records for a child?" He shakes his head. "It's unlikely. And besides, both Sister Cecile and Sarah Dale gave similar accounts—the girl was sent out onto the ledge to clean and then came back in."

"So Missy Graves was sent outside, onto the outer windowsill, to wash the windows—that part is true."

"Yes, but she came back in—the important part."

But I'm not so sure. The windows were two stories up. If Sister Cecile sent a child out there with nothing but a couple of kids holding on to her ankles for protection, it establishes a pattern of behavior. My heart thuds—like I'm about to ask about something off-limits.

"What about Tommy, the boy who drowned?"

Stedsan sighs. "I wondered if it might be that." He steeples his hands together beneath his chin, as if in prayer.

"Let it go. I looked into all this decades ago. There's no record of any of it. Not his death, not even a last name. Concentrate on the material you have."

I reach for my coffee and then let my hand drop halfway there, afraid Stedsan will see how it's shaking. I need to appear calm and professional, but it's taking every ounce of strength. *Let it go.* I know an order when I hear one.

"Children can't just disappear as if they never existed."

"My point exactly," Stedsan says. "If his records existed, they're gone. Poof. For all we know, he ran away and changed his name. Look, I know this is horrible stuff, but I think you'll find the general abuse was well documented."

He looks at me, waiting for confirmation.

I think of the accounts I read. Children slapped with hands and with sticks. A child made to stand in the middle of the room with his arms outstretched for hours after dropping a cup of water. The sameness of the stories. I nod.

"The sexual abuse by Edmund Foster in particular," Stedsan continues. "Children who had never met each other all gave very similar accounts of what happened after they were sent to his office. And they were almost always children between nine and twelve. Even the church couldn't ignore it. He was quietly retired and then died a year after the settlement. But the other accounts"—he looks up, as if searching for a word on the ceiling—"the more outlying violence. Those were slippery. You can include them in the book, but it's going to be more questions than answers. I mean, you've read the transcripts—half of them contradict each other."

I lean forward. "Do you mean Karen Lafayette and Sarah Dale?"

Stedsan winces as if those names were sharp and I'd just stabbed him. "Sarah Dale. She was a tough one."

"What do you mean?"

He sighs. "Her level of recall was impressive."

"Did you believe her?"

"She was very persuasive. And she struck a sympathetic figure— the widowed mother with her boy."

It's a non-answer, a lawyer's answer, but I let it be for now. "And what about Karen Lafayette?"

He shrugs. "She was angry. And I got the sense she was listing off every terrible thing that happened to her or others—real and imagined."

I think of Karen Lafayette's description of the girl going out the window. *She sort of bounced when she hit the ground.* It was such a strange detail. Had she really imagined it? Or is it possible Sarah Dale remembered events wrong, that the death certificate was a fake?

"The allegations against Father Foster were rock solid. Like I said, there was a record of the boy killed on the electric fence, the girl supposedly pushed out the window—but the boy who drowned?" He shrugs with a finality I don't like. "It had happened twenty years before and, well, people at the time suggested Sarah Dale was unreliable."

"Unreliable?"

"Prone to exaggeration. Unstable."

"Well, that would be in their best interest if they wanted the case settled."

"I don't just mean the church. Other witnesses, people who were children at Coram House when Sarah Dale was there."

My stomach sinks. "I see. Was there ever a police investigation into any of this?"

"No. Nothing official, anyways."

"What about other people that could corroborate Sarah Dale's version of that day?"

"The cook was dead by the eighties. And Sister Cecile—all the sisters—always maintained that the boy ran away."

"What about the other children?"

He shrugs. "No one else saw anything."

"No one?"

There's always someone who saw something.

Stedsan's nostrils flare. He holds out his fingers and starts ticking off points. "The day was particularly hot. Everyone was at the other end of the beach—where the trees in the graveyard give shade. You couldn't see the cove from there. The sisters reported the boy missing at dinner. There was no record of Sarah Dale ever making an accusation at the time. By the time she gave her deposition it had been twenty years. A body, any physical evidence, was long gone."

He sits back in his chair, evidently done.

But I'm not finished yet. "What about this other boy—Fred Rooney?"

Stedsan snorts. "What about him?"

"A few accounts suggest he was close to Sister Cecile—a kind of helper. And Sarah Dale saw him going down to the beach that day."

"*Claims* she saw him going down to the beach," he says absently, another lawyer's reflex. "Even if Sarah Dale's testimony was true and Fred was in the boat that day—so what? That makes him less likely to talk, not more."

I taste blood and only then notice I've been nibbling the inside of my cheek. All traces of Tommy are gone, as if he never existed. But it's not that easy to erase someone. It can't be.

"Look, Alex," Stedsan's voices softens as he leans forward. For a second, I'm afraid he's going to pat me on the head.

"I know it's tempting to think you can solve this. And, God knows, it would make for a great story if you could. But it's been fifty years since that boy died or ran away." He turns his palms up in surrender. "Some things—we have to accept that they'll stay questions forever."

"I know it sounds crazy, but what if we dragged the lake? It's possible—"

"Alex." He says my name like he's slapping sense into me. "I admire your"—he pauses—"dedication to the truth. But there's such a thing as taking it too far. I'd think you would know that."

Heat rushes to my face. It was the way he emphasized the *you* so I'd know exactly what he was referring to.

"Look, I'll make it easy for you. Ultimately, it's my book and I'm telling you to drop it. There's nothing there. There—now you can feel you've done your due diligence."

Stedsan smiles at me as if to say, *Problem solved.* Then he glances down at his watch. "Listen, I have to go. I'll see you Wednesday at nine, all right? We can meet at the rectory next to Sunrise House."

"Fine," I bark, knowing I sound like a petulant teenager. But Stedsan either doesn't notice or doesn't care. He pulls on his jacket, saying something about the chief of police and something called a duffer, but I'm not listening, and then he's gone.

I pick up my coffee with shaking hands, but the smell of burnt milk turns my stomach. Stedsan acts like the truth is meaningless if you can't prove it. *Sarah Dale was unreliable. Unstable. Prone to exaggeration.* How many times has someone dismissed the words of a woman or a child as untrustworthy? He thinks this will all come to nothing, but I think I've found a thread that leads to the heart of the story. And the only way to find out is to tug.

4

The room smells like vanilla mixed with old paper, the sweetness of rot. I sit with my binder open before me. Everything I know so far is organized in chronological order and then categorized by what use it might have in the book. Blue for dialogue—hard to come by in a historical book. Green for important events. And then red, the rarest of all. Sometimes it's a particularly vivid description or a scene that propels the story forward. It's not any one thing. But I know it when I see it.

I turn to the first page—my map of Coram House. I've sketched three rectangles: Coram House, the rectory, and the church. Scattered circles represent the graveyard, leading down to a wash of blue for the lake.

My plan is to spend the day reviewing the binder and coming up with questions for the meeting with Father Aubry tomorrow, but I can't focus. Yesterday's conversation with Stedsan—his patronizing speech about getting comfortable with uncertainty—is buzzing in my head. And then his allusions to my last book at the end.

There are two versions of me sitting at this table. The one who knows I should sit down, review my notes, prep for tomorrow, who knows this book is my second chance and doesn't want to think about what happens if I screw it up. Then there's the other me, the one who breaks out in a rash at the thought of sitting quietly when there has to be more information out there. That one wins.

I get dressed. Black pants. A white button-down. Some concealer to cover the bags under my eyes. Perched on the edge of the bathtub, I take in my full reflection in the mirror above the sink. I look like a waiter. So I put on a pair of gold studs and a patterned scarf that Adam brought back from a trip to Mexico. I never wore it while he was alive. Not really my taste. But I couldn't throw it away either. I look at my reflection. Better.

The parking lot next to the police station is mostly empty. I pull in, past the row of black-and-white cruisers, and park in a visitors' spot. The entrance is strung with red Christmas lights, like it's an Amsterdam sex shop instead of a small city's police headquarters.

The automatic doors whoosh open, and I pass into a reception area: a row of plastic chairs and a desk festooned with tinsel behind which an older woman sits typing. Reading glasses dangle from her neck on a gold chain like she too is wound with tinsel. A placard on the desk says BEVERLEY WHITE.

"Good morning, Ms. White," I say. People like it when you use their name.

She stops typing and smiles up at me. "I haven't lost my marbles if that's what you're thinking."

I feel disoriented, like I've wandered into the middle of a conversation.

"The decorations, dear," she says patiently. "It's the twelfth of January. And please call me Bev."

"Right. Of course. They're very . . . cheerful," I say, thinking of my landlord and his bright-purple house.

"Now, how can I help you, young lady?"

Suddenly all business, she reminds me of a thousand other women who have come before her, guarding the gates of administration offices everywhere.

"I'm trying to find some historical records," I say. "Specifically, I'm looking for records of deaths from the 1960s."

She taps a pen against her lips. "Well, the city records would be your best bet for that."

"Yes, well, these deaths might have been suspicious. So I was hoping to see if there's ever been a police investigation."

She pulls a sticky note off a stack and looks at me, pen poised. "What's the name of the deceased and the date?"

"Well, that's the other thing," I say, starting to feel stupid for coming here. "It's only a first name. Thomas or Tommy. But he would have been around ten years old. And it happened up at Coram House."

Her friendly expression is still there, but now there's something else behind the smile. "I see," she says. "Could you give me your name?"

"Alex Kelley."

"Please, wait here a moment, Ms. Kelley."

Bev gestures to the plastic chairs in the corner set among a jungle of potted plants. Then she opens the glass door that separates the reception area from the rest of the station. There's a brief swell of noise—laughter, a phone ringing—and then the door seals shut behind her.

I take a seat, wanting to be seen as following directions, but also because it affords the best view of the office beyond. The station is nothing special—stained drop ceilings, metal desks, chipped fake wood paneling. But behind all that, huge windows frame a spectacular view of the bay, frozen solid as far as I can see.

Bev stops before a desk and starts making dramatic, sweeping hand gestures that I hope have nothing to do with me. I crane my neck to see her audience, but it's no use, her body is in the way. A few seconds later, the glass door swings open again. This time, Bev is trailed by an officer in a navy blue uniform.

I'd put him in his early forties. He's good-looking in a tall, dark, and stubbly way. His brown hair is peppered with gray and he has a long straight nose straight off a Roman coin. But it's his eyes that are arresting—light brown with a circle of gold around the iris. Unfortunately, they're glaring at me. I get the distinct feeling that I'm not about to be offered a cup of coffee and a free pass into their historical records.

"Alex Kelley," he says, "I'm Officer Russell Parker. Please come with me."

He holds the door open for me, but the vibe isn't so much chivalrous as *angry principal inviting you into his office*.

I follow him to a desk tucked in one corner of the open-plan room, right up against one of the big windows. He motions for me to sit in the chair with the view of the water. I wonder why he doesn't turn the desk around.

53

"So, you're the writer." He says it both like he was expecting me and like he's not happy about it.

"Well," I say, "I'm *a* writer."

He doesn't smile. I clear my throat. Better to jump in. "I'm looking for historical records about Coram House. Specifically any investigation around a suspicious death or deaths that would have happened sometime in the late 1960s."

"Up at the House."

"Sorry?" I ask, thrown off.

"Coram House. That's what people called it. The House."

He leans back in his chair and taps a pen against the arm, impatient.

"Oh," I say, fumbling, "I didn't know."

No matter how much research you do about a place, there's certain knowledge that no one ever thinks to write down. *The House.*

"How could you know?" he asks. "You've been here—what—a week?"

"Ten days, actually," I say. "Including today."

He ignores me. The dynamic is clear. The out-of-town writer swooping in. The local cop protecting local secrets.

"I looked you up," he says. "Even read your last book—the one about that lifeguard. My money was on the brother."

The usual greasy ball of shame slides up my throat. I swallow it and force my eyes to meet his. "Mine too," I say. "Too bad he didn't kill her."

"Sure made a good story, though."

Behind him, the lake is a gray mirror. I should be better at this, given how many times I've had some version of this conversation over the last two years. With journalists. With my agent. With myself.

"The book was a mistake," I say. It sounds like an excuse. Sweat prickles in my armpits. I just want to get up and leave, but I can't. Not yet. "Look, whatever you think about my last book, I do actually care about the truth. This isn't just about selling books."

Officer Parker rests his elbows on the table and looks at me. The golden center of his eyes glow. "Is this how you do it?" he asks. "Convince people to give you what you want? You ask for their help telling the truth?"

He says *truth* like it tastes bad.

My stomach roils, but this time it's anger. I've had enough. "Do you know what I've been doing for the last week? Reading depositions. From kids who were abused. Who saw others abused. I read testimony from one woman who saw a child pushed into the water and left to drown—and no one believed her. Can you imagine carrying that around with you?"

He leans back and says nothing. I riffle through my bag and take out a brown envelope, then open it and slide two photos across the desk, right in front of him. The first shows Sarah Dale, head tilted back in laughter. The other the children and nun standing beside the rowboat. I point.

"This woman is Sister Cecile. Sometime in the summer of 1967 or '68, I believe she pushed a child into the water and watched him drown. And this girl"—I point to the photo of Sarah Dale—"saw it all happen. But no one believed her. She was locked in a wardrobe in the attic overnight as a punishment. She thought she was going to die. She was fourteen years old."

Officer Parker picks up the photo. He turns it over, gently. The ink is faded so he holds it up to the window to read the name written there. *Sarah Dale.* I keep talking, wondering if any of this is sinking in.

"The people who did these things—none of them went to jail," I continue. "Some of them are probably still out there. They just— moved on. While the kids at Coram House got—what? A couple thousand dollars in the settlement, if they were lucky. And a lifetime of shitty memories that no one wanted to hear about."

He looks up at me then, and I think I'm finally getting to him. But when he speaks, his voice is granite. "And your book is going to fix it for them?"

Tears burn my throat. But I will not cry in front of him. I'm too tired to be having this conversation. Too many late nights reading about horrible things.

"You don't like me," I say. "Fine. And I get this is your home and I'm an outsider. I get that my last book was shitty and you wish that I wasn't here or that I was someone better. But you haven't read Sarah Dale's testimony. She—" I pause, unsure how to explain the feeling of reading her words—like I was there watching it all happen.

"She saw a boy murdered and no one believed her. I know it's been fifty years and I know it's unlikely I'll find out what happened that day. But I'm going to try. And I'd like your help."

The silence drags on for five seconds, ten. Then he shakes his head and pushes the two photos back across the desk. As if the dismissal weren't clear enough, he swivels his chair toward the window to stare at the smooth ice, the peninsula of Rock Point miles in the distance.

Right there, I want to say. *He died right on the other side of that point, and no one cared.*

I stand and slip the photos back into their envelope. I try to think of something to say that will sting, but my mind is a blank page. Instead, I turn my back on him and leave without a word.

———

I cross the parking lot so fast I'm nearly jogging. Reaching for the door handle of my car, I slip on a patch of ice and nearly go down, but somehow manage to half fall, half throw myself into the driver's seat.

My breaths come in shallow gulps. There's not enough oxygen in the car. I close my eyes and start reviewing things I can touch. The smooth leather of the steering wheel. The cold glass of the window. The tiny ridges on the radio's volume knob. With each, my breathing slows until I can open my eyes again.

My second book has followed me for two years, but it can still ambush me like this, squeeze the air from my chest until I'm drowning. Because I should have known that book was a mistake from the beginning.

No, that's wrong. I did know. But I wrote it anyway.

After the success of *The Isle*, I'd waded through true crime stories for months, waiting for the same spark I'd felt reading about the murders on Channel Isle. Meanwhile, I'd watched the money in our account dwindle. I'd ignored emails from my agent dropping references to my two-book deal. I'd shriveled with the worry that my first book had been lightning, striking only once. All the while, Adam had been getting sick—sluggish, losing weight, strange numbness in his legs—and I'd barely noticed.

Then my editor sent me an email about the unsolved murder of Madeline Curry, a sixteen-year-old girl who had disappeared in 1999. She was a lifeguard at a pond on Cape Cod. It was only her third week of work, but that summer was already sweltering, the pond jammed with children catching frogs, mothers standing up to their thighs in tepid water. On June 17, Maddy left the pond at five o'clock for the two-mile bike ride home, but she never made it.

The police assumed she'd gone off with friends and forgot to tell her parents in the way teenagers do. By the time they brought in blood-hounds the next day, it was too late. It was probably always too late. The dogs tracked her scent to the main road and then it was gone.

No one saw anything.

I read the long email Maddy's parents had sent my publisher—about how badly they wanted to meet me, how they'd been looking for Maddy for a decade, how amazing my last book had been at uncovering leads from a cold case over a century old. I'd have their full cooperation to write about their Maddy. I told myself the spark was there. I agreed to write the book.

From the beginning, it was all wrong. Speaking to people still alive, still in pain, felt like a desecration. So I buried that feeling too, as I kept uncovering the pieces of a puzzle everyone expected me to put back together. Maddy's parents especially. I felt haunted by their expectation, their eyes watching everything I did.

Maddy's brother, Matthew Curry, remembered seeing a man in a white van parked at the beach the day before she disappeared. The police artists sketched a man with a thick mustache. The sketches aired on the national news. Maddy's photo was mailed to seventy-five million people. Authorities offered a reward for any leads. The working theory was she'd been stalked by a stranger who knew her schedule and snatched her on the way home.

They never found him. They never found anything.

I spent months looking for the man in the white van, but came up with nothing. Then, one night, I moved the puzzle pieces around and a new picture emerged.

Matthew Curry was the head lifeguard at the same pond where

Maddy had worked. He'd been the one to tell the police about the man in the white van. Matt was supposed to have been working at the pond the day Maddy disappeared, but had ditched work. He supposedly had an airtight alibi—on security footage at the mall—but what if the police had gotten the timing wrong? She could have arrived home and been killed much later. After all, her parents had been at a party, hadn't arrived home until nearly eleven that night. Most of the time, the killer is someone who knows the victim. What if the answer had been right there?

As Adam got sicker, I spent more time taking care of him during the day, more time working late at night. I slept less and less, but I didn't seem to need sleep anymore. I started looking more closely at Matt. After Maddy died, he had dropped out of college. Had been arrested twice for fighting. Had never moved away from home. Had never married. These could all be signs of a life derailed by a beloved sister's death—or guilt at killing her. Same story, different angle.

The book started to take shape, weaving together two possible stories. The man in the white van. The brother. I congratulated myself on the balanced storytelling, but all along I was sure the man in the white van was a lie.

The book was published. The prosecutor reopened the case just as Maddy's parents had hoped, but this time they pursued Matthew Curry. Adam got sicker. Matthew Curry went to jail. His parents divorced.

Later the publisher used this as an excuse, that my husband was dying while I wrote *Ghost in a White Van*. They said I had a breakdown. But that was just another excuse. The truth is, I'd loved writing the book. Living in someone else's pain, it turned out, was a relief from my own. I was lucky in some ways that Adam was gone before the rest. The only mercy of what came next was I had the freedom to fall apart completely.

The summer Adam died, three months after the book came out, someone in prison stabbed Matthew Curry in the eye with a sharpened pipe. Matthew's father died of a heart attack. And someone found a blue swim cap in the woods five miles away from the Curry house. It had two different sources of DNA on it. Madeline Curry's and another.

It didn't belong to Matthew Curry or some stalker in a white van. The DNA belonged to a man who'd lived three miles down the road and hunted in the woods behind the pond. He'd been convicted for aggravated rape and assault and served fifteen years, but somehow never made it onto the sex offender registry. It had been a crime of opportunity. The man had already been dead for five years. He drove a black pickup truck. I'd been wrong about everything.

The Curry family had invited me into their home, thinking I was there to help them, and instead I'd destroyed them. All along, I'd told myself my responsibility was to Maddy, to the truth. But I'd also wanted lightning to strike again.

My publisher pulled the book and dropped me. My agent was furious. *You were just telling a story,* she'd raged, *based on the evidence. You weren't the prosecutor who put Matthew Curry away. You didn't stab him with a pipe.* But I didn't want to fight it. There's a place between guilt and its opposite.

I called Matthew after he was released from prison. I offered to donate the money from the book, not much by then after Adam's medical bills, in his name or his sister's name. He was polite. He thanked me. He got off the phone. Relieved, I was about to hang up when his mother picked up. *Devil,* she'd hissed at me. *You leave us alone.* And she slammed the phone down.

Maybe I am a devil. Or, at least, I'm someone's devil.

My phone rings. Stedsan. I want to let it go to voicemail, but then I think about the meeting with Father Aubry tomorrow morning.

"Hello?" I sound out of breath. A light skin of frost spreads on the inside of the windshield, a curtain between me and the outside world.

"Alex? Alan Stedsan here. I have some good news."

He sounds buoyant. Well, I could use some good news. "Okay," I say.

"I was at the club last night and Rob Baker, the chief of police, was there as well."

"The club?" I will my brain to catch up.

"Golf. I told you. Anyhow, I told him about our project weeks ago. I assumed he'd forgotten, but he brought it up last night. Turns out he's a history nut. He's out on leave—cancer, very sad—so can't meet you himself, but he's already assigned you a media liaison from the police department."

"A media liaison?"

"I know. He must have heard it on *Law & Order*. One of his officers volunteered for the job. Maybe he's a fan of your books?"

Stedsan sounds giddy. He laughs like all this is the funniest thing he's ever heard.

"Hang on, let me find his phone number." There's a rustling in the background. "Here we go."

A tight ball of dread forms in my stomach like a peach pit. Somehow, I know before he says it.

"Officer Russell Parker."

The name goes off in my brain like a foghorn, drowning out Stedsan's voice.

"Alex? Are you still there?"

"Yeah—yes."

"I'll email you his information."

My mouth is so dry I can barely croak out, "Great."

"All right." Stedsan sounds disappointed. Maybe he was expecting more profuse thanks. "See you tomorrow, then?"

"See you then."

I hang up. Outside, the sky is a watercolor painting of pink and orange stripes. It's going to be a beautiful sunset. My shirt feels clammy where the sweat has dried.

This day has gone all wrong, but it's not over yet.

Tomorrow, we'll meet with Father Aubry. That means I still have this afternoon to try to find something that will lead me to Tommy. A hospital record, a receipt, a goddamn library card—I don't care what Stedsan says, there must be something out there that proves he existed outside a memory. Then I'll track down Sarah Dale, Karen Lafayette, and anyone who's still alive and willing to talk. I don't need Stedsan or Officer Parker.

The defrost is on high, but the hot air doesn't seem to affect the skin of frost coating the windshield. I claw at it with my fingernails until ribbons of white litter the dashboard. An animal trying to escape its pen. Then I throw the car in reverse and drive.

Bill Campbell

Alan Stedsan: Thanks for joining us, Bill. I know you're busy—shall we jump in?

Bill Campbell: Sure.

AS: How long were you at Coram House?

BC: A couple months.

AS: The record says it was six months.

BC: Sure, then.

AS: After that?

BC: My mother got clean and we lived with family for a while. She went back to school to get her nursing degree. She worked hard to get us back on our feet. I have to say, overall I have no complaints about my time there.

AS: And what about the other children?

BC: What do you mean?

AS: You're familiar with the complaints other former residents are making, are you not?

BC: Sure.

AS: And?

BC: I never saw anything and—come on, Alan—even if it happened, it was years ago. Half of them are dead. Is this about Sarah Dale?

AS: Sarah Dale?

BC: Yeah, she's telling everyone about this supposed murder she saw back then.

AS: Supposed?

BC: Jesus, Alan—have you listened to her? Kids set on fire? Pushed out the window? You think they could have kept all that stuff a secret?

AS: There were plenty of secrets at Coram House.

BC: No. There weren't. Everyone knew Father Foster was a pervert, but this other stuff? It's pure imagination. Horror story stuff.

AS: You think she's lying?

BC: Twenty years is a long time. I mean, I can't even remember what I had for breakfast this morning.

AS: It's a point of view.

BC: Whatever happened, happened. It's over. None of it can be proven, so I just don't see who benefits from dredging all this up.

May 13, 1989—US District Courthouse

Sister Cecile Marie

Alan Stedsan: Good morning, Sister Cecile. Thank you for coming today.

Sister Cecile: Well, I didn't have much choice, did I?

AS: All these interviews are voluntary—ah, one moment. Sorry about that.

SC: You didn't let me finish, young man. If I have nothing to hide, I mean. And I do not.

AS: Ah—yes. I see. Well, let's get to it, then. Sister Cecile, how long did you reside at Coram House?

SC: I arrived in 1965.

AS: And you stayed for how long?

SC: Coram House closed in 1977. But you knew that already.

AS: But you stayed on?

SC: Yes.

AS: In what capacity?

SC: I was there to serve God, Mr. Stedsan. And he did not go anywhere when Coram House closed its doors.

AS: Sister Cecile, can you describe daily life at Coram House? What were your responsibilities?

SC: Tending to the children. Overseeing their prayers, their studies.

AS: And discipline?

SC: Yes, of course.

AS: Did you ever hit the children?

SC: Of course. When it was required.

AS: I—ah. I see.

SC: Did your parents ever spank you, Mr. Stedsan?

AS: I—

SC: Mine certainly did not spare the rod. They were different times.

AS: And how would you hit the children? With your hand?

SC: Sometimes. Not usually. A ruler, perhaps.

AS: Were there other instances of violence?

SC: You call that violence. That was instruction.

AS: Sister Cecile, did you ever push a child out the window?

SC: You cannot possibly be serious.

AS: You didn't answer the question.

SC: No. I did not.

AS: Did you ever tell a child to run into the fire to fetch a ball?

SC: Nonsense. Children making up stories.

AS: Did you ever push a child out of a boat?

SC: Let me tell you something, Mr. Stedsan. Many of the children at Coram House were bad children. We did our best to guide them into the light, to show them the path to living a righteous life. Some of them did. Some of them were saved. And many more were not. I have nothing to confess if that's what you're hoping for.

AS: I'm just looking for information.

SC: You're looking for truth. And only God has that.

PART 2

5

At *five minutes* to nine, I pull into the driveway of Coram House. Once again, I'd stayed up too late, first searching online databases for Tommy, which turned out to be hopeless, and then trying to put together an updated contact list for everyone who gave a deposition back in the eighties, which meant hours scouring the internet for addresses and phone numbers, trying to match Facebook profiles to names and locations. Somehow when I looked up, the bottle of wine was empty and the clock said three a.m.

I drive past the construction site, already buzzing with yellow bulldozers, and bump along the dirt until it ends abruptly at a stone wall, where Stedsan stands beside a silver sedan. I smile, wave. Of course he drives a Mercedes.

"Quite the morning," he says when I get out. He gestures toward the expanse of water spread out below us. Unlike downtown, where the bay is frozen solid, the open water on this side of Rock Point feels alive. Waves move in every direction, crashing together in an explosion of white foam.

"The rectory is this way," Stedsan says, raising his voice to be heard above the wind.

He leads us through a gap in the stone wall. Overgrown cedars lean over the path, their branches clutching at my jacket. Past the cedar tunnel, a cottage emerges like something out of a fairy tale—all climbing ivy and puffs of smoke from the chimney. The cemetery comes right up to the path, but most of the gravestones here are moss-covered, atmospheric rather than creepy. I can see the spire of the church rising behind the house, so we can't be far from the street, but it feels worlds away.

Stedsan lifts his hand to the doorknob, then pauses. "Father Aubry has a nervous disposition. I would go easy on him."

I raise my eyebrows, but he doesn't elaborate.

"This isn't my first interview. I know how to read a room."

Stedsan widens his eyes and holds up his hands. *Calm down.* He pushes open the door without knocking. "Ladies first."

I step into a dimly lit entry. The white plaster walls are bare above dark wood paneling, except for a large wooden crucifix. A stained-glass window scatters spots of blue-and-green light on the wooden floor. Stedsan announces us.

"Hello! Father Aubry?"

A door slams upstairs. A breeze rustles the spiderwebs that soften the corners of the ceiling.

A moment later, black orthopedic sneakers appear on the stairs beneath a swish of black fabric. The rest of Father Aubry comes into view piece by piece as he descends: torso, clasped hands, and finally a narrow face dominated by a pair of glasses. He looks shrunken inside the long black cassock, as if he borrowed it from someone much larger.

"Alan," Father Aubry says, holding out his hand. "And you must be Mrs. Kelley. So good of you to come."

I've never been Mrs. anyone, but I don't correct him.

"Thank you for having us, Father Aubry."

He smiles, but his eyes don't quite meet mine. It's like they got stuck on my chin. "Rosa has made us some tea upstairs in the library, if you'd like . . ." He trails off.

"That would be lovely," Stedsan says, his voice growing louder and heartier, as if Father Aubry is part deaf instead of just awkward.

As we follow Father Aubry up the creaking stairs, I wonder how old he is. I'd guess midfifties. He carries himself tentatively, like someone much older, but his skin doesn't have the saggy look of true old age. I do a quick calculation. He might have been here during the case, but he would have been a teenager when Coram House was still operating as an orphanage.

Upstairs, the long hallway is lined with framed photographs, starting with an image of the pope in his white bedsheet robes. Then back in time to a line of nuns ladling out soup, their wimples jostling for space with oversized eighties-style glasses. All the way back to a sepia-tinted photo of children clustered around a font, apparently waiting to be baptized en masse. The girls with their wide eyes and ill-fitting white dresses look like child brides.

"Here we are," Father Aubry says, opening the door so we can step into his study. From a distance, the room looks cozy—a fireplace, an oversize desk, a pair of leather armchairs—but up close everything is shabby. The bubbling paint on the ceiling that suggests a leaky roof. The deep tarnish on the candlesticks. The spring poking out of the chair.

"I'd offer to take your jackets, but it's so drafty in here you'll probably be happier keeping them," Father Aubry says with an attempt at a smile. "Please, sit."

We take our places in two wooden chairs before the desk while he pours tea. The room fills with the smell of something herbal and overly sweet. The silence stretches and I wait to see who will fill it first. My teacup has a chipped edge that feels sharp enough to cut flesh.

Father Aubry clears his throat. "So you're writing a book about Coram House—all the unfortunate things that happened there. I, ah, well, I know the church must seem the villain to you now, but I just hope you won't paint us all with the same brush. There are many of those whose deepest desire was to be of service—to God and those children. The story is not unusual, I think . . ."

He trails off, as if he's not sure where to go now that he's given his talking points. Karen Lafayette's words flash in my head. *She sort of bounced when she hit the ground.*

Father Aubry clears his throat again. His chair creaks like it might collapse. "Alan here tells me that you're a very talented writer."

I paste a smile on my face.

Father Aubry asks a few more questions about how I became a writer, where I grew up, how I like it here. With every answer, he relaxes, leaning back in his chair, nodding, probably thinking to himself that maybe we won't have to touch on any unpleasantness after all.

Sarah Dale stands on the hill, lemonade dripping down her legs from the shattered pitcher. *But Tommy, he never came back up.*

"Father Aubry," I say, interrupting a question he's asking about my writing process. "I'll be reviewing all the materials related to the case and the history of Coram House. Everything Mr. Stedsan has shared, documents from law enforcement, and any additional historical documents I can find. I'll also be speaking to members of the community."

He sits up straighter, clears his throat. "Yes, of course. Yes."

"I know this kind of reckoning can be very uncomfortable, so I want to assure you I'll do my best to be respectful."

It's half true. I plan to be very respectful of my interview subjects. But I can't say I care about the church. From the corner of my eye, I see Stedsan give a tiny nod. *Good job, kid.* I ignore him.

"Anyhow," I go on, warming up to the finale, "I want to assure you that I have no interest in sensationalizing anything."

The story doesn't need my help. There. Olive branch extended.

"Oh, yes, of course." Father Aubry beams. "Well, I expected that Alan knew what he was doing when he hired you. So I was never worried, never, but it's always nice to hear it from the source—as it is. The church is reckoning with its own history, you know, so I want to be helpful however I can."

The smile curdles on my face, but he doesn't seem to notice.

"What I'm really hoping for is any additional records or photos you might have, especially from the fifties on."

Father Aubry's face falls. "There was a fire at the House years ago. Faulty wiring. Most of those records were destroyed."

Disappointment is stones in my pocket, a physical weight.

"I'm so sorry." Father Aubry wrings his hands like he set the fire himself and is so very sorry about it.

I force myself to shrug. *These things happen.* "Perhaps you could tell me a bit more about the children who died while under your care?"

He makes a choking sound. "I— My care?"

"The church's care, I mean, of course."

He stares at me and then back to Stedsan, who's gone very still beside me.

"Much of the sexual and daily abuse is well documented," I continue, parroting Stedsan's words, "but I'm trying to get a better grasp on the more extreme cases. Specifically, a few incidents involving Sister Cecile. You may remember the ones I'm referring to."

At her name, Father Aubry stiffens. His eyes go to the window, as if looking for an exit. *All right, let me jog your memory.*

"There was an incident involving a boy named Tommy. He drowned while under the care of Sister Cecile. And another. A girl who was pushed out the window, again by Sister Cecile."

"Nothing was ever proven," he mumbles. But at the look on my face, he raises his hands. "Not nothing," he says quickly, "I'm not denying certain facts that came to light. I just mean about the incident you're referring to. The boy—"

"Tommy," I say. "His name was Tommy."

But he goes on as if he didn't hear me. "And the other one. The girl and the window. Really—that one was very far-fetched. I mean, you know."

He's babbling now. I'd hoped pressure might uncover something useful, but this is going nowhere. A gale of wind batters the little house, rattling the windows and sending a cold draft of air through the room.

"Do you have more complete records of the residents?" I ask. "So far, I haven't been able to uncover Tommy's last name."

He shakes his head. "The fire."

I notice something yellow and crusty stuck to the front of his cassock. Dried egg, maybe. He waits for my next question, but my energy is gone. All week I've been preparing for this meeting and it's clearly a complete waste of time.

"I want to go inside Coram House." I don't plan to say it, it just comes out.

Father Aubry blinks at me. "It's an active construction site now. I, well, I'm not sure it's safe and I can't— I mean, it's not my–"

"Don't worry," Stedsan cuts in. "I've already spoken to Bill Campbell. We're headed there now."

I turn to him in surprise. This is the first I'm hearing about it.

"I, well, I see." Father Aubry looks alarmed. "And he was . . . all right with it?"

Stedsan smiles. "Of course. In the name of civic duty, et cetera."

"I . . . Yes, of course." Father Aubry laughs. "Very good of him. Well, then, it appears you're all set."

"It appears so," I say, staring at Stedsan, but he doesn't look at me.

As we head back downstairs, I wonder if Stedsan is purposefully trying to keep me off-balance. It seems ridiculous, but he had plenty of opportunity to let me know we were meeting with the developer right after this. I don't know what his angle is, but I don't really care. I don't even care that Father Aubry was a waste of time. Today, I'm going inside Coram House.

———

Outside, the wind skitters a paper cup down the path and into my pants. Stedsan pauses to pull on his gloves.

"Well, that wasn't exactly what we agreed."

"What do you mean?" I wipe at a smear of mud on my pant leg, which makes it worse.

Stedsan angles his head toward the stone cottage. I assume toward Father Aubry's nervous disposition.

I shrug. "I thought it was more of a suggestion. And when exactly were you going to tell me about getting access to Coram House?"

He ignores my clear irritation. "I just heard from Bill this morning." He looks at his watch. "Come on, he said he'd be in the office by ten."

We walk down the dirt track. But I'm quietly stewing. Stedsan could have let me know about the meeting. Instead, he chose to tell me at the last minute in front of Father Aubry. And Monday, the way he ordered me to stop asking questions about Tommy. He's the one who brought me here to write this book, so why do I already feel like he's in my way?

A gust of wind roars around the north side of Coram House, as if it had been lying in wait. But that's not what stops me in my tracks. The extent of the construction isn't visible from the road, but back here it's a different story. The new wing extends like a strange growth, now nearly the size of its host. Slick walls of red corrugated metal and giant sheets of glass take advantage of what must be sweeping views of the lake. The whole thing is sleek and modern, an odd contrast with the solid brick and stone of the old building. But I guess that's the point. A distraction or a fresh start, depending on who you ask.

"Careful."

Stedsan lays a hand on my arm. To our left is a pit filled with frozen water. The foundation for something new.

"Who's Bill Campbell?" I ask. "The name is familiar."

Stedsan raises his eyebrows. "I thought you did your homework," he teases. "I'm sure I mentioned him. He's the developer and a key investor in the project."

He gestures to a pickup truck parked nearby, where the words CAMP-BELL & SONS are stenciled on the side next to a logo of a hammer and shovel crossed in a vaguely Soviet style.

"He also lived in Coram House as a child."

Of course. I'd read Bill Campbell's deposition. He'd been one of the people to throw doubt on Sarah Dale. And now here he was, developing Coram House into condominiums. For a second, I'm too stunned to speak.

"Not for very long," Stedsan continues. "A few months, if I'm re-membering right. His mother had a drug problem, but she got clean. A happy ending."

"And then what?" I ask. "He just bought up Coram House to de-velop it? That didn't bother anyone?"

Stedsan shrugs. "If it wasn't him, it would have been someone else."

He's ignoring the spirit of my question, but he had talked about Bill Campbell like they were friends the other day, so I decide to tread carefully for now.

We arrive at a long white trailer. A generator hums in the back-ground. Stedsan knocks and a gravelly voice tells us to come in.

The small room is crowded with a filing cabinet and desk piled high with papers and an assortment of pens and coffee mugs. The air is damp and stale, like walking into a cloud of someone else's breath. The man sitting behind the desk has white hair buzzed tight against his scalp and a deeply lined face. He looks far too old to be working construction, but the orange vest and wiry forearms suggest otherwise. The man doesn't make any kind of greeting, just goes on reading his newspaper.

"Morning," Stedsan says, his voice flat. That one word is enough to tell me he doesn't like this man at all.

The other man lowers the paper, and widens his eyes in feigned surprise. "Why, it's Mr. Alan Stedsan."

He whistles and leans back in his chair. Then his eyes flick to me, running up and down my body in a way that makes me glad I'm still wearing my parka.

"Bill said you might be coming by," the man rasps. A smoker's voice. "This your writer?"

He says it like I'm a pet.

Stedsan turns. "Alex Kelley. This is Fred Rooney."

The name goes off like an explosion. Sister Cecile. Tommy. Fred Rooney. I try to keep my expression neutral, but Rooney must see something because an unpleasant smile spreads across his face. "Look at that," he says. "I'm famous too."

Anger roils my stomach. How many more former children of Coram House am I going to run into before Stedsan decides to give me a heads-up? It's too early in the morning to be bungling everything this badly.

"Well," Stedsan says, "now that everyone's acquainted, perhaps we could—"

"Not so fast." Rooney wags a finger back and forth. Tick-tock. "Bill said to wait here—wants to take you in himself. Waste of time, if you ask me. But he's the boss."

Just then, the door opens. A man rushes into the office, icy air clinging to his clothes.

"Bill Campbell," he says, pulling off his gloves. "You must be Alex. Sorry to keep you waiting. Alan—nice to see you again."

Droplets of water cling to his hair, which is pure white and leonine.

I'd guess he's in his midsixties, but looks like the kind of person who still goes skiing every weekend.

We shake hands and exchange pleasantries. I thank him for taking the time to play tour guide. "Of course," he says. "Happy to." But his smile looks like someone trying to brave the jab of a needle.

"All right. I'll be off, then," Stedsan says.

I turn to him in surprise. "You're not coming?"

"I have a meeting back at the office. Just wanted to make the introductions. No one knows this place better than Bill. You're in good hands."

Stedsan claps Bill on the shoulder. Despite my annoyance at Stedsan, I'm not sure I want him to leave.

"Well, shall we?" Bill says, ushering me toward the door. Then he turns back to Rooney, as if he just remembered something. "Fred, those lines still need checking along the east wall."

"Sure do," Rooney says without looking up.

Bill waits. The silence stretches. "Right," Bill says, making a production of pulling on his gloves. He turns away, hand on the doorknob, when Rooney speaks again.

"Aren't you forgetting something, boss?"

"What are you talking about?" Bill asks, flustered.

Rooney raps his knuckles on a hard hat sitting on the desk.

"Right," Bill says. "Yes, of course."

He grabs two yellow hard hats from a row of hooks by the door. He holds one out to me, expression apologetic. "We haven't started on the old building yet, but technically it's all a construction site."

"Compliance is very important," Rooney says.

"Yes, thank you, Fred," Bill replies acidly. He turns back to me, his voice now schoolteacher bright. "Ready?"

"Lead the way," I say, wondering what the hell that whole exchange was about.

Bill leads me to the front of Coram House. Both the wind and the sounds of machinery have stopped, leaving us in silence. The doors loom larger up close—ten feet of heavy, polished oak. So heavy I doubt a child could open them, even without the metal chain currently wound through the door handles. Once you went in, someone would have to let you out.

"Got a sign painter up from Boston," Bill says.

At first, I'm not sure what he's talking about. Then I see the words SUNRISE HOUSE painted in gold script above the door. I murmur something I hope he'll take for enthusiasm.

Bill inserts a key into the padlock and the chain slithers onto the steps. He pushes open the door and is immediately swallowed by the gloom. As I follow, I have the sensation that I'm not entering a building at all, but slipping into a dark pool. I take a deep breath and plunge inside.

6

The first thing I notice is the smell: cold and burning metal. The entryway is bright with high ceilings and big windows. A staircase curves around the outer walls, leading up to an open landing on the second floor. An enormous brass chandelier hangs from a chain, each spindly arm holding a single candle-shaped bulb. The wide floorboards are dull and worn, pitted with dark knots, but I can see how they'll glow once polished.

"It's beautiful," I say, because it is. Beautiful and surprising. I'm not sure what I expected. Something more haunted, I guess.

Bill looks relieved. "Yes, it is, isn't it?" he says. "We usually come in from the back, but I wanted you to get the full effect. You can really see the potential."

Sunlight floods through the big windows, each of which is made up of hundreds of tiny panes of glass. I wonder if Sarah Dale had to wash these too. Somewhere, deep in the building, a radiator bangs.

"Shall we go up?" He gestures to the stairs. Each step dips in the center, worn down by children's feet running up and down over the years. *They'd make you stand in the corner with your arms out for hours, until you felt like they'd break.* Maybe children here didn't run.

From the landing on the second story, the chandelier looks like a spider dipped in molten metal, suspended by a thread. Bill leads us into a dark, narrow hallway with low ceilings and an endless stretch of closed doors. I've studied the floor plan of Coram House, but still feel turned around. It's such a different scale, being inside.

"This is where the sisters lived," Bill says. He opens a door, seemingly at random. The room is small and bare except for a sink set directly into the wall. A tiny window lets in the light, but it's set too high to see anything but sky. I stretch out my arms. My fingertips brush the wall on either side.

"It's like a prison cell," I say, but the word in my head is *coffin*.

"The sisters lived spare lives. There would have been space for a bed there"—he gestures to the end of the room—"but not much else."

"Did they all live in rooms like this?"

Bill nods. "This hall leads to the boys' dormitory and there's another set of rooms like this on the other side of the building, outside the girls' dormitory. They're like mirror images."

I try to imagine it, sleeping in this tiny, dark room. Reading the Bible nightly by the light of a lamp. Choosing that life. The air has a faint smell—antiseptic and menthol. Or maybe all this is just my imaginings of what a nun's life would be like.

Bill runs his hand over the door's molding, as if checking its solidity. He clears his throat. Something about this room is making him uncomfortable. I think of when I'd go visit my grandparents—how their bedroom was always off-limits. Then, one day when my grandmother was out, I peeked in. The curtains were closed. The room smelled of hand cream and soil from the lemon tree growing by the window. An intimate smell. I did nothing, just stood there, but my heart beat wildly, as if I was doing something illicit. I wonder if that's how it feels for Bill to stand at the threshold of this room, even five decades later.

"Would you like to see the boys' dormitory?" he asks, already backing down the hall.

"Sounds great."

I snap a quick picture with my phone before following.

"The history of the building is quite interesting," Bill says. "It was originally built in 1879 and designed by a reverend. They really built things differently then. Just wait until you see the trim on these windows."

When we reach the end of the hallway, Bill pauses for dramatic effect and then flings open the double doors. The room is huge and the view is spectacular. Floor-to-ceiling windows frame a snowy hill dotted with gravestones, leading down to the lake. To the left, a peninsula extends into the water. A wooden shack sits on the rocky shore, a green canoe beside it, partially covered in snow.

"That building down there." I point out the window. "Is that the boathouse?"

Bill squints at the view. "Sure is."

"A little cold for a canoe, isn't it?"

He laughs. "It's mine actually. I had a duck blind out there. It's been closed since Christmas but I haven't gotten around to bringing the boat in."

I point to the forested peninsula to our left, reviewing my mental map. "And that's Rock Point?"

Bill nods. "It's all diocese land." He sounds mournful. "But the trails are open to the public. Great views—worth seeing if you get a chance."

I look around, trying to see the room as it would have been. Rows of beds with creaky metal springs. White sheets and scratchy wool blankets. How many beds would have fit? Twenty—maybe more? Light floods in through the windows, trapping dust motes floating down like snow onto the creaky floorboards.

Bill goes on about the history of the building, the slate roof and cupola. The plans to add a rear terrace with lake views, but his voice is background noise. The boys' dormitory. This is where Tommy would have slept. Fred Rooney too. So many children.

"Is this where you lived?" I ask, cutting him off.

Bill blinks in confusion, as if he's forgotten where we are. "I see you've done your homework," he says. "Though I'm not sure I'd call it living here—I didn't stay long."

He walks to a spot in the middle of the room and draws a rectangle with his hands, the ghost of a bed. "Jesus, the windows were drafty. I'm lucky I got here in May. If it had been December, I would have had icicles in my hair." He chuckles, but it sounds forced. "But it's hard to beat the view."

His tone is wistful, but there's something performative about it.

"You were only here a few months then?" I ask.

"My mother, she wasn't a healthy woman. But she got herself clean and came back for me. Coram House was a lifeline for my family. I feel quite grateful, really, that it kept me here in the community and gave my mother a chance to reclaim her life."

I nod along. The speech sounds rehearsed, but maybe his acquisition of the property wasn't just about profit. Maybe he did love this place.

"Do you keep in touch with anyone you knew here?" I ask.

Bill shakes his head. "As I said, I didn't really have time to settle in and make any lifelong friends."

He doesn't mention Fred Rooney. Bill shivers and zips up his jacket. He's right—it is drafty.

"Would you like to see the refectory? The original tables are still there."

I'd like to push him further, but I sense he's ready to be done with this conversation. So I smile. "That would be great."

On the far side of the room, we pass a wall of built-in cabinets. On impulse, I grab one of the brass knobs and pull it open. The dusty shelves inside are empty, but each one has a label holder—the type you might see on a filing cabinet. A few have slips of paper inside, now yellowed with age. *2. 18.* I realize what they are.

"What was your number?" I ask.

Beside me, Bill stiffens. "I don't remember."

I can't tell if he's lying. I snap a picture.

"You know, I'll need to approve those photos before you print them."

Bill looks pointedly down at his watch. It's a TAG Heuer, I notice. Expensive, but not as showy as a Rolex.

"And I do have a meeting in an hour."

Message received. I put away my phone. No more off-roading on his carefully maintained trail through history. "Of course. Lead the way."

Bill guides us down a steep set of back stairs. The kitchen has none of the Dickensian flavor of upstairs. The floor is peeling red linoleum and, instead of counters, the center of the room is dominated by a series of metal rolling tables. The industrial pots look big enough to fit a toddler. The refrigerator, a dirty shade of avocado, is surprisingly small for a kitchen that must have fed over a hundred people.

"There was usually a cook and an assistant on staff," Bill says. He trips on a curled floor tile and looks down at it, angry, as if the floor did it on purpose.

"Did they live here as well?"

"Who? The cook? No, I don't think so. They came in from town."

"So how many adults did live here?" I ask. I know the answer—one or two priests and up to seven sisters—but I'm curious to see if he does. His knowledge seems oddly selective.

"Five or six, maybe?" he says, absently.

"And through there"—I point to a swinging door set in the far wall—"that's where you ate?"

"The refectory."

The door squeals in protest. The long room is filled with scarred wooden tables, benches stacked upside down on top so their legs stick in the air like overturned bugs. A huge fireplace dominates one wall, the brick stained black from years of smoke. On the other wall, tall windows with a view out onto the lake.

"We're thinking of leaving this mostly as is," he says. "Maybe turning it into a cafe or coworking space."

I can see it. A coffee bar on one side. People sitting at the long antique tables, tapping away on their laptops below the pressed tin ceiling, now spruced up with a fresh coat of paint. Worse, I can see myself here. It's somehow easier to conjure than tables full of children. The beauty of this empty place makes it hard to imagine terrible things happening here. As if sweeping water and mountain views somehow preclude human cruelty.

Bill glances down at his watch again. I decide to gamble. "Could I see the attic?"

"The attic?" He frowns. "There's nothing up there."

I shrug. *Humor me.*

"All right," Bill says in the tone of someone bestowing a great favor. "But then I should be getting back."

"Of course," I say. "I really appreciate you taking the time."

He leads me back into the kitchen and up a different set of stairs to another narrow hallway. At least I think it's different. The doors and passages seem to curl back in on themselves like the whorl of a snail's shell.

Then we're in another large room, identical to the boys' dormitory at the other end of the building. But out these windows, I see the new construction that extends toward the lake like a pointing finger. A gust of wind rattles the windows in their frame. It's freezing despite the huge cast-iron radiator that runs along the wall. The dark green paint is peeling off to reveal flakes of silver beneath.

"This was the girls' dormitory," Bill says. He points to a door in the corner with a brass latch. "The attic access is through there."

So that's why they were always locking the girls in the attic. How convenient.

Bill tries to open the latch on the door, but it's stuck.

"Mr. Campbell, you said you didn't keep in touch with anyone during your time here. But out in the office—what about Fred Rooney?"

"Fred?" Bill turns to me. Then he shrugs. "We've worked together for so many years, I didn't think of it. But yes, you're right, we did overlap here if that's what you mean."

"But you weren't friends?" I press.

He shakes his head. "Fred's three years older than me. That's a world of difference when you're thirteen and sixteen."

"What about a boy named Tommy?" I try to sound casual.

Bill goes still. Something in the quality of his attention has changed. "He was the one who ran away?"

Given Bill's deposition and how pointedly he undermined Sarah Dale's story, I have a hard time believing I need to jog his memory. I wonder if he's testing me, to see how much I know.

"That was the official story, but a woman named Sarah Dale suggested that he may have died here under suspicious circumstances."

He waves a hand in dismissal. "She was an old drunk looking for attention and probably extra cash from the settlement."

"She had a drinking problem?"

"In the eighties, at least. She was half drunk the whole time she was here—bottle in her purse, the whole thing. Stedsan felt bad for her and, God knows, it would have been hell for the case if it had come out she was lying."

My insides sink. "So you never heard any rumors when you were a child? That he'd drowned?"

Bill shakes his head. "Pure fabrication, if you ask me." He glances at the door, open now. "Listen, if you want to go up we should—"

"Yes, that would be great."

The door swings open to reveal a set of stairs so steep the runners are only a few inches deep. "If you don't mind, I'll stay here," he says. "Not sure my old knees can take that ladder."

I grip either side and start up. At the top, a trapdoor is pinned open to the wall with a metal hook. My head surfaces into an enormous open room.

"Don't go too far," Bill calls up. "I'm not sure about the floor at the far end."

I imagine punching through a rotten board, falling through empty space. Still, I shuffle a few feet farther, sending up swirls of dust. Outside I can hear the wind, but in here it's barely more than a cold breath on my neck. It smells of dust and resin.

Light filters through windows at either end, but it's still dark. Not that there's much to see. A stack of wooden boards fuzzed with dust. A pile of old rags. What had I been expecting? Those ghostly statues of the saints or the wardrobe that loomed in Sarah Dale's dreams, all here almost fifty years later? Maybe I need to see it, to touch the wooden boards, and remind myself that it's no dark version of Narnia. There's nothing special about the evil in this place. It's just people doing terrible things—same as everywhere.

I cough. All the dust is making my chest feel tight. A soft click echoes in the empty space. It takes me a moment to recognize the sound of a door latching. I walk back to the stairs. The trapdoor is still open, but the bottom of the stairs is dark. "Mr. Campbell?" I call.

No answer.

I climb back down, slowly, in the dark. At the bottom, I feel for the handle, but it's just smooth wood. *There was this old wardrobe. She made you get inside and then locked the door.* I knock, feeling a little ridiculous at how my heart is pounding.

"Hello," I call.

Again, nothing. I knock harder. "Bill!" My voice sounds panicked.

The door flies open, and I stumble out, blinking in the light like a mole.

"Sorry," Bill says. "I just stepped out for a minute—a phone call. The wind must have slammed it shut."

"I'm just glad you didn't go too far," I say, trying for lightness.

"Ready to go? Sorry to rush you, but I really should get back."

"Yes," I say, brushing the dust off my jacket. My heart is still beating too quickly. "Of course."

Bill leads the way at a fast clip, like he can't wait to get out of here. Or maybe just get rid of me. But I don't entirely trust my legs to hold me. I can still feel the smooth wood of the door with no handle. The darkness that tasted of dust. The wind, Bill had said. I think of my grandparents' drafty old house. Every time you left a window open, the wind would suck the door across the hall shut with a slam as loud as a firework going off. The sound in the attic hadn't been a door slamming. It had been a soft click. Like someone on quiet feet who didn't want to be heard gently pressing the door shut.

7

The days after my visit to Coram House pass in a blur of frustration. I search everywhere for Tommy, but he won't be found. First, I drive to the state archives in Montpelier only to encounter the furrowed brow of the archivist who suggests I try ancestry.com if it's family records I'm looking for.

"I tried that already," I tell her.

"Did you check online for death certificates?" she asks.

I nod. I had found 420 Toms, Thomases, or Tommies who died in Vermont between 1965 and 1970. Of those, around a hundred had an unexpected death with a certificate filed by the medical examiner. Ten of those were children. But none matched the Tommy from Sarah Dale's testimony. They were either the wrong age or the cause of death was wrong. Nothing led back to Coram House.

"And you have the birth certificate?" she asks.

"I don't have a last name."

The archivist peers up at me through her purple-framed reading glasses. "No birth or death certificate. What makes you so sure this person exists?" she asks.

My patience hangs by a mostly frayed thread. A soft pattering makes me look up. Hail bounces off the skylight.

"I'm sorry I can't be more help," she says. "You could try hospitals. Some of them have digitized their records."

I thank her and leave. A fuzz of snow coats the sidewalk. My steps leave hollows that follow me back to the car.

I drive home defeated, her words ringing in my ears. After all, what do I have, really? A few mentions of a boy named Tommy scattered across the depositions. Sarah Dale recalling a traumatic incident from twenty years earlier. Or a woman with a drinking problem and a grudge, if you believe Bill Campbell. Either way, not the most reliable witness.

When I get back to my apartment, I pour a glass of wine, even though it's only four. Then I get out the list I made of people who gave depositions back in the eighties. At first, I don't have much luck. Karl Smith died of a heart attack. Christopher Cooper hangs up on me. I can't find a number for Michael Leblanc—he's either dead or off-grid somewhere. But then I get to Karen Lafayette. Not only is her number listed, but it's a local area code.

I dial. Anxiety pulses in my chest with every ring. A woman's voice answers. But it's just her voicemail. I leave a message asking her to call me back, trying to strike the right balance between mysterious and desperate.

Next, I work my way through the Sisters of Mercy, though I don't expect much. Most of the nuns had died years ago. Though I do leave a message at what turns out to be the Alzheimer's floor of a long-term care facility. There's no record of Sister Cecile, which is odd. But she'd originally been from Quebec, so maybe she went back there.

When my phone rings, I stare at it, shocked, as if I've summoned a response. But it's just Lola. I don't really feel like talking, but I never called her back, and if I don't answer, I know she'll worry. I love her, but sometimes I get tired of carrying the weight of her worry. It's like, once you're broken, no one ever really believes that you can be whole again.

"Hey," I say.

"Hey," Lola says. "What's up?"

"Oh, just looking up the addresses of some dead nuns," I say, forcing myself to smile, sound light. I tell her a little about my research, about Stedsan and reading the depositions. About Tommy and all the ways I've failed to find proof of his existence.

"Are you drinking right now?" Lola asks.

"No," I say, not looking at my empty glass. "And besides it's Friday, and it's"—I glance at my phone—"5:03."

"So tell me about this Tommy. Why is he so special?"

Lola does that—jumping from one subject to another so fast it catches me off-balance.

"What do you mean, Lola? He was a kid. They killed him."

I rub at the headache forming behind my eyes. The bottle of wine beckons from the counter, but somehow I know she'll hear it.

"People don't just disappear, Lola. It's like no one cared, so no one came looking. He doesn't even have a grave. So when he died he was just—gone."

My voice breaks and I stop, embarrassed. The silence on the other end of the phone is all I need to tell me Lola is worried. And this is why I didn't want to answer the phone.

"Everyone's gone when they die, Al. Grave or no grave."

"I know that," I snap. My throat feels tight.

"Do you think maybe you need to take a step back for a sec—"

"Lola—"

"I'm not saying give up. Just . . . move forward."

I sigh. She's worried that I'm losing my shit. *It's not like that*, I want to say. *Not like last time.* But, of course, that's exactly what I would say if I was in fact losing my shit.

"Circle back. Change the channel. Put a pin in it. Table that discussion."

I laugh, despite feeling annoyed at her. "Okay, okay, stop please, before my ears start bleeding."

Plus, I have to admit she does have a point. I'm stuck and, right now, I don't have a way to unstick myself.

"You're probably right," I say.

"Forget work for a while," she says. "Take a break. Do something fun."

I promise I will. Lola tells me about the play she's going to see later that night and, finally, we hang up.

I'm going to close my computer, go refill my glass, and maybe watch a movie, I decide. But, as I'm getting up, I hesitate. One more search.

Sarah Dale.

I don't know why I do it.

No, that's not true.

I have this twisting feeling in my guts—like I know I'm not going to like what I find. The search results come up right away. Sarah Dale, deceased in 2010 at age fifty-five. Six years ago. The article is short, but makes my throat ache. A car crash with her two-year-old granddaughter in the back seat. Both died.

I shut the computer and look up at the ceiling, blinking at the cracks until my vision clears. The unfairness burns. I take my empty glass into the kitchen and fill it to the brim. She'd earned an easier death. As if it worked that way. Before I know it, tears are squeezing themselves from the corners of my eyes. I'm glad there's no one to see me blow my nose on the edge of my shirt.

"Enough."

My voice is stern, like I'm talking to a child with a flair for drama. I'm getting sidetracked. I wander back to the living room, where I survey the organized chaos. The stack of VHS tapes, still waiting for a VCR that's been delayed yet again. The table is a grid of index cards and sticky notes around my master binder. Background information on Coram House, the children, the staff.

Usually, by now the story has started to take shape. Shadowy and incomplete, but the beginnings of a form clear within a block of solid stone—something I can take my chisel to. But, this time, nothing is clear. The story is there, but the accounts twist back and forth. Children who deal with real monsters are still children, seeing monsters where they don't exist too. So how am I going to tell the difference? Or maybe all that's just an excuse. Maybe I thought the act of ghost-writing would free me from my past mistakes. But the past is always there.

My agent called this book my comeback, but it could prove that my nerve is gone. Or, worse, that my sense of story has disappeared. I know I'm not a great writer. I'm a good-enough writer. But my ability to find the story within a mess of historical documents has always been my thing. There have been times in my life where I could actually feel it—that warm seeping sensation as the story takes form. Like the warmth that spreads through your body after that first drink.

The wine tastes crisp and faintly grassy. I press the cool glass to my eyes, which are hot and swollen from crying. Maybe I just need a day off from horror stories to clear my head. Tomorrow, I'll go for a long run. Somewhere with trees and fresh air. Suddenly, I know exactly where I'm going. Rock Point. Tomorrow, I'll go to the woods.

8

Even though I knew it would be cold, the air still knocks the breath out of me. My eyeballs sting and my hands ache as I fumble to lace up my sneakers. Getting my gloves back on feels like an emergency. It's past six a.m., but the sky is still navy blue. It would be easy to burrow back underneath my fluffy quilt, but my veins throb with nervous energy.

I'd dreamt of Coram House. Not ghosts or anything like that, just the building. The high, arched windows. Dust motes dancing in the light. Wide pine floorboards with knots so dark they looked burned there. In the dream, the building had been silent and empty. But still, I'd felt a sinking sense of horror. Like all those children—in the hallways, cleaning the floors, doing laundry, whispering, eating their meals, locked in the attic—had disappeared without a trace, leaving nothing behind.

Or almost nothing.

On waking, I'd thought of that cupboard, each shelf bearing a neat label. *They called us by our numbers.* The first thing you learn as a child is how to name things. If someone can take away something as fundamental as your name, it must feel like they have the ultimate authority to do anything they want. God's authority.

I start my run with lazy loops on quiet streets until my muscles feel elastic. Then I lengthen my strides and head north, past the police station, its lights still glowing red. Past quiet, dark houses and trees that scratch at the sky with bare limbs. It's early and most people are still in bed. I have the world to myself.

The sign for Rock Point comes sooner than I expect. And it's a good thing I see it, tucked into the shadows of the trees, otherwise I would have missed the trail entirely. A few steps into the woods, a large sign shows a map of the area. Rock Point sticks into the water like a thumb, with a three-mile trail looping the peninsula. South of the point is the bay with the harbor and downtown. North is the open waters of Lake Champlain. I lean closer. Coram House isn't marked, but the graveyard is shaded in gray and, right in the center, someone's drawn a skull and crossbones. Not far from here—maybe a mile.

My legs are starting to tighten up. I need to move. But the emptiness of the woods makes me uneasy. There are no cars on the street. No one walking their dog. The snow on the trail is fresh and untouched. I could be the last human alive. But I'm not going back to the apartment. The only other choice is to run. So that's what I do.

The snow squeaks beneath my feet, loose and dry as sand. The sky is blue ombre now, but it still feels like night beneath the trees. The path passes between two lichen-covered boulders and widens into a clearing. Another trail joins along with another set of footprints. They're small—a woman's footprints. At least I'm not alone in here.

The trees thicken and the snow gets crisp and hard as if I'm running on a crust of sugar. A sign nailed to a tree promises a viewpoint in half a mile. The trail tilts steeply up and I slow to avoid breaking an ankle on the knobby, buried tree roots. By the time I crest the rise, each breath feels jagged as a shard of glass and I'm hoping this viewpoint will be worth it.

Abruptly, the trees fall away and I'm on top of a rocky cliff, a guardrail all that stands between me and the sweeping expanse of ice and water below. This must be the tip of Rock Point, right at the place where the ice meets the open water. A line between dark and light. A wave moves across the water, then meets the edge of the ice and tunnels beneath like a giant worm. I grab for the railing as vertigo washes over me.

Across the bay, another peninsula mirrors this one. A dock extends into the water where a pair of red Adirondack chairs and a dark lump—probably a BBQ—wait for the return of summer. Perched on the cliff above the dock, I can just make out a house. The shape is boxy and ultramodern, but clad in raw wood that blends into the forest. A house wearing camouflage.

My toes ache. Time to start moving. I turn away from the view, already thinking about a cup of coffee. But there's a monster on the trail. Huge with spindly legs and dark fur beneath a crown of bone. Puffs of white from nostrils big enough to swallow my fist. My heart squishes into my throat.

Moose.

The word takes too long to surface. Then it's gone, crashing off into the underbrush.

In the silence that follows, a laugh bubbles out. A moose. It's so absurd. Are moose dangerous? I have no idea. I listen for the snapping of branches, but all is quiet.

Then it's not.

A raw howl of terror rends the air. Everything in me freezes—legs, heart, breath. Then it's over.

Breathe, breathe, but I can't find any air. My vision swims. I replay the sound in my head, but it's like trying to relive the pain of a broken bone—a dull, faded version of the real thing. And now it's so quiet I wonder whether I imagined it. But my beating heart says differently.

Was it the moose? But, no. I'm sure the sound was human. I don't know how I know, but I just do. Someone out there is hurt. I think of the single set of footprints in the snow.

My breathing slows. I think back, trying to figure out what direction the scream came from. There was an echo to it, as if it were bouncing off something. It was close. And I'm almost sure it was coming from the north, back the way I came.

I retrace my footsteps, scanning the ground. But it's only my footprints. Where had the others left the trail? I speed up. A minute later, I find an offshoot trail I hadn't noticed before. Even with the yellow marker nailed to the tree, I might have missed it if it weren't for the footprints in the snow. The trail leads steeply down toward the water.

"Hello?" I call. No answer. Not even wind in the trees.

Maybe someone fell and broke a leg. *Then why aren't they calling for help?* The voice in my head is all sarcasm and raised eyebrows. It sounds like Lola.

Okay, maybe they just had a scare and screamed. Maybe they saw a fucking moose.

All right, girl, then why aren't they answering you now?

"Hello?" I call again, wondering if I might be losing my mind.

A branch snaps behind me. I whirl around, but there's nothing there. My ears strain with the effort of trying to pull noise from the silence. But then I do hear something, coming from ahead and below—the direction of the water. It's a scraping sound, like something heavy being dragged along a rock. It's different than the other sounds in the woods. Louder. More deliberate. More human.

"Is someone there?" I shout, louder this time.

The scraping gets faster, like someone in a hurry. Like someone heard me.

It's followed by a hollow thunk. Then another.

A faint splash.

Something falling in the water? I look down at the trail. The footprints are even smaller than I'd thought. Narrow and at least three inches shorter than my size-ten running shoes. Definitely a woman or, my heart clutches, a child even.

"Hello?" I call again, hearing the desperation in my voice. "Is anyone there? Are you all right?"

Silence. Only then, like an idiot, do I think of my phone. I pull it out with shaking hands, but there are no bars. How is there anywhere left with no cell phone service?

I'm two miles away from the road. And who knows how long it will take for help to get here. I think of the rocky cliffs below the viewpoint, the freezing water lapping beneath. Then I follow the footprints into the woods.

I half run, half fall down the steep trail. The snow is deeper here, piled up against the trees as if it's all flowing downhill. Every few feet I stop to scan the forest for any sign of movement. The footprints in the snow are steady—someone walking, not running. But they go in only one direction. No one came back this way.

The wind picks up as I get closer to the water. Around me, ice-covered branches sway against one another, making the sound of tiny bells. The woods are still—there's no one here. And yet, I feel eyes. The predatory gaze of something waiting for my back to be turned. My teeth are chattering, which is strange since my insides feel hot and liquid. Like my organs have turned to soup.

I keep walking, back and forth, down endless switchbacks. It's going to be a teenager with a twisted ankle and I'm going to feel like an idiot. I will this to be true.

At the bottom of the hill, the trail emerges onto a narrow rock ledge, blown clear of snow. The footprints are gone, but the only place to go is straight ahead where the path ends at a long set of wooden stairs, leading down to a rocky beach. A cove, really, sheltered by rock ledges topped in tall pines. The beach is empty. Shit.

I turn around, but there's nowhere else to go. The hill is too steep to climb. I scan the ground for any sign a person came this way. The red rocks are pitted with pools of ice, leaves and pine needles frozen inside like museum exhibits, encased in glass. No footprints anywhere, but no snow either.

"Hello?" I call. The only answer is the rhythmic slap of water against rocks. I'm starting to feel ridiculous. I'll check the beach, and then I'll get out of here.

The stairs have seen better days. The railing wobbles and I step over the treads stained black with rot. Tiny pebbles squeak and shift under-foot as I walk right up to the water's edge. There's a crust of ice near shore, but twenty feet out, waves slap gently against the ledges of rock. From down here, they're not as steep as they looked from above—more like a natural staircase that leads into the water. In the summer, I imag-ine this place is full of people sunning themselves on rocks before slip-ping into the cool water. But today, it feels desolate. The water is empty.

Whoever I heard is gone or was never here to begin with. It was probably some raccoon mating call. After all, what do I know about the woods? A knot deep in my gut loosens. But my toes have stopped hurting, which scares me for a different reason. I jump a few times and swing my arms, trying to get blood back into my fingertips. Time to go.

I turn to head back up the stairs. The relief drains out of me so quickly I'm lightheaded. On the ground, right under the staircase, purple flashes against the russet rocks. It comes into focus. A purple jacket. Not just a jacket. A person. Two wide-open eyes stare at me. And blood. So much blood.

9

A scream echoes off the rocks—strangled and wild. Then I realize. It came out of me. The thought breaks whatever gravity roots me in place.

I run forward, then stop. The woman's body—I can tell it's a woman, even through the mask of blood—lies in a few inches of water. You're not supposed to move people with a head injury, or is that a spinal injury? If she fell off the cliff, it could be both. Though I'm not sure that rule applies when they're lying in freezing water.

The woman's jacket is lumpy and dark where water has soaked through. Below, a sliver of jeans, white socks, water lapping against brown boots. You could almost believe it's just a bundle of clothes except for the pale hand floating in the water, fingers curled. And the face. Oh God, her face.

She must have hit her head on the rocks when she fell. One side of her skull looks caved in. Blood is everywhere. In the deep wrinkles around her eyes that are open and staring at nothing, coating the wisps of white hair poking out from under her hat. Threads of blood run from her body into the water and disappear.

She's dead. I'm sure she's dead. But I have to check. I pull off my gloves. My fingers scrabble through her layers of clothing like some scavenger searching for the meat. No pulse, or maybe my hands are just numb. Her skin is warm. It feels good. My stomach heaves and I turn my head away to vomit.

A twig snaps. I stagger to my feet, still wiping threads of saliva from my chin, and scan the pines above me. Some of them are fifty feet tall, but lean over, clinging to the rocks with exposed roots. They've probably grown that way for a hundred years, but they still look like they might crush me any second.

"Hello?" I call, but my voice is a whisper. I try again. Louder this time. "Is someone there? I need help!"

Some distant part of my brain sends off warning signals. I'm miles away from the nearest road. I've been standing in freezing water. I'm wearing leggings and sneakers. I'm pretty sure this woman is dead. I'm the one who's in danger now. I fumble the phone out of my pocket and can't believe it when I see one bar of service. I dial 911. Seconds of eternal silence. *Come on. Come on.*

Then a voice answers. "Nine-one-one, what's your emergency?" He sounds young and cheerful. I want to dig my claws into that voice, cling to it.

"Help." My words are slurred. I sound drunk. "I need help."

Somehow I manage to explain where I am and what's happened. Don't move her, the operator says, and walks me through CPR. I can't do this, I think. But I must have said it out loud because the operator is saying yes you can and assures me that help is on the way. Hang on, he says. Fifteen minutes. But by then, his voice is cutting out. And the line goes dead.

Fifteen minutes. It isn't long, considering.

It's an eternity.

The woman's eyes stare at me. The water around her is pink with blood. I notice a rock near her head the size of a grapefruit. It's covered in blood and chunks of something I don't look at too closely.

Chest compressions only, the operator had said. Something about spinal cord injury. I felt relieved—I can't imagine putting my mouth on hers where the blood is drying to brown. A wash of guilt, for being disgusted, for being alive while she is dead.

I kneel in the freezing water and fold my hands together. I begin chest compressions.

For some reason, I think of this old woman from my neighborhood in Brooklyn. This tiny, hunched figure always pushing a wheeled cart full of things that seemed unrelated. An onion, a potholder, a jar of jelly.

But she was always dressed beautifully in wool suits or silk dresses. Seeing her made me embarrassed to be out in sweatpants. But I felt sorry for her too. For all old people and their dignified decay. Or maybe I was just feeling sorry for my future self.

The woman's bones give beneath the pressure of my hands. A regular thunk thunk thunk echoes through the cove. A woodpecker slamming its head against a tree. I think again of the sounds I'd heard right after the scream. The scrape. The thunk. Different than any other sounds in the woods. The way they'd gone silent when I called for help and then accelerated.

Someone else was here.

Lights bob in the trees, followed by the crackle of static. Blue uniforms appear above me on the rocks. I try to get up, but my legs aren't working. "Down here!" I call. The EMT jogs down the stairs, blonde ponytail swinging. Then suddenly she's there, taking my wrist in her hand, leading me away. "Can you tell me your name?"

"No." I shake my head. "I mean, yes, but it's not me that's hurt, it's—"

I don't finish. Another EMT is already kneeling beside the woman, and calling to his partner. Airway, pulse, eye movement, motor response—negative, negative, negative. Something the opposite of adrenaline courses through me. The feeling of responsibility leaving my body.

Ponytail joins her partner at the water's edge. They unzip the woman's jacket to reveal a flannel shirt, then rip that open too. Buttons plink into the water. I tamp down the urge to pick them up. Beneath is a plain white cotton bra and the pale, spotted skin of an old woman. I turn away.

Ponytail inspects the head injury with gentle fingers. Her partner lifts the woman's limp wrist, where a silver bracelet dangles in the water. "DNR," he says.

"What does that mean?" I ask. Or try to. My lips refuse to cooperate and form words.

The EMTs turn toward me and rise, as if they're one creature. Then they're surrounding me, hands everywhere, feeling my wrist, my neck, wrapping a blanket around me. I want to slap them away, those fingers coated in death.

"I'm fine," I say. They'd just left the woman there, lying on the ground. The blood on her face has dried to rust, nearly the same color as the rocks. "You can't just leave her there."

There's a beep in my ear. "Ninety-two point four," says Ponytail. She shines a light in my eyes.

"You have to help her," I say.

"She has a DNR bracelet," says the partner. His orange hat is pulled low over his eyes, so only his nose sticks out. "Do not resuscitate, which means no CPR."

"Even if you're pushed off a cliff?"

I don't mean it to come out like that—angry and unhinged. They exchange a look. The high wail of sirens comes from the woods.

"There was someone else here," I say, but a motor roaring drowns out my voice.

"We need another blanket," says Ponytail. "And the warmers from the kit. What's your name?"

"Alex."

"Okay, Alex. You're moderately hypothermic and possibly in shock. We're going to warm you up and get you out of here."

I nod, though the idea of walking feels absurd when I can't feel my feet. Her partner returns with something that looks like a giant piece of tinfoil and wraps one around my legs, another around my shoulders. He offers two small papery packets, already giving off a chemical warmth. I press them against my face. The heat feels like coming back to life. I sit and he helps put two more in my shoes.

Both their radios crackle. Then the world explodes. A boat roars into the cove just as a line of police officers appear on the trail above us. They swarm the beach like ants in uniform, all of them shouting to each other or into their radios. When I look up, my medics have been swallowed by the chaos. I can't see the old woman's body anymore.

"Alex."

My head snaps up. One of the officers crouches beside me.

"Sorry," he says. "I didn't mean to startle you."

His face comes into focus—the long nose, the startling eyes with their golden centers. My stomach sinks. Not here. Not today.

He clears his throat. "It's Parker," he says. "Russell Parker. We met before."

If everything wasn't so awful, I might have laughed. "Yeah," I say. "I remember."

Parker unfurls a dark bundle of cloth in his arms. A jacket.

"Here," he says. "I had an extra in my car and thought you might need it." He holds it up so I can slip my arms into the flannel-lined canvas. It's so heavy, it feels like a hug.

"One more thing."

I catch the smell of pine and sweat as he reaches into the pocket for something. "Coffee." He holds up a metal thermos. "It's hot. I haven't touched it yet, if you want some."

And God, do I ever want some. I nod and he pours the hot, dark liquid into the lid. The first sip sears my throat. I take another. "Thank you," I say.

My arms and legs have turned to sandbags. I wonder if I'm going to faint or something else embarrassing.

"Are you all right?" Parker's face is all frown. "Never mind. Stupid question. Let's get you out of here. Do you think you can walk? My cruiser is parked about a half mile back." He looks at me, doubtful. "Or they can take you in the boat."

"The boat?" I picture the solid ice across the harbor, the tiny ice-fishing huts dotting the surface. "But it's frozen."

"Only south of Rock Point," he says. "It's still open water to the north, for now. There's a coast guard station on Grand Isle and they can drive you back to town from there."

I think of being surrounded by all that water with the freezing wind roaring around me. "I can walk."

"One minute," Parker says and disappears into the throng.

I don't want to look at the body. But when someone says don't think about elephants, suddenly it's the only thing on your mind. Then the officers part and the body is gone. I imagine the old woman sitting up, medics sponging the blood from her face. Maybe we made a mistake. Then I see the long black bag lying at the edge of the water.

Parker reappears. "The medics cleared you. My car is closer than their rig. But I promised we'd go straight to the ED if you showed any more symptoms of hypothermia. You sure you're okay to walk?"

I nod. All I want is to be somewhere warm. Somewhere not here. I trudge after him.

At the top of the stairs, an officer wraps yellow caution tape around the slender trunk of a birch. He nods at us as we pass. I turn back to take in the cove, now below us. The ledges of red rocks crowned with green pines. The body bag surrounded by dark-suited officers like mourners at a funeral. Then I look directly down at the shallow water beneath the stairs. I'm standing right where she must have stood. Maybe twenty feet down. I feel a hand on my arm.

"Careful," Parker says.

I take a step back, away from the edge. He lets go.

"Could falling really do that?" I ask. It doesn't feel high enough.

He's silent for long enough that I'm not sure he heard me. "The rocks are slippery," he says, finally. "And it's high enough that a fall—if you hit your head just right—could do real damage."

"There was someone else here," I say.

He looks at me sharply. "You saw someone?"

I shake my head. "No. I—I heard something." It sounds feeble.

"We'll know more soon," he says. "Come on, the car isn't far. We'll blast the heat."

The trail is a slushy mess of bootprints and disturbed earth. "This way," Parker says, guiding us down an offshoot trail. I can feel him there beside me—arm held out a few inches from his body, fingers spread—to catch me if I stumble.

10

The sun is high, the light bright and flat as we take the trail back toward the road. My morning run in reverse. How much time has passed since I left my apartment this morning—two hours? Four? I have no idea.

"Careful there."

Parker points to a patch of ice. Brown maple leaves are curled inside, as if they're still drifting through the air instead of frozen in place. He walks ahead, his boots leaving elephant-sized footprints in the snow.

"What will happen to her now?" I ask. I can't bring myself to say *body*. Neither can I shake the feeling that I'm responsible for her. Like I found a dog on the side of the road and need to make sure it finds its way home.

"They'll bring her in to identify her and determine cause of death," he says. "Or the family will report her missing. Turn left here."

He points down a path that splits off from the main trail. Now it's covered in heavy bootprints—a herd of elephants—but I recognize the spot. "This is the place where she joined the trail," I say.

He stops and looks at me, frowning.

"This morning, I mean. The trail was covered in fresh snow. I thought I was the only one here until I got to this spot." I point at the spur trail. "Another set of footprints joined the trail from down there. They must be hers, right? The woman's."

Parker rubs a hand over his chin. The woods are so quiet I hear his glove rasp against the stubble. "Seems likely. Thanks, I'll pass it along."

I get the feeling that he's humoring me, trying to keep me moving. "Not much farther," he says.

A few minutes later, the trees drop away and we step onto a path lined by rows of headstones stretching up a steep hill. This morning, I felt deep in the woods, but Coram House was right here all along, crouching just out of sight.

A police cruiser sits in front of a white mausoleum. A marble angel keeps watch on the roof. Her legs dangle over the side like a child on a chair too tall for her. The car beeps as Parker unlocks it.

"You'll have to sit in the back," he says.

A prickly ball of fear in my stomach. "Am I under . . ." I trail off, unsure what I'm even asking.

"It's policy," he says quickly. "There's a shotgun rack in front."

Immediately, I feel stupid.

He opens the back door for me. It's warmer inside out of the wind, but this just makes me shiver harder, as if my body can now give up. Parker turns the heat to high and points the vents toward the back. "Should warm up in a second," he says.

I huddle in on myself and look out the window. The gravestones go right up to a stand of birch at the edge of the woods. The silver bark peels away in strips like a snake sloughing off its skin.

"All right?"

A metal grille separates the back seat from the front. I nod back at him from my cage, but the truth is, everything hurts. My skin feels a size too small for the flesh thawing underneath.

Parker rests his hands on the wheel, but doesn't drive yet. "About the other day . . ." He pauses. "I should have told you I was supposed to be your liaison when you came in. That wasn't fair. I didn't mean to come off as—" He searches for the right word.

"Hostile?" I suggest through chattering teeth.

His eyes catch mine in the mirror. The corner of his mouth twitches. "Unprofessional," he says.

"Right," I say. "Neither did I. It was . . . a hard day."

Parker nods and puts the car in reverse. The path hasn't been plowed yet; the only marks are Parker's tire tracks. As we crest the hill, Coram

House appears, one piece at a time. First the gold weathervane, then the long slate roof, the upper floors, the lower, as if the building is rising up from underground. From here, you can't see any of the new construction. It could be fifty years ago.

"I went inside," I say. "Yesterday."

Nothing changes—he's still quiet, eyes still on the road, but his silence takes on another layer. We reach the main gates to the cemetery, and he puts on his blinker.

"It wasn't what I expected," I say. "It was so empty. It was just— a building."

I don't know how to describe what I mean or even why I'm telling him this. It's not that I'd expected some chamber of horrors, preserved in wax. But there had been no sign the building was ever full of children. I'd once been in a school that had been shut down. There had still been drawings pinned to the wall, a pencil jammed between the floorboards, initials carved into the stairwell. The children of Coram House had been erased entirely.

"That's all it's ever been," Parker says. "A building."

We drive down North Avenue in silence. When he pulls into the police station parking lot, I think at first that there must have been a mistake. I thought he was taking me home. He must see the look on my face.

"It won't take long. I—we'd just like to ask you some questions while it's still fresh in your mind. Then someone will take you home. Okay?"

I nod, even though I want to say no. I'm too tired. I don't want to. But what is that in the face of a woman's death?

The automatic doors swoosh open, enveloping me in a rush of warm air. Bev is still there, surrounded by glittering threads of tinsel. But today, she comes out from behind the desk and pats my arm. "It's just awful," she says. "Oh, good lord. Honey, you're frozen. Let me get you something hot to drink. Tea? Tea is hotter than coffee."

She disappears and we go inside. Eyes follow us as Parker leads me through the station and down a back hall. He opens a door and we step into a small room with a single grimy window, set so high, all I can see is a sliver of sky. The drop ceiling is stained nicotine yellow. Parker

104

gestures to four molded-plastic chairs around a metal table. "Here, sit. I'll be right back."

A second later, there's a soft knock and Bev enters, holding a mug. She places it in front of me and then hurries out before I can thank her. The liquid is viscous with sugar, but she's right, the tea's very hot. My chair rocks back and forth every time I shift. I wonder if it's an interrogation tactic or if that only happens in movies.

Parker reappears a minute later with a television remote and another officer, a woman with long braids twisted into a bun and a cherry-red manicure. She smiles at me like we're old friends and introduces herself as Officer Washington. Then she holds out a pair of orange Crocs with white socks tucked inside. "Not the most fashionable," she says, "but better than wet feet."

I peel off my soggy sneakers and socks. My toes look like fat, white raisins. The dry socks feel delicious. I love her a little.

"Alex, just to let you know, we'll be recording today's interview. Is that all right?" Parker gestures toward the camera mounted in one corner.

"Yes," I say. "That's fine."

He sits in the chair across from me, next to Officer Washington.

"Could you take us through everything that happened this morning?" he asks.

I wrap my hand around the mug. "I went for a run this morning—left my apartment just after sunrise, so six thirty maybe?"

Officer Washington writes something down.

"And where did you run?" Parker asks.

"Over to North Ave.," I say. "Then up to Rock Point. I meant to run the loop trail, but I—" My voice cracks and I clear it. "I got to the viewpoint and heard a scream."

"Did you see anyone else at Rock Point?"

"No. It was pretty cold this morning. Just the footprints—the ones I told you about. Oh, and a moose."

Their eyes snap to me in unison. Officer Washington frowns, pen hovering above her notepad. "A moose?" she asks. And I don't think I'm imagining the disbelief in her tone.

My cheeks go hot. "It was just standing there on the trail. When

I heard the scream I thought, I don't know, maybe it had attacked someone."

"Let's back up for a second," Parker says. "Earlier, you said there was another set of footprints on the trail. Can you describe them?"

I picture the trail. The smooth dusting of snow, the way it squeaked underfoot. The place where the other set of footprints joined the main trail.

"They were small. I remember because I was relieved it was another woman. If I was going to be alone in the woods with them, I mean."

Officer Washington scribbles something in her notebook. I try to ignore it.

"Thanks, Alex," Parker says. "That's really helpful. Can you tell me about the scream?"

"I-I was at the viewpoint. At the end of the trail. Did I say that already?"

The laugh bubbles out of me. Inappropriate. I'm just so tired.

"I know the place," Office Washington chimes in, her tone all upbeat encouragement.

"I thought it might be an animal or something," I say, "but it— I don't know—it sounded scared. Human."

"What did you do next?" asks Parker. His expression is neutral. I can't tell what he makes of all this.

"Nothing, at first," I say. "Well, I checked my phone, but I didn't have service. I couldn't tell where it had come from, but it sounded like maybe down by the water?"

My voice rises at the end, as if I'm asking them.

"I was worried someone might be hurt. That they'd fallen and broken their leg or something. I didn't imagine—I mean not then—that someone was dead."

I think of the rock sitting beside the woman's body. Covered in blood and chunks of something I don't want to think about. I try to swallow but the tea sticks in my throat.

"There was someone else there," I say, the words spilling out. "I heard this sound. After the scream, I yelled—to see if someone was there. And then there was this scraping noise. And these echoey thunks."

Parker's face stays neutral, but Officer Washington's eyebrows shoot up. I'm doing a terrible job, I know. But I've never had to describe a sound before—I feel like I'm speaking the wrong language.

Parker's voice is gentle. "Did you see anyone else?"

"No," I say, "just the sounds."

I know what he's thinking. I just finished telling them about the footprints on the trail—the single set of footprints.

Officer Washington leans forward. "Listen, I get it. If you're not used to being out in the woods, all sorts of sounds can—"

"Look, I don't know how to explain it, but they weren't like the other noises in the woods. They were human sounds. There was someone else out there. I think they heard me calling and were trying to get away."

I know it's true as soon as the words are out of my mouth. Someone heard me and was trying to get away. The silence stretches out, until finally Parker clears his throat. "These sounds," he says, his voice even, careful, "could you tell where they were coming from?"

I rub my eyes. My head is pounding, right behind the sockets. I wonder if they'd bring me some ibuprofen. "From the direction of the water."

Officer Washington has stopped taking notes. Now she's squinting at me, as if trying to see something out of focus.

"So after you heard these sounds," Parker says, "what happened next?"

"I followed the footprints down to the rocks. And when I didn't see anyone, went down to the beach. And that's where I found her."

I tell them about the rest: going down the stairs to the beach, how I didn't see anyone at first. And then that flash of bright purple, how she had been right behind me the whole time. I describe the feel of the slippery coat, how her skin had been warm, her glassy eyes staring at me. And the blood. Officer Washington is scribbling furiously now. I take us all the way up to when the medics arrived and then the police. I go to take a sip of tea but the mug is empty. I don't remember finishing it. I shiver.

"We're almost done," Parker says. "Then we'll get you home. Did you see anything that suggested someone else had been down at the cove? Or with the woman before she fell?"

I close my eyes, remembering that feeling of being watched—like the trees had eyes. But had I seen footsteps, a scrap of cloth, anything tangible?

"No," I admit.

He looks at me for one more second. The gold circles around his irises seem brighter in this dingy room. Then he shuts the folder.

"I think that's all for today. Thanks for your time. We'll be in touch if we have more questions. Officer Washington will give you a ride home."

"Oh," I say. "Okay. Thanks."

All I want to do is crawl into bed, but it feels too abrupt, like this can't possibly be it.

The three of us step into the corridor. "This way," Officer Washington says, just as the door we're passing flies open.

A man careens into the hall, knocking the folder out of her hand in a shower of papers. He grabs me for balance, sending us both into the wall. My shoulder connects in a sharp burst of pain. Parker lunges forward, peeling the man off me by his collar. Without the heavy weight, it feels like I'm floating.

Parker grips the man by the shoulders now, but he's not holding him back, I realize. He's holding him up. The man is very, very drunk. The smell of it wafts off him, sharp and medicinal.

"Sor—" He burps. "Shorry about that."

The man widens his eyes and over-enunciates in the deliberate way of someone so drunk they actually think they're fooling you. "Seem to be I lost my balance."

He leans forward, as if to brush some invisible dust off me, but Parker catches his wrist and gently places it back by his side. I wonder what the guy's story is. He looks haggard and red-eyed, but his clothes are expensive. The sneakers a name-brand limited edition and the coat shows a flash of designer plaid.

Another officer comes hurrying down the corridor, holding a paper cup. "Sorry—Jesus, I swear I only left for a minute and he was dead as a rock." Coffee sloshes over the rim. "Shit." He shakes his hand, so brown droplets fly everywhere.

"No harm," Parker says. He looks at me, eyebrows raised in question. I nod. I'm fine.

The drunk man studies me, cocking his head to one side like a dog. "Yer—you're pretty."

"All right, Mr. Nilsson." The other officer takes his arm. "I think that's enough."

Parker grabs the guy's other arm and together they lead him back into the interview room. There's a cot in one corner with a garbage can beside it. A makeshift drunk tank. Drunk guy looks back over his shoulder. "Can I buy you dinner?" he whispers to me, though it's loud enough to carry down the hall. Parker gives me an apologetic look and kicks the door shut.

Officer Washington shakes her head. "They picked him up this morning out on the ice. Half frozen. Probably homeless."

"I doubt it," I say.

She blinks and looks at me.

"Did you see his sneakers? Those were Travis Scott Air Jordans. They go for a thousand bucks."

"Didn't take you for a sneaker head," she says, clearly amused.

"Not me. My husband."

I tamp down the urge to finish with: *He died.* Like I owe everyone the whole story every time I mention him. Maybe that's why I usually don't. But Officer Washington doesn't ask for more. She bundles me out of the police station and into a car—a different car, so I get to sit in front this time. On the way, she keeps up a bright, one-sided conversation about who makes the pizza with the thinnest crust, the freshest bread, the best coffee. It should make me hungry but doesn't.

As soon as I get out of the car, exhaustion settles over me, so intense I can barely make it up the stairs. In the kitchen, I kick off my borrowed shoes and head straight for the shower. Billows of steam fill the bathroom, so thick and hot I feel lightheaded. When I'm the color of cooked lobster, I drop the towel and climb into bed naked.

A siren wails, getting louder until red lights blaze through the curtains, then pass by. A faint smell of smoke hangs in the air. I think of Karen Lafayette's deposition. *There was a little girl who burned up. Sister Cecile told her to fetch a ball from the fire and her snowsuit went up in flames.* I shake my head, as if that will make the picture fall out.

I wonder if I'll hear these voices, these stories, replaying in my head forever. See the bloody tangle of hair floating in the water. Feel warm dead skin. Maybe it's not Coram House that's haunted. Maybe it's me.

I only meant to warm up in bed for a few minutes, but soon I'm sinking into sleep. At first, I fight it, but staying awake is like clawing my way out of a sand pit. The sides cave in again and again until I wonder why I'm bothering when it's so much easier to just let go.

Michael Leblanc

Alan Stedsan: Thank you for agreeing to join us. I know all of this must be very difficult to talk about.

Michael Leblanc: It's not actually. Or it was. But not anymore. Not for me.

AS: Well, I'm glad to hear that. My hope is this will bring others peace as well. Telling their stories.

ML: I'm not sure that's the right word. Stories.

AS: Truths, then. Their truths.

ML: Yes.

AS: All right, let's get started, then. You were at Coram House from 1959 to 1966, and left when you were thirteen. Is that correct?

ML: That's right.

AS: And was Father Foster in residence during that time?

ML: Yes. The sisters took care of the children, all the day-to-day care. But he oversaw the orphanage as a whole.

AS: He was in charge?

ML: Yes. The sisters reported to Father Foster.

AS: A number of former residents of Coram House have made allegations of sexual abuse against Father Foster.

ML: Yes, I'm aware. I'm one of them. One of hundreds, probably.

AS: Could you tell me more about your experience?

ML: Father Foster was a pedophile who used his position of power to prey on children. For me, it started when I was about eight and lasted until I was ten. I'd be brought to his office, usually as a punishment for something I'd done, and he'd force me to perform oral sex.

AS: About how many times did this happen over the seven years from 1959 to 1966?

ML: A dozen. Maybe more. But it stopped the year before I left.

AS: Did you ever share what was happening to you with the other children or an adult?

ML: The kids didn't talk about it, but most knew what was happening. Maybe not the details. But he tended to have favorites. So there was this feeling that once he moved on from you, you were safe. And you didn't want to do anything to risk that. Before me, there was another boy.

AS: And what about the nuns? Did you believe they knew what was happening?

ML: There's no doubt in my mind that they knew. Or if they didn't it was because they didn't want to. I mean, they knew everything else happening in that place. And they knew which boys to take to his office. Which were his favorites.

AS: You mentioned the abuse stopped in 1965. Did anything happen to precipitate it?

ML: I think Father Foster was particular. I think I just aged out of it. Though there was something else. One of the nuns, I think. She put up a fuss of some kind.

AS: A fuss?

ML: I don't know what happened, exactly. I'd met a prospective family. I was just focused on getting out. But I remember she wouldn't send the younger boys to his office anymore. Only the older ones. The teenagers. I'm sure Father Foster didn't like that.

AS: Do you remember her name?

ML: No. She was new, though. And quite young, I remember that. Celeste? Cecilia?

AS: Sister Cecile?

ML: That sounds right.

AS: It sounds like she was a friend to the children.

ML: It's hard to know, really. I don't think any of us had friends in that place. Not even each other. How do you make friends when you're in hell?

Violet Harrison

Alan Stedsan: Good morning, Mrs. Harrison. Would you mind stating your full name for the recording?

Violet Harrison: Violet Dolores Harrison, though I used to be Smith.

AS: Thank you, Mrs. Harrison. How are you today?

VH: Fine, thanks. A little nervous.

AS: Nothing to be nervous about. We'll just be asking you some questions about your time at Coram House—what you remember, things like that. If you don't remember, just say so. It's your memory, so there are no trick questions.

VH: [Laugh] I guess not.

AS: All right, then. Why don't you start by telling us how long you were at Coram House?

VH: I was there for about three years. Until I got adopted.

AS: And how old were you?

VH: I was nine when I got adopted. Then we moved to Massachusetts.

AS: What do you remember of life at Coram House?

VH: Not much. I mean, I was very young.

AS: Of course. Even the smallest memories are helpful. We're just trying to get a sense of your day-to-day life.

VH: All right. Um—let's see. Well, I remember the nuns.

AS: Anyone in particular?

VH: No, not really. They all wore these long dark dresses—or maybe you call them robes? They all looked the same to me then.

AS: And what sorts of things did you do during the day?

VH: Chores. Lots of chores. But—I mean—it wasn't all, you know, *Oliver Twist* [laugh]. Not like it sounds when you hear someone say *orphanage*.

AS: Could you elaborate?

VH: I just mean, I remember having fun too. Like in the summer the nuns would take us down to the lake. There was a beach there, just below the House. I learned to swim. There was this one nun—she'd row kids out onto the lake for swimming lessons. And we'd always try to build sandcastles, but the beach was too rocky. We couldn't get it to stick.

AS: Any of the other children you remember, in particular?

VH: Gosh, it was so long ago. I don't remember anyone's names. There was this one boy—I remember he used to tell these crazy stories. Will? There was one about a lake monster that had us all terrified for weeks. None of us wanted to go near the water after that.

Frederick Rooney

Alan Stedsan: Thank you for being here today, Mr. Rooney.

Fred Rooney: Oh, I'm Mr. Rooney now?

AS: Fred, if you prefer.

FR: So shoot, Alan. What is it you want to know? About the old kiddie fiddler or something else?

AS: We can start there, if you like.

FR: Of course I don't like it. You think I want to talk about that shit?

AS: I understand not everyone feels comfortable—

FR: Is it comfy for you to listen to it?

AS: Why don't we start somewhere else, then? With daily life at Coram House.

FR: You mean shit like what we ate for breakfast?

AS: Sure.

FR: We ate orphan gruel. I know because every goddamn day it was my job to take a bucket of leftover slime we couldn't choke down over to the dump.

AS: You can't smoke in here, Mr. Rooney.

FR: Well, shit. You should be having these little chats outside, then.

AS: If you'd like a break—

FR: I don't need a damn break. I'm not here to cry on your shoulder. I'm still waiting for you to ask a goddamn question.

AS: All right, do you remember going to the beach when you were at Coram House?

FR: The beach?

AS: Yes. With the other children. Or perhaps the nuns.

FR: Why do you care about that?

AS: I told you. Just to get a sense of the rhythms of daily life. What it was like.

FR: That's pretty fucking specific.

AS: All right. Let's get specific, then. What do you remember about Sister Cecile?

FR: What are they saying about her? Those sad fucks out there, I mean.

AS: There are a number of accusations of abuse against Sister Cecile, if that's what you're referring to.

FR: They don't know anything.

AS: Who doesn't know anything?

FR: Them—all them out there. She saved half of them and they don't even know it.

AS: Who saved them?

FR: My turn for a question. When am I going to get my money?

AS: Are you referring to a settlement?

FR: I tell my story with all the dirty details and you go get the money. Am I missing something?

AS: Mr. Rooney, settling a case—if that is the direction things go—is a long—

FR: Oh, that's the direction things are gonna go. Trust me.

AS: Do you have something you'd like to share?

FR: Not a blessed fucking thing.

PART 3

11

My sleep had been deep and dreamless. If the orange Crocs weren't sitting there by the door, I might have thought I imagined everything that happened yesterday. But when I sit down at my table, master binder open in front of me, I keep seeing the woman's face. Her eyes wide and staring. The mask of blood. Like my mind saved my nightmares for morning. I try to push the image into my mental box, but find I can't.

What are the chances that I'd be the one to find her, in that spot, so close to where Tommy drowned? It's as if, in searching for Tommy, I found the woman's body instead. Like I caused her to be there some-how. It's a crazy thought. And yet, there it is.

I take out the black-and-white photo of the children standing beside the boat. The nun's face is indistinct, as if I'm looking through thick fog, but her thin white fingers are in perfect focus, clasped together in front of her. I know exactly the place they're standing now. I recognize the wooden clapboards of the boathouse I saw from the window of Coram House. That places them a few hundred yards from the cove where I found the body yesterday. So much death hiding in those waters. But it's a melodramatic thought—people die everywhere all the time.

The living room's beige walls press in on me, pulsing a little, like they're breathing. I need to get out. I put the photo back in the box and get dressed.

———

The day is cold, but not bitter. Now that I know the feeling of my eyeballs freezing in their sockets, I can recognize the difference. A gray sheen covers the brick sidewalks, moisture frozen to a slippery skin. Still, in my ridiculous sleeping bag parka and furry boots, I move through downtown as if I'm wrapped in a warm cocoon.

I don't have a particular destination in mind, so I wander north, past the little cemetery, and down a hill. I pass a red-brick library with a modern glass addition on one side. It's closed, but I make a note to come back. I've always loved libraries—and, who knows, maybe I'll find something useful. But I know it's wishful thinking.

For two weeks, I've buried myself in dusty archives and stared at historical records online until my eyes throbbed. I've searched the empty halls of Coram House and found nothing. Tommy isn't there. And even if I did find some record of his existence—what then? It wouldn't tell me what I need to know: Did Tommy drown that day? Is Sarah Dale's memory sharp and true or is she telling tales? The answers I need lie in the memories of people who have been dead for a decade.

The road leads past a thrift shop that shares a building with a church supply company peddling gifts, cards, and religious artifacts. I imagine a glass case bearing a dead saint's bones on a pillow. That's probably not what they mean, though. I pass an auto shop and cross a set of train tracks. The road abruptly turns to dirt—as if someone decided the city ends right here.

Fields of snow stretch ahead, pierced by rows of cut stalks, the tips just high enough to catch the sun. I wonder if I should go back. If I should be here. In the distance, a smudge of red floats between the alternating rows of golden stubble and deep blue shadow. Not floating, gliding—a cross-country skier. They disappear into the fringe of trees on the far side of the field. I keep walking.

Soon trees close in again. A river winds below, down a steep embankment lined in tall, dried plants with feathery tips. Everything is dead and dried, painted in sepia tones that make me feel like I'm walking through time. I could be inside one of those photos in the mildewy shoebox. But maybe I don't need to go back in time to get answers.

I think of the conversation I had with Lola just a few days earlier. *Change the channel.* Maybe she was right—just not in the way she thinks. Not everyone who was there that day is dead. Fred Rooney is very much alive.

It seems crazy to reach out to Rooney directly. But maybe it's not. He would have been a minor when Tommy drowned, so there's no way he'd be prosecuted, even if he was involved. If I can make it clear I'm here to tell his story too, he just might talk to me. Yes, he makes my skin crawl, but if talking to him is the only way to get answers, it's worth it.

All of a sudden, I'm aware of my aloneness. The skier is long gone. The only sound is wind rustling dead things. A woman, alone in the woods. A limp hand floating in the water. A face covered in blood. I turn and retrace my footsteps, shivering and not stopping until I've crossed back into the world.

I pass a deli with a long line of college students stretching out the door, waiting for bagels. I go inside, buy food I don't really want, relieved to be somewhere warm with its smell of coffee, lulled by the hum of other people's conversations.

When I get back to the apartment I kick off my boots and head for my computer. A sharp pain in my heel and two beads of blood appear like a snake bite. A staple, hidden in the carpet. I staunch the puncture with toilet paper and, one-handed, type Fred Rooney's name into the Yellow Pages search. No number listed. Disappointment hollows my stomach. I was counting on anyone with white hair having a listed landline. I could go back to the construction site, but my instincts tell me I'll have better luck if I catch him off guard.

I try the number for Campbell & Sons. The girl who answers the phone sounds about fifteen.

"Hi," I say, keeping my voice bright. "I'm looking for Fred Rooney."

"Sorry, he's not here," she says. "He's on site today."

"Oh, shoot. Do you know when he'll be back?"

"Well, they usually finish around three? But he doesn't always come back to the office after."

"Maybe you can help me, then?" I say before she can offer to take a message.

I give her a story about a package that was sent back to me and could she just confirm if his address is 19 or 17 Ivy Lane, Burlington. She'll look it up, she says. But the address she has isn't in Burlington at all, she says in confusion, it's in Huntington and it's not Ivy Lane either. I laugh and say that explains it, and she laughs too and reads out the correct address. I thank her and hang up, feeling a pang of guilt. It's always women who give you more than they should.

Forty minutes to his house, according to my phone. If I leave at three, I should catch him just as he's getting home. For the rest of the afternoon, I work my way down the list of potential interview subjects. Several have died and more have disappeared with no address or phone number on record. I do track down a few people. Hal Stevenson hangs up on me when I tell him I'm calling about Coram House. Cedric Shepherd gives me a polite but firm no. And Violet Harrison agrees to think about it, but I'm pretty sure she's just trying to get me off the phone. I leave another message for Karen Lafayette, with no real hope there either.

By then it's nearly three. I forage for something to eat, but all I find in the fridge is the dried remains of hummus and some old carrots, slightly soft so they bend when they should break with a snap like bone.

I arm myself in professional attire. Slacks. A turtleneck sweater. My blush has gone missing, so I use lipstick. My face stares back at me from the mirror, a red slash on each cheek. Suddenly, I see the woman's face streaked with blood. I close my eyes. When I open them again, the face is my own.

The drive is beautiful, the snow-frosted peaks framed in my windshield like a postcard of a New England winter. The road dips and curves, so sometimes the mountains are hidden and then reappear from a different angle, huge and surprising. My phone directs me to take Exit Eleven and drive south.

After five miles, the pavement disappears and the road narrows. It occurs to me that I should have told someone where I'm going—Stedsan or even Officer Parker. I glance down at my phone. No service. Of course. I pass a few small houses, most with a pickup parked in the driveway. Then a barn with a perfect circle punched in the roof, as if it had been hit by a meteor. A dull pressure in my ears tells me the road is still climbing.

A mile past the barn, I pull into the driveway of a square single-story house. It's painted white with no shutters and has a new front porch, the fresh wood still yellow as unweathered bone. Two round cement planters, now just mounds of snow, flank the front walkway. It's Scandinavian in its bareness. I'd been expecting trash in the yard or a rusted car on cinderblocks outside the garage. I feel a flutter of shame. Fresh tire tracks lead to a black pickup parked beside the house. So much for beating him home.

Before I even turn off the car, a door slams and Rooney is there, standing on his front porch. He crosses his arms and looks at me. Suddenly, I want to back out the drive. This was a bad idea. Instead, I get out.

"Afternoon," I say.

"The writer," he says, as if he's been expecting me. Rooney has a piece of gauze taped to his cheek and a bruise on his forehead, folded in among the wrinkles. Scratches on his neck. He sees me looking and smiles. "I like it rough."

I'm glad for the thick coat, the scarf covering the flush of my neck.

His smile drops away. "So what do you want?"

At least he's not going to invite me inside. "I want to talk to you about Coram House."

He gives me a look like I'm trying his patience. "What about it?"

"I'm interviewing the children—anyone who was connected with Coram House—for the book I'm writing. I'd like to tell your story if you're willing."

It's not much of a pitch, but I feel more nervous than I expected. I've never been good at confrontation.

"That why you came all the way out here? To see if I'm willing."

He emphasizes the last word—*willing*—in a way that makes it sound dirty. I have to stop myself from taking a step back.

"Yes."

He rubs his chin in a pantomime of thinking it over, but his thumb catches on the edge of the gauze and he winces. "What's in it for me?"

This, at least, I'm ready for. "I can't pay interview subjects, if that's what you mean. It would make life easier, but it's not how it works."

"And who decides how it works?"

"If I pay people for their story, it might change the story they tell. Or at least look that way."

"Well, I guess I'll just have to think about it, then. I'm a busy man, you see." He holds out his arms, showing the expanse of his domain.

I don't know what I was thinking coming here. Of course he wasn't going to talk to me.

"I understand."

I hold out a business card. He takes it, but holds on a beat too long before letting go. I catch of whiff of something sharp. He's been drinking. "Call me if you'd like to talk," I say.

"Don't worry. I know where to find you."

I take a few steps back toward my car, but desperation to get something, anything, from him claws inside my chest. "Mr. Rooney—could I ask you a question?"

"You want a freebie?" He looks amused, but motions for me to go on.

"When you were at Coram House, did you ever know a boy named Tommy?"

His expression shifts into a look of interest—like a cat that's been playing with its food and the mouse just did something unexpected. "Maybe," he says. "What's it to you?"

"He would have overlapped with you. I'm not exactly sure when, but sometime after 1965. I'm not sure of his exact age, but probably five or six years younger than you."

"You're not 'exactly sure' of much, are you?" His tone is mocking. "Especially for someone that's probably dug to the bottom of Alan's files by now. Did you come to ask me if he ran away? Then you're stupider than I thought."

My heart speeds up. He's getting angry and people say things they don't mean—or that they don't mean to say—when they're angry.

"A number of the other children talk about Sister Cecile," I say.

"No surprise there."

His tone is nonchalant, but there's a flicker of something in his face. "How she locked children in the attic. Hit them. That it's her fault

Tommy drowned. That there was another child in the boat that day. Maybe someone too young and scared to come forward."

Rooney's face darkens. "Right. 'Cause everything Sarah Dale says is the gospel."

"You were a minor, Mr. Rooney. Whatever happened—wouldn't it be better to tell your side of the story?"

There's a long pause, like he's thinking this over. "You mean like how she said 'Hold him under, Fred' and I did?"

He laughs, his expression pitying. My stomach sinks.

"Look at the face on you. That's what you want me to say isn't it?"

Heat creeps up into my cheeks.

"Maybe I was there that day, maybe not. But I can tell you I never touched that boy."

"The others said you were a particular favorite of Sister Cecile's," I say quietly. "That she loved you."

Fred Rooney's face shuts down like someone turned out the light. "Well, I guess you'd have to ask Sister Cecile about that."

The surprise knocks me back a step. He used the present tense.

After Coram House closed, most of the nuns had gone to convents or retirement homes for members of the clergy. And now all the ones I'd found were dead, except for the one nonagenarian with Alzheimer's. I'd assumed Sister Cecile had died too, probably at some convent back in Quebec. Why?

With a sinking feeling, I know. Because, when I read Sister Cecile's deposition, I'd pictured an elderly nun. And that blurred face in the photo from the sixties—my mind had filled in a sturdy middle-aged woman. Finding Sister Cecile hadn't been a priority because I'd imagined her as old, *all* nuns as old. But if she'd been young, say somewhere between twenty and thirty, I do a quick calculation—she'd be in her seventies or eighties now.

My own blind spot. How stupid.

"I didn't realize Sister Cecile was still alive. I'd love to speak to her. Do you have her contact information?"

I try to keep my voice calm but can tell how eager I sound, like he just put food in front of a starving person.

Rooney throws back his head and roars with laughter. He gently lifts the bandage so he can wipe away tears. "Freebie time's over," he says, smile gone. Before I can say another word, he slams back into his house. I'm left standing alone in the snow.

In the car, I grip the steering wheel, hands shaking. My heart thumps like a rabbit spotting the fox's tail as it disappears into the bush. Fearful with the knowledge that I've been spared.

Back on the main road, the snowy fields glow orange with sunset. A few weeks ago, I would have said snow is white, but now I know it's blue with twilight or the yellow of direct sunlight. White doesn't exist at all.

My phone beeps to tell me I have a voicemail—Parker asking me to call him back. I pull over and turn off the car before dialing the station.

"Parker." His voice is low and raspy, like he hasn't slept.

"Hey. It's Alex Kelley. I just got your message."

"Oh, Alex. Hi." His tone softens. "Look, I'm sure this is the last thing you want to hear right now, but I have to ask you to come back to the station."

He's right. It is the last thing I want to hear. "Now?" I hate the whine in my voice.

"Tomorrow is fine," he says. "We've got a detective from state coming in."

"Oh," I say. "Does that mean— Do you know the cause of death? Sorry, I'm probably not supposed to ask that, but it's, well, I got the sense you didn't believe me. About what I heard—the sounds in the woods."

I shove the heel of my palm into my eye socket, trying to dull the headache gathering there. I'm babbling. The conversation with Rooney's thrown me off.

"Alex, we take all witness statements seriously," he says. "And we treat every death as suspicious if there's any reason to believe it might be."

I hear the reprimand in his tone, but isn't that exactly what he'd done? Dismissed me? Or maybe I'm being too sensitive.

"Alex, are you still there? You're breaking up."

"Sorry." I raise my voice, as if that will help. "I'm out of town. Interviewing someone. For the book. Fred Rooney."

I don't know why I say it. An olive branch, I guess. I'd gotten off to such a bad start with Parker, but after yesterday—it feels like a bridge worth repairing.

"Fred Rooney?" There's a hard edge to his voice, the fatigue gone.

"Is that—a problem?"

"I— Look, I'm sorry. It's just—Alex, that guy is bad news. Stay away from him."

I bristle. "What do you mean, bad news?"

There's a huff of breath on the other end of the phone. "I can't say more right now. But he's dangerous. Just—don't talk to him alone, at least—okay? I can come with you next time."

"Yeah, in my experience bringing a cop along makes interview subjects open right up." A prickle of irritation runs down my spine—what am I supposed to do with half information and cryptic warnings? He's worse than Stedsan.

"Alex, listen to me. I can't discuss an active investigation, okay?" Parker sighs like someone very, very tired.

No one asked you to, I want to say. But then I imagine the sleepless night he's probably had. "Okay," I say. "I appreciate the"—I search for the right word—"information. Anyways, what time do you want me there tomorrow?"

"Is nine okay?"

"Sure."

There's a long pause filled with muffled thumping—Parker tapping his pen against the desk. "Okay," he says. "See you tomorrow."

"See you then."

But the line is already dead. I drop my phone into the cupholder.

The car splutters as I turn the key. For one horrible second, I imagine hiking back to Rooney's house in the dark to use his phone, Parker's warning ringing in my ears. Then the motor catches and rumbles to life. I navigate the car off the shoulder and onto the icy road. Night falls as I drive, the sky a little darker every time I glance in the rearview mirror. There are no streetlights here. No moon. Darkness is following me home.

12

Shit. I wipe at the stain spreading across my shirt with a paper towel. Now I have no coffee, and I'm supposed to be at the police station in five minutes. All morning, I've been distracted, thinking about Fred Rooney and what I could have done differently. And then there's what he said about Sister Cecile. I spent an hour searching various combinations of her name, but came up blank. Could she really be out there, alive? Or was he messing with me? But now it's two minutes to nine and I need to stop thinking about it. I dig through my drawers, but I haven't done laundry yet, so the pickings are slim. Finally, I pull a cleanish sweatshirt on over my bra.

Outside, I hurry to the car. At least we didn't get more snow overnight. The last thing I need right now is to dig out the car. But when I pat my pocket for the car keys, I can't find them. "Shit," I yell, loud enough to get a dirty look from a woman walking her dog. I don't apologize, just dash upstairs.

Fifteen minutes later, I pull into the station parking lot, eyes on the clock, as if that will make it say something other than 9:27. A dark shape appears in front of the hood and I slam on the brakes. A police officer stares me down. I raise my hands in the universal gesture of *I'm sorry, I'm a complete idiot.* He shakes his head and disappears into the building. Sweat prickles down my back. I hate being late. The clock ticks up to 9:28. I jog across the parking lot.

As usual, Bev is sitting behind the reception desk, today in a sweater covered in rainbow pom-poms. She lifts a hand, telling me to wait, and picks up the phone. A few seconds later, Parker appears in the lobby.

His uniform is rumpled and his hair flattened. There are dark purple bags under his eyes. It's unfair how men can continue to be good-looking even when they look terrible.

"I'm so sorry I'm late," I say.

Parker nods, distracted, but doesn't say any more about it. "Thanks for coming. Come on. I'll introduce you."

The station feels busier than before. Or maybe it's just giving off a different energy. Before, it felt somber and restrained. Today, officers are seated at desks, legs bouncing in impatience. One cracks his knuckles as I walk by.

Parker leads me toward a knot of people at the back of the room. They part to reveal a woman in a dark pantsuit, sitting on the edge of a desk. One pant leg is hiked up to reveal a flat black boot. Not one of those TV detectives who run around in three-inch heels, then. Her makeup is minimal, her hair pulled into a low bun. Everything about her feels polished. Professional. Though I do catch a glimmer of gold around her throat. As we get closer I see it's a thin chain with a tiny cross. She catches sight of us and gives Parker a slight nod.

"Thanks, everyone," she says to the crowd around her. "Find me if you have any questions. We'll brief again at the end of the day."

The knot of officers gathered around her breaks apart like athletes going onto the field. She slides off the desk and comes to her full height, which is a good five inches shorter than me. Yet she still projects an aura of authority.

"Alex," Parker says, "this is Detective Garcia. She's here from state."

Detective Garcia holds out her hand and I catch a hint of perfume. Something lush and tropical. It reminds me of one of those expensive candles everyone in Brooklyn has on their mantel. Jasmine. Lily of the valley. Tuberose.

"Thank you for coming," Garcia says. By her tone, I can't tell if she's thanking me for coming or berating me for my lateness. The morning is making me feel off-balance. I half expect to see the floor tiles lifting as a wave moves beneath the surface.

"Let's find somewhere quiet to talk," she says.

Parker leads the way to an interview room. The drunk tank. The bed is gone, along with the guy in the expensive sneakers. Without him, the room is identical to the one I sat in with Parker and Officer Washington two days ago. The table. The four plastic chairs. The only difference is the framed poster. This one shows Lake Champlain at sunset, a white sailboat cutting across the water. The real lake—or at least our little inlet—is obscured by the cinderblock wall.

When I sit, this chair also rocks back and forth. I smile. But when I look up, Garcia is watching me, her lips pressed together into a thin red line. The smile drops from my face.

She sits down and opens a folder. "Let's get started," she says. "Officer Parker?"

Parker adjusts something on the camera mounted to the wall. "All good," he says. He catches my eye and gives me a small smile. My insides settle a little.

Garcia picks up the remote and I consent to being recorded. She asks me to describe what happened that day in the woods. As I speak, she sits very still, her arms crossed and her eyes never leaving me. I feel like an insect trapped under a glass dome.

I've always thought of myself as good at interviews. So much of it is listening—to what someone is saying and what they're not, guiding the conversation so you arrive at the destination you always intended, even if the interview subject isn't sure why or how you got there. But I'm not used to being on the other end. I can't seem to get comfortable in my chair. My story stutters and then bends back on itself because I've forgotten something. God, I really needed that cup of coffee.

With relief, I finally get to the part of the story where the EMTs arrive and take over. Garcia says nothing. The silence stretches out. I want to look at Parker, but I know I'm searching for reassurance and I'm afraid I won't see it on his face. I haven't done anything wrong. Why do I feel like I've done something wrong?

"Alex," Garcia says finally, picking up a pen. "Let's go back for a second. To the minutes right after the scream. Really focus on the scene—tell me what you saw."

My throat feels scratchy from so much talking. "I'm not sure how much more I can add," I say. "There wasn't much to see. The lake. Trees. Snow."

"Tell me about what you heard, then. The sounds. Close your eyes."

So I do. But I hate it. I feel vulnerable sitting there with my eyes closed—like a predator might tear out my throat when I'm not looking. Maybe that's the point.

"Okay, tell me what you hear," Garcia says.

"The trees creaking."

"It was windy?"

"Not in the woods but out on the water."

I hear the pen scratching on paper.

"What else?"

"Something scraping against the rocks."

The scratches of the pen stop. I open my eyes. "It was the rocks," I say. "The sound of something dragging over the rocks. When I called out, the sound stopped. Like they heard me."

In my head, it's so clear, but my voice wavers. It sounds like uncertainty.

"And what came next?" Detective Garcia asks.

I try to go back there. To that moment after I called out. The intense act of standing in the woods and listening. The feeling that every part of my body was absorbing and sensing everything around me.

"Some thunks. I don't know how to describe it exactly. Like something hard hitting something wooden—a drum sort of noise."

Garcia makes a *hmm* noise and writes something down. Then she lays down her pen and folds her hands together. There's sympathy on her face. "You're from New York City, right?" she asks.

I nod, unsure what this has to do with anything.

"How long have you been here? A week?"

"Two," I say, but it sounds silly. Like a child insisting she's not five, but five and a quarter.

"You know, it's very common," she says. "People who don't spend a lot of time in the woods don't understand how noisy they really are. The wind in the branches. Trees creaking. A log floating in the water, smashing against the rocks. Thunk thunk. Then you add in the adrenaline of that moment, and it's completely normal to feel like someone was there."

She smiles at me, gently. And then I understand. She doesn't believe there was anyone else in the woods that morning. "They weren't normal sounds," I say. "They didn't fit."

I don't know how else to describe it. How the sounds felt different from the creaking of branches or the scurrying of animals. How they were deliberate and foreign as a chainsaw. How I could feel myself being watched.

"There was someone else there," I say.

The smile falls off Garcia's face, a discarded mask. She leans forward across the table. "We've got a backlog of murders, you know. An eleven-month-old who was strangled by her mother's boyfriend. Which got put on hold. For this."

I feel a flash of anger. "I'm not trying—"

"Let's review the facts, shall we? One set of footprints on fresh snow." She starts ticking points off on her fingers. "A body discovered within thirty minutes of impact. Cause of death: blunt-force head trauma, likely after an accidental twenty-foot fall."

"Do you know for sure it was accidental? She could have been pushed—"

"I know that you're a writer whose career really needs a good story."

It feels like someone snuck up behind me and dumped a bucket of ice water over my head.

"And I know this will make a much better chapter in your book if it's a murder instead of an old lady who slipped on the rocks. But there's no evidence we should be treating this death as suspicious."

Suddenly, it all makes sense. The simmering hostility. The endless questions about what I heard in the woods. She doesn't think I'm a hysterical witness jumping at shadows. She thinks I deliberately made up some phantom killer in the woods to sell books.

"Thank you for your time, Ms. Kelley," she says, standing. "If we have any further questions, we'll be in touch. Officer Parker can show you out."

I sit there, frozen, while Detective Garcia turns the recording off and leaves. My eyes sting. I blink a few times. Parker clears his throat, but I can't look at him.

"I'll walk you out," he says.

I nod, numb. Parker lifts my coat off the hook and hands it to me. He leads me down a different hall, toward an emergency exit. Gratitude floods me. I don't think I can walk back through the station, feeling all those eyes on me. Not now that I know what they think of me.

Parker pushes open the door. A blast of freezing air makes my eyes water. As soon as I step outside the police station, I feel better. To my surprise, he steps out after me. "Come on," he says. "I'll buy you a cup of coffee. It's better than ours, but it'll burn your tongue off."

I follow him over to the school bus, where cold air mixes with the smell of French fries. A man in a white apron leans out the window and Parker holds up two fingers. A second later the man reappears with two steaming cups. "Thanks," I say as Parker hands me one. I take a sip and wince.

"Told you it was hot," he says.

We sit on the retaining wall that separates the parking lot from the embankment that plunges down to the frozen harbor, which is dotted with fishing shacks. It all looks so solid and permanent. It's hard to believe that just on the other side of Rock Point, the lake is open water and freezing waves. Far out, beyond the ice-fishing shacks, I see something twisted and black. "What is that?" I ask, pointing.

Parker squints and then his mouth hitches into a smile. "Your new friend drove his car onto the lake for some ice fishing the other night."

I frown in confusion and then it clicks. "The drunk guy?"

Parker nods. "When that didn't work out, he managed to light it on fire and then stumble back to his house and pass out on the dock." He gestures with his coffee cup out across the water, to the peninsula that's the mirror image of Rock Point. "And that's where they picked him up. Peeled him right off the dock and brought him in." He shakes his head. "The ice is patchy out there at the break. He's lucky he didn't fall through."

I sip my coffee. It's still too hot. "So who is he?"

"Some rich tech guy. I don't know much else. I guess if you can afford to trash a hundred-thousand-dollar car, you don't need to hand out your résumé."

But I'm only half listening. The truth is, I'm still stinging from the interview with Garcia. I wasn't going to say anything, but I can't help it.

"So what's her problem with me?"

Parker doesn't ask who I'm talking about. "She's just—she has other priorities."

"Yeah," I say. "She made that part pretty clear. Listen, Parker." His name slips easily off my tongue. "Do you think I'm making this up for attention?"

Immediately, I want to take it back, not sure I want to know the answer.

Parker says nothing, clearly considering the question. I realize I'm holding my breath. Finally, he shakes his head.

"No. I don't."

It wasn't quite an *Of course there was someone in the woods if you say so* but it's something.

"But look, she is right. There's no evidence. Two sets of footprints in the woods. Yours and those belonging to an elderly lady with poor eyesight who went on daily walks in Rock Point, according to her neighbors."

I feel momentarily stunned. "You know who she is?"

He nods. "It's not released yet but the obit will be in the paper tomorrow. Her name is Jeannette Leroy. She was seventy years old and lived alone, just across from the cemetery. No family. No money. No sign of a struggle."

I shiver. It makes it more real. Giving her a name.

"That last part wasn't in the paper, so I'd appreciate you keeping it to yourself," he says.

"Of course."

"And, Alex?"

I turn to look at him.

"Detective Garcia is right, about adrenaline. Sometimes we don't see or hear what we think we do."

Somehow it stings less when he says it. Parker drains his cup and tosses it in the trash. "You want my advice?" he says. "Get some rest. Forget about this case and work on your book. If there's anything to find, we'll find it."

I know it's the best I'm going to get.

"Work on my book? Three days ago you were ready to ship me back to New York."

He looks embarrassed. "Sorry about that. I think"—he pauses—"I had your intentions down wrong."

I nod, feeling absurdly relieved and grateful. He rubs his eyes, like he can erase the dark circles.

"You want *my* advice?" I say. "Go home. Get some rest. You look like shit."

He shakes his head, but I see the hint of a smile.

"Here I thought we were getting to be friends."

I hide my smile inside the empty cup.

———

First thing the next morning, I put my jacket on over my sweatpants and dash across to the corner store. A teenager with a fluff of dark peach fuzz lounges behind the register. When I ask where the papers are he blinks at me as if no one's ever asked him that before. I find them on a rack beside the potato chips. I'm not sure which paper runs obituaries, so I grab one of each.

Back in my apartment, I spread the papers on the table. There's nothing in the first one, but in the next, I find it. A two-page spread of obituaries, each with a paragraph of text and a small picture. The woman's photo is grainy and gray, but it's still startling to see her so alive. Her white hair is cropped close to her face, showing off high cheekbones and delicate elfin features. She's staring right at the camera with an expression that's not a smile, but looks expectant somehow. Like someone waiting for whatever comes next.

Beside the photo is a name and a single sentence. *Jeannette Leroy, 1946–2016. For anyone wishing to pay their respects, a service will be held at 11 a.m. on January 23 in the Chapel of Saint Joseph.* That's it. Nothing about how she died or how she was beloved by friends and family.

The lines are so bare. I imagine an old lady living alone. Buying groceries, taking a walk, going to bed—each day blending into the next. How scared she must have been when she lay there bleeding in the woods. Or maybe she died instantly.

Who would want to hurt a seventy-year-old woman with no money and no family? No one. One set of footsteps in the snow. Maybe Garcia is right. Maybe it was just adrenaline.

I pull up the calendar on my phone and add a reminder for the service on Saturday. Then I fold the paper up and set it aside. Time to get back to work. First, I call Father Aubry. No answer, so I leave a message asking him to call me back. Then I try Stedsan. No answer either. I text him instead. *Looking for the last known address or more info on Sister Cecile. Any ideas? Also would have been good to know she's still alive.* I delete the last sentence and hit send.

My desk is a mess of greasy wrappers and crumpled newspapers, piles of notes on index cards waiting to be entered into my binder. You're not supposed to be able to smell your own house, but even I can tell it smells stale, like damp laundry and the garbage I haven't taken out. Something inside me is going to explode if I spend one more hour at my desk. And whatever that thing is, I have to outrun it.

I find my running clothes under the bed. They smell faintly of sweat, but I put them on anyways. It's barely noon, but the clear blue sky outside has the warm light of afternoon. I start up North Avenue, putting on a burst of speed past the police station. I find my legs and run past the houses, a blur of white clapboard against a sky so blue it's indigo at the edges. Flashes of color—a red rug over a porch railing, the lush green of a potted plant in the window. Then the houses fall away and the trees grow denser.

The entrance to Rock Point is strung with yellow caution tape, but there's no one there. What had I expected? An officer guarding the woods? Wind whips strands of hair across my cheeks. I tug my orange hat down over my ears. Lola had bought it for me as a going-away present to keep me safe from hunters. *It's still a city*, I'd said, *you can't just walk down the street with your shotgun.* Now, I think of the moose in the woods and how she'd laugh.

I feel a pang for her or for my life in New York, I don't know which. But it's dull and far away. The way you miss something that doesn't exist anymore. Like childhood or an imaginary friend. Or a life before you had a dead husband, a dead body in the woods, and were floundering at another failing book.

The sun's heat beats down on the crown of my head as I run, even as the wind stings my cheeks. I keep going up North Avenue, trying and failing not to look at Coram House as I pass. No sign of Rooney's truck in the drive, at least.

With every mile, North Avenue narrows—from a busy thoroughfare to a quiet neighborhood street and finally to a dirt road that ends at a muddy beach. A light skin of ice covers the water at the edges. The beach is empty except for a red shack. AUER FAMILY BOATHOUSE, says the peeling paint. Picnic tables are tipped on end, and the boathouse itself is boarded up, for the season or forever, it's hard to tell.

Nearby, a flock of tufted birds feast noisily on red berries. It's been a long time since I've run this far. Too far probably, based on the twinge in my knee. But I wanted to run to the end of something. Any road. Any place.

By the time I get home, my lungs feel torn and my legs are like jelly. The lukewarm shower feels like it's burning, my skin no longer able to tell the difference between hot and cold. It's all just pain.

13

When I get out of the shower, my skin is as pink as a baby mouse. I stand in front of the open fridge, cold air winding around my ankles as I look for dinner, which turns out to be a beer and a bag of nuts. From the desk, my phone pings. I hadn't brought it on my run and now I have two missed calls. Dammit.

The first is from Father Aubry. He's sorry he missed my call, he says. He's traveling but says try him again tomorrow or just come by on Sunday morning—he'll be in the office preparing for the afternoon service. I'd been hoping the second call was Stedsan with Sister Cecile's address and phone number, but it's an unknown number. I hit play. At first it's silent and I nearly delete it, but then a voice speaks.

"Alex, hi."

The man's voice is low and thick, like he has a cold.

"I—um—well, I hope you don't mind me calling. This is Xander Nilsson. We met the other day at the police station. Or, well, maybe *met* isn't exactly the right word. I—well, I wanted to call and say I'm sorry for my behavior. It's inexcusable, really. But I would actually really like to treat you to dinner if you're up for it—to apologize. But I understand if you're not. Anyways, sorry again and—yeah. Just let me know."

Xander Nilsson. Until now, he has felt unreal. A fairy-tale millionaire who set his own car on fire. It's strange to hear the voice of an actual person on the phone. I'm not sure what to make of the fact that he got my phone number. I should probably be creeped out, but mostly I'm curious. Either way, I'm not calling him back, I decide. I don't need any more distractions.

I nurse my beer and riffle through boxes of old receipts. I find Sister Cecile's name on a few documents: an order form for two hundred pencils, a receipt for a donation of flannel sheets. Sometimes she signs her full name, Sister Cecile, and sometimes S. Cecile. Some of the other signatures are illegible, but her looping whirls are identically tidy. It's maddening to have all these pieces of the past and nothing useful. I'm on my second beer when the phone rings. I lunge for it. The number is blocked.

"Hello?" I answer, hoping it's Stedsan.

"Hey, hey."

Lola's voice throws me off. Like she's calling me from a past life instead of just from Brooklyn. "Lola," I say. "Hi."

"Don't sound so excited." Her tone is mock annoyed.

"No—I'm just surprised—your number is blocked."

"I'm at work. Anyways, what are you up to?"

"Going through grocery receipts from 1958."

"Girl, it's almost nine. Even brain surgeons take evenings off."

"I'm not sure that's true." But I move to the couch and lay down. "I'm drinking a beer."

She sighs. "You know there are these places called bars where you can drink with other humans."

I put Lola on speakerphone and listen to her talk about a project at work that's not going well, how the restaurant around the corner—our happy hour spot—is closing, how the weather has been terrible. Her voice is soothing and steady, the backdrop of the last two decades of my life. I listen while I finish my beer and open another, feeling like I'm floating on a familiar sea, warm and relaxed.

"Alex," Lola says. "How are things—really?"

I sit up. I know what she's really asking. Am I still obsessed with the Tommy thing? Does she need to worry about me?

"I'm— It's good," I say, which is what I'd say if I'd just chopped off my leg and was bleeding to death on the floor. But I do the dance. She's just trying to help.

Avoiding any mention of Tommy, I tell her instead about the charming and handsome elderly lawyer and the gruff local cop. I tell her how badly I messed up our first meeting. And I tell her about the moose, which does make her laugh. I don't mention the dead body I found in the water. Partly because I know she'll freak out and partly because the woman's warm, slippery skin still feels too real under my fingers. I'm not ready to package it into an anecdote.

"Officer Russell Parker," Lola rolls the name around her mouth. "It's a movie star name. How old is he?"

"I don't know. Early forties maybe."

"Is he hot?"

"Jesus, Lola. I don't know."

"That means yes."

This line of questioning makes me want to get up and pace, so I change the subject to Xander stumbling into me drunk at the police station. How he's some kind of wayward tech millionaire that washed up in Vermont.

"You're going to go, right? To your apology dinner?"

I can hear how careful she is not to call it a date.

"What?" I laugh. "Of course not."

"Come on!" she says. "You have to go. He probably has a champagne fountain."

"I don't think that's actually a thing."

"It's definitely a thing!"

"All right."

"*All right* you're gonna go?"

"*All right* a champagne fountain might be a thing."

"I'm just saying—once in a while you can do the crazy thing."

"Well, as long as we both agree it would be crazy."

Laughing makes me feel lighter. I like talking like this—at a distance. Like how the thread that connects us is just what we choose to share.

"By the way, I've got next weekend off. I was thinking I could come visit."

I sink back onto the couch. "Visit? Here?"

"Yeah. That's the idea."

The thought fills me with panic. Like a piece of my old life coming to haunt me. Then I feel terrible because I love Lola. "But what about the show?" I ask.

Lola works in marketing for a theater company. The pay is shit, but the people make up for it, she always says. And it's true. She's constantly surrounded by actors, always has an art opening to attend and knows where the coolest bar is before it's the next big thing. It also usually means that her weekends are fully booked from September to May.

"Tech problems," she says. "It got pushed out a week. So what about it?"

"I would love that," I stutter, "but things are just so busy right now. I'm just starting to dig in. I'm working weekends, always on the phone, you'd hate me. Plus it's freezing. Come in a month or two—it will be better then."

I cringe at the way I'm throwing a barrage of reasons at her when one would have been enough.

"Yeah," she says. "Sure." Her voice sounds hard.

"You know I'd love to see you." And I mean it. I do. Sort of.

"Yeah," she says again. "Sounds good. Anyways, it's getting late. I should go."

We say our goodbyes and she hangs up. My phone is hot from being used for so long. Then I pick up the box of receipts and keep reading. As if Sister Cecile might have scribbled some vital clue between the lines of an invoice for canned goods.

———

The next day my stomach feels greasy and hollow. Guilt over all the things I didn't tell Lola. Or possibly a protest that everything I've eaten over the last week has come out of a foil wrapper. Today will be different, I vow. Today I will eat a vegetable. So I get dressed and head for the grocery store a few blocks away.

The aisles are clean and brightly lit, filled with a bounty of boxes in the muted greens and browns that promise local and organic. In the bulk aisle, I decide between seven kinds of granola, and then stop by a refrigerator case stocked with homemade soups and quiches—

homemade by other people, my favorite kind. My basket is overflowing by the time I make it to the checkout, but remembering my vow to eat something green, I wedge in a spinach salad covered in goat cheese.

On the way back, I cradle the paper bag, determined not to let a hundred dollars' worth of organic granola I can't afford fall in the snow. Inside, on the top step, I trip over something, barely catching myself before I plummet backward. My spinach salad goes sledding down the stairs.

When I look down to see what nearly killed me, I find a large cardboard box with a note from my landlord explaining it had been delivered next door by mistake. For a second, I'm puzzled. Then I remember. I unlock the door and push the box inside, groceries be damned. My key slices through the packing tape and there it is: the VHS player.

Twenty minutes of plugging and unplugging and swearing later, I'm staring at a glowing screen on the TV saying *AUX input*. I unearth the box of VHS tapes and lay them out on the floor one by one. Most are labeled with a name and a date, but so faded I can barely read them. I find Sarah Dale's testimony, pop it in, and press play. I've already read the transcripts—I know I'm not going to learn anything new, but I want to see her face and hear her voice. It feels like I'm about to meet a friend, back from the dead.

The only sound in the room is the whir of the tape. I realize I'm holding my breath. At first it's just static, but then a woman's face appears, her mouth moving, but the only sound is a loud crackle. Then the whole picture distorts and turns green. The screen goes black.

"No."

In my head it's a scream, but it comes out a whisper. I want to rip the thing out of the wall and throw it out the window. Instead, I eject the tape and start searching.

According to the internet, either the tape or the heads are dirty from thirty years in a box. I might be able to clean them or they might be too degraded to ever work again. I head out to get supplies.

An hour later, my instruments are laid out like I'm prepping for surgery. Cotton swabs, alcohol, a tiny screwdriver to remove the tape casing. I start with Sarah Dale. A fine white powder coats the tape.

Mold. I swab every inch of it, slowly, painfully. Then I eat my salad standing over the sink while the tape dries. Salad demolished, I wind the tape back onto the spools.

I press play. Static again. Then a woman's face.

"Thank you for coming, Ms. Dale," a familiar voice says off camera. Stedsan. Tears prickle my eyes. Fireworks are going off in my stomach— Ms. Dale. Sarah Dale. She's right here.

Sarah Dale is a tall, slender woman with dark brown hair. Her voice is low, but there's nothing meek about it. Throughout the interview, she never raises her voice or sounds anxious or hurried. Her voice has a distant, dreamlike quality, as if she's telling Stedsan something of no consequence. *Fred, he grabbed Tommy under his arms and he pushed, so Tommy went right into the water.* It's easy to see why the defense attorney went after her, why others believed she was making things up. But I know it doesn't mean anything. People disassociate painful memories all the time.

The only time she shows any sign of emotion is when she describes how Sister Cecile locked her in the cupboard. *She told me to climb inside and she latched the door from the outside.* Sarah Dale's hand goes to the top button of her blouse, just below her throat, and twists, as if trying to loosen the collar. Then she goes still and looks right at the camera. *You can leave Coram House but you can't leave it behind.*

I've read every deposition, hers multiple times. I know what she's going to say before she says it, like she's an actor reading lines in a play, but still—it chills me to hear her say it out loud. When I eject the tape, I'm breathing heavily, as if I've been running instead of sitting cross-legged on the carpet.

Next I tackle the tape for Karen Lafayette's interview. She's the opposite of Sarah—disheveled, nervous, constantly loosening and tightening her scarf. Her anger comes off the screen in waves. I can feel it. And yet, when she tells the story of the girl who was pushed out the window, she's no more or less believable than Sarah. Just different.

After four hours, my back hurts from bending over the tapes. My head throbs from the alcohol fumes. And I've only managed to clean and watch two tapes. My hope that seeing their faces would bring instant clarity feels incredibly stupid now. Years ago, in science class, we did an experiment where we placed a drop of ink in a glass of water. Black tendrils twisted through the water. After a few seconds, they faded and disappeared, leaving the water clear as ever. But the ink was still there, the teacher reminded us, we just couldn't see it. This story feels like that. I can't see it, but the truth is there.

I pick one last tape from the box, one of the unlabeled ones, and unscrew the cassette lid. My cracked skin stings from the alcohol as I swab the tape. I should have worn gloves.

An hour later, I'm done. After this, I decide, I'll stop for the day. I screw the lid back on, feed it into the VHS player, and hit play. The screen is black. I wait, but nothing happens. The tape must be blank. I'm not sure whether to laugh or cry.

My finger is on the eject button when I hear Stedsan's voice. "Good morning, Sister Cecile," he says.

I freeze, heart thudding. I feel as if I'm in that room with them, crouched under the table, eavesdropping instead of here in this dingy apartment thirty years later. There's a muffled screech—a chair being pulled out—and then a sigh, but the screen stays resolutely black. I lean toward the television, as if it's a curtain I can peek behind.

"Thank you for coming today," Stedsan's voice continues. Then another voice speaks, a woman's voice. It's low and gravelly with a faint accent. Sister Cecile. It must be.

"Well," she says, "I didn't have much choice, did I?"

"All these interviews are voluntary—ah, one moment," says Stedsan.

The screen goes bright, the color of a peach lit by the sun. Fingers. Then I get a close-up of a much younger Stedsan as he stares into the camera, lens cap in hand.

"Sorry about that," he says and steps to one side so I can see the speaker seated across from him. Then I'm burning, as if my blood has been replaced by acid. The woman has close-cropped hair and an unsmiling, elfin face.

One I know.

One I saw yesterday in the paper. And before that, streaked in blood, lying in the cold water.

She laces her fingers together and looks right into the camera. "You didn't let me finish, young man."

But I can barely hear the words over the pumping and whooshing in my ears. Every hair on the back of my neck stands up. This woman is the dead body in the water. Jeannette Leroy. Sister Cecile is Jeannette Leroy.

14

I press my fingers to Sister Cecile's face. The TV screen is cold and smooth. Her mouth opens and closes. She blinks. She's alive, yet she wears the face of a dead woman. The blood is gone and the wrinkles are smoothed out, but still—I'm sure of it. Either Sister Cecile is Jeannette Leroy's twin or the woman in this video is the body I found in the woods four days ago. It takes me an hour to get through the first ten minutes of tape. I keep replaying it—because all I can do is stare at her face.

A few weeks after Adam died, I was scrolling through photos, when I accidentally played a video. Adam from a few years before at Thanksgiving. He leaned against the counter between an empty bottle of champagne and the burned turkey, smiling. He was still, posing for a photo, not this accidental video. But then he blinked, shifted slightly onto one foot. It felt like there was a tear in time. Like he might come alive and step out of the phone. The next day I'd uploaded all my photos and videos to the cloud and deleted them from my phone. That's how I feel now, like I could reach out and touch the woman's face. Warn her about what's to come.

A quick search gives me what I'm looking for. Apparently, women usually change their names when they become nuns to signify the transformation of their lives. So Jeannette Leroy became Sister Cecile. And then, at some point, probably after the publicity surrounding the case, she went back to using her given name. It was so simple, and it had been right in front of me. My throat tightens. Stupid. Stupid.

I've read the deposition, so the content of the video is less interesting than the dynamic. Jeannette Leroy is well spoken and calm. But, more than that, she's so perfectly sure that she's right. You can feel it in the way she sits, still and poised at the edge of the chair. You can hear it in the way Stedsan begins to falter and seems to have no answer to her questions—not that she's waiting for one. The woman is a force.

And she's so young. She looks barely older than me. If Sister Cecile arrived at Coram House in 1965, she must have been a teenager or in her early twenties. Barely older than the children she was watching over.

I give up trying to focus on what they're saying. Just the fact of this interview changes everything. Maybe no one had a motive for hiding in the woods to kill Jeannette Leroy, the quiet old lady. But Sister Cecile? I look at the list of names on my desk: all children who lived at Coram House under Sister Cecile's iron cross. If even a fraction of the testimonies are true, any one could have had reason to want her dead. And those were just the people interviewed in connection with the lawsuit. There would be thousands of other children, unknown or unnamed, who passed through Coram House over the years. And there at the top of the list: Fred Rooney.

Fred Rooney who might have helped Jeannette Leroy drown a child fifty years ago. Then there was the bandage on his face the day I showed up at his house. The scratches. The day after Jeannette Leroy's death. My head feels like it's floating off my shoulders.

"Shit." My voice sounds strangled.

What if the cops don't know about Jeannette Leroy's connection to Coram House? I pick up my phone and dial Stedsan. He doesn't answer, of course. Goddamn Stedsan never answers.

"Shit, shit, shit."

I waver, wondering if there's any way around it, but I have to tell someone what I know. I pick up the phone again, but then think of Garcia's face the last time I saw her. The disgust and disbelief. Maybe it's better if I just show up, try to convince Parker in person first, then go to Garcia together.

Outside, a dog barks. A second later, a chorus of answering yips. Then a long, drawn-out howl that makes the fine hairs on my arms bristle. I read somewhere that dogs can sense an earthquake minutes before humans. I wait for the ground to start shaking. When nothing happens, I grab my keys and head for the door.

My stomach is roiling as I pull into the police station's parking lot. Nerves or the pot of coffee I drank instead of lunch, I'm not sure. Bev is behind the front desk packing up her bag. It's nearly five, I realize, not sure where the day's gone. She looks up at me, her face wary.

"Hi," I say with my brightest smile. "I'm hoping to speak to Officer Parker."

"I see."

Bev is wearing another novelty sweater. Dark blue with a sky of patchwork stars.

"I'll just see if he can step out a moment."

She points to the row of plastic chairs beside the potted plants. Just as I'm about to take a seat, someone says my name. "Ms. Kelley?"

My stomach sinks. I turn. Detective Garcia stands framed in the doorway. Snow dusts the shoulders of her black coat. I step toward her, but my shoe catches the edge of the planter and I trip, snapping one of the plant's giant leaves. Based on Garcia's expression, I can see how ridiculous I must appear.

"I have information," I say. "About the case." I wince. It sounds like a line from a bad detective novel.

"I see." Her voice is neutral. "Then I suppose you better come on back."

Relief courses through me. I expected Garcia to brush me off entirely or make me explain standing in the hallway. Just then, the door into the main office opens and Parker comes out.

"Officer Parker," Detective Garcia says. "Do you have a minute? Ms. Kelley has some information for us."

Parker's eyes touch mine, then look away. There's a warning there, but I don't know how to read it. "Of course," he says. "I'll get a room."

Then he's gone.

Garcia walks by me, but pauses in the doorway and turns back, eyebrows raised. "Well," she says, "are you coming?"

I trail behind her like a baby duckling. The office is empty, desks littered with coffee cups like everyone left in a hurry. "Did something happen?" I ask. She doesn't answer. Not a great start.

The door to the interview room is open. Inside, Parker wrestles with the cord of the blinds. When he finally gets them open, I see the sky outside has gone full dark. Garcia closes the door behind us. "Take a seat."

I sit. "I was reviewing depositions—video depositions—from the case against the church back in the eighties, and I found something."

Garcia holds out her palm. *Go on.*

"So I found a video of Sister Cecile. She was a nun at Coram House, from the sixties until it closed in 1977. And when I saw her face, I realized that she was the woman—the one whose body I found. Sister Cecile is Jeannette Leroy. I'd never made the connection before because her real name was never used in any of the other depositions, but some of the things she did—I mean the abuse—I'm sure there are plenty of people who want her dead—"

"Was alleged to have done," Garcia cuts in.

My mouth opens and closes soundlessly like a fish. I have a terrible sinking feeling. "You knew already?" I manage.

Garcia sighs loudly through her nose. It's the noise you make when a child has already used every ounce of your patience and then scribbles on your walls with marker.

"Ms. Kelley, what do you think a police investigation actually involves?"

"I read the obituary," I say. "It didn't say anything about Coram House." I wince at how pathetic the protest sounds.

Garcia shrugs. "She didn't advertise it, but people knew. We thought it was better to keep that information out of the papers. At least until we've investigated any possible connection."

I wonder if I should be encouraged by this. After all, if she is so certain that Jeannette Leroy's death was accidental, why is she still here?

"Look, have you talked to Fred Rooney?" I ask. "I went to his house the day after I found her body and he was all covered in scratches and—"

"I can't discuss an active investigation."

Detective Garcia's voice is ice, any vestige of patience gone. I have a flashback to that day in the car, leaving Rooney's house. It's exactly what Parker said when he warned me off talking to Rooney. Maybe he wasn't trying to fob me off. Maybe he was trying to tell me they are taking me seriously. I risk a glance at Parker and he gives a tiny shrug, like he's read my mind. I wish I could melt into the floor and ooze back into the potted plant in the lobby, hide under its yellowing leaves.

"Listen," Parker says. "Like Detective Garcia said, Jeannette Leroy's connection to Coram House wasn't exactly a secret around here, but if it gets out into national news, our investigation is going to get a lot more difficult."

Detective Garcia leans forward. "The last thing we need is a bunch of reporters getting in the way. And we will absolutely write you up if we find out you've said or done anything to compromise this investigation."

I nod, mumble *yes, of course*. The child with the marker, just grateful to be alive.

"Now, if that's all, we're late for something."

Garcia stands without waiting for a reply.

"I can see her out," Parker says. Garcia nods at him once, a curt thanks. Then she opens the door and leaves without a backward glance.

I cover my face with my hands. Parker clears his throat. "No, don't say anything," I mumble from behind my fingers.

"I did warn you to be careful."

I drop my hands. For the first time, I notice that Parker isn't in uniform. He's wearing jeans and a collared shirt. Like he's going to a party. The sympathy on his face makes me want to throw something at him.

"When you warned me about Fred Rooney, I thought you were just talking about him being"—I wave my hand in the air, trying to summon the right word—"a sketch ball."

He presses his lips together. "He's more than that."

I think again of the way I rushed over here, riding to the rescue to tell them something they already knew. I cringe. "Okay, lesson learned.

Can you please escort me out, so I can die of embarrassment in the parking lot where no one can see me?"

He stands and holds out his arm in an exaggerated, gallant gesture. "Right this way."

I follow him to the side door. But before I can escape into the night, he holds out a hand. "Alex, I think it would be better if you didn't come by here for a while."

"Yeah. I got that. Loud and clear."

"Just . . ." He pauses and gives me a sticky note with a phone number on it. "This is my personal cell. Call me if you need anything, okay?"

My surprise must show because he gives me a small, tired smile. "I'm your media liaison."

I smile back, feeling marginally better. "Right. Thanks."

Then I head back to my car, grateful for the slap of cold air on my hot cheeks.

———

Back home, I fill the kettle. Then I stab a block of ramen noodles over and over with a butter knife, breaking them apart. While I'm waiting for the water to boil, I sink onto the couch. The wood frame groans like I've gained a hundred pounds in a single day. I wait for the horrible feeling of humiliation to pass. I close my eyes, just for a second.

A phone ringing pulls me from a strange dream that I forget instantly, so I'm left only with the impression of dark water, the surface mirror-smooth. The screen of my phone lights up again. Stedsan, finally. I answer, hoping my voice isn't full of sleep.

"Nice of you to call me back."

"I didn't realize it was an emergency."

He sounds amused, but I hear the admonishment too. *I don't answer to you.* I force myself to take a deep breath. "Did you know that Jeannette Leroy was Sister Cecile?" I ask.

"Yes," he says. "Of course."

My anger is a geyser, shooting right up to the surface. "Jesus, Stedsan. Why didn't you tell me?"

"Tell you what?"

"That she was here! Or that the dead body I found in the woods four days ago was a fucking nun at Coram House."

The line is quiet. I wonder if he's going to hang up on me.

"Well, we can start with the fact that I didn't know you were the one that found her body," he says, his voice cold. "Because you didn't tell me. And I only found out Jeannette Leroy was dead this morning when I read the obituary. Voila, here I am calling you back."

I squeeze my eyes shut and open them again. It feels like I'm losing my grip on time. Because he's right. I hadn't told him about finding a body in the woods. Hadn't told anyone. And of course he couldn't have known Jeannette Leroy was dead—her obituary was only published yesterday.

"Did everyone know?" I ask. "That she'd been at Coram House?"

Stedsan is quiet for a few seconds. "She didn't hide it exactly," he says finally. "But she lived quietly on her own. And it's been a long time. So no, I wouldn't say everyone knew."

Still. *It was common knowledge.* I feel myself flushing with embarrassment all over again at the way I marched into the police station waving my groundbreaking information.

"I came by your apartment this afternoon," Stedsan says. "To check in. You weren't home."

I bristle—so he had time to make a surprise visit to my apartment, but not to call me back. But he's right. It's his show and his rules. I'm the one who signed the contract.

"I was at the police station."

Outside, the streetlamp cuts through the darkness. I have no idea if it's eight at night or three in the morning. Tree branches scrape against my window, fingernails tapping to be let in.

"Oh," he says, clearly surprised. "Because of the body?"

"No. I mean, yes. I thought—I needed to tell someone about Jeannette Leroy being Sister Cecile." God, it sounds even dumber when I say it out loud.

"No, I mean the other body."

Now it's my turn for stunned silence. "The what?"

"You haven't heard?" he asks. "Apparently they found it at the dump."

I think of the empty police station, Garcia grudgingly treating this like a murder now. It had nothing to do with me. There's another body.

"No, I haven't heard," I say, trying to keep the edge out of my voice. "Do they think it's connected to Jeannette Leroy's death?"

"No idea," says Stedsan cheerfully. "Dump, body. That's all I know."

"But the body—I mean—it's a murder?"

"Like I said: no idea."

"Right," I say. "Thanks for telling me. And—sorry if I was short with you. It's been a long few days."

"I'm sure it has. And I probably deserved some of it. I'll try to be more available."

"Still, I shouldn't have used the f-word."

"I've heard worse."

I'm sure he has. I hang up and check the clock on the stove. Nine fifteen. I think of my ramen—the water hours cold by now. Then I stand and grab my coat off the hook. Time for a drink.

15

I don't actually know where I'm going, but I figure every Main Street in America has a bar, so I head that way, past rows of brick buildings and trees encased in twinkling lights. I pass the dark windows of a cafe and a used bookshop with a crow stenciled on the window. Down the block, a neon sign beckons me. NECTAR'S LOUNGE. I don't actually know the difference between a bar and a lounge. Except, one conjures up a Hitchcock heroine balancing a martini on her glossy fingernails. The other, a hard-drinking man slumped over a whisky. Tonight, I'll take either.

Through the fogged-up windows, I can make out a bar and the blurred outlines of people. Lots of people. I hesitate. The picture in my head involved sitting quietly in a dark corner, nursing my drink, not elbowing my way through a packed room. On the other hand, there's my cold ramen and the box of VHS tapes and cotton swabs.

I step into a fug of stale beer and bodies. A wood-topped bar runs all the way down the long, narrow room. Behind it, a mirror reflects the crowd, like an old-fashioned saloon. The room is loud, and the bartender is busy serving a large party at the back. I take an empty barstool near the door and wait.

When the bartender appears, I order a double whisky, neat, wanting something with fire. The first sip makes me grimace, but it's followed by the warm glow I was chasing. I breathe in. I breathe out. I take another sip. I wonder what the fuck I'm doing here. Drinking alone in a bar, yes. But not only that.

I try listing what I know as if it has nothing to do with me.

One summer afternoon in 1968, a boy named Tommy got into a rowboat with Sister Cecile and Fred Rooney. Sarah Dale says she saw Tommy get pushed into the water. The next day, the sisters announced Tommy had run away. There's no record of his death. Or birth or existence, beyond the words of a few other people who vaguely remember him.

Four days ago, Sister Cecile was found dead in the woods. There was only one set of footprints in the snow. But unidentified sounds suggest someone else was there. The next day, Fred Rooney had a bandage over one eye and scratches along his arms. Possibly from a struggle. Except, even if Rooney magically erased his footprints, the depositions suggest he was Sister Cecile's favorite. And, even if that changed sometime in the last few decades, she's lived here quietly as Jeannette Leroy since Coram House shut in 1977. So why would he or someone kill her now? None of it makes sense, but I can't shake the feeling, deep in my bones, that Fred Rooney knows more than he's saying.

The bartender reappears. "Another?"

I'm surprised to find my glass is empty. I nod yes. "Wait—hey, do you know anything about those condos they're building north of downtown?"

He frowns. "The ones out on North Ave.?"

I nod. He refills my glass. The first sip burns its way down.

He shrugs. "Out of my price range."

He turns away, but I'm not done yet. "Do you know what it was before—the building?"

I hear my tone. Like I'm testing him. I'm not sure why I'm pushing so hard. Who cares what the bartender knows.

"No idea," he says, backing away.

How do you not know, I want to shout at him. But I let him go.

I nurse my drink and let the hum of conversations wash over me. Then my eyes catch on a face I recognize. Parker leans against the other end of the bar. Around him, a group of people are zipping up coats and pulling on hats, clapping each other on the shoulder. I recognize a few of them from the station. Officer Washington is there, this time wearing jeans and long dangly earrings that catch the light. She smiles and leans closer to say something in Parker's ear. He tips down his head to listen over the noise. I don't see Detective Garcia, but it's hard to imagine her drinking in a bar. Or wearing jeans.

I look for a place I can hide until they leave, but when I glance back, it's too late. Parker is squinting down the bar in my direction, head cocked to the side like he's trying to make sense of something. Then he looks away. Disappointment and relief.

I turn the barstool so my back is to the door as the officers filter out behind me in a stream of ribbing and inside jokes. I drain my glass. I'm trying to decide whether to order another when someone takes the stool beside mine.

"You look like you could use a drink," Parker says.

"That's why I'm in a bar."

I intend it as a joke, but my voice is flat. He holds up two fingers to the bartender, who pours us both a whisky, then retreats as fast as he can. *That's right, back away from the crazy lady.* Parker's cheeks are flushed, but he doesn't sound drunk. Then again, I'm probably not the best judge.

"You're glaring at me," he says.

"Sorry."

He leans forward onto one elbow. "Did I do something to piss you off, Kelley?"

I don't think he's ever said my name like that. Like we're colleagues. I don't hate it. "Not lately."

He raises his eyebrows. "But someone did."

It's not a question, but I let the silence hang there. We sip our drinks. Finally, I say, "Maybe everyone. But right now mostly myself."

That earns a small smile. "And Alan Stedsan," I say. "Plus Xander what's-his-name who called me up and invited me to dinner and now it's just sitting there in my brain."

His eyebrows shoot up. "The tech guy?"

"Oh, and also Detective Garcia, who clearly hates me."

Parker shrugs. "I wouldn't worry about it. We've all earned a time-out or two this week."

"I get that we're all supposed to stay in our lane, I do," I say, hearing the anger in my voice but not caring, "but shouldn't she be encouraging people to share information? Because last time I checked you hadn't arrested anyone. Or are you still trying to convince me that Jeannette Leroy slipped and fell?"

"I can't—"

I hold up a hand to stop him. "Discuss an ongoing investigation. Yeah, I heard. But come on. Even with another body at the dump?"

His surprise lasts only a second. So Stedsan was right. There is another body.

Parker rotates his glass so the brown liquid catches the light. "I'm not going to ask how you know that."

I hiccup. Dammit. "Stedsan."

He sighs. "I said I didn't want to know. Aren't you supposed to protect your sources?"

"Maybe if my source didn't piss me off so much. And anyways, someone else is dead and I know Jeannette Leroy is connected to all this crazy shit somehow and—"

He puts his finger to his lips, asking me to lower my voice. I glare at him.

"It's not a body," he says. "Not exactly."

Well, that shuts me right up. Not only because he's clearly saying something he shouldn't, but also what does that even mean? I look at him closely. "Are you drunk?"

He coughs into his fist. Or maybe it's a laugh. "We did get an early start," he says. "Retirement party. But no."

"Because I don't want to be taking advantage of you."

That gets an actual smile. He clears his throat. "It's not a body—it's bones. We haven't identified them yet, but they look old." He shrugs. "There's no reason to think this has any connection to Jeannette Leroy."

"Bones," I say. "At the dump."

"Another?" The bartender appears out of nowhere again. How does he keep doing that?

I look down at my glass. Empty again. I nod, mutely.

"We'll take them to go," Parker says. "Come on. Let's get some air."

———

The slap of cold doesn't dull the buzz of the whisky exactly, but it sharpens everything else. The pinprick stars in the black sky, the smell of woodsmoke in the air. We cross Church Street, the boutiques and bakeries shut down for the night, and cut through an alley that spits us into the park behind city hall. It's empty and dark, except for pools of light cast by the streetlamps, a long chain of yellow circles. We walk in silence, but it's not heavy with anything.

The night is still—no wind blowing off the lake—and I assume that's where we're headed. That huge expanse of ice has its own gravitational pull. I sip from the paper cup. The whisky's warmth spreads through my body like a tree putting down roots.

Two blocks later, the street cants sharply downhill and crosses a set of train tracks. Then we're on a boardwalk, heading for the pier that juts into the harbor. Patches of ice crunch beneath my boots. A row of empty bench swings are positioned to take in the view. At the end of the pier, we stop. Surrounded by ice on all sides. Nowhere left to go.

"This feels illegal," I say, sipping my drink. "It's going to look very bad for me if I get arrested."

"I hear the cops have other things on their minds these days," Parker says, and raises his cup in a toast. He leans on the railing so the arms of our jackets are almost touching. Warmth radiates off him.

It's so quiet. There's the soft groan of ice shifting as water moves underneath. I imagine all the fish asleep for the winter, floating in place.

The night is clear with no moon, just a scattering of stars, but it's light enough to make out the dark shape of Rock Point in the distance. Out there, I know, the water is still moving. Still alive. Behind the point, the sky glows softly. Like the early hours of sunrise. Or industrial construction lights. Coram House.

He follows my gaze. "So, what do you think of it?"

"I wouldn't want to live there."

He takes a long sip. "Why? Because it's haunted?"

He doesn't ask it like he's making a joke, so I don't answer that way either.

"Not haunted exactly, or not by ghosts, at least. But sometimes I wonder if all those feelings—cruelty, terror, happiness—can sink into a place. Change its character somehow."

It's certainly how I felt about our apartment after Adam died. It was sad. Empty. Colorless. Or maybe that was just me. "Plus," I go on, before he can laugh at me, "it would make me feel complicit. Like I was benefiting from the things that happened there."

He looks surprised. "People could say the same about this book you're writing, you know."

I nod, ready for this. "Maybe. But it's not how I see it. It's not how I want it to be."

"I know," he says quietly. I laugh. I hope it doesn't sound too bitter. "Now," he adds. "I know that now." He nods in the direction of Rock Point. "So, as your official media liaison—how goes the research?"

I sigh deeply.

"That good?" he asks.

"No, I mean, it's fine. I'm lucky in some ways. There's lots of source material. Historical documentation, transcripts from the case. I have enough detail to make a book out of it."

"But? It sounds like there's a *but*."

"There are inconsistencies. Stories—memories—that contradict each other."

"You think the kids made them up?"

"No!" It comes out harsher than I meant. "Sorry—I just—I don't think anyone is lying. But trauma does strange things to memory. And there's so much that's missing."

"Like the boy in the boat?"

"Tommy." I sigh. At least Parker had been paying attention. "I can't find any record he ever existed outside the depositions. No birth certificate, no paperwork, nothing. If Sarah Dale is right, then they didn't just kill him, they erased him. And no one even went looking. Like his life meant that little."

I take a sip of my drink to cover the crack in my voice.

"And then there are other depositions that frame Sister Cecile as this heroic figure. The nun who bravely stood up to the pedophile."

Parker stares out into the night, his eyes two dark pools. "Why can't both things be true?"

I huff. "Tommy either went into the water or he didn't, Parker. This isn't some philosophical exercise about a cat in a box."

He shrugs. "Maybe not that, but with Sister Cecile. I'm just saying, plenty of us have good and bad in us. Just depends which way the balance tips that day."

I consider this. "So you're saying she's both a child killer and a holy savior? That's going to be hard to fit into the tagline for my book."

His response is halfway between a laugh and a cough. "Maybe you need to talk to your star witness."

"You sound like a cop," I say. "Anyways, I can't. Sarah Dale died a few years ago."

I'm embarrassed to hear the catch in my voice. I avoid his eyes, clear my throat.

"And that's a whole other problem. The only people left aren't exactly cooperative. Most won't even talk to me. Then there's Fred Rooney"— I hold up my hand before he can say anything—"who I haven't interviewed again. But I'm sure he knows something he isn't sharing."

"Like what?"

"About what happened to Tommy in the boat that day. I think he was there, Parker. That Sarah Dale was right—he might even have pushed Tommy into the water himself."

Parker considers this. "There's no statute of limitation on murder, you know. If he did do something, he's not going to just tell you."

"I know that," I say, annoyed. "This was back in the sixties. He was a minor. But what if it's more than that? What if he had something to do with Jeannette Leroy's death too? She's the only other person who was there that day, according to Sarah Dale. The only other person who could incriminate him."

"So you think, what? He killed her?"

"Well, he could have, couldn't he? He knew her. Knew her habits. He could have waited out in the woods until she walked by. And he had all these scratches on his face—it sure looked like he was in some kind of a struggle."

Parker looks skeptical. "There were no footprints on the path."

"It had just snowed that morning. He could have waited overnight."

"And why now? After fifty years?"

And that's the real problem, isn't it? Sister Cecile was already dead when I went to question Fred about Tommy. So unless someone else happened to be digging around, had already spooked him, the timing doesn't make sense.

Parker is quiet for a few seconds. When he speaks again, I can tell he's choosing his words carefully. "It would be easier if he killed them both," he says. "But that doesn't mean he did it."

"It doesn't mean he didn't either," I say, stubborn. But I don't have any real fire behind it anymore. "This book—it's like trying to weave together a story, but every strand turns to smoke in my hands."

"Can you write the book without knowing what happened to Tommy?"

"Yes," I say flatly.

"But you don't want to."

His tone is neutral, but still I feel defensive. "How many other kids are there just like him? Who just disappeared? I know it's been half a century and I sound crazy, but if I can just . . ."

I trail off, because what I almost said is: *If I can just help this one kid.* But, of course, I can't help him. He's dead.

"I don't think it's crazy," Parker says softly. "Every kid should have someone to stand up for them."

"Fifty years too late."

"Sometimes too late is the best we can do."

I smile at him, grateful, but he's looking out at the water. I think of all the things he's seen in his years on the job. How many flavors of sad and terrible exist in the world.

The silence hangs, not awkward, but full of something. For a second, I think he's going to take my hand. I clear my throat.

"So, these bones," I say.

Parker laughs and turns his eyes back to me. "Nope."

"They were really at the dump?"

"I can't discuss an—"

"All right." I hold up my hands in surrender. "But I can't tell you how tired I am of hearing that."

Nothing I can do, his shrug says. He has a good smile, a little crooked so it always looks like one side of his mouth wants to look more serious than the other.

I sigh for effect, but the truth is I'm tired of talking about bodies and bones. "Fine," I say. "Tell me about something else, then. What was it like to grow up in this promised land of maple syrup and sledding?"

"Probably pretty great." He sips his drink. "But I couldn't tell you. I grew up in the city—Brooklyn—at least until my dad died."

"I had no idea." It bothers me. I'm supposed to have a sixth sense for people's stories. "So how'd you end up here?" I ask.

Parker turns, leaning his back against the railing. He nods at me. "How'd *you* end up here?"

I shrug, not sure I'm ready to go where this conversation is leading.

"What—only you get to ask the questions?" he teases.

"Well, I got offered this book deal. After my last book, it felt like a fresh start."

It sounds hollow. He lets the silence hang there.

"And my husband died."

The words always feel like a line in a play. At first, Parker looks surprised, but then his expression changes. Not the melting eyes and cocked head of sympathy. Something else. He looks knowing. Grim. "I'm sorry to hear that," he says.

"It was—he was sick. It was fast, but long enough to say goodbye. So that's something, I guess."

Suddenly, I feel embarrassed—like I've taken off my clothes in front of someone who never asked to see me naked. And it's a lie besides. It was all terrible. There was one night, near the end, just before Adam went into hospice. He got stuck in the bathroom and I had to help him get up. He was so angry with me, and then he cried. In that moment, I wanted it all to be over more than I've ever wanted anything in my life. Our wedding is barely more than a series of snapshots in my head, but the shame of my wanting in that one moment is always fresh. It makes me so angry—that of all the memories of our life, that's the one I'm left with.

"It's something," Parker says quietly. "But it's not enough."

I shake my head, not trusting myself to speak. I know, in that moment, that he's lost someone. It's like there's some secret underlying sadness I can recognize. Another member of the club no one wants to be part of.

"My kid died," he says. "And then my marriage—well, I'm not married anymore. It was time for a change. So I came here. A few years ago."

He says it matter-of-factly. Like reading out loud from a history book, but the pain is there in the stiff set of his shoulders. I feel a mirroring stab in my chest. Adam and I had lives before we met and then a decade together. But losing a child is losing the future. A piece of yourself carved off. So much pain for so little time together.

Guilt leaves a bad taste in my mouth. I wonder if I used Adam's death to get the information I wanted from him. I'm honestly not sure.

"I'm so sorry," I say. "I didn't mean to dig things up."

Parker shrugs. "They were never buried to begin with."

The wind has picked up and drifts of snow blow across the ice. "What I said before." I can't say *husband* again. Can't say *dying*. "That wasn't the only reason I came."

He looks at me, waiting.

"I mean, I'm not just here to hide. Those kids—this story—it matters to me. I know you didn't think that when you met me, but it does."

Parker nods, but doesn't reply. The silence isn't tense, though—it's the opposite. Like something's been released. I drain my drink. Next to me, Parker crumples his cup and throws it in the bin. Then he takes mine and does the same. "Thanks," I say with a shiver. Either it's getting colder or the whisky is wearing off.

"Come on," Parker says. "Let's call it a night before we both freeze."

We hike back up the hill and, even though I tell him he doesn't need to, he walks me the three extra blocks home. "This is it?" he asks when we get to the purple house. "Your landlord has interesting taste."

I laugh. "You should see the inside. It looks like a dorm room."

Immediately, I flush at how it sounds. "Anyways—good night," I say quickly. "Thanks for the drink."

"Wait," he says.

I turn back. Parker's hands are buried deep in his pockets. His breath billows, a cloud of fog. My chest feels tight. I'm suddenly aware of how many inches there are between us. Tiny ice crystals have formed on his eyelashes.

His phone rings. He pulls it out of his pocket, and I see a name on the dark screen. *Washington.*

"Sorry," he says. "I'm on backup. I have to get it."

I think of how she leaned into him at the bar, whispered in his ear to be heard over the noise.

"Parker," he answers.

I turn and retreat up my stairs. Fish inside my pocket for the keys. Behind me, Parker murmurs into the phone. Sirens ring out in the distance. I wonder what Washington is telling him, know that I can't ask. I turn back just as he's hanging up.

"Listen, Alex—"

"Thanks for this—the drink, the walk. I think I needed it. Sorry for keeping you out so late—have a good night."

My tone is light, but it feels forced. Like someone trying to recapture a feeling of levity. As easy as catching snowflakes.

Parker pauses for a second and then nods. "All right, good night. Talk to you soon."

Then I'm inside, taking the stairs two at a time as if I'm trying to outrun something. Upstairs, I twitch aside the curtains to see if Parker is still there. But the sidewalk is empty, just the dark hollows of our footprints, filling up with snow.

My skin feels hot with anger or embarrassment or relief—I don't want to examine the swirl of emotions too closely. I'm worried I said too much, revealed too much of myself. I feel exposed. Like someone's peeled off my skin to reveal a mass of twitching nerves and muscle.

I want to call Lola, to have her tell me about her night. But I can't call her this late. She'll think it's an emergency. And I know what she'd say anyways. She'd say I need to get out more. To get my mind off dead kids and bodies and cops. *Once in a while, do the crazy thing,* she'd say. *Or, in your case, I'd settle for a slightly out-of-the-ordinary thing.*

I reach into my pocket for my phone and pull up Xander's number. Before I can hesitate, I type.

Got your message. No apology necessary, but I never say no to a good meal.

I hit send. There. Crazy thing, done.

I'm brushing my teeth when the reply comes.

Definitely apologies necessary. How about tomorrow? 7pm?

My stomach sinks. All at once I'm both sober and full of regret for my impulse. But it's too late now.

Sounds great.

Three dots and then a response.

sg. Will send details tmrw.

I put my phone away, trying to ignore the queasy feeling in my stomach, unsure if it's regret or whisky. Probably both.

June 5, 1989—US District Courthouse

Karl Smith

Karl Smith: Do I remember Tommy? God. Sure. Been a long time since I thought about him. You know, that little bastard left without a word. I'm kidding, mostly. We all did what we had to do. I wondered, actually, if I'd find him here. Saw some of the others already. People brought their whole families—it's like a reunion out there. Twenty years now.

Alan Stedsan: So you believe he ran away?

KS: I mean, it makes sense. All of us would have run away if we'd had anywhere else to go. And Tommy had it worse than some of us.

AS: What do you mean by that?

KS: Look, he was a small kid. And on top of that he was scared of everything. Spiders, stories, water. And he wet his bed all the time. You can imagine how the older kids—the tougher kids—were.

AS: But you were friends?

KS: You make it sound like we were, I dunno, blood brothers or something. But yeah, we were. He was a wizard at building stuff. Forts, rock castles, that kind of stuff. That's why I remember the day he left. See, we were supposed to meet up. All the kids were down on the point, playing in the woods. The sisters hardly ever gave us time like that just to play, but it was so hot. I think they just wanted to get rid of us. Tommy was supposed to meet me and Willy, but he never showed up.

AS: Meet you where?

KS: We'd started building this fort out in the woods. Over on Rock

166

Point—you know it? It was real woods back then, no trails or anything. Willy was in trouble—he'd gotten suckered into helping one of the sisters with something, so he was out. Tommy was supposed to meet me, but he never showed. It was supposed to be this perfect day, you know—three boys building a fort in the woods—but then it was just me, all alone. I was pretty sore about it. But when I went to find him at dinner, let him have it, he wasn't there. I figured he got sick or something. And then the next day, they said he ran away.

AS: Who said he ran away?

KS: You know, the sisters.

AS: And you never saw him again?

KS: Like I said, I was sore about it for a while. But we all would have done it if we could. Maybe he ended up somewhere better. You never know.

AS: Did you ever look for him?

KS: Nah. Once I left, I wanted to put it all behind me, you know? Start over. It's not like we were going to get a beer and talk about the shit that happened in there. It's not the kind of stuff you want to go back to.

March 16, 1988—US District Courthouse

Linda Bessette

Linda Bessette: Fred Rooney? Yes, I knew him. He was a monster. A nightmare.

Alan Stedsan: Can you tell me what you mean by that?

LB: He was always beating up the smaller kids. And not just hitting them—saying things to them. He liked to see us scared.

AS: What kinds of things?

LB: That he'd tie them to a tree in the graveyard and leave them there. Cover their feet with honey and wait for the ants to eat them off. Stupid stuff. It doesn't sound that scary now.

AS: What was his relationship like with the sisters?

LB: I don't think they liked him any better than we did. Except Sister Cecile. But no surprise there. He worshipped her.

AS: What do you mean by that?

LB: Fred would have done anything she asked. [Laugh] God, the way he looked at her. Like she was Jesus Christ made flesh. It was almost funny. She was tiny. Maybe five feet. And he was tall, even back then.

AS: Were there ever allegations of sexual abuse at the time?

LB: [Laugh] Sure. What flavor? I mean, there was Father Foster. Everyone knew about that. Though it was only the boys who had to deal with him. People said there were things going on with the nuns too. And, God knows, no one wanted to be alone with Fred. I don't know how much was true, but there was lots of talk.

AS: And Sister Cecile?

168

LB: No, never her. Not sex stuff. Sometimes, I think she might have been the only one out of any of them that actually believed in God.

AS: It sounds like there was a lot to be afraid of. A lot for a child.

LB: [Laugh] And that's not even counting the ghosts.

AS: Ghosts?

LB: I know it sound ridiculous. Maybe it is. But there was this attic off the girls' dorm. They used to put us up there as punishment sometimes. I never saw anything myself, but I know girls that did. And one time this girl got sent to the attic and came down with bruises all up and down her arms and neck. I swear to God, they were in the shapes of fingers. We all asked but she never said a single word. Scared silent, if you ask me.

PART 4

16

My hangover is brutal. I feel shriveled, desiccated—my tongue Velcroed to the roof of my mouth. I didn't feel that drunk last night. Really, I'd swear I wasn't drunk at all. Then again, three whiskys on an empty stomach probably wasn't a great idea. Or maybe it was four.

After a handful of ibuprofen and a blistering shower, I'm almost able to think about food without throwing up. My binder sits on the table, notes and papers spilling out. But as soon as I sit down before it, my mind strays back to last night's conversation with Parker. The body at the dump, yes, but the rest of it too. It's all a warm blur until the end, then it's white-hot humiliation. Why did I run upstairs? What did I think was going to happen? And why on earth did I accept a dinner invitation from the drunk guy who set his car on fire?

Air, I decide. Fresh air will help.

I put on my parka and start walking south, not for any particular reason other than it's away from the lake. I can't face that expanse of water. Not this morning. I consider stopping by Stedsan's unannounced, but what good would it do? He either doesn't know anything else about Tommy or doesn't want to help me. Either way it would just piss him off. And my head hurts too much for that.

Instead, I follow the smell of baking and cinnamon into a cafe and order a triple shot of espresso, which burns my stomach like acid. I take the back door out, thinking it will save me a block of walking, but it doesn't open onto the street at all. Instead, I wander through a maze of alleys that winds among brick warehouses. The windows are cracked and missing half their panes, but the walls are covered in murals. Enormous bees climb up one wall, dripping with glistening honeycombs so real-looking I expect my fingers to come away sticky. On another wall, someone has stamped a field of blue flowers.

Waves of heat pulse out an open door. A man in a metal mask and thick gloves twirls molten glass on a long rod. Behind a window, a woman manipulates clay on a wheel, her dark skin covered up to the elbows in pale mud, so it looks as if they've been erased. Through another window, papier-mâché whales hang suspended from the ceiling, each lit up to reveal a skeleton inside.

I feel the thrill of being lost, of crossing into another world nested inside my own like the crystals of a geode hidden inside a dull gray rock. I stop. Ahead of me, a tree made of mirror shards covers a two-story wall. Its branches reflect blue sky and then the white of cloud. It's unreal, a portal to somewhere else.

Ice on Parker's eyelashes. Tommy going in the water. A woman's face covered in blood.

Leave it alone. But it's a scab I can't stop picking.

My phone pings. Reality intruding. I unlock it to find a message from Xander.

Still on for tonight? 7pm at Lands End. At the end of Harbor Rd.

I think about canceling, but then I'd just have to reschedule, dread this dinner for another week. Better to get it over with. I write back.

See you there!

I walk closer to the mirrored mosaic, touch a long sliver of glass that makes up the tree's bark. It's cold and smooth, the edge sharp enough to slice skin. Real, then, after all.

———

At six thirty, I trade my sweatshirt for a cable-knit sweater and swipe on some mascara. Good enough. Then I pull up directions to Harbor Road. It's on the other side of the bay, running up the peninsula that extends toward Rock Point. The road ends at a marina, so at least the restaurant will have a water view.

After driving south for ten miles, I turn onto a smaller road that follows the curve of the bay back north. It's quiet and dark. Most of the houses are wrapped in shadow and set back behind high fences. One fence has individual notches cut out for the limbs of an ancient hedge to pass through.

I arrive at the marina, but a sign nailed to the fence announces it's closed for the season. No restaurant in sight. Ahead, the road is narrow and pitted with potholes. I wonder if I've taken a wrong turn, but my phone doesn't have a signal. So I drive on.

After another minute, the road ends at a stone pillar topped with a brass carriage lantern, giving off just enough light to read a plaque fixed to the side: 4539 HARBOR RD., LANDS END. A black metal gate bars the way forward.

Okay, so it's not a restaurant. It must be a hotel or some kind of private club. The gate swings open silently. I know there must be a camera or a sensor, but it feels like dark magic.

The drive is lined in tall, spreading trees whose branches form a tunnel above the car. After a minute, a building appears lit from below by hidden spotlights. The roof is flat and the angles are modern, more like a series of connected boxes than a house. But the structure is wrapped in cedar shingles, weathered to silver, so it blends into the forest despite the size.

The driveway widens into a circle with an island of dried plants in the center. I park and get out. Tall grasses glow silver in the moonlight. To one side, a shrub droops under the weight of purple berries. I run my finger up the golden bottlebrush of some kind of dried flower. It's all dead and beautiful.

And empty.

I turn to take in the driveway, free of cars, the front stairs with a single pair of muddy boots sitting outside. That's when I realize my mistake.

Lands End.

This isn't a hotel. This is just the kind of neighborhood where houses have their own names. I'm at Xander's house. Alone.

I'm trying to decide whether to get back in my car when the front door opens.

"Alex?"

He's wearing jeans and a blue hoodie. He looks so different from the sloppy drunk I met in the police station, I barely recognize him. He's handsome with symmetrical features and clear blue eyes behind glasses—a nerdy quarterback.

"Just admiring your garden," I say. *And hoping you're not going to murder me at your isolated mansion.*

He comes down the walkway. Up close, his skin has the tender look of someone who doesn't shave often. He's made an effort.

"What's your favorite?" he asks.

I point to the bush with the purple berries. His smile is shy. He shuffles his feet in the gravel.

"Beautyberry," he says. "I got deep into native plant gardening when I first moved here. Planned most of this myself."

His broad gesture could mean the driveway or the estate beyond, hidden by darkness.

"Anyways, dinner will be a little bit." He nods to a lit window and I see a woman in a white apron flash past. Relief rises in me—at least we're not alone.

"Do you want to start with wine?"

Definitely.

"Sure," I say and follow him inside.

Knotty pine floorboards lead from the entrance to the huge stone fireplace that dominates the center of the open room. On the other side, a wall of glass windows reveals a patio where flames leap from a stone fire pit. "I thought we could sit outside, if that's okay?" Xander says.

"Sounds great," I say casually, but in my head I'm already draining the glass of wine, feeling the edges of the world soften.

Xander leads me past overstuffed leather couches and an enormous coffee table made from a cross section of some ancient tree. The bar already has a decanter of red wine and two glasses waiting on it. He pours. It smells expensive. I try not to finish it in one gulp.

Outside, we settle into Adirondack chairs and watch the coals of the fire glow orange. Xander turns his glass around and around on the arm of his chair, not looking at me. "So," he says, "I just—I want to say I'm so sorry for the way I acted in the station."

Even in the low firelight, I see the deep crimson of his blush.

"It's okay," I say. "I'm sure it wasn't your best moment, but we've all had those."

He tugs on the strings of his hoodie, looking so uncomfortable that I actually feel better. At least I'm not the only one.

"Look, the last couple days haven't been great for me either. And this wine is delicious, and I really don't want you to spend the whole evening apologizing. Can we just—can we consider that part done?"

I can see the relief on his face. "Deal."

"So how long have you lived here?"

I don't know if it's the wine or the setting, but everything about this place feels unreal.

He shrugs. "On and off for a couple years. It took two years to build the house, so I'd come back and forth from San Francisco to check on things. I meant it to be more of a retreat, but after the IPO flopped, things got kind of messy."

He says it like I should know what he's talking about. "The IPO?"

"Videara. It was—is—a video-sharing platform. I founded it, but exited last year after we took the company public. It wasn't, well, it wasn't great. I mean, I made shitloads of money, so it's not like you should feel bad for me or anything."

He says it reluctantly, like it's the last thing he wants to talk about, but also like it somehow explains him, so he needs to get it over with. A feeling I know something about.

"At least they let you keep the hoodie." I point to the logo on his chest, a bright-purple *V*. His laugh lights up his face.

"Yeah," he says. "There's that. Anyways, after I left, this seemed like a good place to regroup, you know? Wait for the next big idea to find me."

"And has it?" I mean it as a joke, but he looks down at the ground with a mournful expression, as if the thought that he might not jump from one success to the next had never occurred to him.

"I have some ideas," he says, "but nothing solid yet."

"Well, there are worse places to live out an early retirement."

His eyes widen. "It's a break."

"Of course. Sorry, bad joke."

I take a sip of wine. A big sip. I'm not used to being around some-one who shows exactly what he's thinking. It's like he's managed to get through life without any of his edges being filed to sharpness.

"No, wait." Xander rubs a hand through his hair, making it stand up like a hedgehog. "It's just—you really saw me at my worst the other day. This was supposed to be my apology for all that. And I'm being a shitty host."

The evening is balanced on a knife's edge. I feel lightheaded, drunk not on wine but on knowing that whatever I do or say will topple us one way or the other. And not caring.

I hold up my empty glass for a refill. "Well, at least the wine's good. Let me guess—it's from your vineyard in France?"

His face goes bright red. "It's in Napa," he says quietly.

It's not that funny, but suddenly I'm laughing so hard my stomach hurts. "Of course it is," I gasp.

At first, Xander looks uncertain, then he too starts laughing with the kind of unhinged hilarity that comes from releasing tension. I feel like an empty balloon.

Behind us, a door opens to reveal a tall woman in a white chef's jacket. She frowns down at us, laughing like kids. "Dinner is ready," she says.

"Yes, sorry, Cara," Xander says, getting ahold of himself. "We'll be right there."

We both wipe our eyes and go inside.

The dining table looks like something a medieval king would sit at—rough-hewn wood and long benches, high-backed seats at the end like thrones. Cara enters, somehow balancing six dishes on her arms at once. Oven-warm pita served with whipped feta and nutty muham-mara. Chicken sticky with a honeyed brown sauce and a salad over-flowing with roasted sweet potatoes and crunchy radishes. After weeks of living on cereal and frozen burritos, every bite is like an explosion. Dinner is nice. The food, yes. But it's also surprisingly nice to be eating with a real live human, someone who doesn't know me at all. I could be anyone.

While I eat, Xander tells me about Silicon Valley like he's summoning memories from a past life. There's something adrift about him. Like this estate is Avalon, unmoored from time and space. He asks about my life in New York, which I don't want to talk about. So I tell him about the book: Coram House, the case against the church, how I'm here to shape it all into a story. History for true-crime fans, I say, trying it out and hating how it sounds. I've never been good at marketing-speak.

He nods as he refills our glasses, looking politely interested. But when I mention the condo development, his eyes light up. "You know," he says, "there's something about the project that draws you in. When Bill first took me to the site, I could see it. It was such a blank slate. So much possibility."

My wine goes down the wrong pipe, and I cough a spray of red droplets onto my napkin. "The project," I say when I can breathe. "You mean, Coram—Sunrise House?"

His brows furrow. "Well, yeah. I'm the largest investor, apart from Bill. Sorry, I just assumed you knew."

I take this in with a burst of anger but no one to direct it at.

"It's going to be really cool when it's done."

Xander goes on to describe the green roof, the communal gathering spaces, the fire pit. I think of the brochure Stedsan gave me. The good-looking, racially neutral yuppies drinking wine under the shade of trellised vegetables someone else would be caring for. I should have known all that didn't come from Bill Campbell.

Xander makes a broad gesture—saying something about affordable housing units—and knocks over his wineglass. The red liquid pours into the cracks in the wood, oozing toward me across the table. Xander rushes to soak it up with his napkin. The stain spreads across the white linen.

"The history of Coram House," I say, because I can't bring myself to use the word *sunrise* again, "it doesn't bother you?"

He frowns like he doesn't understand the question. "Of course it's terrible," he says. "But that's the point—it's history. We're building a new future. A quarter of the units are going to be affordable housing and the whole thing will be net-zero. That's where the name came from. I wanted something the opposite of what it used to be. A new beginning."

He looks at me, waiting. So I paste on a smile while I think. I mean, he's not wrong. What would be the best use of that space? To molder away? Become a museum of horrors? But still, it bothers me. It's not a blank slate.

"Look, I think we can find a way to honor the history while still harnessing its potential," he says.

I imagine what the plaque will say. Some quote about beauty and suffering probably. *After the rain, comes the rainbow.* I feel a mad urge to laugh or to throw my wineglass at him just to hear something smash. But I know Cara would be the one cleaning up the mess.

Xander pushes back his chair and gestures for me to follow him. "Come on, I want to show you something."

I look at the platters of uneaten food—far too much for two people—the ruined napkin, the half-finished bottle of wine that probably costs a week of my salary. I wonder what the hell I'm doing here. Then I get up and follow him.

Xander leads me down a back hall and into a library with matching tartan armchairs and floor-to-ceiling bookshelves. The spines of the books are all arranged by color, so it gives the impression of a wall wrapped in rainbows. A massive coffee table is littered with stacks of photos, newspaper clippings, and a leatherbound notebook. The mess reminds me a bit of my own workspace.

I pick up one of the photos. It's Lake Champlain. Rich, deep black in the shadows, but the surface of the water has the sheen of mercury. Probably a silver gelatin print. It's dusty; everything on the table is, as if someone abandoned whatever project this is halfway through.

"I was thinking we could frame these," Xander says, pointing to the photos. "And hang them throughout the buildings. I figured they'd give the historical flavor."

I lay aside the landscape and lift another photo. Children sitting in a pew, dressed in dark jackets and dresses. *Sunday Service*, it says on the bottom. I frown.

"Xander, where did these come from? Father Aubry?"

He shakes his head. "Most of that stuff burned up, I guess. But these are from the right time period."

The photo isn't from Coram House at all. It's a prop. Some picture unearthed at a thrift shop or, more likely, bought online.

"Here, check this out."

Xander slides a photocopy of a newspaper clipping across the table. A grainy black-and-white photo shows a man in a suit and two children in front of a building, a ribbon stretched across the doors. *Orphans open new library wing*, says the caption.

"I'm trying to talk the library into giving me the original. They've got it framed in some back hallway, where no one can see it. And I figure there's got to be more stuff like this out there."

He goes on, but I'm not listening anymore. I hold the photocopy gently, as if it might crumble to dust. The two children in the image are dressed formally. The boy in a dark jacket, the girl in a dress and frilled ankle socks. I would have assumed the photo was from the fifties based on their clothes, but the caption says 1967. No Swinging Sixties here. But it's not the clothes that have grabbed my attention, it's the rest of the caption: *Mayor Francis J. Cain cuts the ribbon on the new Mary Fletcher Library wing with some help from Elizabeth R. (7) and Thomas U. (8), children of Coram House.*

I feel like I've been punched in the stomach. The image is grainy. But the boy's age is right. The year is right. It could be him. *Thomas U.* A last initial. I grip the paper like someone might try to tear the photocopy out of my hands.

"Can I take this with me?" I ask.

Xander blinks at me. I've interrupted him, I realize too late. My mouth is dry, afraid he might say no.

"I've been looking for someone—my research—this might help."

"Of course," he says, and he looks so genuinely happy, that I feel bad for wanting to throw a glass of wine at him only five minutes before.

"Take anything you need."

My phone vibrates. I pull it out to see a text from Stedsan, asking if I'm going to Jeannette Leroy's funeral tomorrow.

"Do you want a coffee?" Xander asks. His voice is overly bright, like a kid who knows he's in trouble but isn't sure why. "I could show you the lake before you go. It's a great view of downtown at night."

I feel guilty—he's obviously trying—and also something close to euphoric at having the photocopy folded safely in my pocket. *Tommy U. It could be him.*

"Sure," I say. "Coffee sounds great."

We wind our way back through the dark house to the front hall, where I pull on my jacket and hat. Xander disappears into the kitchen and reappears with two thermoses. Outside, liquid dark presses against the windows. We could be in a submarine, deep in the ocean. When Xander opens the door, I half expect the darkness to flood inside—to drown us. But it's just the freezing air, the mineral tang of impending snow.

Outside, Xander taps his phone, and a soft glow rises from the ground, illuminating a path that leads into the woods. Uneasiness creeps up my spine. It's the darkness of the trees, the flicker of shadows. Nothing particular. Just monsters in the woods.

The path winds beneath the trees to a set of stone steps cut into a steep hillside. Gravel and salt crunch underfoot. At the base of the hill, a dock stretches into the black night. Two red Adirondack chairs sit at the end, waiting for summer. The sight triggers something in my brain, some sense of familiarity.

"Careful, it might be icy," Xander says, as we step onto the dock's wooden boards.

The moon emerges from behind a cloud and illuminates the rocky cliffs across the water. And I understand, now, why the chairs felt familiar.

The cliff across the water is Rock Point. Five days ago, I stood right over there, looking across the ice at a huge house nestled in the trees. At a dock with two red chairs. This house. This dock. I feel untethered, as if I've stepped through the looking glass.

Xander is still talking and I force myself to return my attention to the present. "What?" I say.

"Oh, nothing, I'm just babbling," Xander says, laughing. "I was just saying—there's something hypnotic about the water. It's always the same, but always changing, you know? It just froze out there, so we should be able to ice sail in a few days if the cold weather holds."

"Out there?"

I look at the flat ice beyond us, beyond Rock Point, and realize what's different. Everything out there was open water just five days ago. Now it's all frozen solid.

"And to complete tonight's tour, that's downtown over there."

Xander raises his cup to a scattering of twinkly lights to our right, resting in the curve of the bay.

In the distance, I make out the fishing shacks that dot the ice, but there's something else out there too. A shadowy lump. Snippets of what Parker told me at the police station come back. A car on the ice. A fire. I point. "Is that—"

"My car, yeah." Xander clears his throat, embarrassed.

"And you walked all the way from that to here?" I ask, incredulous. Now that I'm standing here—it's not a funny story anymore.

"The ice is solid," he says, defensive. "I drink my coffee down here every morning. Sure it was open water beyond the point, but the bay has been frozen for weeks."

"Right."

"It's not like I'm the only one. People are out there fishing all the time. Skating. I mean, I saw someone paddling a canoe around the point last week."

"The canoe thing isn't exactly supporting your argument."

Xander sighs and rubs his hand over his eyes. He's silent for a few seconds and I wonder if he's mad at me. When he takes his hand away, his smile is rueful. "I don't know why I'm trying to recast my bad, drunk idea as something logical. I guess I just don't want you to think I'm a total idiot."

"I don't," I say. "Think you're an idiot, I mean."

He smiles at me. "I don't know if that's true, but I appreciate you saying it either way. Come on, I'll walk you back."

At the car, Xander opens the driver's side door and I slide inside. I thank him for dinner, for the photo, and wait for him to close the door, but he doesn't.

"Sorry, can I just ask something? My therapist—I'm working on being more direct—and I just, did I say something wrong before, at dinner? You seemed annoyed at me."

I have a ridiculous urge to hit the gas and drive until he's forced to let go of the car. But, of course, I don't. Xander is so direct—no room for subtext. Maybe this is what people are like in California. Everyone's on the road to self-actualization.

"I just have a hard time seeing Coram House turned into condos for people who want a water view."

He opens his mouth—I think to protest—but I'm not done yet.

"Look, Xander, I know your plans go beyond that and, on some level, I do agree with you. There's no good to anyone in letting the building rot. I just—I'm not comfortable with it. Not with the condos, not with the framed photos, none of it."

I wait for him to explain all the reasons I'm wrong, but he just nods. "Okay," he says. "Thanks."

"Thanks?" I ask, unable to cover my surprise.

He shrugs. "I'm glad you told me. And I hope you'll come see it when it's finished—decide what you think then."

I smile. Hard to argue with that. "Deal."

He shuts my door with a soft click. I roll down the window. "Thanks again for the newspaper clipping. And for dinner."

"You said that already," he says, but he's grinning. "I'm going to call you about ice sailing. It's the best. You'll see."

"I don't think so," I say with a laugh, and start the car.

As I pull away, I glance in the rearview mirror and see Xander standing in the driveway, waving. I raise a hand back. I feel a rosy glow, relief at being in my car, at having the evening I dreaded not be so bad after all. Nice, even. And, most of all, at the photo that might be nothing or everything, tucked safely in my pocket.

17

At a red light, I stop and inspect my reflection in the mirror. My red lipstick has settled into the cracks in my dry lips, making them look raw and bloody. When I opened the curtains this morning, the street was covered in a thin blanket of snow, but now, just a couple hours later, it's already gray with dirt. I thought about wearing my black flats to the funeral, my only nice pair of shoes, but now I'm glad I opted for my clunky snow boots.

The rest of my clothes aren't ideal funeral wear either—black leggings and a dark gray turtleneck sweater—but I threw away my one black dress after Adam's funeral. Anyways, it's not as if Jeannette Leroy cares what I'm wearing. I'm not even sure why I'm going. I feel a responsibility for the defenseless old woman brutally murdered in the woods. But what about the nun who ordered a child to push another child out of a boat to drown? Same story, different angle, but always ending in the same place. With a body.

Not just a body, a boy. And now, thanks to Xander, I may have a face.

A car honks behind me. "Yeah, yeah, calm down," I say to no one and drive on.

I accelerate past the police station and the entrance to Rock Point, not slowing until I get to the large church—the Chapel of Saint Joseph—that shares the graveyard with Coram House. Two looming brick bookends.

Instead of pulling into the drive, I park on the street so I can get a better look at the building. The chapel has an air of neglect. The nook above the doors is missing the statue of whatever saint should be watching over it. Underbrush presses against the wall, growing right through the fence, as if the woods are trying to swallow the building. On the top step, a priest welcomes a pair of elderly mourners, his purple-and-gold vestments a contrast to their somber black. When he turns, I recognize Father Aubry.

Five cars are parked in the lot, including a police cruiser. A small crowd, then. I turn off the ignition. My hands shake a little. Too much coffee. I wonder if I should have brought flowers. Adam's service had so many. Giant wreaths of white lilies. The green buds poked out from behind the star-shaped blooms like the chrysalids of some giant insect. The smell was strong and sweet, melted vanilla ice cream. A smell used to cover the smell of something else. When I die, I don't want any flowers or a funeral. I'd like to fade instantly into the air. Poof.

Knuckles rap against my car window. "Morning," Stedsan says, voice muffled through the glass. "I wasn't sure you were coming."

Shit. The text last night when I was at Xander's. I'd never written him back. After all my grumbling about how he needs to be more responsive, there goes the high ground. I scramble out of the car and mutter *sorry.*

Stedsan wears a dark overcoat with a gray suit and dark blue tie peeking out. "Shall we?" He holds out an arm. I fight the urge to smooth my hair. It's annoying to be standing beside someone always perfectly dressed for the occasion, but the truth is I'm grateful not to be walking into the church alone.

"How have you been?" Stedsan asks.

"The outline is coming along," I lie.

Stedsan gives me a strange look. "Alex, you found a dead woman a week ago. Then this body at the dump. I wasn't talking about the book."

"Good morning," Father Aubry interrupts. His hand is dry and cold when he clasps mine and ushers us into the dim vestibule.

A tapestry of Jesus hangs on one wall, finger held up like he's about to make an important point. The cheap threads are overly bright, so he looks like a painted clown—face too white, lips too red. We pass into the nave, which is light and open. Tall white columns support an arched ceiling. Filigreed white lanterns dangle above the pews. Stedsan tightens his scarf. "It's freezing in here," he says.

The casket sits before the altar on some kind of wheeled metal cart. Like the kind you see in the morgue on crime shows. I try to remember the name for the flower arrangement that goes on top of the casket. I knew it once.

A dozen silver and white heads sit scattered among the pews. Sitting halfway to the altar, I recognize the three officers. Detective Garcia's tight black bun and suit. Beside her, Parker is a full head taller. Then Officer Washington next to him, toned shoulders in a fitted black dress.

Bill Campbell is here too. He beckons us forward and shakes hands with Stedsan before turning to me. "Good morning, Ms. Kelley," he says. "Care to join me?"

He moves over to make space in the empty pew.

Stedsan and Bill talk in low voices of golf and the mayoral election. Across the aisle, a few elderly women sit with bland expressions, as if they're in a doctor's waiting room. I wonder if they're friends or neighbors, here to pay their respects. Is it possible they're connected to Coram House? Though it's hard to imagine any of the former children coming, and all of the other nuns are dead now. There's no sign of Fred Rooney. I'm not sure if I'm disappointed or relieved.

Father Aubry passes up the aisle in a swish of robes and steps up behind the lectern. He welcomes us, then opens the red leather Bible. "The righteous perish, and no one takes it to heart," he begins. His voice isn't loud, but it echoes in the empty room, as if there's another Father Aubry crouched beneath the casket, speaking on a slight delay.

"The devout are taken away, and no one understands that the righteous are taken away to be spared from evil."

The righteous. The urge to laugh bubbles up, so strong I pretend to cough, and bite the heel of my hand.

The psalm done, Father Aubry produces a vial of holy water from the folds of his robe and sprinkles it over the casket. He motions for us to rise. There's a rustle of clothes and a few grunts as people haul themselves up, using the pews for leverage.

Father Aubry opens his mouth, but his words are drowned out by a sharp crack from behind us. A blast of freezing air blows up the aisle. Every head turns.

The church's doors swing open wide, revealing a figure standing in silhouette. It lurches forward into the light.

Fred Rooney.

He takes two steps up the aisle and then stumbles into a pillar. "Sorry," he says, patting it like a dog. "Must—lost track of time."

He burps into his fist and adjusts his tie. His buttons are mismatched and I notice he's not wearing socks.

"Is he drunk?" Stedsan whispers.

"Jesus Christ," Bill Campbell mutters. He closes his eyes and tilts his face up to the ceiling, as if in supplication.

Rooney weaves his way up the aisle now, toward the casket. The bruises on his face have turned a sickly yellow beneath his shock of white hair. "Go'on," Rooney calls to Father Aubry, who's staring at him from the altar, speechless. "I'll just sit right here."

He tries to slide into the pew in front of the cops, but can't seem to figure out how to wedge himself in. Parker stares at Rooney, a mix of surprise and interest on his face. His eyes meet mine and he gives a tiny shrug. Rooney finally sits.

"Ah, well, shall we," Father Aubry says. He adjusts the Bible on the lectern and smooths his robes. An elderly lady, puffs of white hair above a blue dress, walks briskly toward the open door, but before she can close it, Rooney is back on his feet, roaring, "Leave it open, ya dumb cow!"

The woman freezes, one hand on the door, her face pale under too much blush. Parker's face has lost any trace of amusement.

Then, like he's turned off a switch, Rooney begins to laugh. "It's the bullshit—the smell of the bullshit's too strong. Needs some air."

People whisper and shift in their seats, clearly waiting for someone—someone else—to do something. "Now," says Father Aubry, a quaver in his voice. "Now I think that's enough."

But Rooney just laughs harder. He's started forward again and seems to grow more sober with every step toward the casket. A foot away he stops and reaches out toward the smooth wood, but just leaves his hand hanging there.

Garcia leans over and whispers something to Parker. Rooney is so close that I could touch him, but he's not looking at me. He's staring up at Father Aubry. "This is a fucking joke," he says. "Up there—in your robes. You should be in the ground with all the others."

He spits on the floor. The glob of phlegm sits there, wet and shiny.

"Then I'll dig you up too—like I dug up that kiddie fucker. Take a shit on your bones too while I'm at it."

"Oh, God," Bill Campbell mutters. I turn to look at him. His face is white.

"Mr. Campbell?" I whisper. "Are you okay?"

He replies as if in a trance. "I— A couple days ago, one of the smaller excavators was missing. I didn't— Do you think?" I think of what Rooney just said. *Like I dug up that kiddie fucker.*

"Shit," I whisper.

Stedsan looks from me to Bill. "Does someone want to fill me in?"

In the aisle, Rooney fumbles at his belt buckle. "Or, you know what," he says, "maybe I'll just do it right now."

A woman in the front row screams and covers her eyes. Bill is on his feet now, pushing past me, into the aisle. "That's quite enough, Fred," he sputters, his face now red with outrage. "This is a funeral. Your behavior is completely inappropriate."

Rooney lets go of his belt and turns to Bill. "Inappropriate, is it? That's pretty good, Bill." He leans forward and drops his voice, so low that I barely hear him. "Especially coming from you."

Beads of sweat roll down Bill Campbell's face. I wonder if he's having a heart attack.

Garcia and Parker move up the aisle, closing in. Sensing something behind him, Rooney spins just as the officers grab him. Somehow, Rooney gets one arm free and throws a wild punch, but he overbalances and goes down hard on the marble floor. I wince, imagining brittle bones snapping. In a flash, Garcia has his hands cuffed behind his back.

I step into the aisle. Bill Campbell's face is bloodless again and he's swaying. I take his arm. "Mr. Campbell," I say, "you have to tell them about the excavator."

He looks at me like he doesn't recognize me.

On the ground, Rooney has stopped struggling. I step closer. "Detective Garcia," I say.

She looks over her shoulder. When she sees it's me, her mouth presses into a thin line. I speak quickly, before she can turn away.

"The bones you found at the dump, I think I know where they came from. Or, well, Mr. Campbell here does."

From the ground, Rooney cranes his head back. He doesn't look hurt, despite the fall. Invincible as a roach.

"Lookie, it's the writer," Rooney says cheerfully. "Come a little closer and maybe I'll spill my guts for you. Tell you all about that boy who drowned—what was his name?"

He smiles. I want to rake my fingernails over his face.

Bill Campbell appears at Garcia's shoulder. "Can we please get him out of here?" he whispers through gritted teeth.

Garcia nods and together, Parker and Officer Washington haul Rooney to his feet. "Dunno, Bill," Rooney shouts, laughing as the officers half carry, half drag him toward the door. "They can't even manage to find a huge fucking hole in the ground."

Garcia waits, looking from me to Bill Campbell. "You and you," she says, pointing. "Come."

Then she stalks down the aisle without waiting for a response.

Father Aubry raps on the lectern, trying to regain control. He lifts a Bible into the air. "If you would turn to John 14," he says in a shaky voice.

Stedsan looks from me to Bill, amused by the whole disaster. "Well," he says. "Don't keep the lady waiting."

Bill straightens, as if steeling himself, and walks briskly to the exit.

I slink down the aisle after Garcia, like a dog summoned by a very pissed-off master.

Outside, the sun stabs my eyes. In the parking lot, Parker is pushing Rooney's head down so he doesn't hit it on the roof of the police cruiser.

Garcia stands at the base of the stairs, watching us descend. She looks furious. "All right, let's hear it," she says.

Bill Campbell shuffles his feet but doesn't say anything. My stomach flutters. "I think the bones you found in the dump belong to Father Foster," I say. "He was a priest at Coram House when Fred Rooney lived here. He abused the children."

Garcia's hand goes to the gold crucifix around her neck. "And where did you get this theory from?"

"Inside—what Rooney said about digging up the bones." I leave out the shitting part. "Mr. Campbell"—I gesture to Bill—"mentioned they're missing an excavator from the construction site where Rooney works."

Garcia nods slowly, connecting the dots, then turns to Bill Campbell. "Is this true?"

He clears his throat and nods, but can't seem to find his voice.

"Why didn't you report it?" Garcia asks.

"I—well—I didn't know it was stolen," he says. "I thought record-keeping—maybe it was left at another site—"

Garcia raises a hand, cutting him off. "All right, we'll talk about it later. Where would we find this Father Foster's grave, then? If we wanted to test this theory."

Bill clears his throat again and rolls his shoulders like he's trying to work a kink out of his neck. "I'm not sure exactly, but he'd likely be in the southwest corner. Most of the clergy are buried there."

It seems strange that he doesn't know or is pretending not to know. But his expression gives nothing away.

"All right, let's go." Garcia steps onto the path that leads into the graveyard, then stops. She looks down at her black heels, now full of snow. Her cheeks turn red, in fury or embarrassment, I'm not sure.

Parker joins us. I notice a tiny spot of blood on his chin where he must have cut himself shaving. Garcia turns to him.

"Officer Parker, you check it out and then report back. I'll take Mr. Rooney back to the station. Question him once he sobers up."

Garcia climbs into the cruiser, slamming the door behind her rather harder than necessary. As she pulls onto the street, Rooney turns to look out the back window. He waves, at me or at Bill, I can't tell.

"Lead the way," Parker says, gesturing to the graveyard. Bill Campbell looks from Parker's boots to his own flimsy black dress shoes.

"It's a long walk," Bill says.

Parker pulls a pair of leather gloves from his pocket. He glances down at my own sensible boots, then up at Bill. "Then I guess we had better get started," he says.

As we follow the path away from the church, I wonder at what Garcia said. Why didn't Bill Campbell report the missing excavator? The only answer that makes sense is he knew and was protecting Rooney. But why?

We reach the iron gate that marks the entrance to the graveyard. Two stone angels flank it, making a very dramatic show of weeping. Just in case you forget a graveyard is supposed to be sad, I guess.

The main path only has an inch or two of snow. It must have been plowed sometime this morning, but most of the gravestones are buried under soft mounds, like turtles tucked in under a white blanket. We pass through a circle of evergreens with a stone bench in the center. It's sheltered from the snow, so brown pine needles crunch underfoot. On the other side the view opens up to reveal the lake. Last time I was here, the water was dark and churning. Today, it's been replaced by flat, endless white. Without the breeze rattling the bare branches, the landscape would be still as a photograph.

"What's that?" Parker points down the path. I scan the snow-frosted gravestones, but don't see anything out of place. Not at first.

"I don't know," Bill says. He sounds nervous.

Then I spot a flash of yellow at the edge of the woods. A crust of snow crunches underfoot as we step off the path. Bill's feet must be soaked, but he follows us without complaint.

"Stop." Parker holds out his arm to block our way. Tire tracks. Not fresh, they're covered in a layer of snow, but still visible. We give them a wide berth.

At the edge of the woods, a yellow backhoe lies tipped on one side in a mess of broken saplings and underbrush. The machine is covered in a thin layer of undisturbed snow, so it must have been here since at least last night, maybe days. But all around it the earth is torn up and stained brown with mud. A small tree has been dug up and cast aside, dirt still clinging to the roots. The ground is covered in chunks of stone, some bearing fragments of text. *Sister. Beloved. 19.*

Gravestones.

"Oh my god," Bill says.

In the middle of the debris there's a deep wound in the ground. I drift closer until Parker puts a hand on my arm. "It's a crime scene," he says. "And I don't know if the ground is stable."

But I don't need to go any closer to see the splintered wood and torn satin lining, black with age and mud. The remains of a coffin. A gravestone lays on its back, miraculously unbroken. *Fr. Edmund Foster. 1914–1994.*

There's a clicking sound. Bill's face is pale with cold or shock. His teeth are chattering.

"Parker," I whisper and nod toward the older man.

Parker frowns. "Mr. Campbell," he says. "Are you all right?"

"What?" Bill snaps. "Of course I'm not all right. Look at this mess." His speech is slightly slurred.

"It's cold out here," Parker says. "Why don't you wait back at the church?"

Bill looks like he's going to protest but then spins on his heel and trudges back to the path.

"Give me a second," Parker says. "I have to call this in."

I take a few steps away. My eyes follow the tread marks that lead back up the hill, a straight line to Coram House. Not a single other section of graves looks damaged. I'd pictured Rooney drunk, taking the excavator on a whim. But maybe not.

"Copy that," Parker says into the phone and then hangs up. "They're sending a team. We should clear the area."

I nod, but don't move. "This has been here for days," I say.

Parker's smile is wan. "Thanks for the reminder."

"No—I just mean, look at this place. It's a mess. And the ground must have been frozen solid. It would have taken a long time to do this.

Plus, how much do those things cost?" I point to the excavator lying on its side. "A hundred thousand bucks? If it was your business, wouldn't you report it missing? Unless you knew exactly where it was."

Parker seems to consider that.

"Campbell and Rooney have known each other a long time," I say.

"You think he's protecting him?"

I think of the way Rooney acted toward Bill Campbell in the office the day we met. How rude he was and the tension in the room. Then there was that strange moment when I'd asked Campbell about Tommy. He'd dismissed Sarah Dale's testimony, sure. But he'd also looked scared.

"Or maybe he's afraid of him," I say.

"Afraid?" Parker frowns.

"Think about it," I say, getting excited now. "We can't prove Rooney did anything to Jeannette Leroy. Campbell knows we can't. Even if he suspects Rooney—he's not going to come forward. I've seen them together, Parker. They're not friends. And Rooney undercuts him in public. Why would he put up with that?"

Parker's frown deepens. I think he's going to tell me I've gone too far, to butt out of the case and cut out the *we* stuff. But he doesn't.

"Rooney works for him—has for decades," Parker says. "Why would Campbell employ him all these years?"

"I don't know," I admit. He's right. It doesn't make sense. Maybe Bill Campbell has suspicions about what happened to Jeannette Leroy, maybe he's afraid of Rooney now. But why give him a job in the first place? From everything I've read, Rooney has always been monstrous. But a certainty is blooming somewhere deep inside me. Bill Campbell knows more than he's saying.

Sirens sound in the distance, faint but getting louder. "Let's go," Parker says. We return to the main path. Nearby, a bird alights on a branch dotted with red berries. It plucks one off and tosses its head back, swallowing it whole.

"Alex," Parker says. He looks uncomfortable. "I—know you're going to keep digging into this—this connection to what happened back then. Will you let me know what you find out?"

"Of course I will," I say, surprised.

Just then, Parker's phone rings. He looks down at the number. "I have to—"

"Yeah," I say. "Of course."

I walk the rest of the way alone. Coram House looms above, casting a long shadow across the snow. The moment I'm inside the shadow, the air grows suddenly colder, as if I've passed through a ghost.

18

I unlock the door to my apartment. My feet feel frozen from standing in the deep snow at the graveyard.

"Shit."

The word floats into the room, a puff of cloud, because it's cold enough inside to see my breath. The floorboards groan as I cross to the heater in the living room and touch it. Warm. It seems to be working.

Then something on the desk catches my eye. My laptop sits in the middle of the table, surrounded by black-and-white photographs. Earlier, I'd been going through them, trying to build a visual storyboard to run with the book. One image per chapter. Except the photos aren't in a stack anymore. They're scattered across the table. Had I left them that way? I'd swear I hadn't.

My throat tightens. Both windows are locked. Next, I check the bedroom. Also locked. I'm being paranoid. What do I think happened, exactly? Rooney got drunk and stopped here for a little breaking and entering on the way to the funeral? But, in the kitchen, I find the window wide open. My heart beats hard enough that I swear I can feel the muscle slamming against my breastbone.

I stick my head out the window and peer down into the narrow, overgrown yard. There are no footprints in the snow. And no ladder marks. So unless Rooney can fly, no dice. I shut the window and stare at it. A second later, it creaks open again. The latch is broken. I sigh, feeling stupid, and rig something with a rubber band until I can call the landlord.

I clean up the windblown photos scattered on the floor. I was lucky the weather wasn't worse. With an open window, the apartment could have been full of snow, the pictures ruined. I come to the photo of Sister Cecile standing beside the boat. By now, I've memorized every part of it, but something is bothering me. Some tickle in my brain. I take in her black habit, the blur of her face. Maybe it's the incongruity of knowing I stood beside her coffin just a couple hours ago. I nestle the photo back in the box with the others.

I'm halfway to the bedroom to get another sweater when I stop. It feels like the air has been sucked out of the room. In three steps I'm back at the box of photos.

Sister Cecile. The boat.

I pull out my phone. I don't want to call Xander, would much rather let yesterday remain where it is—something to tell Lola about next time she calls. But I dial anyway.

"Alex," Xander says. He sounds pleased. "How's it going?"

"Xander, what you said last night—about seeing a canoe on the water—when was it?" I'm breathless and speaking too fast. "I mean, do you remember exactly what day it was?"

"Well, yeah," he says, sounding baffled. "It was the night—well, I guess it was probably morning by then—the whole thing with my car—"

"You saw the canoe from the dock that morning? Before the police brought you into the station?"

"Yeah. I was sort of just, you know, sitting on the dock—well, no, I was probably lying down, to be honest. Anyways, yeah, the canoe was out there, off the point."

He sounds so embarrassed that I feel a trickle of guilt. I plug it up. A girl with her finger in the dike.

"What time was it?" I ask.

He clears his throat. "I don't know exactly. I was pretty out of it."

"But you saw it across the water, off the far shore. So there must have been some light."

"That's true," he says, with effort, as if pulling the memory up from a hole. "I don't know. Seven, maybe?"

I run through the timeline in my head. I got up at six that morning, was heading into Rock Point around six thirty, just like I told the police. The timing works.

"Did you see who was paddling it?"

Xander laughs. "Alex, I was shit-faced. It was barely sunrise. And it was half a mile across the lake."

"Just—try. Please."

He sighs. "I don't know? A man? It was just a dark shape."

"But just one person?"

"Yeah, that part I'm pretty sure of."

"Did you tell the police?"

"About what? About the canoe?" He sounds baffled. "I don't know, to be honest. I mean, I'm pretty sure I gave them my whole life story. I don't remember much."

"Thanks, Xander. I have to—"

"Wait, Alex—what is this about?"

I owe him an explanation, but right now I'm itching to get off the phone. "Maybe nothing. I just—I don't know exactly. Not yet. Look, I have to go. I'll call you."

I hang up before he can say anything else. Then I exhale a long, slow breath and go back in time to last week. The quiet, still woods. A single set of footprints on the trail ahead. Dim, predawn light. The scream. I shut my eyes—Garcia's trick—and hear the other sounds too. The scrape of something against a rock. A hollow thunk.

I play it again, this time with a figure, a hood pulled up so their face is in shadow. But with blood on their hands. After all, they just smashed a woman's head on the rocks. There would be blood. The figure drags a canoe over the rocks with a long scrape. Once it's in the water, they lift a leg over the side and step in. Thunk. Then they paddle away, emerging from the cove just in time to be seen by Xander, half passed out on his dock. They stash the boat back on the beach in front of Coram House, where it has been sitting unused for months.

Fred Rooney could have left that canoe on the beach and been back in the office in minutes. No footprints in the woods. No witnesses. The lake froze over a few days later. No one would have suspected. Except Xander happened to be looking in that direction.

Before I can change my mind, I pick up the phone again and dial Parker. He answers on the second ring. "Sorry," I say. "I know you're busy."

"It's all right," he says. I hear muffled voices in the background.

"I know how he did it, Parker."

"How who did what?"

"Fred Rooney. How he killed Jeannette Leroy."

He inhales sharply. "Hang on a second."

The click of a door shutting. The background noise disappears.

"You still there?"

"He used a canoe. Bill Campbell left one at Coram House, sitting on shore by the boathouse. Rooney would have known it was there. All he had to do was paddle a couple hundred yards, stash it on the rocks, and wait for her there. She went every day—you told me yourself—so he easily could have known. It explains why there weren't any footprints, why no one saw him. Everything."

I pause, waiting, triumphant.

"A canoe?" Parker says. His voice doesn't contain the urgency I'd hoped for.

"I'm not making this up," I say. "Xander saw a canoe that morning before the police picked him up."

"The drunk guy? He saw a canoe at Rock Point?" Parker asks. Now he sounds fully awake. "Did he get a look at who was paddling it?"

"Well, no," I admit. "It was dark." *And he was drunk*, I don't add. "He said it was definitely one person. He couldn't make anything else out."

"Alex—" Parker starts, but I cut him off.

"Just . . . bring him in. Talk to him."

"We did talk to him. He was so drunk he barely made sense."

"Try again. Please." I hear the whine in my voice, but I can't stop. "I believe Sarah Dale. I think Fred Rooney was in the boat the day Tommy drowned, all those years ago. What if he pushed him in? He could have killed Sister Cecile to cover it up—"

"Alex—"

"Rooney must have known about my book. I mean, didn't everyone around here know? He must have been afraid I'd find Sister Cecile eventually, figure out what happened. Jesus, Parker, I showed up at his house the day after she died. He was covered in scratches like he'd been in a fight. And he laughed when I asked if Sister Cecile was alive. He laughed."

There's a long silence on the phone. I hold my breath. I can't go to Garcia about this, she'll think I made it up. If Parker doesn't believe me, it's over. Finally, he sighs. "All right. I'll talk to your Xander. Then we'll see."

"He's not my—"

"Look, Alex, I'm at work. I have to go."

"Right, yes. Okay. Thanks."

He hangs up. I look down at my desk, at the photo sitting there. I'd been gripping the edge so tightly my fingernails left little half-moon indentations in the paper. Above them, Sister Cecile stands in her black habit, but the blur has been replaced by the bloody face of the woman in the woods. I blink the image away.

Even though I know they're the same person, it's hard to hold them both in my head. Jeannette Leroy, the frail old woman. Sister Cecile, the nun who abused children. What had Parker said the other night? We all have good and bad inside us. I think about Fred Rooney. The sad boy, abused by the adults who should have taken care of him. The teenager who took joy in hurting the other children. The hot, sick feeling of his eyes running over me. The cold sound of his laughter at his house that day.

Maybe goodness is like a tank of gas—enough bad stuff happens and one day you just run empty. Or maybe evil is a seed, born inside all of us, waiting for the right conditions to thrive. I wonder if you feel it—that moment it starts to bloom.

————

In the morning, there's a text waiting from Parker. Sent after midnight last night. *Arresting FR on a drunk and disorderly. Wanted you to know.* Then another text a few minutes later, also from Parker. *It's a start.*

A sense of lightness fills me. For a minute, I lie in bed, staring at the ceiling cracks as I try to parse it. Happy, I finally realize. I feel happy, though I have no real right to be. Sister Cecile is dead and I'm no closer to proving Sarah Dale was telling the truth. And the photocopy I found at Xander's has turned out to be no help at all. None of the birth or death records for Thomases during that time period in Vermont have a last name that starts with U. Plus, I'm supposed to present a preliminary outline to Stedsan in a few days and I'm nowhere near ready. But Fred Rooney has been arrested. And Parker is taking me seriously. And right now, I have to focus if I'm going to drop in on Father Aubry. Sunday morning, he'd said, but it seems indecent to show up before nine.

I pull on my spandex leggings and sneakers. I run under a gray sky, heavy with unfallen snow. I'm getting used to the weather patterns here. The blue-sky days with sunshine that camouflages the biting cold. Then gloomy days like this where the clouds act like a blanket, trapping any vestiges of warmth, holding them close to the earth.

By eight, I'm showered and dressed, my hair blown dry so it doesn't freeze into icicles. My instincts tell me Father Aubry might still be useful, even if I'm not sure exactly how. At the very least, if Jeannette Leroy attended church, he would have met the woman, might be able to tell me what she was like.

Coffee mug filled to the brim, I sit down in front of a blank notepad and try to focus. I write Sister Cecile's name in the center of the page. Father Aubry badly wants to be relevant—I sensed that from our first meeting—and to come out looking like the good priest. It's too late to find Sister Cecile, obviously, but maybe if he knew her he can help me understand how she fits into all this. For starters, what was her relationship like with Fred Rooney? The depositions suggest she was an authoritarian who played favorites. So what did it mean for him to be a favorite? And could she still have had some kind of hold over him, even after all these years? If I can understand that, maybe it will help me understand why he killed her.

I look down at the paper and see I've drawn a constellation of questions around Sister Cecile's name, a line connecting each of them to her like the rays of the sun. The clock on the stove says quarter to ten. Time to go.

Coram House is busy today. Yellow hard hats dot the scaffolding, bright smudges against the gray sky. The high whine of a blade cutting metal fills the car as I drive past, down the dirt track. The rectory looks even shabbier in the flat light. The bricks are worn down at the edges and missing huge chunks of mortar. Without the tendrils of ivy that cover the building, I wonder if the whole thing would crumble.

I knock, and the door swings open to reveal an older woman wearing a long dark skirt and sweater, which remind me of a nun's habit despite all the appliqué birds.

"My name is Alex Kelley," I say, stepping inside. "Father Aubry is expecting me."

She frowns at the slush gathering at my feet, as if I should know better than to walk through snow. "Follow me," she says and begins to haul herself to the second floor, grunting on each step, as if it hurts.

Hours later, it seems, we make it to the door of Father Aubry's study. "He's on the phone," she says. "You may wait here."

Then she's gone, limping down the dark, creaking floorboards. And I'm alone in the hall, listening to the low murmur of Father Aubry's voice through the door.

I wander back down the hall a little, not wanting him to think I'm eavesdropping, and inspect the photo of the smiling nuns at the soup kitchen. The black habits made the photos oddly timeless. Apart from the oversize eighties glasses, you could plop these same nuns in the sepia photo of the baptism and they wouldn't look out of place.

The study door opens. "Ms. Kelley," Father Aubry says, coming into the hallway. "So good to see you. Ah—I see you've had a little wander through our history."

Immediately, I think of Xander. *Historical flavor.*

"We run the longest continuously operating soup kitchen in the state, you know," he says.

Gold star for you, I think, then feel ungenerous. He didn't murder any kids, at least that I know of.

"And this one," I say, pointing to the antique photo of the children gathered around the font. "A baptism?"

He pushes his glasses up his nose and leans closer. He smells musty. Like a damp towel. "Ah, yes," he says. "They used to baptize the orphans at Coram House when they arrived."

He makes a face when he says the name like it tastes bad. "There weren't always records, you see, on who had been baptized before they arrived. Some of the children came from out of state. So they baptized everyone, just to be safe."

So Tommy would have been baptized.

"Records," I say, looking from him back to the photograph. "The church keeps records of baptisms?"

"Of course," he says.

My mouth goes dry, but I try to sound casual. "And would you still have those records? From the 1960s?"

He nods. "Most likely. Those would have been kept here at the church. Why don't you come in and sit? It's warmer by the fire."

He leads me into the office and we settle into the armchairs facing the fireplace. Moaning wind pours down the chimney—like some poor creature is trapped up there. I tell him about the photocopied news article, about finding Tommy's last initial, about my search for a boy lost to history and how much I'd love his help. He nods and then phones down to Rosa, asks her to take a look at the baptismal ledgers. I'd prefer to do it myself, but don't push him.

I try to focus on why I'm here. It's maddening to think that just a week earlier I might have been sitting across from Sister Cecile in a different drafty room. Alive. If only I'd known. If only I'd asked the right questions.

"Thank you for meeting me today," I say. "You must be busy, especially after the funeral."

He looks pained. "That was terrible. But grief takes many forms."

"Did you know Sister Cecile well?"

He looks wary, but I keep my expression bland. I wonder if he's heard yet about Fred Rooney's arrest.

"She led a quiet life, but remained a devout member of our congregation. She helped at the soup kitchen every week, you know. The community gardens. But kept mostly to herself."

"Was it usual for the sisters to change their name?" I ask. "For example, Sister Cecile, I assume she was born Jeannette Leroy?"

He leans back in his chair. "Oh, yes. It was quite common, especially then. It's symbolic, you see. A new name to symbolize their commitment to our Lord Savior. Their new life."

"And the fact that she went back to her birth name? Was that the custom too?"

Father Aubry sips from a glass of water. "Generally," he says, "sisters do not revert to their birth name upon retirement. But, ah, this was a somewhat special case."

"Oh?" I ask, all innocence.

He puts down the glass. I notice a dried film on the rim in the shape of lips.

"It's a rather delicate matter, of course. But given the case, the church thought Sister Cecile might be more comfortable living out her retirement at another locale."

So they tried to hide her somewhere else. Unsurprising. "That makes sense," I say.

"Yes," he replies absently. "But she—ah, well—she had lived here for nearly thirty years. And felt very strongly that God was calling her to remain. She wished to retire and live a life of quiet service, so I believe the name change was decided upon to avoid any unpleasantness."

In other words, she refused to go and they decided this was the best way to avoid bad PR. I nod along as if this was the only possible course.

"And people here didn't mind—about her history?"

"People tend not to care who is putting soup in their bowl."

I wonder what she would have said to him in the confessional. What he absolved her for.

"And you have to remember," Father Aubry continues, "Coram House had been closed for fifteen years by the time the case was settled. Most of the sisters had retired elsewhere. And, well, people simply didn't talk about the things that had happened there. There was a collective desire to move on."

"To make the case go away, you mean," I say. *Whoops.*

He sighs. "Did you ever pause to consider that we—the church—agreed to settle because we thought it would be the best thing for the community, for the children themselves?"

Father Aubry must see my skeptical look, but he presses on.

"Did you know most people involved wanted to settle? It's not as if the church forced them to take some sort of deal. Alan was instrumental to the plan, of course, but so was Bill."

"Bill? You mean Bill Campbell?"

Father Aubry looks at me warily. If he were an insect, his antennae would be waving in the air, searching for a threat.

"I truly got the sense that most of the former children just wanted to move on with their lives," he says. "Including Bill Campbell, yes. It's not a surprise really—no one wants to linger on the most terrible moments of their life."

But plenty of people have no choice.

"But you mentioned Bill Campbell specifically."

He frowns. "Bill and Alan were the de facto leaders, I suppose. The others listened to them, took their advice."

My mind is whirring. Could Bill Campbell have had his eye on developing the property, even then? Why else would he convince people to settle for next to nothing? And Stedsan was on board with this. Not exactly the crusader for justice he painted himself as, then.

There's a knock at the door. Father Aubry stands, barely concealing his relief as he lets Rosa in. Her long skirts swish around her ankles as she thumps the ledger on the table. The spine of the book cracks as Father Aubry opens it. "Around 1967, you said? Tom or Thomas," he murmurs.

I hover over his shoulder as he flips through the brittle, dusty pages.

"We're in luck." Father Aubry stabs the page with his index finger, as if the name might wriggle free. "Here you are. Thomas Underwood, aged eight."

I go to lick my lips but my tongue is dry.

Thomas Underwood. The name is printed right there. I don't know what I'm expecting—the clouds to part? Angels strumming harps?—but there is something there. A tiny light. Two days ago I had nothing—no face, no name. Now, both.

I take out my phone and snap a picture. Father Aubry clears his throat. "Did you have other questions, Ms. Kelley? It's just, with everything that happened yesterday—I haven't had much time to focus on my sermon."

"Of course," I say, standing. "Thank you for your help."

As we shake hands, Father Aubry looks down at the ridged gold band on my right hand. "Ah, I didn't realize you were married."

I want to pull my hand back. "My husband died," I say.

Father Aubry squeezes my fingers. "My condolences for your loss. I will add you both to my prayers."

It feels like a violation. I don't want his prayers. But I thank him again and show myself out.

Back in the car, I blast the heat to get the chill of the rectory out of my bones. My mind is spinning. *Thomas Underwood.* Finally, a name. But it's hard to enjoy my victory when I think about everything else Father Aubry said. *Alan was instrumental to the plan, of course, but so was Bill.* What does that mean?

I could ask Stedsan about Bill Campbell's involvement in the settlement, but Father Aubry made it sound like they were working together. But surely Stedsan wouldn't have brought me here to write a book if he'd been involved in some kind of corruption? He's smarter than that.

My phone rings, cutting through my thoughts. It's a local area code. "Hello?" I answer.

"Is this Alex Kelley?" It's a woman's voice, but deep with a hint of gravel. Older but not elderly.

"Yes," I say. "This is Alex. Can I help you?"

"This is Karen Lafayette. I hear you want to talk to me."

"Karen," I say. "Karen Lafayette."

My brain takes a moment to process the name. Karen who was a child at Coram House. Karen who knew Sarah Dale. Karen who saw Sister Cecile push a girl out the window.

"Yes," she says. "You called me? Left a message. Two messages, actually. I've been on a cruise. Just got back yesterday."

"A cruise," I repeat. My heart thumps absurdly, not quite believing she's here, alive, on the phone.

"Do you want to tell me what this is about? Or should I start guessing?"

She sounds amused.

"Right," I say. "Yes, of course."

I'd kept my messages vague, hoping to pique her curiosity enough to call me back. "I'm writing a book about Coram House." I pause, waiting to see if she's going to hang up.

Instead, she lets out a long breath. "Well," she says. "It's about time somebody did."

Before I know what's happening she's agreed to an interview tomorrow and is giving me directions to her farm. "All right," Karen says. "So I'll see you tomorrow sometime around eleven. Are you in a truck?"

"A—what?" I ask.

"The roads up here are pretty slick, but you should be all right, as long as you have four-wheel drive."

"Oh, right." I look around my car, trying to figure out if I have four-wheel drive.

"Otherwise, you might want to wait a week. Give the plows a chance to catch up."

Not going to happen. I try to fill my voice with confidence. "No problem. I'll be there tomorrow."

We hang up and I drop the phone into the cupholder. Fireworks are going off in my stomach. For weeks, I've been looking for some proof of what happened to Tommy. But every time I think I find a way in, a window open just a crack, it slams shut. And now, finally, a door.

19

My appointment with Karen isn't until eleven, but I'm out the door by eight. After reading the manual, I'm pretty sure my car doesn't come with four-wheel anything, so the plan is to drive slowly and hope for the best. But first, I fortify myself with coffee and an egg sandwich from the corner store.

In line to pay, I text Stedsan to reschedule tomorrow's meeting, tell him I have a promising interview and need a few more days. I'd already been dreading our check-in since the outline was nowhere near ready, but now I don't know how I can sit across from him knowing he might have colluded with Bill Campbell to settle the case. My poker face isn't that good. Stedsan writes back immediately, saying great, just let him know.

I eat with the heat blowing full blast to melt the rime of frost coating the windshield. My fingers itch to text Parker for an update: Did he call Xander about the canoe? What's going on with Rooney? But I don't want to hear that he can't discuss an active case. The grease from the sandwich turns to jelly as it goes cold. I wrap the rest in foil. Time to get going.

Westfield doesn't look far on the map, but my route follows a snaking maze of country roads into an area called the Northeast Kingdom. The name conjures enchanted castles, but an hour into the drive, I've only seen barns that fill my car with the animal tang of livestock.

My phone loses service, so I pull over at a crossroads to scan the map. Fields of snow stretch in all directions. Not a car or house in sight. The only sign of habitation is a split-rail fence that runs along the road.

Each post is weathered to gray and covered in patches of pale green lichen. The fence could be a hundred years old. Then I spot the pile of rocks rising from the middle of the field like a cairn. Karen told me about this spot. According to her directions, I should go straight for two miles and then turn into her drive. The only problem is that the road ahead is covered in a layer of snow.

I get out of the car and cross to the unplowed section of road. The snow is loose and squeaks underfoot. Far across the field, pines sway. A few seconds later the wind reaches me with eye-stinging cold. The air rings with quiet. The places I used to seek solitude—a bench in Central Park—seem crowded and noisy in hindsight.

Two more miles to Karen's. So close and yet impossibly far. I could drive and get stuck, end up having to walk the rest of the way. Can you freeze to death in two miles? Probably. Or I could do the smart thing. Go back to my apartment and try again in a few days. All the options are bad. I turn back toward the car, and then stop.

A white owl perches on a fence post, watching me with yellow eyes. *Where the hell did that come from?* Wind ruffles its feathers, which are speckled brown like someone shook pepper on them. The owl shifts and black talons peek out from feathery boots.

It's magnificent. I don't move, don't breathe.

The owl cocks its head at me and then unfurls its enormous wings. The span could envelop me entirely. The feathers at the end spread wide like fingers. The bird flaps once and launches into the air, soaring pale and silent over the field and into the trees beyond.

I get back into my car, feeling as if I've just had an encounter with a unicorn. The unplowed road stretches ahead. *Fuck it.* I step on the gas. The snow scatters like baby powder.

By some miracle, I make it the two miles without getting stuck, but I'm sweating with anxiety by the time I park behind the yellow farmhouse. I walk up the steps onto the wraparound porch. A pair of rocking chairs creak back and forth, buffeted by wind. It's the kind of place where you'd sit on a summer night, listening to crickets and watching as stars appear one by one over the hills. But summer is impossibly distant.

I knock. A chorus of barking comes from inside. A few seconds later, the door flies open. A woman with wild gray curls smiles at me. Karen Lafayette. Her legs are spread to contain the herd of dogs jostling behind her. "You made it! Get in here before we all freeze. This old place is a bitch to heat."

Somehow I squeeze past her. The floor is littered with muddy boots and piles of gardening tools. Three black Labs present their silken ears to be scratched and lick my wrist with soft pink tongues.

"Hang your jacket anywhere you can find a spot."

Karen waves her hand to indicate the wall hooks already crammed with sweatshirts and raincoats. Her hair is held back by two sparkly butterfly clips—the kind I loved in middle school.

"Come on, gang. Out of the way!" Karen shoves aside the clambering dogs and strides into the kitchen.

I hurry to follow. "Thank you for meeting with me," I say.

"Happy to," she calls over her shoulder as she fills the kettle. "Not much to do around here in the winter except feed the horses."

I force myself to stop shuffling my feet. I'm a bundle of nerves, whereas Karen seems entirely at ease. She must be in her sixties by now, but there's something decisive in her movements that make her seem younger. She doesn't wear makeup but her clothes aren't frumpy. A long gray sweater over black pants. Bangles that sing up and down her arm as she gestures.

"There's a fire going in the living room," Karen says. She holds up a box of tea bags. "Do you drink tea? I'm afraid I don't have any coffee. Gave it up years ago."

"Tea sounds great," I say. "I'll drink anything warm."

Once the water boils, we take our mugs through the low doorway into the living room. "Watch your head," Karen says. "People in the 1800s must have been Hobbits."

The living room is ten degrees warmer thanks to a wood-burning stove. The dogs lie in a pile on the rug, only inches from the flames. Except for the soft snoring, you'd never know they were alive. All the furniture is overstuffed and faded by years of sun, and every flat surface is covered in photos. Karen on a beach. Karen at a long table full of people, a giant turkey in the center of the frame. Karen and a cluster of women holding matching pink cocktails.

"I don't think I've ever been in a cozier room," I say.

"As long as you don't sit too close to those drafty windows." She laughs, but I can tell she's pleased.

Karen talks for a while about the history of her house, the farm, how they inherited it from her husband's aunt before he passed. As she talks, she walks around the living room, straightening a stack of magazines, fluffing a throw pillow. She has the kind of barely bottled energy you see in children, stuffed into fancy clothes and made to sit through long dinners, legs under the table bouncing up and down. I think about steering the conversation to Coram House, but don't. Some people need to get there on their own.

Finally, she seems to run out of steam and sinks into a chair. "How was your drive? Not too much trouble getting here?"

I picture the unplowed road, but shake my head. "No trouble. Oh—I did see an owl, a white one."

Karen claps her hands, which makes all three dogs sit up. When it's clear we're not about to take them on a walk, they settle back down on the rug.

"A snowy owl," she says. "How exciting. You must be good luck."

I laugh. "I don't know about that." But I'm pleased that she too recognizes the strange magic.

Karen looks out the window. "Well, you've let me go and tell you my whole life story."

But, of course, that's not true. She hasn't mentioned Coram House. Nothing at all from her childhood. I've done enough interviews to feel the moment when it comes. I wait, silent.

"Truth is," she says, "ever since you called, I've been thinking about the House. Remembering all these tiny, stupid things that don't matter to anyone. It's strange the way they just come back into your head like that. I hardly ever think about it anymore." She turns back and looks at me like she just remembered I'm there. "Anyways, I imagine you have questions."

Only hundreds. But I force myself to appear relaxed. I take out my phone and put it on the coffee table, hit record, so she can see. "Karen, is it okay if I record the rest of our conversation?"

"Yes, of course," Karen says.

I clear my throat. "I'd love to start with what it was like. All those tiny things you mentioned, they do matter—to me. I've read all the depositions from the case, but most people who actually lived at Coram House are gone or don't want to talk to me—which I completely understand."

She waves away my concern. "God, no. I'm happy to talk. Always have been. But no one ever wanted to hear it. I think you should put everything in your book."

Karen takes a deep breath as if she's about to plunge underwater. And then she starts talking. The stories pour out of her. Some are terrible—being made to strip naked and stand outside in the snow as punishment, the other children watching from the windows. Kneeling on the icy floor of the chapel until her knees bled. Other memories could be from children anywhere. Smuggling crackers from the kitchen in their pockets. The nuns taking their lessons outside on a sunny day. Watching the leaves change and blanket the graveyard in red. A time when the bakery in town brought cider donuts for the children and they each got a half. With every story she sits up a little straighter, like it's a stone she casts off in the telling.

Two hours and two cups of tea later, I get the sense that Karen could keep going forever. I wish I could let her, but there's a snowy road to travel before dark. And I feel the tapping of someone at the window, waiting to be let in.

"Karen," I say when she pauses to sip her tea. "I want to ask you about a boy named Tommy."

Karen sighs. "That poor boy," she murmurs. Then her expression changes, sadness replaced by something grim and hard. "Poor all of us."

"Did you know him?"

"We all knew each other at least a little. Tommy was, well, he didn't have many friends. He used to pee his bed—and we didn't bathe very often—so he smelled. And he was always carrying his sheets down to the laundry. Those were the worst punishments, you know. Not the hitting. Shame."

I remember one of the other depositions calling him the bedwetter. It had cracked my heart—for a little boy to be remembered only for that.

"I saw him that day," Karen says. There's something eager in her voice. "With Sister Cecile."

My mouth goes dry. "The day he died?"

"Early that morning. It was his turn for swim lessons. Sister Cecile was telling him to put on his swim trunks, to come down to the beach. And he said no." Karen laughs, but there's no humor in it. "It stuck in my head for years because you didn't say no to Sister Cecile. You just—didn't."

"But he did go in the end."

Karen nods. "Yes. He did go in the end. Stupid kid. To think he ever had a choice."

There's venom in her voice. She swipes at her eyes with the heel of her hand, though I don't see any tears.

"The next day they told us he ran away. Even then, I remember thinking it was odd. He wasn't the type—always afraid of everything. And then, when I found out what Sarah saw. Well, it all made sense."

Something in the story feels off. "Karen," I say, "why do you think he refused to go in the boat that day? From what you're saying, that seems out of character too. Wasn't he afraid of Sister Cecile?"

"Oh, he was terrified for sure, but I guess the water was even scarier than Sister Cecile."

Now I'm even more confused. "The water?"

She leans forward. "Bill used to tell these stories. There was this one about a monster in the lake that gave the kids nightmares."

"Bill Campbell?" I ask, trying to imagine it.

She snorts. "I know. Doesn't seem like he'd have the imagination. I don't remember it all, but something about how the monster would come up underneath and pull you into the dark water, never let go. Once Sister Cecile found out, she let him have it, though. Devil's tales. So no more stories after that."

Wind howls outside the window. I shiver at the cold draft on my neck. "So Tommy—you think that's why he refused to go in the water?"

Karen nods. "Like I said, he was a fragile kid. That type didn't last long there." Her voice is as matter-of-fact as a shrug.

"Sarah Dale saw three people in the boat that day," I say, choosing my words carefully. But it turns out to be unnecessary.

Karen snorts. "If Sister Cecile was there, you can be sure Fred was too. He was like her shadow. Listen, I didn't see what happened that day. I'm not going to pretend otherwise. But I do remember what Fred was like the day after. After they announced Tommy had run off, he seemed different. Angry. Well, angrier than usual. He walked right up to Bill and knocked him down. A real gut punch. For no reason at all."

Based on my experience with Fred Rooney, I can't say this surprises me. "Karen, were they friends back then—Bill and Fred?"

She shakes her head. "No one was friends with Fred. Besides, Fred was always such a loose cannon, and Bill, well—he's the opposite. Everything he does is always for a reason. Whatever you call that."

Calculating, I think. That's what you call it. The picture she's painting doesn't fit with the jovial man who gave me a tour of Coram House. But maybe that's just how he wanted me to see him.

"Karen, can we go back to the case for a second? Do you think Bill wanted it settled out of court?"

She looks at me blankly for a moment and then her face cracks down the middle. A big, boisterous laugh bursts out. "I-I'm sorry. I just—the look on your face. Oh, honey, didn't anyone tell you?"

I stare at her, trying to catch up. "Tell me what?"

She leans forward, as if she's going to tell me a secret, but her voice is almost a shout. "Bill Campbell paid people off to make the case go away. Even back then, he had a plan. He was starting a business with his wife's money and always needed to be bigger and better than everyone else."

The air is knocked out of me. "Paid people off," I manage. What had Father Aubry said? *Alan was instrumental to the plan, of course, but so was Bill.* Is this what he meant?

"But—who?" I stammer. "What people?"

The fire crackles. Karen's spoon clinks against the mug as she stirs her tea, though it must be cold by now.

"Whoever he could get away with. Listen, I can't prove it. He's too smart for that. But you hear things." She raises her eyebrows meaningfully.

"So he didn't offer you money?"

She gives me a stern look, like I'm a child who hasn't been paying attention to the lesson. "Of course not. He knew I'd have thrown it right back in his face."

I don't know what to think. Karen sounds so sure, but she'd sounded sure on tape when she talked about the girl being pushed out the window. A girl whose death certificate says she died of the flu. An event Sarah Dale said never happened.

Karen puts down her mug and looks at me intently. "Look," she says. "He pushed hard to convince every last one of us to take the settlement the church was offering. And I mean, pushed. And for people like Fred, he did a lot more."

"You're saying he paid Rooney off?"

She studies me. "You've met Fred, I'm guessing."

I nod.

"Well, then you can probably guess how I know. Fred would do anything for a crumb of power he could wield over the rest of us. That never changed."

I can picture it—Rooney as a teenager with that snarl, an enforcer on the littler kids. His power both shield and weapon. "But why didn't Bill get in trouble if he was bribing people?" I ask. "If you knew, others must have too."

Karen shrugs. "Who was going to prosecute him? Besides, Fred never came out and said it. Just dropped hints. Just enough to make it clear that he got a bigger slice of the pie than the rest of us." She snorts in disgust. "Like we were competing to see who could get more of that blood money."

"Is that why you didn't take the settlement money from the church?"

"Of course I took it," she says. "I needed a new truck."

"But the NDA," I say, my stomach sinking. Everyone who took the money had to sign a nondisclosure agreement that they wouldn't discuss the details of the case, an agreement she was in violation of right now.

"Fuck the NDA," Karen says. Then she looks at me, hard. "Was that all it was worth? Those years of our lives. The down payment on a truck?"

I think the question is rhetorical but it becomes clear she's waiting for me to answer. "It wasn't fair."

She looks disappointed in me. "Life hardly ever is," she says. "Hang on, I need to feed the fire."

Karen opens a door on the stove and tosses in a scoop of wood pellets from a bucket nearby. The dogs are still a smelly snoring pile on the floor. My mind spins with what Karen has told me. Bill Campbell, bribing people to drop the case. This goes a step beyond anything I'd guessed. I wonder how Stedsan fits into this mess.

Karen settles back into her chair. "You know, I read about Sister Cecile in the paper," she says. "So the old hag slipped and fell off a cliff?"

"That's one interpretation." I sip my tea, buying time while I decide how much to share.

Her eyes are hungry. "But not yours."

"No. I think someone killed her."

"Well, I'm not surprised someone wanted her dead. Hell, I poured myself a drink to celebrate. Someone should have put a stake in her heart years ago."

I wince at the image of pierced flesh and spurting blood. For a second, I consider what I'm about to say, wondering if I'm violating my promise to Parker. But I know I'm going to say it either way.

"Karen, what if I told you that Fred Rooney was a suspect?"

Karen's eyebrows furrow. "For killing Sister Cecile?"

I nod. She lets out a low whistle and leans back in her chair. Then, silently, she gets up and fetches a bottle of whisky from a cabinet in the corner. She pours some in her mug and then holds it up to me. The bottle looks old and dusty. I want some, desperately, but shake my head no. It's a long drive home.

Karen takes a long sip. "No. I don't see it."

There's no waver in her voice, no hesitation. It wasn't the answer I was expecting. Not by a long shot.

"What do you mean?" I ask.

"Look, at the House, Fred was Sister Cecile's dog. She'd tell him what to do and he'd do it. *Fetch that boy. Lock her in the attic. Take away his food. Tear up her book.*"

"It's been decades," I say. "Things change. People change."

Karen looks at me with sympathy, like I've said something very naive.

"No, honey. No they don't." Her expression darkens. "And definitely not in Fred's case. You know, I used to drive by her house sometimes— Sister Cecile, Jeannette Leroy, whatever she was calling herself." She smiles and shakes her head. "That's a lie. I used to go all the time. I'd park on her street and just sit there. I didn't care if she saw me. I wanted her to see me. To be scared. But she always acted like I wasn't there. The last time I went was, oh, I don't know, maybe fifteen years ago. Summer. I got there and parked as usual. And there was Fred, up on a ladder, fixing her roof. I thought I was hallucinating. He didn't ignore me like her. He looked down at me in the car and got this big smile on his face. Then he waved at me. That asshole waved. I never went back."

"He was fixing her roof?"

"What I'm saying is—he loved her. She saved him. He never would have hurt her."

I absorb what she's saying. It doesn't fit. Rooney was so angry when he showed up at her funeral. The story seemed so clear. The boy who was abused. Revenge coming thirty years later. But maybe this is actually more plausible. Maybe they had a fight. Maybe he never intended to kill her. *Then why did he take the canoe?* Why go to all that trouble to hide his presence there if he didn't plan to kill her? A headache is beginning to throb behind my eyes.

"He dug up Father Foster's bones," I say. "And took them to the dump."

Karen tilts her head back and laughs until she's gasping and has to use her sleeve to dry the tears streaming down her face. "Oh, that's almost enough to make me like him," she says.

I see no point in holding anything back now, so I tell her about Sister Cecile's funeral—how Rooney showed up drunk, taunted Bill Campbell, and rubbed it in the face of the police. Karen nods along, looking thoughtful. "It's interesting," she says, "that he'd do it now, I mean. After so much time."

She blinks a few times and then murmurs, "That creepy fucker."

"What do you mean?"

"It makes sense," she says. "Sister Cecile hated Father Foster—never stopped trying to get rid of him."

I frown. "She hated him? Why?"

"Because he was raping little kids—not that anyone else seemed to have a problem with it. It was the only good thing about that psycho bitch. She put a stop to all that."

So it's true. It feels like someone's turned the world on its axis, so that the sky is the ground and the ground is the sky. Sister Cecile, who used to strip children naked and make them stand in the snow for talking back, who dangled a girl out a window as punishment, who beat children and starved them and locked them in the attic. Who pushed a little boy out of a boat and watched him drown. She really was the one who stopped Father Foster from preying on the children. *Plenty of us have good and bad in us.*

"Spare the rod, spoil the child," Karen says. "That part's in the Bible, so it was just fine with her to knock us around. But the Bible has a few things to say about sodomy too."

"Karen, did Father Foster abuse Fred Rooney?"

Karen looks surprised. "Oh, yes, definitely. I think Fred was one of his favorites."

"So the fact that he dug up the bones—or the fact that he dug them up now, I guess—"

"It was a present for her, I think. One last present."

Unease trickles down my spine—like someone cracked an egg on my head. All the evidence is there. Rooney had access, a history of violence, and what looked like motive too. It all fit together seamlessly like a puzzle. Or at least I thought it did. Now I'm not so sure.

But all of this is based on Karen's memory, and I'm still not sure I can trust it.

"Karen," I say, "in your deposition, you talk about a girl who was pushed out of a window. Do you remember that day?"

Karen gets a faraway expression. "I was washing the windows that morning with Eleven."

Eleven. She means Sarah Dale.

"And the other girl. It kills me that I can't remember her name. Sister Cecile came in, on the rampage about something. She yelled at us about how the windows were still filthy. The other girl was standing on the windowsill already. To reach the top panes." Karen mimics reaching up.

"She said something to Sister Cecile about how the smudges were all on the outside where we couldn't reach. She wasn't sassing her or anything, just trying to explain, but it was a stupid thing to say."

"What happened then?"

"Well, Sister Cecile grabbed the girl by the ankles and shoved her out onto the sill. Said something about how she could reach now. I don't know if she just meant to scare us and lost her grip, but the girl fell."

"You saw her fall?"

Karen nods. "She was just lying down there, not moving."

I try to reconstruct the scene in my head. In her deposition, Karen said that she actually saw the girl bounce as she hit the ground. But that would have been two stories down. There's no way she could have seen it unless her head was already out the window.

"And what did Sister Cecile do after?"

"Nothing. She just left. Didn't say a word."

"Karen." I need to tread gently for this next part. "In her testimony, Sarah Dale said the girl never fell. And Melissa Graves's death certificate says she died of the flu."

Karen shrugs, seemingly unbothered. "We all blocked a lot of shit out to survive that place. You don't always get to pick what you remember and what you don't."

Her face lights up like she's had a great idea. "You should find Sarah—ask her again. You never know what else might have surfaced after all this time."

She must see something on my face. "What is it?" she asks.

"I'm so sorry, Karen, but Sarah Dale died a few years ago. A car accident."

Karen looks sad, but unsurprised. "I saw her once, you know? Years later. It was during my travel-the-world phase—Paris, New York, San Francisco. We just ran into each other on the street. Can you imagine that?"

I smile. "It must have been nice to see each other again."

Karen laughs. "God, no. She was horrified. Like I'd crawled out of the grave. She tried to hide it—was polite and all that, but I could tell."

"I'm so sorry. That must have been hard."

"It was my fault. I never should have sprung on her in the street like that, especially when she had her kid with her—of course she didn't want to go into all that. But I didn't have kids. I was still so young. I didn't understand."

Her gaze is back out the window now. "So many of us died before we should have."

"I'm so sorry," I say again. But it's meaningless. Just something to say. I'm aware of the deep orange color of the light outside and how little I want to be driving these roads after dark. "I should go," I say. "I can't thank you enough for your time."

Karen waves away both my thanks and offer to help with dishes and walks me to the door. As I pull on my boots and coat, I decide to take a gamble. "Karen, can I ask you one more thing?"

She nods. "Shoot."

"Do you remember Tommy's last name?"

Karen looks up at the ceiling, like the answer might be written there. She takes a deep breath and shakes her head. "No," she says, "sorry."

I force a smile—I knew it was a long shot. "Thanks anyways."

"One last thing from me too," Karen says. "When this book is published, make sure you send a copy to Bill Campbell with a big *fuck you* from Karen Lafayette."

She smiles at me, but it's not a happy smile. It's the look of a scorpion hoping its sting found the killing spot. She shuts the door behind me.

The cold sucks the air from my lungs as I trudge back to the car. I'm about to slide into the driver's seat when Karen shouts my name. I turn to see her running across the driveway with no jacket.

"Karen, is everything—"

"Under-something," she says breathlessly. "I remember because the kids used to call him Tommy Underwear. Because of the bedwetting and because kids are little shits. Funny how things just pop into your head." She frowns. "But I don't remember the last part. Something nature-y. Underhill?"

"Underwood?" I ask, heart thumping.

"Yes!" Karen shouts and then smacks me on the shoulder. "That's it!"

We grin at each other and then she pulls me into a tight hug. "Good girl," she says in my ear. To my embarrassment, I start to tear up as I hug her back. Karen lets me go and waves one last time before closing her front door. I climb into the car, feeling hollowed out, so exhausted I'm not sure how I'll make the drive back.

Tommy Underwood. It's the closest I'm going to get to confirmation. But my bright mood dissipates when I think of everything else Karen said. If she's right, then Fred Rooney had nothing to do with Sister Cecile's death. So what do I do now? Call Parker—and say what, exactly? *Oh, after weeks of trying to convince you that Rooney did it, I've changed my mind. And by the way, Bill Campbell has been paying out bribes.*

Parker would be justified in kicking me straight into the nearest snowbank. Anyways, it's all theoretical. My phone doesn't have service here. I put the car into drive and pull back onto the snowy road.

The story feels like a tree. Every time I manage to answer one question or find a new piece of information, the story branches out into three more questions, ten more, growing thinner and harder to grasp as it grows toward the sun.

20

Shadows play on the ceiling—branches trapped in the yellow glow of the streetlight. Outside, a gaggle of girls stumbles home from a party. Peals of laughter ring out like the call of a strange flock of birds.

I'd taken a wrong turn on the way back from Karen's and somehow added forty minutes to my drive. By the time I got home, I was so tired I shoved some food in my mouth and collapsed into bed. But now, I'm wide awake in the indefinable space between night and day. I can't stop thinking about Fred Rooney. Both the child and the old man in a prison cell. The present, haunting the past.

Rooney had seemed so angry at the funeral. It had confirmed everything I thought I knew about him. He was full of rage, wanting to punish someone for what had happened to him. My coming here was the catalyst. But what if it had only looked like rage? What if it had been grief—raw and terrible. But if he didn't kill Sister Cecile, that means one of two things is true: either Garcia was right all along and I imagined what I heard in the woods. Or I was right and someone else was there instead.

Giving up on sleep, I glide into the kitchen over icy floors to put on the coffee. A nutty, sharp smell fills the air. Then I shove everything to one side of my desk, except for a pen and blank pad of paper. In the center of the page, I write *Fred Rooney.* Beneath his name, I write *canoe.* So, what do I know about the boat? That it's Bill Campbell's, but he stores it at Coram House. It's visible from the construction site, but not from the road. You'd have to either know it's there or get lucky.

Beneath *canoe,* I write *motive.* Fred Rooney was at Coram House for seven years. He was abused by Father Foster and was a particular favorite of Sister Cecile. If I can trust Karen's memory, he was also repairing Sister Cecile's roof fifteen years ago, which suggests they maintained some kind of relationship long after Coram House closed. And, even if Sister Cecile was abusive herself, if she put a stop to Father Foster, that could easily explain Rooney's devotion to her.

But love doesn't negate violence. Plenty of people murder in a fit of rage or passion. But then there's that other word right above. *Canoe.* If Rooney knew her habits, was waiting in the woods, then it was planned. I look down at the page to see that I've drawn a circle around the word *motive*, over and over again, so that the ink is bleeding through the paper. That same headache from yesterday thrums behind my eyes. I get up to refill my coffee.

Maybe I'm looking at this from the wrong angle. Maybe I need to search for the connection points instead—the places where their stories collide. In one corner of the page, I write *Father Foster.* In another corner, I write *Tommy.* Then, after a long pause, I write one more name. *Alex Kelley.* Because, as far as I can tell, the only thing that's changed in the last month is me. Or maybe none of this has anything to do with Tommy or me or even with Coram House and I'm trying to force puzzle pieces together because I want them to fit. In a fit of pique, I throw the pen across the room, where it leaves a single black dot on the white wall.

Feeling stupid, I fetch the pen. In the last blank corner, I write another name. *Bill Campbell.* He paid Rooney off to drop the case and he's employed him for decades. And, most damning, he looked scared when I mentioned Tommy's name. *Thomas Underwood*—that thrill again, of having a name, a picture to beat back the darkness. Maybe Bill knows more than he's saying. Or maybe he's the only lead I have left. Either way, I need to at least try to get more before I go to Parker with this. If Rooney is in jail, out of reach, then Bill's who I have left.

The paper before me is an insane constellation of lines and words. I tear it up and let the pieces fall onto the rug. Then I get dressed.

At eight, I pull into the driveway of Coram House. Thick clouds have muddied the bright morning sunshine, so the snow looks gray and dirty. Coram House is quiet. The windows reflect back the sky like mirrors. I drive around the side of the building and park in front of the office. The metal blinds are half open, showing light inside, but no movement.

I slam the car door louder than necessary to announce my presence. I'm lifting a hand to knock when the door opens. Bill Campbell stands, coat on, blinking at me in surprise. "Ms. Kelley," he says my name like a question.

"Please, call me Alex," I say, putting on my most winning smile. "I'm sorry to drop in on you so early, but I had a favor to ask."

He nods, but looks preoccupied, as if he didn't really hear me. "I was just on my way to walk the fences. We've had some trouble with vandalism."

"Oh, I'm sorry to hear that."

He waves a hand in the air. "Nothing serious. Just some kids and spray paint, that sort of thing."

Nothing like your foreman stealing equipment to dig up graves.

"I could come with you," I say. "We can talk and walk."

He blinks a few times and frowns, like he's trying to find a way to say no.

"It'll be quick, I promise. Where are you headed? This way?"

I point toward the skeleton of steel girders protruding out of the old brick building.

"Well, all right, then," he says. "I'm always happy for company."

Though he doesn't sound happy.

We follow the fence that stretches along the southern edge of the property, weaving through gravestones tilted at crazy angles. A limp angel sits on the roof of a mausoleum, her wings drooping like a bird waiting to be plucked. Bill slips his fingers through the chain-link fence and shakes it. Checking for holes, I guess. Or pretending to.

"You mentioned a favor?" he asks without looking at me.

"I was hoping to take some more pictures of the interior of Coram House," I say. Not a total lie. "We have some historical photos, but none of them are great. I think it would really help ground readers in a sense of the space."

"Oh," he says, sounding relieved. "Yes, of course. That would be fine."

I ask him some innocuous questions about the building itself. Does he know anything about the history of its construction? Not much. Did they find anything of historical interest during renovations? Some statues of the saints stored in the attic—given back to the church. But not much else, unless you count the mouse poop, he says with a laugh. His tone is light, but he still seems uneasy.

The fence ends in a stand of scrubby pines. "We're going to clear all this out," he says, motioning to the choking undergrowth. Glimmers of water are just visible between the branches. "So residents will have direct access to the water and then the trails at Rock Point just through there." He points to a gap in the fence, the woods beyond.

"Access through the graveyard?" I frown, surprised. I'd assumed they'd move the graves at some point.

Bill shrugs. "This piece of land is deeded over in perpetuity to the church, and it's too close to the water, so we couldn't build on it anyways. Besides, it's a piece of history. Think of it like a park."

So the new residents, the young professionals with lakeview balconies, they'll be looking down at the graves just as the children did.

"I met Xander Nilsson, by the way," I say.

He perks up. "Xander? He's a wonderful guy. A real visionary. He really understands what we're trying to do here."

I nod. "When did he get involved with the project?"

Bill thinks. "Two or three years ago? Once things really got going."

"Seems like the property sat here for a long time, then."

He looks at me, and I detect a hint of wariness. "We acquired the property ten years ago. But there's a lot that goes into a project of this scale. A lot of planning. Red tape."

I nod, but say nothing. We follow a path through the scrub and emerge at the water. The beach is narrow and rocky, covered in dirty piles of snow. Bill crouches down beside a hole filled with blackened chunks of wood and crushed beer cans. "Idiot kids," he mutters. The fire pit stands barely three feet from the side of the wooden boathouse. "They could have burned the whole thing down."

I scan the beach but the canoe is gone. "You put the boat away," I say, keeping my voice light. "Finally decided it was too cold?"

He looks distracted. "The police took it. You know, I didn't take it out once this summer. I thought my grandkids would use it but it just sat there on the beach."

I keep my tone nonchalant like the news hadn't sent something surging inside me. "The police took it?"

"To dust for Fred's fingerprints, I assume. I told them of course they'd find them. I'm the one who asked him to put the boat in the shed. Thanks to you, actually."

It sounds like an accusation.

"The day you noticed it from the window," he says. "I'd completely forgotten it was down here." He looks at me, coldly. Like my casual act isn't fooling anyone. "Why are you really here, Ms. Kelley?"

It's now or never. "Are you close with Fred?"

He frowns. But it's not consternation, it's confusion. This isn't the question he was expecting.

"What do you mean?"

"Well, you were at Coram House together as children. And you've employed him for—what—twenty years? Even after he wrecked your equipment, when he showed up drunk at a funeral, threatened a priest. I'm not sure most people would be so charitable."

Bill shrugs. "He's had a hard time of it. And I—well, I've been lucky. I'm in a position to be charitable, as you say."

It's a convincing portrait of a man carrying guilt for profiting when so many others suffered. Or it would be if I didn't know how ruthlessly he'd fought to make the case go away. We face off over the fire pit.

"Mr. Campbell," I say. "Did you pay Fred Rooney and others to drop the case?"

A curtain comes down over Bill's face. Gone is the affable, thoughtful expression. His eyes narrow and his mouth sets into a firm line. "I don't know what you're referring to, Ms. Kelley."

"Did you give people money so they'd drop the case against the church?"

Color creeps up Bill's neck. "I think we're done here."

But he doesn't leave. Maybe he expects me to blink first.

"They trusted you to be on their side," I say. "To have their best interests in mind."

"You talk about them like I'm not one of them," he snaps. "Do you think it would have been better to have the case drag on for decades? A case that we could never win? Or to take the money the church was offering and get on with our lives?"

Hatred washes over me. My mouth fills with the taste of metal. He's so smug, so sure it was the right thing to do because it's the thing he wanted to happen.

"If that's all, Ms. Kelley, I'd like to get on with my day," Bill says coldly. "I assume you can see yourself back to your car. And any other questions you have for me, you can send to my lawyer."

Bill turns and stands with his back to me, looking out at the water. I knew this is where we'd end up. I just wanted to see his face when he denied it. Because I can be sure of at least one thing now: he's a liar.

"Bill," I call.

He turns automatically at the sound of his name.

"I hear you're a good storyteller. That you have one about a monster that lives in the lake and hunts children."

I'm not sure why I say it. Maybe it's instinct. Or maybe I just want to ruffle his smooth surface. Either way, it works. Instantly, his cold anger is replaced by a look of terror so pure it stuns me. Then it's gone. Maybe for a single moment he remembered what it feels like to be a child here, alone and afraid.

"You have five minutes to get off my property," he says. His voice is so full of hate that I feel a spike of fear and, for the first time, think about how alone we are here. Then I turn my back on him and walk as quickly as I can up the path. Thorns grab at my jacket like sharp claws, trying to drag me back.

In the car, heat blasting, I wait to feel regret, but it doesn't come. Bill Campbell won't talk to me again. And I'll probably never get back inside Coram House, which gives me a pang. But I got what I came here for. Bill denied paying people off but there wasn't a flicker of surprise on his face. People always make that mistake—jumping straight to denial when confusion is the first reaction of true innocence.

So what do I do about Stedsan? The chances that Bill Campbell paid people off and Stedsan didn't know about it seem slim. So why bring me here to write this book? Why dig up the past at all?

Because you fucked up your last book. And because I happily signed a contract with an NDA giving him total control of the story. He can fire me and write it however he wants.

The answer feels like a gut punch.

He didn't bring me here in spite of my failure, but because of it. Because he knew I'd go along with whatever story he wanted to tell. *His legacy*, he'd said. Tiny pellets of snow patter on the windshield.

I can gather all the truth I want, but I can't do anything with it. But I know someone who can. Without giving myself a chance to second-guess it, I call Parker. When I hear a gruff hello, I'm lightheaded with relief. "Parker? It's Alex. Can we talk?"

"Alex, this isn't—"

"Look, I know this isn't a good time. But there are some things you need to know. It's about Rooney."

The line is silent for five seconds, then ten.

"All right. I get off at six. But dinner is on you."

The laugh that bursts out of me sounds unhinged. I think of Parker, standing outside my apartment in the snow. That strange current between us. It feels like a hundred years ago.

"Deal. Just tell me where to meet you."

He gives me the address of a Vietnamese restaurant near the station. By the time I pull back onto the road, the heat has been blasting long enough that my whole body feels warm, like I have a tiny sun glowing inside me.

21

The restaurant where I'm supposed to meet Parker is only a few blocks away from my apartment, so I decide to walk. The night is bitterly cold, the streets empty. Still, I pause beside the cemetery—the one I can see from my bedroom window. It looks smaller and sadder up close. The gravestones are overly shiny with laser-cut initials. There's no fence around the perimeter, so the snow is crisscrossed with footsteps and yellow patches of dog pee. It seems dirty and haphazard after Coram House's weeping angels and marble mausoleums.

Further down the block, a streetlight stands sentinel among dark warehouses. Somehow the small circle of light is worse than nothing at all. I feel uneasy walking alone, accustomed to the protection of streets bustling with people at all hours. It's an illusion, I know. Anyone can be violent. And plenty of people will stand by and watch.

At the intersection of two roads, I turn left onto North Winooski. All the roads here seem to be north this and south that, all named for the place you're going, not where you are now. The warehouses along this stretch have gotten a makeover—fresh paint and new windows, zinc washtub planters around patios.

The restaurant is straight ahead. EAT PHO orders a neon sign above the door. Tall black windows surround the booths like picture frames. One table is crowded with college kids, laughing and tipping back bottles of beer. A girl reaches her chopsticks across the table to steal a shrimp. At another table, an older couple sits, heads bent low over steaming bowls. And there, in the last booth, is Parker.

Two plastic menus sit on the table, but he's looking out the window. I wave, but he doesn't see me. It's dark and I'm too far away, whereas he's lit up on display. He's wearing jeans and a flannel shirt with the sleeves rolled up to his elbows. He looks terrible—black circles under his eyes and hollows under his cheekbones like he needs a good meal. But the relief I feel on seeing him is immediate and overwhelming. For a second, I actually sway with it. I need to tell someone about Karen and Bill and all of it.

A bell chimes as I open the door. The air inside is steamy and delicious—thick with the tang of lemongrass and fish sauce. A lanky guy with a shaved head and muscle tee sits behind the counter. A vine tattoo starts at his knuckles and winds up his arm, unfurling in a brilliant flower just below his shoulder. I point to the corner booth and he waves me ahead.

My reflection in the window must alert Parker as I approach the table because he turns to look at me. Something flickers across his face—sadness maybe—and I wonder what he was thinking about before I interrupted. He stands.

"Thanks for coming," I say, sliding into the booth across from him. He sits back down.

"To be honest," he says, "I'm glad you suggested it. It's been a while since I ate a meal anywhere besides my desk."

"Me too."

We exchange a smile. I'm aware of his knees, knocking against mine under the table. I study the menu. "So, what's good?"

"Everything."

Our server arrives—the same guy with the vine tattoo. I order a beer, but Parker shakes his head when I look at him. "On backup," he says and lifts his water like he's making a toast.

We talk about the food, about the snow, about nothing. It's nice to pretend that we're friends catching up over dinner. Parker seems more relaxed. Even the way he sits is different, arm stretched out along the back of the booth, running his fingers through his wet hair when a strand falls over one eye. But I feel the pull of why we're really here—the case, the past, Bill Campbell—all black holes exerting their own gravity.

"I think I found Tommy," I say, unable to keep the smile off my face. It feels so good to say it out loud, to someone who understands what it means.

He smiles back. "How?"

I tell him about the baptism records and then about my dinner at Xander's and the newspaper clipping, all the while feeling slightly ashamed, like I owe Parker an explanation.

"He wanted to apologize," I say, even though Parker didn't ask.

He makes a skeptical noise. "So what was he going to do with the photo anyways?"

I sigh. "He was going to use it for . . . historical flavor."

Parker laughs and, for once, it doesn't seem like he's trying to hold it in. But I feel a bubble of guilt at making Xander the butt of my joke. He was nice, he means well. Then again, the world is full of people who think good intentions give them a blank slate to do what they want.

The server arrives with my beer. It's cold and the bubbles make my nose fizz. As he turns away I see the vine tattoo isn't just a vine. A thin green viper winds its way through the greenery on his shoulder, its red tongue licking the dark stubble of his shaved neck. When I look back, Parker is studying me. I busy myself peeling the wrapper from my chopsticks, but I know it's time.

"I went to interview someone yesterday. Someone who was at Coram House as a child. She knew them all—Fred Rooney, Sarah Dale, Bill Campbell, and Tommy too."

Parker nods for me to go on but doesn't say anything.

"I wanted to know more about Rooney—about back then but also now. Why he might kill Jeannette Leroy after all these years."

Parker's frown sharpens, so I continue before he has a chance to reprimand me. "Look, I swear I'm not trying to meddle. I just—I think we're missing something, that it's all connected somehow. What happened to Tommy in the boat, Sarah Dale's testimony, Sister Cecile, Rooney, and me. I need to understand how."

Parker nods, but he looks unhappy. "And did you—learn how they're connected?"

"No," I admit. "But from what she said—I'm worried that I got it all wrong, Parker. I assumed Rooney killed Sister Cecile to cover his tracks. Or for revenge. Or, I don't know, some combination of the two."

"And now?"

"My source confirmed that Sister Cecile put a stop to Father Foster's sexual abuse. And she told me that Fred loved Sister Cecile, was loyal to her, even now."

Parker gives me a skeptical look. "You know, you worked pretty hard to get us to look at Rooney as a suspect. I'm not saying it's up to you we arrested him. I'm just trying to understand. Are you saying you think he didn't do it after all? Because he loved her?"

He doesn't sound angry. Worse. There's something closed off in his voice. Our food arrives—a steaming pile of vermicelli noodles topped with grilled pork, and fish in a clay pot smelling of garlic and caramel. It smells delicious, but I don't want any of it.

"No," I say. "Well, I don't know. Doesn't it bother you—that we don't know why he killed her?"

Parker shrugs. "Motive is just a story. It doesn't matter if you can prove someone committed a crime."

I taste blood. I've chewed the inside of my cheek to shreds. Snow flutters against the window, melting as it makes contact with the glass. He's right, of course. Technically, motive doesn't matter. But how can you ever be sure, really sure, what happened if you don't understand the why of it?

"Look," I say, ready for a change of subject. "This isn't the only reason I asked you here."

Parker uses his chopsticks to pick up a piece of glistening pork. "There's more?"

I tell him what Karen said about Bill Campbell, how he paid people off so they'd settle the case. How Rooney used to brag about getting the largest slice of the pie. My suspicion that there might be more to Bill's acquisition of the Coram House property—that maybe Rooney knew it and was using that information to hold power over him.

Parker is sitting up straight now, arms crossed over his chest, the easiness from before gone. I might as well have shoved an iron rod up his back.

"So you think Bill Campbell is crooked," he says. "Does this source have proof that he paid people off?"

I wonder if I should tell him about my conversation with Bill earlier today but decide against it. It's not like I learned anything new. I shake my head.

"No proof. And my source signed an NDA, so I'm not sure if she'd be willing to testify more officially."

"What does Alan say about it?"

I was afraid he'd ask that. I shrug. "Father Aubry said something about how Bill and Alan worked together on the settlement. I wasn't sure what to think of it. I mean, Alan was their lawyer, so of course he was involved. But now I'm wondering if there's more to it."

I think of the words Father Aubry used: *they were instrumental to the plan.*

Parker lets out a low whistle. "Alan too, huh?"

I tear my chopstick wrapper into tiny pieces until the table is littered with confetti. "I don't know, Parker. That's the thing—I don't know who did what or if any of this is even true."

My voice cracks and, to my deep embarrassment, I feel tears gather at the back of my throat. I pick up my chopsticks and chase slippery noodles around my plate, so I don't have to meet his eyes.

"Alex."

I wipe my nose with a napkin and look up. Parker is sitting with his elbows on the table, looking at me. "Thank you for sharing this," he says.

"But?"

"But this isn't your job. There's a whole police department out there working on this case."

"I know that, I—"

"If any of this—Rooney, Campbell, these bribes—is connected to a murder, we're going to find out. But what about this boy who drowned? No one else is looking at him."

"I can't prove anything."

"That's not what I'm saying, Alex. You don't need proof. You're not here to solve some fifty-year-old crime. You're here to tell their story.

To make people—care. You have his name, his picture—what are you waiting for?"

The words fall on me like a blow. He thinks I'm failing them. But how can I make sense of the past if I can't figure out how it's connected to the present?

"Coram House is at the center of this all. What happened then and now. I can't understand any of it until I know how."

Parker sighs and rubs his eyes. I recognize his expression—frustration, disappointment, and, the one that cuts deepest, resignation. He glances down at his watch. I feel desperate to keep him there, to explain that I haven't abandoned the book. That it's the opposite. My greatest fear is failing those kids, but it seems like every road leads me back to the body of Jeannette Leroy in the water.

"It doesn't matter," he says. "We've got CCTV footage from the construction site that puts Fred Rooney's car there at six a.m. the morning Jeannette Leroy was killed. His prints are all over the canoe."

My heart lifts—he must have talked to Xander.

"We also found an empty bottle near the cove where you discovered her body. It tested positive for his DNA. His prints are also all over the machinery used to dig up the grave, and he's refusing to give an alibi for either time period. He's in custody now, waiting on bail. Fred Rooney is going to jail, and you helped put him there. This is a happy ending, okay?"

I nod and try to summon some kind of happiness or at least satisfaction, but it won't come.

Parker's phone rings. He frowns down at the screen. "Parker," he answers in a clipped tone. The voice on the other end is speaking quickly. Parker nods along. "Right," he says. "I'll be there in fifteen."

He hangs up. For a second, he stares down at the dark screen. It's something bad. I can see it on his face. "What is it?" I ask.

"They just released Fred Rooney."

The clinking of silverware, the laughter, all the sounds of the restaurant disappear, as if someone turned down the volume. "What do you mean, released him?"

"He has an alibi."

"But the fingerprints, his car—you just said—"

"Yeah, I did. Turns out he was at a bar that night. Took a friend's car and smashed it up pretty good. He ended up in the ER down in Middlebury, but ducked out before officers arrived. He never gave his name so they couldn't track him down. His car was parked at the construction site all night."

A car accident. I think of the bandage on his face the day I went to see him—the day after Jeannette Leroy's death. The scratches all over his hands.

"So he refused to give his alibi for a murder because he didn't want a DUI?"

Parker slowly shakes his head. "Honestly? I don't think he cares about the DUI. I think he was just waiting until the last minute to make us look bad. Which we do."

"And they're sure about the timeline?"

He shrugs. "They're still trying to nail down security footage from the hospital to get an exact time stamp. But we have the doctor who stitched him up. So yeah. It's solid."

I let out a long slow breath. "Jesus, Parker. I-I'm sorry."

I feel responsible. I'm the one who pushed him to look at Rooney.

He shakes his head, grim. "Like I said before. Not your fault. It's on us."

"Are you allowed to be telling me any of this?"

His mouth hitches up at one side. "Do you care?" He stands. "I have to go in."

"Right," I say. "Of course."

Parker fumbles in his pocket for his wallet.

"Stop," I say. "It's on me, remember?"

For a second, he looks like he's going to protest. Then he pulls on his coat. "All right. Thanks for dinner." He turns to go, then stops. "And I'll look into what you said—about Bill, the money. Okay?"

I nod. "Thanks." I want more, but at this point I should be grateful he's even speaking to me.

Parker weaves between the tables and steps outside into the night. He walks south, toward the police station. Snow settles on the shoulders of his parka until it looks like there's some furry white creature curled up there. Then he's gone.

My head is spinning. I'd been so sure there was someone else in the woods that day that I latched on to Rooney and his connection to Sister Cecile. Now this is the second time in my life someone's been arrested for a murder they didn't commit. Because of me. I feel a familiar tightness in my chest. Maybe there was no one in the woods that day. Maybe the canoe is just a coincidence. Maybe that's been the answer all along—I just didn't want to admit it.

The noodles slither around my plate, cold and slimy. The server comes by and I hand him my credit card, nod when he asks if I'm done.

I can't eat anymore. Because it's not just Rooney's life I ruined. There's Parker too. He says he doesn't blame me, but maybe he should. I pushed him to look at Rooney. And now, what is my mistake going to cost him? The server reappears with the receipt and all the untouched food, neatly packed into Styrofoam containers. I smile and thank him, even though I don't want any of it.

The dark streets are so quiet that it feels much later than eight. I'm on edge, jumping at every shadow, at the sound of snowflakes rustling the plastic bag of leftovers. But what am I afraid of exactly? I imagine Rooney waiting in an alley, out for revenge, and immediately feel stupid.

From half a block away, I spot a box at my front door. When I get closer, I see it's a wooden crate, like something that belongs in an antique store. The card, thick as a wedding invitation, has my name on it.

Alex—I know you told me to stop apologizing, but sorry. Again. Thanks for coming. I hope we can do it again. Anyways, here's some wine. From NAPA!! —Xander

Xander added a tiny curve under the exclamation points, turning them into a smiley face. My stomach twists—guilt at making fun of him at dinner.

I try to lift the crate, but it's too heavy. Somehow I manage to get the door open and wrestle it into the vestibule, but there's no way I'm getting it up the stairs without dismantling it with a crowbar first. I feel a surge of anger at Xander, at people who give without stopping to think whether they're sending a gift or just one more burden.

Upstairs, I make sure all the windows are locked, including the brand-new latch on the kitchen window. The curtains in my bedroom are half open, so a wedge of light falls across my pillow. I pull them shut. Then I go back into the kitchen and check the deadbolt again. I feel stupid and paranoid. I bet Karen doesn't even lock her doors. Though, to be fair, she probably has a shotgun under her bed.

My phone vibrates in my pocket. The caller ID shows a local number. I don't know who would be calling me this late, but I answer.

"Hello?" I answer. "Alex Kelley."

Silence on the other end. Then I hear the slow exhale of breath. Someone smoking.

"Hey there, writer."

My stomach drops. I lean my back against the door and slide down until I'm sitting. The floor is freezing.

"Mr. Rooney. How can I help you?"

He laughs. "Oh, so now you're looking to help me, are you?"

His voice is dripping with sarcasm, but he doesn't sound angry.

"Listen, I don't know if your cop boyfriend told you, but they let me go. I got what they call an alibi."

"All right," I say, but he continues as if he didn't hear me.

"There are some things you should know."

My heart thumps. He's probably playing me, almost definitely playing me. "Is this about Tommy?"

"Jesus," he snaps, so loud I flinch. Then he sighs. "A lot of shit happened back then. Why are you so obsessed with this one kid?"

He sounds more curious than angry now. The silence stretches out. He's waiting for an answer.

"They tried to erase him," I say. "Like he never existed."

"Yeah, well. Like I said, there are things you should know."

I take a deep breath, worried that he's going to hang up on me. "I can't pay you, Mr. Rooney. That hasn't changed."

"I know. We're past that. I've got other shit to think about."

Shit like what? I want to ask, but instead I wait. There's a quaver in his voice that wasn't there the last time we talked. He's desperate or—maybe I'm imagining it—but he sounds scared.

"Bill Campbell," Rooney says. "He's not what you think."

"All right," I say, trying to keep my voice even. "Let's talk."

"Face-to-face," he says. "Tomorrow. My place."

Alarm flashes in my brain. Being alone with him is not a good idea. "Listen—"

"Calm down, writer. Nothing funny. I just need to talk to you like I said."

To my surprise, I believe him. "Okay," I say. "I'll come by your place in the morning. Around eight?"

"Fine," he says.

The line goes dead.

I climb into bed and pull the covers up to my chin. My heart gallops, every beat like hooves. It's fear, but not of Rooney, not attached to any particular person. It's like when you're a kid and you have to go to the bathroom, but don't want your bare ankles exposed to whatever is hiding under the bed. It's just adrenaline, I know. Maybe it always comes back to monsters in the dark. Real or imagined.

I close my eyes. The lake monster floats just beneath the surface of the water. A long neck rises from a smooth, gray back. Orange eyes glow in the murky water. They fix on a skinny pair of legs treading water in the shallows. The monster's body undulates like a snake across the bottom, stirring up swirls of mud. It strikes silently.

I wonder if that was Tommy's last thought as he slipped below the surface. The tug of gravity must have felt like a monster, jaws clasped around his ankles, pulling him down into the deep. I lie there for hours, exhausted, brain spinning, sure I'll never sleep again. But sleep pulls me under eventually. And I wonder what monsters I'll dream about.

22

The fields of snow flanking the highway glow gold with sunrise, but the forested edges are still black, shadows stuck to the trees like cobwebs. I didn't tell anyone I'm going to see Rooney. I sat at the table with Parker's number pulled up on my phone, but couldn't hit call. I knew he'd tell me that it's stupid to go alone, might even insist on coming. He'd be right. But I heard the desperation in Rooney's voice. This time, he has something to say, and he wants to say it to me alone. So I wrote a note explaining where I'm going and why—just in case. Sitting there in the middle of the table, it looked like a suicide note.

On the drive, I play the recording from Karen's interview. I'd only meant to review the section where she talks about Bill and Rooney, to make sure there's nothing I missed. But her voice feels like history is playing out in front of me. The opposite of a black-and-white photograph in a dusty box. I'm riveted. I can't turn it off. I wonder if I should include parts of the depositions in the book—to let the children of Coram House speak for themselves. Maybe entire sections interspersed between chapters. I feel the tiny thrill of a puzzle piece clicking into place.

In college, I took a writing class with a famous investigative journalist. He had a Pulitzer and a dozen bestselling books, which entitled him to make all sorts of pronouncements about what writing should or shouldn't be. At the time, I took notes like it was a recipe for success. Now, I think most of it was garbage. He had talent and he worked hard and was lucky. Whether or not he stood at his typewriter barefoot for four hours a day like Hemingway was beside the point.

One thing he said stuck. *You have to write for an audience of one*, he said. *All the other people you hope will read your book don't matter. You're writing only for this one person.* Now, I wonder if that's what made me feel so directionless after Adam died. He was my one. And who is my one now? Tommy would be the easy answer. The lost boy, found. But it's not his voice I hear in my head; it's Sarah Dale. Sarah, who spoke the truth and was dismissed again and again. Locked in a cabinet. Silenced.

The turnoff to Rooney's comes sooner than I remember, and I slam on the brakes. The car skids on a patch of ice as I swing left. It's just a small skid—I correct it easily—but still my hands are shaking by the time I pull into Rooney's driveway. A fine layer of snow covers his black pickup. But the driveway itself is freshly plowed and the walkway to the front door is already scraped clean of snow. I turn off the engine. My stomach twists, but it's not fear—it's anticipation. I get out.

The morning is still. A quiet cabin in the woods. Snow layered on the roof like cotton batting. I step onto the porch, and knock—three raps that echo inside the house. My phone says quarter past eight. I wait for footsteps or a gravelly voice telling me to hang on a second, but it doesn't come. I knock again, louder this time. He's probably just in the bathroom. And yet, an alarm is going off in my brain.

The snow on Rooney's truck suggests he hasn't gone anywhere since the snow fell overnight. Maybe he just overslept. A flash of movement in the front window sends my heart into my throat. But it's nothing, just the flutter of a curtain. And that's when I realize what's wrong. The window is wide open.

The curtain moves again, caught by a current of air. And it's not just the one window. All four windows along the front of the house are open.

My hand goes to the doorknob, somehow knowing that it will be unlocked even before it turns under my hand. The door swings open with a loud creak.

"Hello?" I step inside. The floorboards groan. It's freezing inside.

Straight ahead a sliding door leads onto a snow-covered deck. To the left, the kitchen. Bare tile floors and empty counters. It looks like no one has ever cooked a meal. I cross back into the front hall and then to the living room. This room, at least, looks lived in. The faded red couch bears an indent in one cushion, as if someone just got up. The television is on, but muted. A bottle of beer lays on its side on the rug, a dark stain spreading outward from its mouth. I turn to the dark hallway beyond.

"Hello?" I call again.

The nearest door is half open, revealing the foot of a bed. I don't want to go in there, don't want to smell Rooney's bedroom or see the twist of sheets on his unmade bed. But the alarm in my brain is screaming now. Something is wrong.

I force myself to take three steps forward, counting each one. The door opens easily under my fingertips. A flash of movement makes blood thud in my ears, but it's just another open window above the bed. More curtains blowing. Who would have expected a sixty-something bachelor to have so many damn curtains. I'm about to retreat into the hall when I see something that makes me stop.

On the far side of the rumpled bed, a pile of clothes sits on a chair—pants, shirt, and a sweatshirt folded on top. On the floor, peeking out from behind the bed skirt, is a sock. An icy prickle of sweat trickles down my armpits. Not a limp twist of fabric. A sock on a foot.

My legs take a step forward and then another. It's as if someone else is driving my body. All along, I'm staring at that sock. At the worn patch on the bottom where the flesh peeks through. As I round the bed, I see the ribbed top of the sock, then a few inches of smooth calf, hairless and speckled with age.

Rooney lies on the floor in boxers and socks, arms and legs splayed out as if he fell that way and stayed put. His skin has the bluish tinge of someone in a fairy tale, frozen by the ice queen. Cloudy eyes stare up at the ceiling. Along his neck, a thin red line. Cut or bruise, I can't tell. But there's no blood. I swallow down the bile rising in my throat.

I back away—*bang*—straight into something. My scream comes out as a squeak. But it's just the bathroom door. I look back. Rooney hasn't moved.

Then I'm stumbling into the hallway, running so the rug slips and I slam into the wall. I stagger outside, down the front walkway, and wrench open the door of my car. I fall into the driver's seat and lock the doors.

For a mad second I wonder if I can just leave. Drive away. Let someone else find him. He's blue. It's not like anyone can do anything. And the last thing I need is for the police to find me here with another body barely a week after the first one.

I try to put the key into the ignition but my hands are shaking too hard. My breathing is ragged. There's no air in the car.

"Fuck," I yell at no one.

I can't leave. I know I can't leave.

I lean back against the headrest and wait for my lungs to fill. Then I dial 911 and go through it all again. Tell the operator where I am, how the body looked. *You're getting good at this*, says a voice in my head. The operator asks me to stay on the line until help arrives, but I hang up.

Rooney is dead. I probe to see how I feel. It's like pressing my tongue against a sore tooth. When the pain comes it's acute, but satisfying too. I don't feel sad exactly. The world is probably better off without Fred Rooney. But with Sarah Dale and Jeannette Leroy dead, he was my last chance to learn what really happened the day Tommy drowned. And he wanted to talk. I was so goddamn close. A door into Coram House, into the past, has closed forever just when I was about to peek through.

Then there's that red line on his neck. What was that—a cut or bruise? Maybe he just died of a heart attack. Or maybe there's another option.

Rooney is dead and someone killed him.

I let this sit for a second.

All this time, I thought we were hunting whoever killed Jeannette Leroy. That they were the rabbit, going to ground as we got closer. But what if I had it wrong? If whoever killed Jeannette Leroy came back to kill Rooney too, that changes everything. It means they've always been the hunter, not us.

It means they're real. And they're still out there.

Sarah Dale

Sarah Dale: Did you know that mold grows roots? So even if you scrape it off the surface of a piece of bread, you're too late. Invisible roots have already grown all the way through.

Alan Stedsan: I'm not sure I—

SD: I wonder if the House was like that. You leave. You start a new life. You think you'll be able to wipe it all away, but it's already too late. It's already inside you.

AS: Whatever happened back then, it's not your fault.

SD: Maybe. But it doesn't change a thing.

AS: Ms. Dale—

SD: Sometimes, I wonder if sadness can spread. Like spores. If it's not just us—the ones who were at the House. Maybe we're infecting everyone around us.

PART 5

23

I stay in the car, heat blasting, until I hear sirens. When the police turn into Rooney's driveway, I'm waiting on the front walkway. Two officers climb out of a car marked RICHMOND POLICE—both men past the middle part of middle age. One gives off Aryan Nation vibes with his cropped blond hair and blue eyes. The other is taller with a paunch and a mustache like a furry caterpillar. Both men rest one hand on the butt of their gun.

"You the one who called this in, ma'am?" Paunch calls in my direction.

I nod, or try to, but I'm shivering too hard. "He's inside," I say, gritting my teeth to keep them from chattering. "Fred Rooney. He's dead."

"You touch the body?" Blue Eyes barks.

I shake my head, thinking of the bluish tinge of his skin. I didn't need to touch him to know he was dead. "No. He's in the bedroom."

"There's an ambulance on the way," says Paunch.

Blue Eyes unbuckles his holster. The gun is like a pit bull—ugly and threatening, even at rest. "Wait here," he says. The officers go inside.

More sirens. An ambulance pulls into the driveway. Two medics get out and jog into the house with their orange bags. *Don't rush*, I want to tell them. *There's no point.*

The cold feels like it's inside me, leaking out. A car door slams. I turn to find Detective Garcia standing beside the door of another police car, dressed in her usual dark suit. No sign of Parker. Still, I'm surprised to feel a lift of relief. Now she can be the one to explain this tangled mess to the officers inside.

Detective Garcia's eyes flick over the scene, finally landing on me. Beyond a faint lift of her eyebrows, she exhibits no surprise. She has a good poker face. Just then the officers reappear and converge on her. Snippets of conversation drift over. *Scene is clear. DOA.*

When the group disperses, Garcia walks toward me. Her jacket is open at the collar, and I notice a smudge of pink on her shirt, as if she tried to wipe away a dollop of ketchup.

"Ms. Kelley," she says, "I'm getting used to finding you at crime scenes." I'm not sure whether to smile. It doesn't sound like a joke.

"Fred Rooney called me last night," I say. "I came by to interview him this morning."

Her gaze sharpens. "What time did he call?"

"Around nine p.m."

"Did he say what he wanted to discuss?"

I shrug. "Only that there are 'things I should know.' He wanted to talk to me about Bill Campbell. He said, 'Bill isn't what you think he is.' That was it."

"Do you know what he was referring to?"

I pause, wondering if Parker already shared what I told him last night at dinner—about Bill Campbell and the bribes. Maybe I got him into trouble and that's why he's not here.

"Maybe," I say, hedging. "I have some ideas—but I'm not sure if they're relevant."

Garcia stares at me. How is it she never seems to blink?

"All right," she says finally. "We can talk back at the station. It's freezing out here. Hold on a second."

She rejoins the knot of medics and police officers now gathered on the front porch. Another squad car shows up, tries to find a place to park in the driveway, then gives up and backs into the road. I resign myself to slowly freezing to death. An image of blowing curtains pops into my head. Then that angry red line on the loose skin of Fred Rooney's neck. My mouth fills with saliva. I swallow it down.

"Officer Davis will drive you back to the station."

Garcia is standing in front of me again, this time with Officer Paunch beside her. Where had they come from?

"I'll follow shortly," she says. "And another officer will bring your car."

I nod and hand over my keys, but before she can leave, I call out, "The windows were all open when I got here."

She pauses, turns back.

"Why would someone do that? Open all the windows."

She frowns at me. "Turn up the heat. She's turning blue."

"Sure thing," Paunch says and opens the passenger door of the cruiser.

He does indeed blast the heat the entire way back to Burlington, which makes me wish I'd given him a kinder nickname.

Turn up the heat.

I think of the groaning floorboards and Rooney's blue skin. Whoever opened the windows was trying to turn *down* the heat. But why? To buy more time before someone discovered the body? If I hadn't been there, I wonder how long until someone would have noticed Rooney missing.

By the time we arrive at the station, I've finally stopped shivering, but feel wrung out. In the lobby, Bev sits at her desk in a plain black sweater. It feels like a bad sign. "They're waiting for you," she says. "Go right on in."

Paunch holds open the glass door. A few officers sit behind desks doing paperwork. The room smells stale—like old coffee and unwashed bodies. Parker's desk is empty. No mugs. No pens littering the surface. I scan the room, but don't see him anywhere.

"Alex. Hi, how are you doing?"

Officer Washington has traded her uniform for jeans and a fluffy pink sweater. It should look ridiculous—Officer Barbie—but instead it highlights the smoothness of her skin and the flecks of gold in her braids. Her smile is wide and warm. Right now, I want to take a bath in it.

"How are you holding up?" she asks. "Come on, let's find a room. Technically, I just got off duty, but we're short-staffed. I'll keep you company until Detective Garcia arrives."

I turn to thank Paunch for the ride, but he's already gone.

Once again, I drag myself down the hallway to the interview rooms, feeling like someone stuffed my boots with rocks. Officer Washington opens the door at the end of the hallway. The room looks the same as the others—the same plastic chairs and generic art. But this one has a huge window that looks out onto the lake. The VIP room. Today, the ice is streaked white and gray, like an expensive marble countertop.

"Can I get you a cup of coffee?" she asks.

I nod, grateful, and sink into the nearest chair.

Crows gather in the tree just outside the window. One lets out a guttural cry as it lands, then another and another, until the tree is a mad cacophony of flapping and jostling.

Rooney died at home. Rooney was murdered.

Jeannette Leroy slipped and fell. Sister Cecile had her head smashed in with a rock.

Tommy ran away. Tommy drowned.

Some or all of their deaths were an accident. Or they weren't. The thread connecting them is meaningful—or not. It all depends on what angle you look from. What story you want to believe.

One afternoon, when I was in Maine working on what would become *The Isle*, I stood on shore and watched black clouds roll toward me. I could actually feel the pressure building. That sense of electricity—that something was about to happen—that's what I feel now. The difference is, this time it's coming from inside me.

Since I got here, I've told myself that I'm the outsider looking in. That I'm impartial, a reporter. That it's not my story. But it's not true anymore. I don't know when that changed exactly. Maybe it was when I heard that scream in the woods. Maybe it was finding Rooney's body this morning. Or maybe the moment came before. The first time I read Sarah Dale's deposition. Now it's my story too.

Officer Washington reappears with a paper cup and tells me Detective Garcia is on her way. I'm about to ask where Parker is, but her phone rings and she ducks into the hallway. I watch the crows. For a while they flap and caw, adding more to their numbers. Then, all at once, they go quiet. It's eerie. A waiting kind of silence.

I hold my breath.

One crow lifts into the air. Then a hundred other silent shadows fill the sky. By the time Garcia comes in, the tree is empty.

"Thanks for your patience," she says, taking the seat across from me. Stray hairs poke out of her bun like spikes. She's unraveling.

There's a knock and the door opens. Office Washington holds out a folder. "The rest of the files just came in."

"Thank you," says Garcia, flipping it open. "You should go home."

"Can I get you anything, Alex?" Officer Washington asks. "Water? More coffee?"

"No," I say. "Thank you." I'm already jittery.

Officer Washington gives me a smile and then shuts the door.

"All right, Alex," says Garcia. "Let's get started."

I take a deep breath and walk her through everything again. How Rooney called me last night. How he seemed different—scared, like he'd lost his bluster. How I'd gone out to meet him this morning and found him like that. Garcia nods along, occasionally taking notes.

"That mark on his neck," I say. "Was that how he was killed?"

She looks up. I brace myself for her to be annoyed, but she looks thoughtful.

"His body is with the coroner, waiting final determination on the cause of death."

I think she's going to leave it at that, but she sighs and tucks a few loose hairs behind her ears. "But it's looking that way," she says.

Her eyes wander to the window like there might be some critical piece of information she missed out there, trapped beneath the ice. Then, as if making a decision, she slides the folder across the table.

"Alex, the truth is, I was going to ask you to come in today, even before all this." Her finger rests lightly on the folder, holding it in front of me, but closed. "I'd like to discuss the allegations you made against Bill Campbell."

My throat feels dry. "Allegations?"

"That he bribed certain participants in a trial that was settled out of court in 1993."

"Look, I didn't make any allegations," I say. "I reported information that I uncovered during an interview. For my book. Because I thought it might be relevant."

Garcia takes her finger off the folder and waits. I want to leave it there, refuse to play this game. But I can't. And she knows it. I open the folder. Inside are pages of bank statements with a few rows highlighted.

"When we arrested Mr. Rooney, we pulled his financials," Garcia says. "He has a series of unexplained deposits going back over the last decade—around ten thousand dollars a year. Together they add up to over a hundred thousand dollars."

"Over the last decade," I say. "But the case was settled over twenty years ago."

She nods. "We've requested the documentation going further back but don't have it yet. Most of it's not electronic, so it may take a few days."

I think of what Karen said about the bribe money. "It's a lot more money than I would have expected," I say, carefully, "based on what my interview subject said about Bill Campbell. And the timing doesn't fit."

Garcia nods. "That's what I think too. But we have to check it out." She leans forward. "Mr. Rooney was into some nasty stuff. Mostly opioids. A little dealing, a little using. The money could be from a number of sources."

It doesn't add up. Annual deposits don't sound like drug money to me. It sounds more like a salary.

"This has been helpful," Garcia says abruptly. "Thank you for coming in."

She closes the folder and then, as if it's an afterthought, she adds, "Oh, and could you put us in touch with your interview subject? It sounds like they might be able to shed some more light on this."

I pause. Of course. This is what she's been angling for. My stomach sinks. On the one hand, Karen was happy to have me use her interview in the book. But she's angry. I'm not sure she fully considered the consequences of accusing a person, especially someone as well connected as Bill Campbell, of bribery.

"I'll have to talk to them first," I say.

"Look," Garcia says, her tone friendly as a knife in its sheath. "I understand you have to protect your sources. But this is a murder investigation."

I almost laugh. I don't even know which case she's referring to anymore. Which body. I open my mouth, but then shut it again. I can see the look of betrayal on Karen's face when the police show up at her door without warning. No. She trusted me with her story.

"I understand that," I say. "Which is why I'll call my source as soon as I leave and urge them to get in touch with you."

Garcia sighs loudly. "Is there anything else you learned during the course of your interview that might be relevant? Anything at all?" There's a hint of desperation in her voice.

"I don't know," I say. "I haven't transcribed the interview yet, but I can do that today. Right after this. I'll redact the name and email you a copy."

Garcia looks surprised. "That would be very helpful. Thank you." She glances at her watch. "Sorry to rush you, but I have a call in five minutes. Let me walk you out."

She sweeps the folder and notebook into her hand. We stand to go, but she pauses with her hand on the knob and turns back to me. "Alex, I'd appreciate it if you'd give the investigation some space."

She doesn't sound angry this time, just exhausted.

"I never stopped trying," I say.

She nods, but doesn't look convinced.

Garcia walks me to the front desk where Bev hands over my car keys. "Stay warm out there, honey," she says. "They say a big storm's rolling in tomorrow."

"Thanks," I say. The sliding doors open and spit me into the cold, but I don't feel a thing.

Snow crunches underfoot as I walk toward the parking lot. No one's plowed the sidewalks yet. My little gray car is parked on the far side, waiting like an old friend.

"Alex," calls a voice behind me. My stomach lifts like I'm in a plane that's just dipped in midair.

Parker is dressed in his dark blue uniform. "I was off this morning," he says. "They sent me home—too many hours this month. I just heard what happened. You okay?"

I feel hot and cold at once, as if I've touched a live wire. "What the hell, Parker?"

He looks as surprised as if I'd slapped him, but I'm so angry I don't care. "I'm in there and Garcia starts going on about the 'allegations' I've made against Bill Campbell. What did you say to her?"

"I had to tell her about the money, Alex."

"But did you have to make it sound like I was on a witch hunt? No wonder she thinks I'm some psycho spotlight hound."

Absurdly, tears burn the back of my throat. Parker looks away, which gives me a chance to really look at him. The circles under his eyes are so dark they look like bruises. I try to harden myself against it, but just like that, my anger is gone. Two dead bodies. A hundred thousand dollars of unexplained deposits. The thankless balancing act of trying to do his job and help me. However hard the last few weeks have been on me—he hasn't gotten off unscathed.

"Look, I'm sorry," I say quietly. "I know you had to tell her."

Parker turns back to me. There's an intensity to his gaze that wasn't there before. "I won't pretend I'm sorry Rooney's dead," he says. "But I am sorry that you were the one who found him."

His voice is thick. I wonder if he also has the feeling of being trapped in a whirlpool—going around and around, pulled down no matter what he does. He clenches his jaw like there's something else he wants to say. I step closer.

"What?" I ask, but my voice is barely louder than a whisper.

Our eyes lock and we stand like that for a second, almost but not quite close enough to touch. That feeling comes again, of pressure building.

Then Parker clears his throat and takes a step back. "Just—be careful out there, okay? Give this all some space."

I laugh, but it tastes bitter. "Garcia said the same thing five minutes ago."

"Alex."

"I have to go."

I turn away and fumble in my pocket for the keys. Behind me, his footsteps crunch away over the ice. When I turn back, he's halfway across the parking lot. I want to shout for him to wait, but I don't have anything else to say. I just don't want him to go yet. I'm like a child who wants to yell and beat my fists and be comforted all at once. The station doors open and swallow him.

Forget the car. Walk. I need to walk. I cross Battery Park, and then follow the street as it slants downhill. At the bottom, I pass a cluster of stores. Two coffee shops and a vintage clothing store with a glossy, headless mannequin in the window. All the while, my brain is spinning. *What the hell were those deposits in Rooney's account?* They could have been drug money like Garcia said. But why would she bring it up unless she suspected otherwise? I have all these puzzle pieces, but no matter how I put them together, nothing quite fits. It makes me want to scream.

The sidewalk ends at the rail yard, a huge expanse of dirt with a maze of train tracks crossing in every direction. There must be a method to it, but it looks like chaos. I turn right, into the marina's parking lot, and walk until I reach the pier. It's empty, except for a bench at the end and some kind of sculpture—an undulating line of green copper.

At the end of the pier, I stop and look out at the harbor. The ice isn't whole, but made of many pieces that fit together like the shards of a shattered mirror. Seagulls nap on the frozen surface, heads tucked under their wings. It's perfectly still until I look closer. The gulls are bobbing gently up and down with the movement of the ice. Indigo water gushes up from a crack between the floes like blood pumping from an alien heart. It's not really solid. It's just an illusion.

I picture Fred Rooney paddling the canoe around the point, pulling himself up onto the icy rocks. Hiding among the trees in wait for Sister Cecile's footsteps in the snow. But that never happened. He had an alibi. Drunk in the ER. The figure slowly changes shape. Instead of Fred Rooney's flannel shirt and worn boots, I see a black cashmere coat, leather dress shoes, Bill Campbell's face.

Bill bribed people to drop the case more than twenty years ago. What if those deposits are also from him? He could have kept paying Rooney, either to keep him quiet about the hush money or some other shady dealing. He paid him and kept paying him. But what changed?

Then, with a sinking feeling, I know.

I showed up, and Rooney saw an opportunity. If I wouldn't pay him for the story, maybe he could squeeze more money out of Bill in exchange for keeping his mouth shut. Maybe none of this was ever about Tommy or about Coram House at all, at least not directly. Money is the oldest motive in the books. And I'd missed it.

Admittedly, it was hard to imagine Bill Campbell crouched in the bushes or—what—strangling Rooney with a rope? But isn't that what people always say when their neighbor turns out to be a killer? *He was the nicest guy. Salt of the earth.* Bill has already proven the lengths he'll go to get what he wants. Maybe murder is just one step beyond bribery. Or maybe I've totally lost my mind. Either way, I'm not going to find the answer here, staring at the ice while my toes freeze.

As I turn to go, the sculpture catches my eye. It's nearly as tall as I am, but its long, undulating form is curled up like a snake about to dive into the water. I run my hand over the surface, which is rough like fish scales rubbed the wrong way. Its face is something between a dragon and snake with tufts that could be ears or feathers, a long snout, and a forked tongue.

My phone vibrates in my pocket. I pull it out and see it's Xander. I'm tempted to let it go to voicemail or, better yet, drop my phone in the lake, but then I think of the case of wine and how I never called him back. "Hey," I answer too brightly.

"Alex. Hi—um—hey, how's it going? I wanted to see if you got the wine."

"I nearly broke my foot on it last night."

"Shit. I'm sorry, I—"

I wince. "Xander, it was a joke."

"Oh. Right."

"Sorry. Not a very good one. I'm tired. Thank you for the wine. And thank you again for dinner. Really. It was great. And sorry for grilling you about the canoe thing, but I think it was helpful."

"Great, great," he says in a way that makes me think he's not really listening. "Actually, I called to see if you wanted to come ice sailing."

"Ice sailing?" Confusion pushes other thoughts from my head. "Now?"

He laughs. "Tomorrow. It's been so cold, the bay is frozen solid. Perfect conditions."

I scrabble for an excuse. I need time to think—I have too much going on. "I heard there was a storm coming tomorrow."

"Not until tomorrow night," he says, dismissively. "We'll go in the afternoon. It'll be fun, I swear. Seriously, there's no feeling like it."

He goes on about the wind and the type of boat and what to wear and some strange alchemy turns his excitement into my own. Garcia asked me for space. Even Parker is trying to get rid of me. I've found two bodies in as many weeks. Maybe it would be good to step away from all this—just for a few hours.

"Okay," I find myself saying. "I'll come."

By the time I hang up, I've agreed to be at his house tomorrow at two. Before I can change my mind, I also text Stedsan and tell him I'm coming by his office tomorrow, that it's important. It's time to find out what he knows about Bill Campbell.

I brace for the long walk back up the hill to my car, but then a glint of metal catches my eye. At the base of the statue a small brass plaque is engraved with three words: *The Lake Monster*. I have an odd sensation—like vertigo—as if the lines between real and not real, past and present, are blurring together. It's like being a child and knowing there's no monster in the closet but believing it anyway. Knowing only that your fear is real.

24

The air smells cold. I never thought of cold having a smell until I came here. I hoist the laundry bag out of my trunk. The laundromat isn't the most glamorous place to spend the morning, but I'm meeting Stedsan at noon and don't have a single pair of clean pants left.

Plus, I'm exhausted beyond the help of coffee. My interview with Karen had been more than five hours of tape, which had taken me until three a.m. to transcribe and send to Detective Garcia. I'd also called Karen and left a message explaining the situation and asking her to call the police.

I fill up three different washing machines and then just sit, letting the mechanical hum and the smell of soap lull me into a kind of stupor until it's time to transfer the clothes to the dryer. The laundromat is empty. I guess other people have somewhere better to be on a Thursday morning.

Outside, a line of children waddles up the sidewalk, each stuffed into a snowsuit and holding on to a long red cord in one mittened hand. A teacher at the front of the line walks backward, murmuring encouragement. They pass in front of the window like a giant centipede.

My phone pings. Lola.

Sooooo? Champagne fountain yay or nay?

Another ping.

Your report is a week late. I start to type and then slide it back into my pocket. Another ping.

I can see you typing.

Ping.

Don't make me come up there.

I put my phone on silent. I'm lucky to have a friend who cares about me—I know that—but sometimes I just wish she could care about me from a distance. I should never have told her I was going to Xander's. *It was fine,* I type.

Fine bad?

No, it was fine. Just some other stuff going on right now.

Immediately, my phone rings.

"What kind of stuff?" Lola asks instead of hello.

I try not to sigh. *Oh, just a couple of dead bodies I haven't told you about.* "I'm at the laundromat, can we—"

"Alex, what's going on? You never call me, text me, anything. You don't want me to visit. And when you finally pick up, I get mono-syllables like a robot. Just . . . tell me what's going on."

I waver. I've drawn a line between what's happening here and my life out there—what's left of it. I'm not sure I'm ready to blur it. But I hear the worry in her voice.

"Lola, do you remember that boy I told you about, Tommy?"

"The kid who drowned."

I sigh and plunge in. I tell her about finding Sister Cecile's body in the water. About Rooney digging up the bones at the dump. About Bill Campbell bribing people. About going to Rooney's house to find out what he knew and finding his body instead. When I'm done, Lola is stunned into silence. For maybe the first time in history.

"This could be dangerous, right?" she says, finally. "You should come home. You can stay with us. Or don't come home, go sit on a beach somewhere. Leave it to the police."

"I can't just leave, Lola. I signed a contract—"

"Jesus, Alex. Fuck the contract. People are dying. This is real."

"Yeah, thanks. I found the bodies. I noticed."

"This isn't a joke."

I bristle, little hot spikes of fury pushing themselves out through my skin. "No shit, Lola."

"Is this about something else? Do you have feelings for this Xander guy?" Her voice softens, hopeful. It makes me furious.

"Jesus, Lola. I'm not staying for some guy. What's wrong with you?"

"Would that be so bad?" she yells into the phone, so loud I have to move it away from my ear. Her anger is so sudden and blistering it shocks me.

"I just want you to do something. To live. You're just—existing. You used to be sarcastic and funny and weird and now you're just like—this ghost. I mean, you're so afraid no one remembers this kid, but you won't even say Adam's name."

My throat tightens, so I can't speak. She doesn't understand how memories lose substance when you think about them too often. A favorite pair of jeans, worn thin at the knees. How it's safer to keep them all, good and bad, locked away. I feel itchy, like my skin is crawling with ants.

A bell jingles above the door and a woman comes inside, balancing a baby and a laundry bag. The baby's face is covered in a dried river of snot, which it wipes on her shoulder. The woman looks too tired to notice.

"I have to go," I say.

"Look, Alex, all I'm saying is that chasing your own happiness is not the same as giving up. And I think maybe you need to hear that."

The baby starts to cry. Loud, long wails that turn its face purple with rage.

"I have to go," I say again, my voice so tiny I wonder if she can hear it at all. I hang up before she can say anything else.

I feel wrung out. Lola doesn't understand. She can't—she's outside this. The binder is sitting there on my desk. It's all there. Everything I know about Coram House. I'm so close to the truth.

Tommy Underwood. Sarah Dale. Jeannette Leroy. Fred Rooney.

One by one, they've died and taken what they know with them. But still, I have the sense that everything I need to know is there in front of me if I could just see it.

My laundry is warm and smells of rain. I shove it back in the bag and imagine I'm taking my whole conversation with Lola, balling it up, and shoving it in there too.

After a quick trip back to the apartment to change, I head back out to meet Stedsan. The day is cold, but doesn't have the same bite as last week. There's a heaviness in the air that makes me think of Bev in her ominous black sweater. *A big storm's rolling in.* I lock the front door and head down the steps to my car.

"January thaw, eh?"

I look around, startled. My landlord is in the driveway, leaning on a snow shovel.

"Didn't mean to sneak up on you," he says. Then he scoops up a pile of slush and nods at it like its evidence. "January thaw. Always happens this time of year. A few days of warm weather blows in and then out again. Used to give my Eileen the most awful headaches."

"Oh," I say. "Good to know."

I wish him a good day and hurry to my car. Driving away, I glance in the rearview mirror and see him there, watching me as I go.

I drive to Stedsan's house, too fast, and park in front. His walkway hasn't been shoveled in a few days, so I wade through soupy brown slush to the front door. The mailbox is overflowing and marketing postcards litter the porch. I knock.

The door opens. "Come in, come in," Stedsan says, and steps back so I can pass. Then he locks the door behind me.

Inside, the air is hot and dry as an oven. Sweat prickles my skin in the time it takes to unzip my coat and peel it off.

"Can I get you anything?" Stedsan asks. "Coffee?"

"No," I say, stepping out of my boots. "Thanks."

He coughs into his elbow. "Apologies. I've been under the weather."

He does look terrible. His skin is sallow and his eyes are red and puffy.

"Sure you don't want any coffee?"

I shake my head.

"Well, I'd like some. Go ahead in. Be there in a moment."

He disappears in the direction of the kitchen. I notice his clothes are rumpled in the back, like he just woke up from a nap.

In the living room, I find the same subtle disarray. A stain on the coffee table drying to mud. Smudges on the sliding doors that frame the apple tree out in the garden. The way the branches are pruned to curve down makes the tree look hunched and twisted. Tortured to make the apples easier to reach.

A few minutes later, Stedsan reappears with two cups of coffee on a wooden tray. "In case you change your mind," he says. The couch sinks beneath his weight. "Well, now, your message made this meeting sound very urgent."

"Fred Rooney is dead."

It just comes out. Like there's so much building up inside me I needed a pressure release valve. Something passes across his face—not sadness, weariness maybe. He sighs deeply and looks out at his garden.

"You don't look surprised," I say.

"I'm not. Fred was old and sick and taking God knows what on top of that."

"He was murdered."

Stedsan looks at me sharply. "You're sure?"

An image flashes into my head of Rooney's age-spotted legs, his blue lips, the red welt on his neck. I nod.

"It could be a coincidence," he murmurs. I can almost see the gears turning in his head, thinking of Sister Cecile, trying to make sense of it. This is as off guard as I'll ever get him.

"Alan," I say. "Did you know that Bill Campbell paid people off to settle the case back in 1993?"

The silence stretches out. He sips his coffee and then nods at the other cup. "It's going cold."

"Alan—"

"Yes," he says. "I did."

Fury surges through me. My fingertips tingle with it. It feels good. "Why didn't you say something?"

"It's called attorney-client privilege, Alex," he says sharply. "If you haven't forgotten, Bill Campbell was my client too. At least at the beginning."

He places the cup carefully back on its saucer.

"And by the end, the case was such a goddamn mess that it didn't matter anymore. It was never going to go to court. We were never going to win. Settling was the only way. The only question was how much money we could wring out of them. I didn't see the harm in letting Bill add his money to the pot too."

"So Bill Campbell gets to make millions off developing the property while Karen Lafayette gets a down payment for a truck."

I expect him to meet my anger with his own—or at least with defensiveness—but he just shrugs. If anything, he looks sorry for me.

"That's the way these things work sometimes. Bill always did play the long game. Always knew what he wanted."

There's a note of admiration in Stedsan's voice that makes me sick.

"It was a different time, Alex. Everyone wanted the case to go away. Not just the church. No one wanted to think about it anymore."

"So why bring me here? Why write this book at all? You must have known I'd find out."

"Well, no," he says and gives me a sad smile. "I didn't. Based on your last book, I rather hoped you wouldn't."

I knew it was coming, but the sting is real. My last book. All the sloppy research and mistakes, but still a bestseller. He assumed I'd take only what I was given, wouldn't dig any deeper. I was perfect for the job. Still, he must have known I might find details that would make him look bad. So he needed a writer desperate enough to sign the NDA.

He sighs. "I'm retiring this year. I suppose the idea of this book—of leaving a legacy—was too tempting to pass up. And I had faith in your ability to write a great story. I still do."

If he's trying to mollify me, it's not working. "You failed them."

"Ask yourself how many of them were happy to settle the case," he says sharply. "To get what they could and have it go away. Vengeance doesn't pay the bills."

"How much did Bill offer them?"

"I don't know exactly." He holds up a hand when he sees I'm ready to interrupt. "Truly. I didn't want to. But, from what I inferred, I'd guess a few thousand here or there. The kind of money that could be easily passed off as a helping hand. A loan that never got repaid. That kind of thing."

I frown. That's a long ways from the hundred thousand dollars in

Fred Rooney's bank account. "And these were onetime payments? They weren't ongoing after the case?"

Stedsan's brows knit together. "I assume so. What possible reason would he have had to pay them after we settled?"

"What about Fred Rooney? Did Bill pay him?"

Stedsan snorts. "Fred was never one to let a dollar out of his grasp."

"They worked together for years. Why?"

Stedsan frowns. "You know, I've often wondered. Maybe Bill felt bad for him. But more likely he wanted someone around who wasn't afraid to get his hands dirty."

"Alan, why did you tell me not to look into Tommy's death?"

Alan swallows. "We could never prove anything. And Fred—he was my client too. I had to be careful about anything that hurt our case."

His face, which had been made of stone, starts to crack. Suddenly, he looks old.

"There was no proof, Alex. No body. Nothing except a witness who couldn't make out anyone's faces for sure on a day nearly twenty years before. It never would have held up in court and the church was happy enough to make the whole thing go away."

I sit there for a moment, stunned, as I realize what he's saying. "You used Tommy's death to negotiate the settlement."

"I used everything at my disposal," Stedsan snaps. Two spots of color burn in his otherwise pale face.

Tommy's story was more useful as a bargaining chip, so that's what he did. Bargained. That's why he tried to steer me away from the story. The optics for his legacy aren't great.

We sit for a moment, staring at each other. I want to scream. I want to pick up the glass paperweight off his fancy coffee table and throw it through the window. Tear the branches from the trees. I want to destroy something.

"I believed Sarah," he says, "but the case was over. My support wouldn't have changed anything."

I think of her obituary. Of what Bill Campbell said. *An old drunk.*

"It might have changed something for her," I say.

To that, he has nothing to say.

"And what happens if I include all this in the book?"

Stedsan smiles sadly and shakes his head. "No," he says. "I don't think so."

It's all there in the contract. His final editorial approval. The consequence of breaking my silence—money I don't have and legal problems I can't afford. The only thing I can do is quit, which we both know I'm not going to do. Suddenly I can't be in this house for one more second. I stand and stalk into the front hall, slam my feet into my boots.

Behind me, Stedsan clears his throat. "Do they have any theories about who killed Fred?"

Something in his tone makes me turn back to look at him sitting on the couch, legs crossed, sipping his coffee. Behind him, water drips from the icicles hanging from the roofline.

"You're the one who's friends with the chief of police," I say. "Ask him."

He sighs at me, as if I've disappointed him. My hand is on the doorknob, but I turn back.

"You were wrong, you know. I found Tommy's last name. His photo in the newspaper. I'm going to find out where he was from, if he had family."

"Good for you," he says. "The past is never dead. It's not even past."

"Don't quote Faulkner at me," I spit. "You shouldn't have brought me here if you wanted it to stay past."

I open the front door and walk into the gray winter day, leaving it wide open behind me.

———

Two blocks from Stedsan's house, I have to pull over. Rage courses through me. It started out as anger at Stedsan—for lying to me about what he knows. For hiring me because he thought I'd do a shit job. For being a smug old man who thinks money and powerful friends means he can buy whatever legacy he wants. But it's beyond that now. The anger is crushing. It's intoxicating. I could open my veins and bleed molten lava. I lay my head against the cool of the steering wheel and will myself not to cry. Crying when you're angry feels so pathetic.

Instead, I call Parker, without letting myself think about how I'm mad at him too. He picks up on the first ring. "Hey," he says. He sounds wary.

"I just met with Stedsan," I say. "He confirmed what I told you. Bill Campbell wanted the case settled. So he paid people off—including Fred Rooney. Alan knew what was going on and, on top of that, he knew Bill was trying to discredit Sarah Dale's story. And he used it all, Parker. He used Tommy's murder to negotiate the settlement."

There's a moment of silence on the other end. I wonder if Parker is as stunned as I am. Or if he's about to tell me it's not relevant to the case. To go home and stay out of it. That might kill me.

"Does he have proof?" he asks finally.

"Not that he's going to share, trust me."

"That's what a subpoena is for," Parker says, his voice hard.

It feels good to hear my anger mirrored in his voice.

"Attorney-client privilege," I say. "Bill was his client. They were all his clients." I lean my head back against the seat. "But you knew this already. I—I don't know why I'm calling."

Except I do. I take a deep breath.

"Parker, what if Bill Campbell killed Rooney? What if Rooney had been blackmailing him all this time and that's what the deposits were? Maybe he'd—I don't know—he'd had enough."

"Fred was blackmailing Bill for paying *him* a bribe? That's pretty ballsy."

I laugh. "Did you meet Fred Rooney?"

It's exactly something he would do, and Parker knows it.

"And how does Jeannette Leroy fit into this theory?" He sounds curious.

"I don't know," I admit. Bill had access to the canoe, but the rest—Bill crouching in the woods, smashing Sister Cecile's head in with a rock—without a motive, it's hard to imagine.

"There's something else, Alex." His tone makes me sit up straight.

"We're starting to get some press interest in this. Local reporters, mostly. But there have been a few calls to the station."

"Do they know about the history—about the connection to Coram House?"

He pauses. "No."

But I hear what he doesn't say: *not yet.* My throat feels like someone is squeezing it. Time. I need more time.

"Alex, I need you to sit on this. Not forever. Just for a day or two. We're getting the rest of the financials from Rooney's accounts. And we'll know more then. It will all be over soon."

"I'm not good at sitting on things."

"I know. That's why I'm asking."

I glance at the dashboard and see it's past one o'clock. I'm supposed to be at Xander's for ice sailing at two. "Shit," I say.

"What's wrong?"

"Nothing." I sigh. "I'm just— I'm late for something."

"I should go too."

He sounds far away, like his mind is already somewhere else. I picture his face outside the police station yesterday, so tired and worried. The glint of silver in the stubble on his chin.

"Okay," I say. "Talk to you later, then."

The line goes dead.

For a second, I have the disorienting feeling that I've traveled forward in time and I'm looking back at myself sitting in this car, feeling confused and at a dead end. This used to happen to me sometimes with Adam, at the end. Memories would play out in my mind, as if time was no longer a straight line, ever moving forward. As if I could go back and change things.

Moving into our first apartment. How we used packing crates for a table. How grown-up we'd felt buying a brand-new IKEA couch instead of one we found on the street. The apartment had a fireplace, but I didn't think to ask whether it actually worked. It's New York City—of course it didn't work. But Adam went to the bodega and bought two boxes of candles to put inside it. We kept them lit all winter.

Adam was forever coming home with things he found on the street. A hat stand. A single velvet dining chair. Swollen paperbacks no one wanted to read. We used to fight about it—how he was always bringing home strays that I had to put down. But I think it actually hurt him, to see those things abandoned on the street.

After Adam got sick, he brought home a horrible painting he'd found somewhere of children trick-or-treating, their empty eyes like ghouls. He'd grinned at me and said, *A dying man's last wish*. And I'd laughed and then cried while he held me. I was always too hard on him for all the places he was soft and I was not. No one appreciates gentleness until faced with its opposite.

Our wedding. The months planning, the input from our families, all wanting something different. Different chairs. A church. Their name on the invitation. A longer dress. A different flavor cake. How much I hated all of it. Until Adam took my hands, and said, *No, we're not doing any of it.* How we got married in a field outside a friend's house upstate and ignored the grumpy looks on our mothers' faces. How our friends brought fried chicken and tortilla chips and cheap wine and we stood in the tall grass and watched the sunset turn the sky electric pink.

How few truly perfect moments we're given in this life. And those are the ones that rip the heart from your chest later. The ones to lock away the tightest. But something has broken and now I can't.

I take deep breaths until I'm back inside my body. How can Adam still be dead? How can I have only been here, in this place, a month? How can the murder of a boy over fifty years ago feel this vital?

Time doesn't mean anything at all.

It's cold enough inside the car that I can see my breath. I shiver and start the engine. January thaw, my ass. There's still time to call Xander and cancel, but then what? Sit alone inside my apartment, going over my notes for the thousandth time, trying to think of anything that doesn't hurt.

No. If I leave now, I can make it to Xander's only a little late. *Ice sailing.* As I pull away, I wonder what half-insane version of my past self agreed to this. *Do the crazy thing. Lola, if I drown, I'm blaming you.* But thinking about her hurts too, so I stuff the thought away, in the box in my head, though I fear the lock is broken.

25

The sun is low in the sky and too big, as if the earth is hurtling toward it. As I drive to Xander's, my anger drains away, leaving frustration in its wake. I know so much—I'm so close—and yet I'm missing something.

Fifty years ago, Tommy Underwood drowned in the lake, while Sarah Dale watched. When she tried to come forward, she was locked in the attic. When she tried again twenty years later, her claims were dismissed.

Twenty years ago, Bill Campbell paid people off to settle the case. Ten years later, his company purchased Coram House and began building. Alan Stedsan knew about it all, but said nothing.

Fred Rooney received regular payments of $10,000 a year for at least the last ten years. Bill seems like a likely source, but why would he give him all that money?

Someone killed Sister Cecile.

Ten days later, Fred Rooney himself was also killed.

Bill had access to the canoe, but the rest—Bill hiding among the trees, bringing the rock down on Sister Cecile's head, strangling Fred— it's hard to imagine. By the time I pull into Xander's drive, I've worn a groove in my brain going over and over the same facts.

My stomach sinks at the sight of the other cars parked in front of the house. A salt-splattered pickup towing a boat trailer, and another car, forest green with the aerodynamic lines of something built for speed. I instinctively dislike its owner. Xander hadn't said anything about other people. I wonder whether it's too late to turn around.

Just then, the front door opens. Xander steps out wearing an outfit that looks like race-car-driver-meets-astronaut—a long orange jump-suit, thick with insulation, and a silver helmet tucked under one arm. I look down at my own jeans, which I'd stuffed myself into over my only pair of long underwear, and feel deeply skeptical about this whole excursion.

"Alex!" Xander calls with a grin. I wave back, and force myself to take my hand off the key.

"You made it!" he says as I get out. He sounds both happy and surprised, like he doubted I'd actually show up, which makes me feel guilty for plotting my escape. Maybe it will be fun. Detective Garcia and Parker had told me to lay off, so here I am, laying off.

A shriek rends the air. A second later comes the deep boom of a man's laughter. "You're such an asshole!" yells a woman's voice, but in a tone that suggests she's flirting rather than being murdered.

Xander looks at me, nervous. "A couple friends dropped in for the weekend. Kind of a surprise."

I force a smile. "That's nice."

"Come on," Xander says, "we're all headed to the boathouse."

The path down to the water is solid ice, but he walks right over it without slipping. *Magic*, I think, until I realize he's wearing some kind of cleats.

"Xander," I say, gesturing to my outfit. "I'm not sure I took your directions as seriously as I should have."

He swishes a hand through the air—as if shooing a fly. "You'll be fine," he says. "When I get a new toy, I just like to have all the acces-sories."

He says it with an embarrassed smile that makes me smile back, for real this time. Maybe this will be fun. Maybe for a few hours, I can forget about the case and everything that goes with it.

See, Lola, I know how to have fun.

Xander holds out a hand. "It's a little slippery on the way down," he says. "But you have to see this thing. It's *en fuego*."

"I have no idea what that means," I say, but I take his hand and let him lead.

And it's a good thing I do because the path is ice all the way. With every step, Xander's cleats make a sound like breaking glass. At the bottom, where it's too narrow to walk side by side, I cling to the fence. A cardinal lands at my feet. It pecks at the snow, then, finding nothing, takes off into the trees. A flash of red, there and gone.

"You okay?" Xander calls from ahead. He's nearly at the dock. I flash him a thumbs-up and half walk, half slide the rest of the way.

The boathouse buzzes with activity. Two men, nearly interchangeable with their stubbly faces and mirrored sunglasses, stand on the ice, near a contraption that's not quite a sailboat.

"This is Dan and that's Chris," Xander says as he hops down onto the ice. Both men raise their hands, so I have no idea who's who.

The boat looks like a sailboat, sort of. The sails are white and angular with indecipherable letters and numbers printed on the canvas. But the body of the boat is so sleek and narrow it's hard to believe it accommodates a person, let alone multiple people. A perpendicular crosspiece reaches out from either side for balance, giving it an insect-like appearance. The name of the boat is painted in neat red script on the stern. I look at Xander.

"*CodeRunner*? You didn't."

"It's like *Blade Runner*, but—"

I groan. "Yeah, I got the joke. It's terrible."

But he just grins at me. Someone giggles. That's when I notice three other people standing in the shadow of the boathouse. A man—tall and broad in a former linebacker kind of way—and two women with matching blonde waves cascading down their backs. All three look dressed for an après-ski photoshoot: fur-lined parkas, fur headbands, shearling boots. One of the women wiggles her fingers in a wave. "Hey," she says, drawing out the *y*.

"Hi," I say. The other two look at me and then turn away. A dismissal. I want to be anywhere but standing here looking like an overstuffed sausage in my long underwear.

"Ready?" Xander calls from the ice. He plonks a pair of cleats at the edge of the dock.

"Is that thing really safe?" I nod at the boat.

"Totally," Xander says. "See, we have helmets!"

He holds up something that looks like a motorcycle helmet. But I'm not sure how much weight this should carry, coming from the guy who drove his car onto the lake. Behind me, one of the women lets out a high, annoying laugh. I take the helmet. I'd rather risk death than be stuck here with them.

Xander pumps his fist in the air. "Let's do this thing!"

Both members of his crew grin and roll their eyes, but it doesn't feel mocking. Xander's unfiltered enthusiasm for whatever's in his line of sight is both ridiculous and infectious.

I pull on the cleats and then hop down onto the ice. There's a sick second where I'm sure my feet will plunge through the surface, but they connect with a click. It feels like walking on stone.

Up close, the boat is elegant—all sleek, smooth wood and shiny pulleys. "I assume the useless luggage goes there," I say, pointing to myself and then the bench seat in the front.

"Best seat in the house."

Xander holds out a hand to help as I haul myself over the side. I nod to his friends on the dock. "What about them?"

He glances over his shoulder as if he'd forgotten they were there. "Spectators," he says dismissively. Clearly he's used to having an audience.

One of the crew comes over to tug on a rope. I feel around the seat. "Should I have a seatbelt or something?" I ask.

Chris or Dan shakes his head. "Nah, you wouldn't want to be strapped in if the boat turned over."

Okay, wrong question.

I look out at the view. The sun hovers over the Adirondacks in the distance, as if balanced on the peaks. Beyond the point, the lake is a flat open field of white.

"Are we going out there?" I ask.

"Yup," says Xander. "But not past that island." He points to a tiny smudge in the distance. "Reports this morning said open water a couple miles offshore."

I check the faces of the crew, to see if they're alarmed by any of this, but no one seems to be. "Ready?" Xander asks.

I nod, surprised at the thrill of anticipation. Then, we start to slide.

Xander and a crew member run alongside the boat, pushing until we catch the wind. Then Xander hops in—much more gracefully than I did—and it's just the two of us.

The boat picks up speed until we're flying. It's amazing to be moving this fast with nothing but the wind and the slice of the boat gliding over the ice. I imagine Bill's lake monster, woken from its winter sleep, green scales trapped beneath the ice, teeth scraping against the hard surface in its hunger to catch us. But we glide right over.

When I turn back to Xander, he's grinning at me. "Look," he shouts. I do, just as we round the point, out of the bay and onto the open ice. Coram House stands on the hill, sun glinting off the windows so it looks like it's on fire. The sky right above us is clear, but dark puffy clouds loom to the north. The promised storm on its way. We fly along in silence. The only people in the world.

"This is amazing," I shout over the wind. "Is it always like this?"

I point out at the ice, the mountains, the sky.

"Nope," he yells back. "Must be for you."

I roll my eyes, but I'm smiling. The freezing wind stings my cheeks. The sky blazes orange. The speed clears my mind. It feels like we could keep gliding forever, fast and freezing, straight into the sunset.

When we get back to the dock I'm not sure if it's been minutes or hours, but I've never been so cold. My arms and legs jerk like a poorly coordinated puppet as I climb out of the boat. The clouds have taken over the sky, eating the sunset. The dock is empty, the others probably sitting in front of that enormous fireplace by now.

"I got this if you want to head up," says one of the sunglassed crew. "She looks half frozen."

Distantly, I resent being talked about like I'm not here. But he's not wrong. I do feel frozen.

"All right. Thanks, Dan."

Xander takes my hand as we climb the steep, icy slope. The smell of woodsmoke drifts on the air. My ears ring in the quiet now that we're not tearing across the ice. Xander stops at a landing cut into the earth, a small stone bench tucked under the pines. It's probably a lovely place to rest in the summer. Today the stone is a cold slab.

"So," Xander says, turning to take in the lake behind us. "What did you think?"

"Of the sailing?" My speech comes out slurred. "It was—it felt like flying."

He smiles. "When you're out on the ice with no one else around—it's like the closest I ever get to feeling free."

Before I can reply, he kisses me. His lips are warm, but my face is so cold I barely feel it. He leans back and looks at me. "You're really cold, aren't you?" He rubs my arms.

I nod, grateful that I don't need to say anything else.

He takes my hand again. "Come on, let's go up," he says. "They'll have a fire going."

I let him pull me the rest of the way.

When we reach the house, Xander flings open the door and leads me into the great room. The two women lay in a tangle on the sofa. Orange flames leap and crackle in the huge stone fireplace. The man gazes into the flames, one arm resting on the mantel as if posing for a portrait.

"Jesus, Xand," he says. "Shut the door, would you? It's freezing."

He speaks like someone used to owning the attention of every room he walks into. He comes toward me, hand outstretched. "We haven't officially met. I'm Bill."

Another Bill. Just what I need.

"And that's Evvy and Nat." He gestures toward the women on the couch. One of them, Nat, I think, lifts her glass to me.

"Nice to meet you," I say. My cheeks tingle as they defrost.

"Let's get you a drink," says Bill. "The rest of us are having cognac."

I don't really want a cognac at four thirty, but I take it anyway. Bills sets another down by Xander, who is in the process of taking off his spacesuit. "God, it feels good to warm up," he says. His boots sit, melting snow onto the sisal carpet. *It will be ruined*, I want to say. But it's not my carpet.

I unzip my jacket, but all I want to do is leave. They all seem so relaxed. It could be because they know each other, but I have the feeling they're the sort of people who feel at home in any room they walk into.

The joy I felt out on the lake is draining away at the prospect of sitting here making small talk.

I'll stay fifteen minutes, long enough to be polite.

As I look for somewhere to put the whisky down so I can take off my wet boots, Bill launches into some story about their undergrad days. Xander gives a loud, hearty laugh—different from his usual laugh. Bill grabs a beer from the bar's fridge and looks around for a bottle opener.

"Yo, Willy, catch."

Xander lobs something across the room that looks like a ceramic duck. Bill catches it easily in one hand. The beer opens with a hiss.

But I barely hear it. It feels like all the blood has drained out of my head. "What did you call him?" I ask.

Xander turns to look at me and the smile falls off his face. "Are you okay?"

The room blurs at the edges. "Your friend—Bill."

Xander stares at me blankly, but then it clicks. "Willy? It's a joke. Bill is short for William, but in college there was another Bill so sometimes we used to call him Willy."

The glass slips from my fingers and smashes on the stone floor. Shards reflect the dancing firelight in flickers of orange.

"Party foul," says Bill, looking down at the puddle of cognac.

Bill. Willy.

Is it possible? Was it really there in front of me all this time?

Xander jumps to his feet. "No worries, it's just a glass."

In my mind, I'm already in my car, driving away. Because if I'm right—if Bill and Willy are the same person—this changes everything.

"I have to go."

The two women exchange a look and scoot back into the deep cushions, as if my insanity might be catching. Ignoring Xander's call to wait, I pull open the front door. The hood of my car is covered in a dusting of snow.

"Alex!"

I turn. Xander has followed me outside with no shoes or jacket. "What the hell is going on?"

He's annoyed, verging on angry.

"You're acting all weird." He drops his voice. "Is this—was it because I kissed you?"

This isn't about you, I want to shout. But of course it is. This house. This life. Those friends. How could he not, somewhere deep down, believe he was the sun.

"Look, it's important," I say, opening the car door and sliding into the driver's seat.

He steps forward quickly, grabs the door before I can close it. "I'm sorry for—whatever. Just don't go yet."

I look at him. My urge is to apologize, to promise to call him later, to thank him again—for dinner, wine, sailing. I feel the obligation of holding someone's attention, the value it gives me, the desire to keep it even if I'm not sure I want it.

"Thank you for today," I say. "But I don't want to be here."

It's maybe the first fully honest thing I've said to him. He steps back, surprise on his face, and I slam the car door. Pebbles spit beneath my wheels as I pull onto the drive. When I glance in the rearview mirror Xander is still standing on the steps, watching me drive away. Then I round the curve and he's gone.

26

My wheels send a wave of slush over the curb as I turn too sharply onto the main road. Still, I accelerate until the fast-food restaurants are a neon smear out the window. *Bill. Will. Willy.*

I think back to the depositions in my head. A boy had described the day Tommy died—how he was left in the forest to build a fort all alone because neither of his friends—Willy or Tommy—showed up. Willy who got suckered into helping the nuns. Bill who got in trouble for telling the devil's tales. I'd assumed they were different people, but what if they were the same? What if Fred was never the boy in the boat at all? What if it had been Bill forced to help Sister Cecile with swim lessons that day? I feel the clunk of the missing piece sliding into place. But I need to get back to my desk, to see the words in front of me. I need to be sure.

The sky is fully black with clouds now. Snowflakes smack against the windshield like insects. The radio jangles pop music until it's interrupted by a weather report warning about a dip in temperatures and high winds. I hear the word *bomb cyclone* and turn it off.

I park crookedly and take the stairs two at a time. At my desk, I lay out the transcripts one by one. Sarah Dale. Fred Rooney. Karl Smith. Karen Lafayette. Violet Harrison. I open the binder to a map of Coram House as it was in 1968 and review the places I'd marked in red. The kitchen. The boathouse. The cove where Tommy drowned. The dump. The old oak.

First, Sarah Dale. On the day Tommy died, she described waiting by the back door to the kitchen when she saw Fred Rooney.

I'd just seen Fred outside the kitchen, on the path down to the water.

I'd been scared. He'd had this huge knobby stick through the handle of his bucket. A boy like that doesn't carry a stick unless he means to hit someone with it.

The first time I read it, I'd focused on the stick—what it said about Rooney that she'd been so scared of him—and the fact that he'd been headed down the path to the beach. When Sarah Dale looked at the water, she'd seen two boys in the boat with Sister Cecile—of course she'd assumed one was Fred. But I'd missed the mention of the bucket.

Next, I pull out the transcript of Stedsan's interview with Fred Rooney.

We ate orphan gruel. I know because every goddamn day it was my job to take a bucket of leftover slime we couldn't choke down over to the dump.

On the map, I trace the most direct route from the kitchen to the dump. It starts out as the same path to the water, but then splits off to the south. Rooney had never been heading to the cove at all; he'd been taking the bucket to the dump, same as every other day.

So Sarah Dale saw Fred leave down the path and then waited for the lemonade. For how long? Ten minutes? More? I try to retrace the path from Coram House to the water in my head. Would Rooney have had enough time to empty the bucket and then run to join Sister Cecile and Tommy in the boat? The timing seems unlikely. And Sarah Dale herself said she never saw their faces. She'd just assumed it was Fred and no one had questioned it.

My panic is gone. I pick up Karl Smith's interview and turn the pages until I find the spot where he talks about the day Tommy died.

See, we were supposed to meet up. All the kids were down on the point, playing in the woods. The sisters hardly ever gave us time like that just to play, but it was so hot. I think they just wanted to get rid of us. Tommy was supposed to meet me and Willy, but he never showed up.

That afternoon, Tommy would have been with Sister Cecile at the cove. I'd skimmed over his mention of the other boy—Willy. It hadn't seemed relevant. But I scan farther down the page.

Willy was in trouble—he'd gotten suckered into helping one of the sisters with something, so he was out. Tommy was supposed to meet me, but he never showed. It was supposed to be this perfect day, you know—three boys building a fort in the woods—but then it was just me, all alone.

It's not much to go on. But maybe it's enough.

Quickly, I turn to Violet Harrison's transcript. *There was this one boy—I remember he used to tell these crazy stories. Will? There was one about a lake monster that had us all terrified for weeks. None of us wanted to go near the water after that.* I don't need to review Karen's transcript to remember what she'd told me about Bill Campbell. *Bill used to tell these stories. There was this one about a monster in the lake that gave the kids nightmares.* The same story. The same kid.

My mouth goes dry. I've read the transcripts a dozen times. All the words are the same, but suddenly the story is different. Before I know what I'm doing, I pick up the phone and dial Karen Lafayette. She picks up on the first ring.

"Karen, this is Alex Kelley." I'm breathing heavily, like I've been running. "I'm sorry to call like this. I just—I had a question for you."

"Is this about the police?" she says. "Because I called that detective back and—"

"No," I say quickly. "This is going to sound strange, but did Bill Campbell ever have a nickname?"

There's a moment of silence and I'm worried Karen's hung up, but then she laughs. "God, I'd forgotten all about that. Kids used to call him Little Willy. There was another Bill at the House already. And he was so tall for his age, I think the *little* part was a joke."

Bill Campbell was supposed to meet his friend in the forest the day Tommy drowned, but he didn't show up. Because Bill got in trouble for telling stories and had to help Sister Cecile with swim lessons.

Sarah Dale saw Fred Rooney go down to the water. A few minutes later, she saw two boys in a boat with Sister Cecile. One was tall and lanky like Fred Rooney. Or like Bill Campbell.

Tommy went into the water and never came out.

"Alex?" Karen asks. "Are you still there?"

"Yes," I say. "Thank you."

It's as if my brain is split in two. One half is thanking Karen and saying goodbye. The other half is in 1968. The day after Tommy disappeared, Karen saw Rooney punch Bill Campbell. He must have known what really happened. All these years.

I hear Fred's voice the day I showed up at his house. *Maybe I was there that day, maybe not. But I can tell you I never touched that boy.* The way he smiled at me, like he was toying with me. I'd assumed he was lying. But what if he'd told me the truth right from the beginning? Someone else had pushed Tommy into the water. And Fred, like Sarah Dale, had been watching from shore.

I think of how pale and sweaty Bill had looked when Rooney stumbled into Jeannette Leroy's funeral drunk and shooting off his mouth. He must have been terrified that Rooney was spiraling out of control—that he'd say something. Because Rooney's blackmail had never been about the case. It had been about hiding what happened the day Bill Campbell pushed Tommy into the water and watched as the little boy drowned.

For a moment, I have to remind myself to breathe. Even if I'm right—Bill had been a minor and under coercion. Would he really kill Fred to hide what happened? *He paid Rooney for decades to keep quiet,* says a voice inside my head. *He made sure to buy that property and then sat on it for ten years. He cared deeply about keeping the secret.* Maybe Stedsan wasn't the only one worried about his legacy.

A hundred thousand dollars was too much money to pay Rooney just because he wanted the case settled. Garcia was right about that. But to hide murder? My stomach sinks. And not just one murder. Sister Cecile and Fred Rooney were the only other people who knew what happened that day. And now they're both dead.

I'm not sure how long I sit at my desk staring down at the map of Coram House. It all makes sense, but at the same time, my mind protests that it's not possible. Had my last book felt like this—like a puzzle piece finally snapping into place? I'd been wrong then. My mouth fills with metal, as if uncertainty has a taste.

Then I realize my mistake.

Parker is bringing Bill Campbell in to ask about the bribe money. But it's going to be the wrong line of questioning. We only have one chance at this and he's going to blow it—because of me.

Shit shit shit.

I dial Parker but it goes straight to voicemail. It's nearly six p.m. I hang up and call the station instead.

"You've reached the police department," Bev chirps.

Oh thank Christ.

"Bev. Hi, it's Alex Kelley. Is Officer Parker there?"

"Hold on a moment, dear."

Before I can tell her it's urgent, staticky hold music blasts my ears. After two infinite minutes, Bev picks up again.

"I'm sorry, he's not here right now. Can I take a—"

"What about Detective Garcia?"

"Hold, please," Bev says, sounding clipped now.

"Wait—"

She's gone longer this time. Finally, the hold music stops and she comes back on the line. "I'm sorry, she's not available right now. Can I take a message?"

"Shit," I mutter.

"Could you repeat that?"

"Nothing. Sorry. I just— Can you ask them to call me? As soon as they can. It's really important."

"I'll pass along the message."

The line goes dead. I imagine Bev writing my message on a Post-it and sticking it to Garcia's desk. How she'll find it tomorrow and toss it straight in the trash. I'm the girl who cried *important information* too many times. Everything is about to fall apart, and I'm powerless to do anything.

Then I have an idea. A stupid, desperate idea. I dig through the papers on my desk until I find Bill Campbell's home number.

"Hello?" A woman answers. Her voice is commanding.

"Mrs. Campbell?" I ask.

"To whom am I speaking?"

I clear my throat. "Sorry—my name is Alex Kelley. I'm a writer working on a local history project. I met with Mr. Campbell last week and he was so helpful. I was hoping he could answer a few last questions."

"Oh," she says. "Well, he's not here right now, but I'm happy to pass on the message. Alex, did you say?"

I grimace. "Do you think it would be worth trying him at the office? It's just a quick question."

"No, I'm afraid not," she says. "He's at a dinner party this evening."

"Ah—I see. I'll try him tomorrow, then. Thank you for your help."

I hang up. The phone sits in my hand, dark and inert. This is good news. Bill is at a party. Nothing is going to change before morning. I should eat some dinner and wait for Parker to call me back. But there's one more thing I need to do. Before I have time to think about all the reasons this is a stupid idea, I grab my jacket and my car keys. And I head for the door.

I back down the driveway too quickly. A pickup truck slams on the brake and honks. The driver shakes a fist at me. My heart is pumping twice as fast as usual. I back out the rest of the way onto the now-empty street. And I drive toward Coram House.

From upstairs, the falling snow looked gentle. At twenty miles an hour, each flake tosses itself against the windshield like it's trying to break through. If I can time myself on the path that Rooney would have taken to the dump and after to the cove, I can prove that he couldn't have been the one in the boat with Sister Cecile in 1968. Then, when Parker or Garcia calls me back, at least I can be sure of that one thing.

As I turn onto Battery Street, a gust of wind comes off the lake, rocking the car back and forth. I pass a snowplow, driving in the opposite direction. North Avenue stretches ahead, dark and empty. Then Coram House appears on its hilltop etched into the sky by the spotlights. I pull into the driveway over slushy tire tracks that have hardened to ice. The temperature must be dropping.

I pull around the back, so my car won't be visible from the street. The wind stills. The snow hangs suspended, as if time has stopped. A black SUV is parked in front of the office. CAMPBELL & SONS, it says on the door. Beside it is a police cruiser. Panic squeezes my throat.

The cruiser could be here for any reason. Could belong to anyone.

I stop the car and call Parker. It goes to voicemail again. I text him instead. *At Coram House. Are you here? Call me. It's important.* I hit send and get out of the car.

The office is dark. There are no footprints in the fresh snow leading up the steps. But still, I knock. "Mr. Campbell?" I call.

Silence. I try the handle, but it's locked.

The cruiser could belong to anyone, but I know it doesn't. Parker is the only one who suspects Bill Campbell of being connected to the murders. Could he have come here to try to question Bill at work? To catch him off guard? Parker is younger, stronger, sure—but Bill killed two other people and has the element of surprise. The air is cold enough to tear my lungs, but I take it in huge, deep gulps.

Bang.

I jump, then spin around. The driveway is empty. A tornado of snow blows across the empty road. Another bang—loud and sharp. It's coming from Coram House.

I backtrack down the drive, zipping my coat against the cutting wind. I need time to speed up to the moment I find Parker. But I also want time to slow. Because what if I'm too late.

Coram House's heavy front door slides open until it's a yawning hole. It hits the wall with a loud bang. Then it starts to slide closed again, sucked by the wind.

I walk up the front steps. "Hello?" I call into the empty front hall. "Parker?"

There's no reply but the wind. A faint glow comes from upstairs, like there's a light on up there. The door presses against my outstretched arm, trying to slam shut. *Make up your mind*, it seems to say. *In or out.* But it's not really a choice. Before the door can close, I slip inside. The wind slams it shut behind me.

27

I'm plunged into darkness. *Like a coffin lid shutting.* A laugh bursts out of me. The short hysterical bark of a trapped dog. As my eyes adjust to the dark, I listen for sounds—voices, footsteps, anything. But all I hear is my own breathing and the wind moaning outside.

I pull out my phone and dial 911, but my finger hovers over the call button without pressing. What am I going to say? *I'm breaking and entering. Oh, and the developer who owns the property might be on-site. Also he might have killed two people.* I'd sound like a lunatic. I lower the phone, but keep it in my hand.

Suddenly, the room is bathed in a faint glow. The white orb of the moon shines through the window. The snow has stopped for now, the clouds gone. But not the wind. If anything, it sounds more violent. A gust rattles the windows, as if frustrated I'm out of reach.

What had the radio said? Rapidly dropping temperatures followed by heavy snow. Bomb cyclone. The kind of storm where people freeze to death. And I'm wandering around an unheated building at an empty construction site, hoping to find a killer. *Dumb to the last,* my tombstone will read. I'll look around for ten minutes. Then I'll go home. Wait for Parker to call me back. I'm sure he's fine.

"Hello?" I call. But of course there's no answer. The brass chandelier sways back and forth. The wind, finding a way in.

Then I hear it. A murmur rising and falling. I can't make out the words, but I'm sure it's a voice. Someone upstairs. My thumb hovers near the call button again.

The banister is cold and smooth as stone under my hand. The stairs creak and groan beneath my weight. At least I'll hear if anyone follows me. *They're not behind you, they're already upstairs, idiot.* I lick my lips and find that my mouth has gone dry.

At the top, I pause on the landing. All the doors are shut, except for one. The door to the girls' dormitory at the end of the hall is half open. A faint wedge of light spills into the corridor. I wait, my heart beating. There it is again. It's faint, but the rise and fall is unmistakable. Not voices, though. Not even words. Someone in the room beyond is humming.

I drift down the hall, closer. It should be terrifying, but it's not. The song is familiar, but I can't name it. Something I heard as a child, maybe. The knob is ice under my hand as I push the door open.

The room is empty. I don't need to see the floorboards lit up by the moonlight spilling in through the tall windows. Don't need to tug on the door leading up to the attic to know that it's latched shut—though I still do. I know it's true as soon as I step inside. It has the feel of an empty room. There's no one here to see me, but still heat floods my cheeks. What had I expected? Someone sitting up here, waiting for me and humming? I'm a little old to be turning every gust of wind into a ghost.

Time to go home, Alex.

But as I turn back toward the hall, movement outside catches my eye. The windows look out onto the graveyard and the frozen expanse of lake beyond. Trees bend and snap in the wind. Maybe that was it. Still, I scan the gravestones for footprints or the shadow of someone hiding.

Then I see it. A figure down by the water. Quickly, I step closer until my nose is pressed against the glass. It could be a rock. A trick of the moonlight.

The figure steps onto the ice. It's walking strangely, hunched and monstrous. Then I see why. It's dragging something large and unwieldy. It takes a few more steps. The picture snaps into focus.

The hunched figure isn't dragging *something*. It's dragging *someone*. Out onto the ice.

Suddenly, I think of the police cruiser parked in front of the office. I imagine Parker arriving to question Bill Campbell with no idea what the man is capable of. I bang on the window. "Stop!" I shout to the empty room. For a second, I stand, paralyzed by my distance, my powerlessness. Then I turn away from the window. And I run.

Instinct takes over. I burst onto the landing and sprint through the narrow hallway so quickly I bounce off the wall. Time slows down. I run across the boys' dormitory, wrench open the door, and take the steep, dark stairs down to the kitchen two at a time.

At the bottom, I shoulder the door. But the knob doesn't turn and I'm thrown back, landing painfully on my hip. The door is locked.

No. No. No. No.

Just then my phone vibrates. I stare down, shocked to find it still clutched in my hand. It's the police station. With immense relief, I answer. "Parker?"

"Alex? This is Detective Garcia."

Her voice is breaking up.

"You have to get here," I shout. "You have to hurry."

Some jumble of words falls out of my mouth. About Bill Campbell and Parker. About the canoe. And hiding in the woods. About a boy who drowned in 1968 and this moment in a dark back staircase, trapped behind a locked door.

I'm not sure if I make any sense at all or if Detective Garcia just thinks I've gone insane, but after a pause her voice comes back on the line, clearer this time.

"Stay right where you are, Alex."

I can hear her shouting orders at someone.

"We'll be there as soon as we can. But the weather—emergency services are delayed."

My phone beeps. The line goes dead.

I try the door again, shouldering it as I turn the knob. This time it opens easily, and I tumble onto the kitchen floor, landing hard on my knee. The pain is so sharp that, for an instant, my vision goes black. I pull myself up, using the counter for leverage, and hobble to the door. The heavy antique key is in the lock, waiting. I throw the door open and step into the night.

The wind is a punch in the gut. Thick clouds cover the moon now.

My eyes rake the ice below, searching for movement, but everything is shadow.

I have been here before.

Except not me. This is where Sarah Dale stood while she watched Tommy drown. Pressed down by the heat of the day, her ears full of the chirp of crickets, she felt her feet grow roots. Everything and nothing stopped. But I'm not rooted to the ground.

There on the ice, a dark shape is moving. My eyes find the gap in the underbrush at the bottom of the hill—the path to the lake. I limp forward, knee throbbing, through the gate flanked by weeping stone angels, and then I begin to run.

The snow in the graveyard is deep. It cakes my boots until they're heavy as bricks. I'm slow, too slow. The snow is blowing, blinding. I've lost the path. My foot catches on a headstone hidden beneath the snow and I go down. When I stagger to my feet, my bare hands sting with cold.

Finally, I reach the hedges that separate the graveyard from the beach. Branches catch my jacket and tangle in my hair. Then I'm through, standing on the rocky shore. Without the shelter of the underbrush, the wind howls. All is darkness, but the ice—so much ice—stretches ahead, glowing with its own light.

In the distance, I can make out two dark shapes. One upright, the other on the ice. My heart squeezes into my throat. The prone figure is struggling. It's not a body. It's not too late.

"Stop," I yell. But the wind carries my voice into the sky.

At first, I assumed they were making for the nearest point of land, which would be Xander's house, though it's hidden now by blowing snow. But they seem to be walking out onto the lake. Could it have frozen all the way across since this morning? Or maybe there's a boat out there waiting.

I look down at the spot where the ice meets the shore. It's thick and lumpy. When I look up, I can barely see the dark shapes. I put a foot on the ice and test my weight. It holds. I take another step and then another. *Don't let me be too late.* I think it over and over like a prayer. Because I know there's no boat waiting for them. That's not how this story ends.

From a distance, the ice looked smooth and blown clear of snow. But it's covered in ridges and holes, crevasses where plates come together. Out here, it's an alien landscape. I try not to think about what I'm doing. How insane this is.

Ahead of me, the two figures struggle on the ice. Faster. I have to go faster. But I'm afraid. Of sliding, of falling, of going into a hole and slipping quietly below the ice.

"Stop," I scream. But they can't hear me over the wind. I break into a run.

Finally, I get close enough to see Bill looming over a dark shape, both blurred by snow. I hear weeping. See a hand smeared in blood. Parker. Alive. I'm not too late.

"Bill," I shout. "The police are on their way. Don't do this."

The looming figure straightens. Slowly, he turns around, giving me a clear look at the man down on the ice.

The world tilts on its axis. Because the man bleeding on the ice, his eyes wide and terrified—that man is Bill Campbell.

"Oh, thank God," he moans, wiping at his face, leaving a red smear on his cheek. The figure in the black coat stands over him, one booted foot on Bill's neck to keep him down.

"No," I whisper.

The monster I've been chasing has brown eyes ringed in gold. It's not Bill Campbell, of course. It never was.

"Hello, Alex," says Parker.

28

The wind dies. The storm, shocked into silence. "You," I say. My voice is barely louder than a whisper. "I can't— I don't understand."

Parker looks at me with so much sorrow that I wonder if I've misunderstood somehow. But his voice doesn't waver.

"I told you to go back to New York," Parker says. Below him, Bill thrashes like a fish on a hook. His cheeks are smeared in blood, now freezing to his face. *Please*, he moans over and over.

"Let him go," I say. "Please."

Parker looks down at Bill as if he'd forgotten he was there. "Stop it," he says coldly. Bill stops struggling, but he begins to sob. I wonder if I'm going to throw up.

Parker looks at me. "You know he bribed people to settle the case, but do you know all of it? How he wheedled and paid and threatened them. How he set them against each other, called her testimony a lie. All to protect himself."

Parker kicks Bill sharply in the side. The older man cries out.

"Tell her," Parker says. "She deserves to know."

I should speak, tell him to stop, but not a sound comes out.

"I— It wasn't supposed to be me," Bill says, "in the boat that day. If Fred hadn't been late, it never would have been me."

"Tell her."

Bill winces as though Parker had kicked him again. "I pushed Tommy into the water," he says. "I—held him down."

I see it like it's happening in front of me now. The ice is gone. The sun is shining. A hot summer day. Tommy goes into the water. He shouts for help.

"He tried to get back in the boat," I say.

Bill begins to sob. "She told me to hit his hands. Make him let go. She said it's how you learn."

"And you did," I say.

"Please," Bill says, but he's not looking at Parker anymore, he's looking at me. Pleading with me. My stomach lurches again.

"He was a child," I murmur, but I'm not sure if I'm talking about Tommy or Bill. I look at Parker, my voice firmer now. "Bill was a child too."

Parker's face is stone. "And was he a child when he lied about that day over and over? He called her a liar. She drank herself to death while Sister Cecile tended her garden."

My brain feels sluggish with cold. "She—you mean Sarah Dale?"

"Nothing happened to them. While my mother suffered—" Parker's voice cracks.

Gears turn until it all snaps into place. The thing I couldn't see. The same story, but from a different angle. Sarah Dale drinking too much. Sarah Dale dying in a car crash. Her two-year-old granddaughter in the back seat. *My kid died*, Parker had said that night with the whiskys.

"Parker, I'm so sorry." I choke on the words.

He nods but his face doesn't change. "After the case, she started drinking. Just a little at first to help her sleep. I don't know when it went beyond that. I didn't notice, I—" He breaks off. "I should have noticed."

"It's not your fault."

"When you have a kid, you have all these firsts. First steps, first words. You just expect the rest to come. And then it was just—over."

It feels like a hand is squeezing my throat. I can't speak. Can't breathe. But the words are pouring out of him now. Maybe he's never been the silent type. He's just been living behind a dam he built between his mind and voice.

"I tried so hard to hate her. But I knew all the things she was trying to forget. It was like this chain of terrible things, one leading to another, but if you followed it all the way back to the beginning—to the people who did this—what happened to them? Nothing." His voice is blazing. "They all got exactly what they wanted."

"This isn't the way," I say, but I sound unconvincing, even to myself. There's some part of me that agrees with him. Jeannette Leroy didn't earn a life of peace. She abused children. Watched a boy drown. She should have died in jail. But there are other kinds of justice.

Parker looks at me. For a moment, it's like everything else disappears. The wind. The cold. The bleeding man at his feet. "There was nothing left for me but darkness," he says. "At least, this way there would be a point."

Something inside me breaks. Maybe my heart. *I understand*, I want to tell him. I too have looked into the mirror and seen an empty container, filled with grief.

Red and blue lights flicker on the ice. I turn. Coram House stands sentry on the hill. Police lights strobe the sky. I didn't hear the sirens over the wind.

"You called Garcia?" Parker asks.

I don't trust myself to speak, so I just nod.

"All right," he says. "Okay."

"Parker, let him go. Please. I don't want another body."

Our eyes meet for a long second. Then he looks down at Bill. He steps back.

It takes Bill a second to realize he's free. Then he scrambles across the ice like a crab. "Help," he shouts. He slips and falls and then gets to his feet again. "Here, I'm down here."

He takes off toward the flashing lights at a limping run.

I face Parker, ten feet of ice between us. He doesn't step toward me, doesn't move. Tears make warm tracks down my face. It's incredible what a person can carry inside, unfathomable from the outside.

"I'm sorry," he says.

But I can't find my voice, couldn't forgive him anyways. It's not up to me. But I can't hate him either.

"Parker."

His name comes out as a whisper, but his eyes are trained ahead, where the mountains would be if there was enough light to see them. Now it's just darkness.

"If you knew you'd die horribly," he says. "If you knew how it ended—would you go back and undo the moment you were born?"

He turns to look at me with those brown eyes ringed in gold, waiting for my answer.

I think about Tommy, his short life, his terrible death. Parker's daughter, two years old, crushed in a totaled car. Adam, who lived with his own slow death rolling toward him. Would I erase them, knowing what I do about how their lives ended? Then there's the bottomless sadness of my own heart. Would I go quietly into oblivion or do it all again?

"No," I say. "I wouldn't undo it."

"Why?" he asks.

"Because, what else is there?" It's not a good answer, but it's the only one I have.

Parker nods. "I'm sorry, but I don't regret it. You tell them that."

He starts walking, slowly, bent against the wind. Toward the darkness. Toward the open water. Toward nothing.

He's twenty feet away. Forty.

"Parker!" My voice is a sob.

The snow falls between us like a veil. And then he's gone. There's no crack. No splash. Just darkness. As if he was never there at all.

I have no idea how much time passes. A minute. An hour. Then voices. Shouts. The crunch of footsteps. Flashlights. My eyes don't leave the darkness.

"Alex!" Someone calls my name over the wind, but I can't look away. Strong hands grip my shoulders, turn me around.

I stare into Garcia's face. I take in a ragged breath, as if I'm surfacing from underwater. Then I begin to shiver. "He's gone," I say through tears and chattering teeth.

"Russell Parker," she says. It's not a question. "On foot?"

I nod. "Out there."

Someone drapes a blanket around my shoulders and I'm half-escorted, half-carried across the ice. I'm aware of Garcia shouting instructions as we go. *Fan out along the shore. Set up a perimeter on the road. Crime scene. Boats. The storm.* But I know they won't find anything. Not on this side of the ice.

Garcia helps me into the back of an ambulance parked beside Coram House. Bill Campbell is already inside, a bandage taped over his forehead. He pulls down his oxygen mask. "I'm not riding with her," he mumbles.

"Shut up," Garcia says.

Their words are far away. I'm still out there on the ice, listening for the distant crack of the world breaking apart.

May 1, 1988—US District Courthouse

Karen Lafayette

Karen Lafayette: That's the thing with anger—you have to figure out what to do with it. You control it or it will control you. I'm not talking about forgiveness—okay? Fuck forgiveness. I'm saying you have to make something with that rage. Do something. If you keep it inside, it will change you until you don't even recognize yourself anymore.

July 31, 1968—Coram House

Tommy

It's dark. Not outside. Outside there's a full moon. The gravestones glow white on the black grass so they look like they're floating. Some stones are so old you can barely read them. One just says *Baby* on it. Like they didn't care enough to give him a name.

Outside is noisy with summer sounds. The crickets are singing like crazy. In here, the only sound is breathing, which should be quiet, but there are too many of us. And anyways, the quiet doesn't mean anything. Something could still be waiting in the dark. Listening for me to get out of bed just like I'm listening for it.

I pull the blanket up to my chin, even though I'm sticky with hot. But it doesn't help. The darkness is inside already. I can feel it coming from all the scary places. Under the beds. Inside the cabinet with the door that never latches.

It's all the new kid's fault. He brought it in with him. The darkness. He says it's slimy and slithery with sharp teeth. He says it lives in the lake but I can feel it breathing. It's inside Coram House. I know it is. I try so hard not to think about it. Because I really have to pee. But I can't put my legs down on the ground. Can't walk through all that dark to get to the bathroom.

It's just like today at the beach. Sister Cecile told me to get in the water with the others. I tried, but all I could think of was what was waiting in the down deep. Swimming and waiting. And I couldn't move. I tried. I really did. *There is no* can't *in the eyes of our Lord,* Sister

Cecile said, right before she said *I'll deal with you tomorrow* in a voice that made my skin get goose bumps.

No, I wanted to say. Tomorrow, we're going to build a fort. Deep in the woods with branches for a roof and sticky sap for glue. Or maybe burn out a hollow tree like the kid in that book. Catch one of the falcons that nests on the cliffs and teach it to hunt rabbits. It will be far away. So deep that no one will ever find us. Tomorrow we're going to do it. Or maybe not tomorrow but a tomorrow that comes after that. One of these tomorrows, we'll do it.

EPILOGUE

The packing tape screams as it comes off the roll. That's the last box, sealed shut. My suitcase is stacked at the foot of the bed and now my work is all packed away—binder organized, index cards wrapped in rubber bands, laptop zipped into its case. I'd hoped to leave yesterday, as soon as the police gave me the green light, but it was late by the time I got back from Xander's.

He'd been waiting for me, standing outside in his driveway when I arrived. Like everyone else, he knew what had happened, wasn't sure what to say. So we talked about the weather—cold—and about where I was going next—somewhere warm and then somewhere else.

I told Xander how, thanks to his newspaper clipping, I found Tommy's name. Found out he was born in Port Henry, New York. He still has cousins alive, an aunt who'd come looking for him, but never found him. People who would have remembered him if given the chance.

He told me how the Coram House development is at a standstill, mired in red tape. I imagined the building years from now, standing on the hill, abandoned and half-finished, rusting steel beams sticking out like naked bones. Maybe it's a more fitting end, but what a waste. When it was too cold to stand outside any longer, we hugged and said goodbye. I felt lighter leaving.

As I zip up my suitcase, a knock from downstairs makes me freeze, as if someone might see me up here. In the two weeks after that night on the ice, a few reporters had found my address and come knocking, but I'd ignored them. Finally, I'd taped a piece of paper to the door that said: *I can't discuss an ongoing investigation.* I had read it and then cried.

But they left me alone. Probably it would have petered out anyways. Another news cycle. Fresh blood somewhere else.

After that night, I'd been briefed and debriefed, questioned first about everything that happened in the hours preceding and then the days and weeks before that. Time was sand inside an hourglass, flowing ever backward. My throat was raw with talking by the time I left the police station and stepped outside, blinking in surprise at the sun. *When had it become morning?* I'd come back to my apartment, slept. And then gone back the next day and started all over again as they—as we—tried to untangle the knot of what had happened and why. Or maybe I was the only one wrestling with the why. Motive is just a nice-to-have, after all.

Officer Russell Parker had taken a canoe to Rock Point and killed Sister Cecile. He was the one I'd heard in the woods. He'd killed Fred Rooney and had tried to kill Bill Campbell, working his way down the list of anyone who had hurt his mother or profited from what happened at the House. The evidence was there once you knew to look for it. Same story, different angle.

The knock comes again. I pull on my coat and drag the suitcase into the kitchen. Might as well make the trip count. Whoever is outside must have heard me wrestling the suitcase down the stairs because they don't knock again. For about the hundredth time, I curse the absence of a peephole. Instead, I fling open the door—*No comment* already on my lips—but it's not a reporter.

Detective Garcia stands on the porch. Instead of her usual black suit, she's in jeans and an emerald-green coat. She has a coffee in each hand.

"Hi, Alex. I hope it's okay—me coming here like this."

I nod to the cup. "If one of those is for me, it is."

She smiles, but it doesn't quite reach her eyes. I step outside, hoisting the suitcase onto the porch after me. The cup warms my fingers.

"How are you doing?" Garcia asks.

I shrug. "Honestly? I don't know how to answer that question. You?"

She shakes her head. For a while, we just stand there, not saying anything.

After that night, the police had asked me to stay in town for a few weeks. It was easy to agree when leaving and staying had seemed equally unimaginable. Lola came, and Kay too.

I'd spent the next week in stasis, lying in bed until hunger forced me out, then burrowing into my blankets as soon as the sun went down. Not that sleep was a refuge. I dreamed of ice and the cold water beneath and whatever lay beneath that. Lola rubbed my back and made me shower, while Kay cooked soup on the only burner that worked. For another week they stayed, until the day I woke up and something felt different.

That morning, I'd gotten out of bed and brewed a pot of coffee. My laptop felt cool under my fingers as I began to type. The words just came. Not as if I was assembling the pieces of an outline, but as if the story had been there all along, whole and waiting for me to begin. Lola had smiled at me. *Nice to see you back,* she'd said. *Guess it's time for us to go home.* I'd held on to her, knowing her friendship has been the tether that anchors me to earth and also thinking how exhausting it is to keep incurring debts I'll never be able to repay. But maybe that's what love is—debt.

Garcia takes a long sip of coffee. "The DA isn't going to press charges against Bill Campbell for the bribery," she says.

She's watching me, waiting for a reaction. But I'm not angry. Hell, I'm not even surprised. From a certain viewpoint, he's a victim of blackmail, who was almost murdered by a serial killer. The optics of going after him for bribery and obstruction wouldn't be great.

"Is that why you came?" I ask. "To tell me that?"

Garcia sighs. "And because I owe you an apology."

"I never thought you'd arrest Bill," I say. "Even I know there's no case there."

"No, not for that." She's struggling with whatever she came here to say. "I've—well, I treated you badly—before. I believed you were involving yourself in the case for attention, to make a better story for your book." She pauses, clearly deciding whether to go on. "Officer Parker, he—well, he said a few things."

My teeth grind so hard I feel a sharp pain in my jaw. "Yeah, I'm sure he painted a nice picture."

Garcia shakes her head. "I was the one that filled in the gaps, Alex. I need to take responsibility for that. For not seeing—for not looking."

I swallow a lump in my throat. "I gave him everything he needed to know about them. Rooney. Bill Campbell. What they'd done. Jesus, I sent him to Xander's house to ask about the canoe."

I bury my face in my hands.

"You didn't know."

"Do you think— I mean, none of this started until I got here. Do you think it was me?"

Is this my fault? I can't quite get the words out. Maybe I don't want an answer.

Garcia considers this, then she shakes her head once, decisively.

"Maybe your coming sped something up, maybe not. But we searched his house. We found notes, documentation, some of it years old. He moved here for this. I think it was too late long before you got here."

I'm sure she's not allowed to tell me any of this, so I smile, grateful, even though it doesn't make me feel better. The silence stretches out. I try to decide if I'm going to ask it—the thing I want to know but am also afraid to.

"Did you ever suspect?" I ask.

Garcia goes very still, as if she's watching a replay of the last few weeks in her head. Finally, she shakes her head. "Never. Not for a minute."

I wonder if this should make me feel better or worse.

Garcia nods at the suitcase. "Where are you headed now? Back to New York?"

I shake my head. She doesn't press.

"Have you found anything?" I ask. My lips are dry. I lick them and taste blood where the skin has cracked. "Out there."

Her eyebrows unknit as she realizes what I'm asking. Then she shakes her head. "There's too much ice. In the spring, they'll drag the lake, but . . ." She shrugs. "It's deep. We may never find him."

"Do you think— I mean, is it possible . . ." I trail off.

Her expression softens. "There was nothing out there but open water, Alex. Nowhere to go."

I force the words out, but they're sharp and they tear. "I know."

302

Garcia looks away. I take three deep breaths. I count the stairs. One to seven and then back down to one.

"I didn't know Officer Parker well," she says, "but I don't think he was ever planning to escape. I think"—she pauses, choosing her words—"I think he was just trying to get to an ending."

My mind has gone black. Not a single thought in it. I barely feel it when Garcia gently squeezes my hand. "I'll call you if we have any more questions. Good luck, Alex."

They're strange parting words. Not *take care of yourself* or *goodbye*. As luck goes, I think I've made it clear mine is either great or terrible, depending on your perspective.

Garcia tosses her cup in a trash can. She turns west, toward the police station. I watch until she's an emerald smudge in the distance. Then I heft the heavy suitcase and load it into my car. Five boxes to go.

Then I have to make one more stop.

———

The porch lights are on at Stedsan's office, despite the sunny day. They look like two glowing eyes. The knocker becomes a twisted nose. The mail slot a slash of mouth. The face is monstrous and impossible to unsee.

I'm taking a chance just showing up like this, but I didn't want to let him know I was coming. Didn't want him to ask why.

I lift the knocker, for a second expecting flesh beneath my hand, but it's cold metal. The thunk echoes inside the house. Then the door opens. Stedsan wears jeans and a gray sweater. His hair is wet, making it look much darker than his usual white blond.

"Alex."

He sounds surprised and looks behind me like he expected me to bring a date.

"Can I come in?" I ask.

He steps back and opens the door wider. "Yes, of course."

Stedsan offers coffee, leaving me plenty of openings to tell him why I'm here, which I decline to use. I do take him up on the coffee, though.

While he's gone, I wander into the living room. The back garden is blanketed in fresh snow. The twisted apple tree looks like an enormous white-capped mushroom—something from the wrong side of the looking glass.

Stedsan reappears with the tray and hands me an espresso in a delicate blue cup. It's smooth and nutty. Delicious.

"How are you holding up?" he asks. "The last few weeks can't have been easy."

"No," I say.

"If this is about our contract," he says, "I don't want you to worry. Given the circumstances I think we can alter the timeline to be—"

"That's not what this is about." I set the cup on the table.

He looks up at me, his expression curious, but not worried.

"How much did you know?" I ask.

Stedsan frowns. "I told you, Alex," he says slowly, as if speaking to a child. "I always believed Sarah's version of events, but I never had any proof. I'm as surprised as you are that Bill was involved."

I can't tell if he's lying, but it doesn't matter. It's not what I'm here about.

"You know, I've had a lot of time to think over the last few weeks," I say. "And there's this thing, tiny really, I don't know why it stuck in my head, but it did. Something Russell Parker said to me."

He waits, eyebrows raised. The silence stretches out, but he doesn't squirm.

"His dad died when he was a kid. I checked, just to make sure, but it's true. Lewis Parker died in 1987, when Russell Parker was ten years old."

I wait to see if this means anything to him, but Stedsan just frowns.

"It got me thinking. Sarah Dale was a single mom, an orphan with no family, when she gave that deposition in 1989. Days of interviews. Who would have taken care of her son back in New York? Or maybe she brought him along."

I see it in his eyes—the moment he realizes what I'm getting at.

"He would have been, what, twelve? Still a kid, sure, but I'm betting he was still recognizable to someone who met him again twenty-five years later. Especially if that someone was paying attention. And you strike me as someone who is always paying attention."

Stedsan's expression doesn't change, but he goes so still he could be a statue. This is risky, I know it is. It's a wild conjecture that he'd be crazy to confirm, but I can't get the idea out of my head. The way he'd laughed when he told me about my media liaison and his strange reaction to Fred Rooney's death, like he knew something he wasn't saying. It could add up to nothing. Or to this.

"I think you always knew who Russell Parker was," I say. "And I think that you suspected what he was doing and decided to let it play out."

Stedsan says nothing, but that foxlike expression is back. "You can't prove any of this."

It feels like someone's punctured my lungs. "People died."

"You know," Stedsan said. "If Bill Campbell had just told us everything he knew from the beginning, all this might have been avoided. Why don't you save your lecture for him. As it stands—drugs, sexual assault, blackmail, murder—I'm not sure the world is worse off without those two."

I can see it from his perspective. Justice from another angle. But I think of the dark sadness in Parker's face. The world *is* worse.

"What makes you think he wasn't coming for you next?" I ask.

Stedsan laughs. "What makes you think he wasn't coming for you too, Alex Kelley?"

And if he had come for Stedsan, would some part of me have thought it was deserved? The part that right now thirsts for Stedsan's blood. That wants not just justice, but retribution. As for me, Parker had his chance out on the ice and he walked away. But maybe that had less to do with my innocence than his sense of mercy. Or maybe he knew that being left was a punishment of its own. Either way, I'll never know.

"I'm leaving," I say. "Today. I'm going to write my book somewhere else."

He raises his eyebrows. "Our contract clearly stipulates you remain here for the full six months or until the first draft is done."

"I'm not finished," I say. "Our financial arrangement will remain the same. You'll get your royalties, but my name goes on the cover and the final edit is mine too."

"And why on earth would I agree to any of this?"

"Because I think you want to keep this conversation out of the book."

He shrugs. "Allegations with no evidence. And you'd be in violation of your NDA."

I look him right in the eye without flinching. "Fuck the NDA. I've done some research and there's a good shot it wouldn't hold up in court. Plus this story is so good I'm sure one interview with the press would more than cover my legal costs."

We look at each other, not saying anything. Behind his eyes, I can see the gears of his mind turning, looking for the way out.

"Or you could let me write the book my way. The rest of it goes in, but this part we'll keep between us. Your choice."

A smile spreads across his face. He shakes his head. "I'm not too big to admit when I've been outmaneuvered," he says. "Very well. Go where you wish. Write your book."

He sighs but I'd swear he looks a little relieved.

"This book was supposed to be my legacy, but I have a feeling you'll do the subject justice."

I still hate him, but feel a pang. He looks so old suddenly. "We don't get to write our own legacies, Alan," I say. "That's not how it works."

He stands to walk me out. I let him go first. He doesn't seem the type to hit me over the head with a bookend, but then who knows?

"What were you doing inside Coram House that night anyway?" Stedsan asks as I slip on my jacket. "Just luck?"

I consider the question. The slamming door. The sound of humming drifting down the stairs. The moon lighting my way. "Do you believe in ghosts?" I ask.

He looks surprised. Well, that's something, to finally surprise him. He raises his eyebrows, waiting for more.

"Me either," I say. But I'm not sure that's true anymore.

I'm halfway down the walkway when Stedsan calls out, "I always liked him, you know. Officer Parker."

I turn back. "Yeah. Me too."

"How do you think he'd feel about the book you're going to write?"

A deep pain twists in my chest. I think he'd tell me the why doesn't matter, only what he did. But I think the why is everything.

"Goodbye, Alan," I say. "I'll send you a copy when I'm done."

On the way to the car, tiny chunks of ice crunch beneath my feet like pieces of broken glass. I feel Stedsan in the doorway, still watching, as I climb in and turn the ignition. But I drive away without turning back.

I've thought a lot about the question Parker asked me on that last night. Around and around in circles. What I'd do if given the power to turn back time, to lick my fingers and snuff out a life and all the pain that came with it.

No, I'd told him, I wouldn't do that. And not just because there's nothing else. But because love is a debt paid only in loss eventually, one way or another. You cannot open the door to one without the other. But you also never know what will come next. Joy on the heels of sorrow on the heels of joy. And we don't get to pick. We're given so few perfect moments in this life, and sometimes you don't see them for what they are until after. But how do you put the pain and the perfection of a life on a scale and decide how they stack up—which lives are worth living? Maybe someone else can, but not me.

The highway is quiet. I drive until there are no more office parks or big-box stores, just a road snaking through mountains. In the rearview mirror, my file boxes sit patiently on the back seat, waiting for me to unpack them in a new place. My fingers tingle to begin writing. I come around a bend and see the mountains, framed in my windshield. The snow and shadowed branches would look like a black-and-white photo were it not for the pure blue backdrop. Blue that goes on and on forever. I drive into it.

Acknowledgments

To my agent, Alexandra Machinist: from our first conversation I knew you were the one to launch this book. Thank you for your steady leadership and for holding my hand when I needed it, which was often. Thank you also to the rest of the team at CAA, especially Katherine Flitsch (you read it first!) and Sarah Harvey.

To my editor, Loan Le, thank you for knowing exactly what questions to ask. This book is so much better with your fingerprints on it. I also want to thank the rest of the team at Atria, especially Lindsay Sagnette, Elizabeth Hitti, Maudee Genao, Holly Rice, Paige Lytle, Shelby Pumphrey, Katie Rizzo, Claire Sullivan, and Linda Sawicki. This book has been touched by so many thoughtful hands along the way, for which I will be forever grateful.

Thank you to my parents, Peggy and Crossan Seybolt, for getting me my first library card and believing in me always. And to all the writers and friends who have shared encouragement over first drafts and glasses of wine, thank you. I especially want to thank Liz Parker and Flynn Berry for reading my book and fielding my frantic questions with humor and patience.

Thank you to Vermont, my adopted home. We have been so lucky to live, build a community, raise our children, and find inspiration in this beautiful state. To everyone in Burlington, sorry for all the liberties I took with our town's geography.

And, finally, to my family. Tim, thank you for your love and encouragement and for making time for me to write no matter how many jobs or kids we were juggling. Claire and Seb—you are everything. The best part of publishing a book is showing you what happens if you dream big and just keep going.

Author's Note

While Coram House is a work of fiction, the story owes a debt to the real history of St. Joseph's Orphanage in Burlington, Vermont. Between 1854 and 1974, more than thirteen thousand children passed through its doors. They were abused and silenced by the people who were supposed to protect them. The legacy of orphanages and residential schools has proven that power lies in controlling what is remembered and what is forgotten. May we remember.

To learn more about the historical context of this book, visit www.stjosephsrjinquiry.com.

About the Author

Bailey Seybolt grew up in New York City. She studied literature at Brown University and creative writing at Concordia University. She's worked as a copyeditor and travel writer in Hanoi, a tech copywriter in San Francisco, and many writerly jobs in between. She now lives with her family in Vermont, not far from Lake Champlain and its monster.

Learn more at www.baileyseybolt.com and @baileyseybolt on Instagram.